WARNING

This book contains sexually explicit scenes and adult language. It may be considered offensive to some readers. This book is for sale to adults ONLY.

* * * * * * * * * * * * * * * * * * *

Please store your files wisely where they cannot be accessed by underage readers.

ISBN-13: 978-1988083551
ISBN-10: 1988083559

Other Books by Darla Dunbar:

<u>The Romeo Alpha BBW Paranormal Shifter Romance Series</u>

Amanda Walker thinks that she has a normal and boring life. That is until after her 24th birthday. Everything changes when she meets the man who says he was supposed to be her husband. Denying everything the man says, she fights him every step of the way. But after he kidnaps her, Amanda discovers that there are some things about her family that her parents kept a secret all these years. Among the history of the family she learns secrets she thought only happened in story books. Can Amanda tell the difference between truth and lies or is she this mysterious woman that holds the key to a legacy?

<u>The Daemon Paranormal Romance Chronicles</u>

The daemon infighting can only be stopped when a strong leader emerges to calm the different factions. Juno appears to be at the heart of the conflict. Things become complicated when Phoebe and Supay try to negotiate with the siren, Juno. The love triangle among Phoebe, Supay and Apollo become tense when Juno's meddling threatens to destroy any romance that develops.

The Mind Talker Paranormal Romance Series

Ananda finds herself on the run and she's not alone. With help from Jared, a stranger that she just met, the two evade capture by an organization that is intent on hunting her kind. Ananda and Jared are able to read minds. When an unfortunate incident happened involving a disturbed individual that resulted in the death of his schoolmates, the secret organization decided to take action.

The Leather Satchel Paranormal Romance Series

Valtina is stuck in Middle World, unable to pass on to The Afterlife. In order to redeem herself from past deeds done, she must help bring romance back into the world and stop The Dark Side from destroying love in its entirety. Following orders issued by Ladaya and armed with a leather satchel filled with the appropriate tools and weapons, Valtina embraces each mission with enthusiasm.

Get the latest update on new releases from the author at:

http://darladunbar.com/newsletter/

This book contains all the stories of "The Alpha Packed BBW Paranormal Shifter Romance Series"

Book 1

Darlene has led a quiet life since suffering through a terrible break-up. She wants nothing more than to spend her time in front of the TV, away from any sort of trouble. But all that goes down the drain when handsome, rugged and rough Idris comes into her life. He is a werewolf on the lookout for his missing pack leader. Darlene quickly finds herself pulled towards this mysterious man and at the same time finds herself falling deeper and deeper into the world of the supernatural.

Book 2

Darlene finally has Idris all to herself. But with forces outside her control threatening her safety, will she be able to juggle both Idris and her newfound powers? Idris is being threatened with exile over telling Darlene about his world. With pressure mounting from both packs, he tries to protect Darlene from whatever he can. But Vivica, his old vampire girlfriend, will stop at nothing to get him back into her life – or else.

Book 3

With Idris facing a life time as an Exsul, Darlene finds herself trying to cope with her own power of seeing and connecting with spirits. Idris is tormented by his life choices and where he ends up at the risk of shoving Darlene away from him. Then Idris' maker turns up on his doorstep with a seductive promise – to lead a pack of Exsuls for the purpose of changing the future of all werewolves to come. Will Idris and Darlene be able to survive these trying times?

Book 4

Just as Darlene thinks her life has settled down, a terrible old foe returns for revenge. Darlene is still learning how to control her abilities with the spirit world when Jacob returns with an army of his own werewolf/vampire hybrid creatures. He has only one goal... get his revenge on Darlene and the packs that ruined his plan with Lucian the first time around. Darlene and Idris find themselves fighting for survival for the final time – but will they both survive?

Alpha Packed - A BBW Paranormal Shifter Romance Series

Books 1 to 4

By Darla Dunbar

© **Revelry Publishing 2016**

Table of Contents

Book One

Chapter One

THIS WAS a huge mistake. Darlene should have known better, but in utter and total desperation, she agreed to this date. Now the guy in front of her—what was his name again? Steve? Mike? She couldn't even remember now—had been talking non-stop about pro wrestling. But not even actual real wrestling. The stuff that was fake and basically just soap operas with some terrible phony fights thrown in.

"So then the Ice Cube challenged The Man to a battle!"

"Wow, really?" Darlene replied, feigning interest on every possible level.

This was her mistake. She had been spending way too much time at home lately, curled up on the couch, binge watching reality television shows because they made her feel better about her boring life. Darlene would leave for work in the mornings, do eight hours at a boring local bookstore, come home, eat and watch TV. She also stayed up far later than any normal human should, which resulted in limited forms of social communication.

That was how Darlene ended up on some free dating website. She deleted most of the messages she got. They were mostly from guys who seemed to think of her as a sexual fetish instead of an actual human being. Getting messages from guys who were into her being overweight made her feel uncomfortable. Darlene either got disgusted looks or sexual lust over her size. Both sucked. She had been about to delete her page for good when a guy who appeared to be normal messaged her. He hadn't made any gross comments about her size and even made her laugh once or twice with his messages. It had been eight months since her last relationship blew up in her face. *Why not try something different?* She decided to accept his date.

The guy was so boring that Darlene wished the restaurant would go up in flames so she could flee. She was flipping through her options on how to end the date early when he finally pushed his plate away.

"That was delicious," he said.

"Oh yeah. It was great," Darlene lied, thinking the potatoes were too dry for her liking.

The check came and the guy—what was his name!—made an effort to search for his wallet. *Oh here we go...*

"Oh man. I forgot my wallet at home!" he said with fake surprise.

"Yeah, yeah, I got it," she mumbled, slamming her debit card on the table.

It didn't take a genius to figure out this asshole had asked her out to throw her what he thought was a "pity date" and get a free meal out of her. He would probably go home to all his idiot friends and talk about how he gave the fat girl a date because he was just so nice. Darlene felt like punching him in the face.

She paid, and they walked out of the restaurant in silence. He escorted her to her car and then glanced around, as if checking so that no one could see him, before he tried to kiss her.

"Yeah," Darlene lifted up her hand to block him, "I don't think so. Thanks for nothing though, seriously."

The man scowled and before he could say something back, Darlene got into her car. She pulled out of the parking lot as quickly as she could, wanting to forget the entire terrible date.

What a mistake. What an absolute mistake. Not even just the date. The last couple years of her life had been a huge mistake. She wished she could travel back in time and re-do everything. The first thing she'd do would be to say a resounding *no* when Austin proposed to her.

Darlene pulled into her apartment complex five minutes later. She had picked a nearby restaurant so she could make a quick escape home if needed. She walked up to the second floor. The couple by the stairwell was fighting again. They were constantly screaming at each other over everything. Some nights, Darlene wanted to yell back at them to just break up. Other times, she wanted to tell them to make it work, because being alone was terrible.

She opened the front door of her apartment and glanced around. Her computer was on in one corner, and a few blankets were thrown on the couch for maximum comfort for those times when she drowned herself in ice cream and terrible reality shows. Everything else was clean though. Darlene couldn't stand her apartment being messy or dirty. She wanted it to be perfect, as if she could make her apartment look like how she didn't feel.

Darlene yanked off her high heels and plopped down in front of her computer. She deleted the online dating profile and stared out the window. That was it — she was going to become a hermit. Well, as much of a hermit as one can be if they still had to go to work and grocery shop and run errands...but other than that she was totally going to be a hermit from now on. People were not her thing. People were just terrible all around. And she'd had enough of terrible people.

She moved to the couch, wrapping herself up in a blanket. Darlene mused over what she would watch. Terrible shows about being tricked into online dating seemed like a good end to the night. It'd make her feel better at the very least.

***

Her cellphone rang loudly. Darlene jolted awake, startled. She wasn't used to her new ringtone. It used to be the theme song of an old cartoon she liked, but after everything went to hell she changed it to a normal ring in an effort to seem more adult. Now the ring was bleating loudly and annoying her. She looked at the front of the screen... her boss.

"Hello?"

"Hey, sorry, did I wake you?"

"No, Maria," Darlene lied. "What's up?"

"I had to fire Jacob. Can you cover his shift? You'd be working till three."

Darlene glanced at the clock to see it was a little past eight in the morning. "That's fine. I'll leave now."

She hopped in the shower, letting the warm water rush over her. She wasn't surprised that Maria had to fire Jacob. He was constantly late and unable to help any of the customers who came into the shop. The bookstore was small and dealt with books that couldn't be found at any of the chains. Business was slow, but the books were rare enough that Maria only needed to sell a few each month to keep the business going. Darlene liked how quiet it was and the fact that human interaction was minimal. She knew she needed to get over this slump she was in, but felt no desire to. Almost everything Darlene did as of late seemed to feed into it — her lifestyle, her job, even the stupid things she spent time watching and looking up online.

The bookstore was only a ten-minute drive to downtown and located between a coffee shop and a cheesy massage parlor. Maria hated the massage parlor. She thought it was tacky and ruined the charm of the street. Darlene usually liked to watch to see how many guys went in there. She swore it was a front for some hookers.

Darlene parked her car and headed toward the bookshop. She could already tell no one was in the store. She walked inside and waved to Maria.

"Oh, I am so glad you are here!" Maria exclaimed when she saw Darlene. "I'll have to hire someone right away, but you and I will have to work extra in the meantime."

"No problem," Darlene replied, shoving her purse under the front counter.

Darlene had worked here for almost four years. Maria was a good boss. She always treated Darlene with respect and even gave her an entire month off after her father passed away three years ago. She was an older Native American woman with a bushy head of white hair that she barely cared enough to run a comb through. She wore large glasses that looked like they were from the seventies. Her fashion left a lot to be desired. Maria seemed to put on whatever she grabbed first and didn't look twice in the mirror afterward. For instance, today she had on a blue shirt with an off-color green skirt and black shoes. Her earrings were painted octopuses she had probably made herself — she liked making crazy jewelry.

"So," Darlene asked. "What happened with Jacob?"

Maria scowled. "He comes into work high as a kite, stinking of weed. Starts rambling to me about how he was in the woods last night and *like, totally felt something, like, man,*" Maria said, mimicking Jacob's slow tone. "He was an hour late on top of it. I can't have someone late, stinking of weed and scaring off the few customers I get each month... especially after the last incident."

"Yeah, that was a mess." Jacob had hit on one of their regular clients in such a crass manner that she had threatened never to return again.

"Anyway, thank you so much for covering. I'm going to head off now. One of the grandkids is having a birthday party. You'll be okay?"

Darlene cast a sarcastic glance around the empty bookstore. "Wow, I hope I can handle it."

Maria laughed and grabbed her purse, heading to the door before stopping. "Hey, how was your date?"

Darlene frowned. "A total mess."

"Sorry, love. Hang in there, okay?" Maria said before leaving.

Hang in there. Darlene sighed. She has been hanging in there for way too long. When was she going to get a grip on her own life again? She walked around the shop to make sure everything was in its proper place. Darlene knew it would be, of course. It wasn't as if they had a ton of customers come through.

Maria had the marketable books up front, which brought in some tourist traffic during the summer. The farther back in the store one went, the stranger the books became. Darlene ended up in the back again, like she always did. Maria kept the supernatural books back here — books about ghosts, werewolves, mermaids and all sorts of paranormal creatures. Darlene always felt drawn to these; she never knew why. As a kid, she liked to pretend to be a ghost hunter. Nowadays, she liked to watch terrible B-movies about ghosts.

She trailed her fingers along the spines, letting the musty old-book smell wash over her. Darlene stopped in front of one book about ghosts, pulling it off the shelf. She had just flipped it open to a random page when the tiny bell on the door jingled. Surprised, Darlene looked up.

A tall man in amazing shape walked in. He had brown eyes, a beard and scruffy hair and wore a leather jacket. Darlene found herself gawking at him. He was so handsome her knees turned to jelly.

"Hi!" she said, but her voice sounded too high pitched, like she was eleven. "Hi, sorry, back here." She walked up front to him.

"Hello," he said in a deep voice that sent shivers down her back.

"Hi," Darlene repeated and then tried to get a hold of herself. "How can I help you?"

"I'm lost. I'm trying to find Roman's Tavern."

Her eyes widened. "I don't know if it's open yet."

Was this guy a hardcore alcoholic? It was still early in the morning, and he wanted to find a bar. Roman's Tavern was the only bar in town that Darlene hadn't ever gone to. It brought in a wild crowd that made her uneasy. Any time she drove past it and saw the crazy partying in there, she realized how much she wanted to go and that scared her. She was never much of a partier. The fact that such an overwhelming urge to go when she drove by made her nervous. What if she went and lost her head?

The cops were there often, breaking up fights. Bike gangs were always seen there. Sometimes, if she left work at closing time, she'd drive by it and hear the thumping music and smell the cigarette smoke. She thought about going in every time. What would happen? Would she get hurt? What if she was missing out on something?

To Darlene, Roman's Tavern represented a life she could jump into if only she wasn't afraid. But she *was* too afraid. Life as a hermit was too comforting.

"Do you know where I can find it anyway?" he asked.

"It's down the street. On the corner, kind of pushed back a bit. It has this rundown broken sign that you might see if you drive by it."

"Thanks a lot, Miss…"

"Darlene." She held out her hand.

He stared at it for a second and then shook it. "Idris. Thanks for the help. You guys sell books about ghosts?" He pointed to the book she was holding when he came in.

His hand was so warm that Darlene had to snap herself back to the conversation. Was he sick? Shouldn't he be resting instead of going to some bar?

"Yes," she managed to respond. "We have a supernatural section in the back. Ghosts, vampires, werewolves…the usual."

"Werewolves, huh?" he replied. "Okay, well, nice to meet you."

Before Darlene could say anything else, he was gone.

She stood there, clutching her book to her chest, thinking about the feeling of warmth from his hand. What in the world was that about?

Chapter Two

Idris stopped in front of Roman's Tavern. It was located so far back from the road that it was easy to miss during the day. But he knew exactly how to get to Roman's Tavern — he had been there tons of times before he left town. Today though, something had pulled him toward the bookstore and before he knew it, he was standing in front of the cute and friendly girl who worked there. In his old life, he would have shamelessly hit on her. But that was before everything changed. Instead, he lied and said he had gotten lost and needed directions.

He took a deep breath and walked toward the entrance of Roman's Tavern. This bar was the local haunt in town for anyone who fell in the "paranormal" group, as Darlene would have called it. Idris had stopped coming to places like this. They made him feel out of control and he hated it. He loathed anything that made him remember what he was — a werewolf. If he could have, he would have lived in seclusion, but no one would let him do what he wanted. Now he was being dragged into yet another scuffle between the pack here in Waterfall Grove and his own pack in Hedge Hills.

The door opened with a creak. Roman, the leader of the pack here, owned the bar and had a place to crash upstairs. His girlfriend often kicked him out due to their constant and vicious fights, but they never broke up. Idris knew he'd be here. The bar looked terrible in the daylight. The floors were dirty, and it smelled of old cigarettes and booze. Occasionally, vampires would come into the tavern, but only if they were craving a fight. This bar was a werewolf haunt.

Mark, Roman's second-in-command, rounded the corner as soon as Idris entered. He had a missing eye from a vicious fight with Roman six years ago, when Roman was vying for pack leader. Mark bowed to Roman after that fight and agreed to drop his claim.

"What the hell are you doing here?" Mark hissed.

"I need to speak to Roman," Idris replied, skipping the pleasantries.

"Roman doesn't want to speak to you or anyone else from your shitty pack," Mark said, crossing his arms.

This was what Idris hated the most. The stupid pissing contests between the packs. It all felt so childish. It reminded him of being ten years old and fighting with his friends at the playground. In the end, all of this amounted to absolutely nothing. Idris' patience began to wear thin.

"I need to speak to him," he repeated.

Mark scowled. "Are you deaf? You're not going to speak to him."

Idris took two steps forward, inches away from Mark's face, trying to control the urge to Change right in front of him and tear his throat out. "You are going to let me talk to him right now, do you understand? Or I'll leave you dead on the floor of this shitty fucking bar."

Mark shrugged. "Have it your way for now. Whatever has your panties in a twist isn't our problem." He moved to the side and avoided looking at Idris again.

Idris wasn't surprised that Mark backed down, given their history. There was no one in this entire area who didn't know about them. And now he had used fear to get what he wanted instead of taking the time to try to act like a normal human being. *But you're not a normal human being.*

Idris took a metal staircase in the back up to the top. The bar's second level overlooked the dance floor and offered a lot of dark corners where people could make out and drink. Idris opened a door off to the side, stepping into the offices and the one room that made up Roman's makeshift bedroom.

"Roman?" Idris called out.

There was a grunting noise of surprise and then Roman stuck his head out of the office, looking down the hallway. He was an incredibly large man, with scars down his cheeks from scratches from other werewolves. Roman had scars and marks all over from head to toe, from all the battles he had gotten into. He looked like a gladiator from ancient times. His hair was messy and sticking out at different angles. He had a jacket pulled on tightly but it looked as if his shoulders were going to pop right out of it.

"What the hell are you doing here?" Roman asked, echoing what Mark had already barked at him.

"I need to talk to you."

"Mark let you by? You didn't kill him, did you?"

Idris ignored the jab and tried not to let it get to him. "He let me by."

Roman looked him up and down, as if debating if he wanted to push this into a fight or just talk and get rid of Idris quickly. "Come in here."

Idris walked into the neatly organized office. There was no way that Roman put this together himself.

"Where's Julie?" Idris asked, trying to see if Julie had kicked him out again.

Roman shrugged. "I'm staying here tonight."

So she had. That explained his downtrodden spirit. Normally whenever Idris had to deal with Roman, it went as well as teaching a cat how to swim. Idris sat down across from Roman at his desk.

"Why are you here?" Roman asked, leaning back in his chair.

"The pack sent me," Idris replied. "Lucian has gone missing."

Roman's bushy eyebrows shot up. "Your pack leader is missing?"

"Yes, that's right. You're the closest pack. I wanted to know if you saw him pass through here."

"No, I haven't seen that son of a bitch pass through here. If he had, you'd know about it. He'd be dead up front in the bar."

"Charming," Idris replied dryly. "You have anything you can give me besides threats of what you'd do to a missing man?"

"When he go missin'?"

"Four days ago. Was leaving his shop and never came home." Idris glossed over most of the details.

Roman shrugged. "Haven't seen him."

"Nothing you can tell me?"

"You calling me a liar, boy?"

Breathe in, breathe out. Idris tried to control the urge to Change. "No. Roman, I am not calling you a liar. I am just trying to see if you happen to know anything."

"Well, I don't. And I don't appreciate you coming in here accusing me of knowin' something." Roman was getting angry now, having found an outlet for his anger about Julie.

Idris stood up. "I'm not accusing you of anything. Don't be pissed off at me because Julie kicked you out again."

Roman stood up as well, growling. "How do we know that you didn't do it?"

"Excuse me?"

"You! We all know you used to kill anything that moved. You tricked everyone into thinking you were fine and recovered, but what if you snapped and killed the pack leader to get his spot?"

Idris started counting to ten in his head in order to stop himself from reaching across the desk and dragging Roman over it. He was different now. He had to keep telling himself that.

"I'm done with this," Idris said, turning around.

"You are done speaking to me when I say you are, pup," Roman growled. "You're in my land now, not back at home."

Idris ignored him, leaving the office. He waited for Roman to burst through the door to attack him but there was nothing. Just like he had thought — a bunch of bravado. Still no closer to the truth about what had happened to Lucian. As Idris walked out of the bar, he thought at least he had kept his promise to himself — he didn't hurt any of the other werewolves, even if they did piss him off.

***

Darlene came home and plopped her purse on the floor. She turned the oven on to heat up a pizza. Her social interaction with the one lone person who had come into the bookshop was quite enough for her, thank you. It was funny, most of the time when a customer came in, it felt like there was a glaring spotlight on her size. But Idris made her forget all about her size during their brief conversation. If only all conversations could be like that.

She wandered off to her computer, sitting down in the chair and staring out the window next to it. After Idris left, she had idly flicked through books about ghosts for the rest of the shift. Darlene couldn't help but think about Roman's Tavern. The man didn't seem like some sort of booze hound. And his hand was so warm! He was tall and built like a tank. She normally didn't like guys like that but she found herself drifting off thinking about him the rest of the day.

Darlene would have remembered a guy like that if she'd ever seen him before. He must have been passing through town. She wondered how long he was going to stay. Why was she thinking about this guy so much? She rubbed her eyes, sighing a bit, before booting up her computer. Darlene typed *Roman's Tavern* into the search bar and watched the results pop up.

The first was where it was located on the map, along with its rating. It wasn't rated that hot. She flicked through the reviews quickly.

"Everyone seemed to glare at me in unison when I came in..."

"Fight broke out while I was there and the guy walked out with a broken nose..."

"Dirty floors that looked like dog fur was the main décor..."

"The regular crowd here seems a little rough for my taste."

"Drinks sucked!"

Darlene went back to the search results page, staring at it. Why was she even looking this up? What was she looking for? She clicked on the homepage for the bar and found herself staring at some website that looked straight out of the 90s back when Geocities was still a thing. She expected to hear MIDI music start to play. Was there *clip art* on this page?

The main page said the bar offered a *"well stocked bar as well as busy dance floor. Second story offers great places for low-key conversations"*. Somehow she doubted that. The address was wrong, and there was no phone number on the main page. Darlene clicked through more of the pages but almost all of them were dead links. One page said Roman's Tavern was better suited for locals instead of tourists. It seemed an odd thing to write on their page. Darlene got a vibe that this place only wanted a certain group of people as patrons… even less of a reason for her to go try it out then.

She went through a few more pages of search results but they got less relevant as she went on. Darlene paused at one that caught her eye though — *Roman's Tavern theory?* She clicked on it and it loaded a post from user 'SunnyWerewolf' from five years ago on an old message board labeled *The Dark Side of Night*, whatever the hell that meant. Darlene read the post:

Went here finally from the tip of user XOreal. What a trip! It was a terrible bar and I didn't see anything supernatural about it at all, honestly. I got there around eleven pm and it was packed but mostly by regulars.

When I got inside it was like everyone began to glare at me all at once. The rumor was this place had some sort of supernatural vibe to it, like vampires or faeries or something, but it was just a bunch of pissed-off bikers acting superior to anyone who wasn't a local. I have always identified as a werewolf and was saddened to see I wouldn't be meeting any of my kin here!

Identified as a werewolf? Darlene felt out of her element. People identified as mythical creatures? She read the replies to the post but most of them were generic. There was one final reply though, six months after the original post. All it said was: *Come on a full moon.*

There was no reply. Out of curiosity, Darlene brought up SunnyWerewolf's profile. His post about the tavern had been the final post he ever made. She searched his name on the board and got a couple of other posts popping up, all about him.

Anyone heard from SunnyWerewolf lately?

Hey, whatever happened to SunnyWerewolf?

I guess he must have moved on to another board.

Darlene thought about the final reply to his post. The user who had made it had no other posts. It looked as if that reply to SunnyWerewolf was the only reason that account was created.

On a hunch, Darlene opened a new search window. She was acting ridiculous, of course. She remembered a murder that happened in town a while ago. The body had been found in the hills, maimed by wolves. The police never figured out why the guy wandered into the hills near the town. They were dangerous and ended in cliffs that could send a person who was not paying attention over into the ocean. Darlene's imagination always ran wild at night. When it did, she usually went on some online game and talked to strangers — no one minded a person acting odd online. But she started typing into the search bar instead.

Old articles about the case popped up. Five years ago. She flicked back between the post telling him to come on a full moon and when SunnyWerewolf had gone missing. The dates synced up. SunnyWerewolf had gone missing on the full moon and was last seen at Roman's Tavern.

Had the police known about this post? The case was concluded as a drunken accident but what if they had never seen this before? Darlene's heart began to beat very quickly. She couldn't just ignore this. What if there was a link? Did the person who posted, asking

SunnyWerewolf to come to Roman's Tavern, kill him and make it look like an accident?

Darlene exited the browser windows quickly, as if they suddenly had eyes watching her.

Chapter Three

Idris walked into the police station when he saw Darlene from the bookstore being led out of the back office with a detective. She looked upset and frustrated. Understandable, Idris thought, since she had just been talking to cops. He didn't want to be here either, but he wasn't able to pick up Lucian's scent at all. At least if he filed a missing persons report, he'd be notified if someone found him.

As he walked up to the main desk, Darlene spoke to the detective. "You don't find it curious he believed he was a werewolf and vanished on a full moon?"

The detective mumbled something non-committal, with an expression that said he was sick of talking about it. But Idris froze. Why was she talking about that old case? He knew it was that because she mentioned that guy who thought he was a werewolf. Brent had shown up one night to Roman's Tavern, rubbing everyone the wrong way, claiming he was a werewolf looking for a pack. He wasn't a werewolf. Idris happened to be there that night, back when he still ran with Roman's pack. He wanted to rip the kid apart for invading their spot, claiming to be one of them, when no one in their right mind would want to be one of them.

Brent left soon after, and Idris didn't see him again. But he turned up dead in the woods six months later, on the night of the full moon, when everyone was Changed. The cops ruled it a drunken accident, saying Brent had pissed off some wolves. But everyone knew better. The kid had been mauled by werewolves and left for dead in the woods. No one came forward to admit they had killed Brent. Roman blamed Idris, saying he had lost it and had wanted to kill the kid previously. That was when Idris broke free from the pack, which kicked off more trouble.

"Hello?"

The voice snapped Idris out of his memories. The assistant in front of him looked irritated — she probably said hello to him at least three times, judging by her tone.

"Sorry, excuse me." Idris turned around, following Darlene.

She left the police station and walked toward her car.

Idris jogged after her. "Excuse me?"

Darlene stopped and turned around. She was pretty. Her features were girlish with large, bright blue eyes and chestnut brown hair swept back out of her face. Everyone in his pack used to make fun of him for his penchant of falling for bigger girls who ended up breaking his heart, probably because he used to be an ass and deserved it, but Idris ignored the teasing. He always liked his girls on the thicker side and was proud of it. Darlene fit into that box nicely.

"Oh, hi, Mr. Idris," Darlene said, blinking those pretty blue eyes at him. "Did you find Roman's Tavern?"

"Yes, thank you," Idris replied. "I couldn't help but overhear you mentioning the murder that happened a few years ago."

Her face fell. "Yeah, I thought I found something new to the case but they weren't interested." She shrugged. "How did you know what I was talking about?"

Idris wasn't sure how to lie properly to her without mentioning the tiny little fact that it all had to do with werewolves. "To be honest, my friend just went missing. Seemed like a long shot but someone mentioning an old case like that at the same time my friend went missing…" He trailed off, but realized it was true — that was why he came after her, wasn't it?

"Your friend is missing? I'm really sorry to hear that," she exclaimed. "Is that why you were checking out that bar yesterday?"

Idris nodded. "Yes, I was checking to see if he passed through. No luck though."

"Yeah, I just…I found this post online telling the kid — I guess his name was Brent but he posted as SunnyWerewolf — to come to that bar on a full moon. And then he vanished. What if the police didn't know about the post? Someone telling Brent to come back to the bar and then he vanishes and shows up dead, you know?"

Idris' heart started beating very hard. There was a *post* telling Brent to come back to the bar? He didn't know about that. The case suddenly burst wide open in front of him. After everyone had denied responsibility for it and tried to pin it on Idris, no one seemed that interested in finding out the truth. But now…

Darlene's phone suddenly rang and she looked down at it. "Oh, this is my best friend. I've been blowing her off lately. I have to take this or she'll kill me."

"I understand," Idris said. "When do you work again? I'd like to hear more about what you found about Brent."

"That was mostly it. The police blew me off. Said the case was closed and a post wasn't enough to warrant opening it up again. But I start work tomorrow at ten in the morning." She looked down at her phone. "Okay, I'll see you later!"

Darlene answered the phone, turned around and walked off. Idris caught himself staring at her bottom as she walked away. He shook his head before returning to make the report about Lucian. As he walked into the police station again, Idris wondered — what was Darlene doing that made her find that post in the first place?

***

"Why are you vanishing again?" Rebecca demanded when Darlene answered the phone. "Every time I try to pull you out of the hole, you're back in real life for about two weeks and then you go back to being a hermit," Rebecca said loudly into her phone as Darlene sighed. "Was it that terrible date you went on?"

"I'm trying. You know I am," Darlene replied.

"You know I love you, Darlene," Rebecca said after a long pause. "But you can't keep letting what happened with Austin hold you back from living. I'm not sure how else I can help you except by telling you the truth. You need to find a way to move on with your life and stop living by yourself and closing everyone out."

After Darlene hung up, she returned home and curled up on the couch, with a bowl full of ice cream and some terrible reality show about gypsy brides who loved toddler beauty pageants or something. She had known Rebecca for over ten years now. They met online before they realized they lived only thirty minutes from each other. Rebecca lived in Hedge Hills and often wanted to see Darlene. They used to see each other all the time back when Darlene was dating Austin. But everything went to hell, and she hadn't seen Rebecca in over six months.

Rebecca meant well and wanted Darlene to get better and to get her life together. But Rebecca had a good job and a steady boyfriend. Rebecca was adorable and chubby in a way that guys didn't mind, unlike how Darlene felt about herself. Rebecca didn't think Darlene was trying to get better. And to be honest, Darlene didn't think she was trying to get better either.

She didn't know how to move on after losing Austin. They had been together for five years and she loved him every second of the day, more fiercely than the last second. Austin was tall, blond and handsome. He made Darlene feel as if she was the most beautiful woman on the entire planet. They used to spend time reading books together or laying by the pool of his parent's house, letting the sun cook them as they sipped cocktails. It had all been amazing.

And then Austin proposed. The ring was enormous. Austin had been saving up for it since their first date because he knew she was the one. Life couldn't have been better.

Darlene tried to shut the thoughts down before they came back in full force. She did herself no favors when they did and ended up drinking. Rebecca meant well by her tough love talk but it just depressed Darlene. She pulled her blankets tighter around herself and thought about how the police officer had blown her off completely with her information about Brent aka SunnyWerewolf. He told her the case was shut and had been solved for quite some time and not to be playing detective at home.

It pissed her off. She wasn't playing detective at home. Darlene was still bothered by the post. And then Idris showing up…

He said his friend was missing. The first place Idris looked for his friend was Roman's Tavern. It just seemed odd to Darlene that Brent had gone missing there and Idris checked there first. And now Idris was going to stop by to see her again to talk about what she knew about Brent.

That was another thing that Darlene didn't want to think about. When she was actually talking to Idris, she didn't feel self-conscious at all. Idris was gorgeous in a rugged way. But she couldn't just walk away when someone started a conversation with her. She was terrible with people but not *rude.*

There was just too much social interaction for Darlene today. She wanted nothing more than to cover her head with the blankets and ignore everything going on in her life.

***

The next day, Maria held interviews to replace Jacob so Darlene watched the front shop. There were no customers, as usual. The applicants who came in were college kids looking for a part-time job or tiny, little old ladies looking for something to do. Darlene didn't care who Maria hired. They never needed two people to man the store at one time. The best employees were the ones Darlene never had to hear about, unlike Jacob, whom she only met once and felt as if she knew him like a brother from how often he had messed up.

Darlene was idly flipping through a book about werewolves when the front door chimed. She looked up and saw Idris walk into the bookstore. He looked tired, with bags under his eyes. His jacket was zipped up tightly but Darlene could still see the muscles rippling beneath. His hair was messy, and stubble graced his chin. His eyes were a dark gray, like storm clouds. Darlene tried to ignore the butterflies in her stomach.

"Hey," he said, walking over to her.

"Hi," she replied, hoping her tone was casual. "How are you?"

"I'm good. Tired."

"How did the police report go?"

His gaze fell on the book in front of her. "What are you reading?"

"Oh!" Darlene looked down at the book. "It's called *The Werewolf Code*. Just…it's silly…I like reading in that section…you know. Um, I find it interesting to read about things that probably aren't around us. I said probably, I meant — not at all. No one is like that. I…"

She trailed off, mortified with how much she was rambling on to him.

"I've read it," Idris admitted.

"Really? You've read *The Werewolf Code?* That's great —"

"Who's this?"

Darlene turned around to see Maria come from the back office and look Idris up and down. "Oh, Maria."

"Somehow I don't think this is the next person I am supposed to interview — Mabel Rodgers."

"I'm Idris," he said, holding his hand to Maria. "Darlene's friend."

Maria's eyebrows shot up. "Darlene's friend, really?" She glanced over at Darlene with an expression that said *I hope you tell me about this later.* "Nice to meet you." She shook his hand.

"I was just talking to Darlene about *The Werewolf Code.*"

"Oh," Maria sighed. "Darlene just loves all that paranormal stuff. Especially ghosts. You into that stuff, too?"

"It's interesting," Idris replied.

"Glad you found someone else interested in that stuff, Darlene," Maria turned to head back to the office. "Let me know when the next person gets here."

Idris looked at Darlene. "The cops filed the report but they haven't seen anyone matching my friend's description."

Darlene sighed. "I'm sorry. That sucks."

"I was wondering about the post you found online," Idris said.

"Oh, yeah." Darlene pulled out her phone. "I found it last night on here to show you."

Idris looked down at Darlene's phone. He'd been surprised to find her looking through *The Werewolf Code* or that there was even a copy here. Idris hadn't seen a copy of that book in a long time. Every pack leader had one and gave it to anyone who had been turned. Idris remembered after the first time he Changed he spent a full week going through the book page by page, trying to find a way to reverse the curse. Idris couldn't find one, and he never looked at it again.

But there were only so many copies of the book in existence — one for each pack that had been together since the Dawn of the Change. If a pack didn't have a copy of the book then they'd reach out to share one from a friendly pack. The fact there was one just sitting here concerned him. He wanted to ask when the book was acquired.

Nothing about the post on Darlene's phone seemed to have come from anyone he knew. But there was the proof, staring at him right in the face, that someone had lured Brent back to Roman's Tavern to murder him.

"I don't know much about computers," Idris said, looking up at Darlene. "Is there any way we could track this?"

"That was the only post by that user. It looks like the account was created just to post that."

Idris looked back down at it, frowning. "Strange."

"Did the same thing happen to your friend? Did he think he was a werewolf, too?"

Idris wanted to laugh, but knew he couldn't. Lucian was a good pack leader, tough when he needed to be and knew when to bend to make sure the pack saw him as fair. His wife, Liara, was also a werewolf and was beloved by almost everyone in the pack for her gentle nature, even when they all had naturally violent sides. She cried so hard over Lucian going missing that Idris worried about drowning in her tears.

"No," Idris replied. "How did you get this book, by chance?" He pointed to *The Werewolf Code*.

Darlene looked at the cover, running her fingers over it. "Someone sold it to us, actually. About a month ago."

"Really? Did you see the guy?" Idris pressed, knowing he didn't sound casual at all but not caring.

"He was tall and wearing a suit. Although I remember the suit didn't fit properly. I notice weird things like that." Darlene shrugged, and Idris tried to ignore his desire to flirt with her yet again. She crinkled her nose when she was nervous, and it was adorable. "Anyway, he had glasses on with large frames. And he had this cellphone that looked like it was from the late nineties. A relic. He could have donated that instead. Anyway, he said he had this laying around and it took up too much room so he dropped it off here. Said someone would come by for it one day."

Idris felt numb all over. *Lucian,* Idris realized with a jolt. *Lucian was here and dropped the book off.*

"And that was it," Darlene finished. "Been sitting on the shelf just gathering dust. I mean, it is a huge book. I started looking at it and it's like…rules for being a werewolf and stuff."

"Can I see it?" Idris asked stiffly.

Darlene slid it over to him. At that moment, a woman who looked roughly a thousand years old, came into the bookstore. Probably Mabel Rodgers for her interview. Darlene excused herself to help the visitor. She walked with a cane and took a long time to cross the store. She had an open umbrella as well, which she seemed to be fighting to close. Idris thought the umbrella was weird, but old people were strange in general.

Idris turned back to the book. He opened the cover and checked the bottom of the first page. Lucian's initials were there. Idris' head felt light for a moment. This was his own pack's book. Why did Lucian disguise himself and drop it off here? *Said someone would come by for it one day, but who?* Idris trailed his fingers over the initials. Did Lucian mean Idris?

"Yes, right through here," Darlene said to the tiny old lady. "Maria, this is Mabel — okay, thank you." She shut Maria's office door with a soft click and let out a sigh.

As she walked back over to him, Idris looked up. "How much is this?"

"Let me look. No one has even asked before." She went over to the computer on the front desk, typing quickly before stopping. "$2,000."

Idris' eyebrows shot up. What was Lucian thinking? If he meant for Idris to find this, did he forget Idris wasn't exactly rolling in money? Darlene was looking at Idris patiently. He found himself admiring her blue eyes again before shaking his head.

"I want to buy it," Idris said. "But I don't have that sort of cash on me."

"You want to buy it?" Darlene replied, surprised.

Idris nodded, trying to come up with an excuse. "Yes, it looks interesting."

The way Darlene was looking at him made him nervous. There was no way she was going to buy any excuse he gave her. But he couldn't tell her the truth either. No one was supposed to know about the packs if they weren't one of them.

"Books that much are usually bought by high-end collectors. That's why they don't mind the price. It's not for casual reading."

"You can't wiggle on the price?"

Darlene shook her head. "Sorry, Idris. We're barely breaking even as it is. I don't know why Maria paid so much for it."

Idris found that curious but knew he hit his question limit for the time being. "Well, if she changes her mind, can you call me?"

Darlene's big eyes blinked. "Oh, sure."

They pulled out their cellphones and exchanged numbers. Idris hurried from the bookstore, leaving with more questions than ever.

Chapter Four

Darlene was doing the last walkthrough of the night. It didn't really matter, but Maria liked knowing that everything was in its proper spot and Darlene didn't like lying. As she slid *The Werewolf Code* back onto the shelf, she found herself thinking about Idris for the millionth time that hour alone. His phone number, now safely stored in her own phone, seemed to be burning a hole in her purse behind the counter. She knew he had given her his phone number for reasons other than any desire for her, but Darlene had never received another number from any guy since Austin — and that tragic date she was just on… but she liked to think that didn't count.

But Idris, no matter how good looking he was, was strange. His behavior seemed just off enough to make Darlene think he was hiding something major, not only about him but his missing friend, too. And his sudden desire to buy the book out of nowhere — one look inside told the reader that they were in for dry reading and a lot of strange jargon that made no sense.

Darlene's hand rested against the spine of the book. She took the book out again, balancing it with one hand then flipping it open with her other. The book was massive, at least 1,000 pages and had an old smell to it that was more than just that of a musty old book. She opened it to the first page, which was all Idris had looked at before suddenly deciding to buy it.

Darlene couldn't find anything out of the ordinary. Certainly nothing that screamed "Spend $2,000 on me!" She ran her fingers down the page idly, and saw something that wasn't part of the print. Initials — *LC.* Darlene suddenly knew that was why Idris wanted to buy it.

Darlene shoved the book back onto the shelf and went back to the computer. Maria stored data on everyone who sold any book to them for possible donations or sales in the future. She typed quickly and a page on the screen popped up about the book. The seller's name was *Luke Craig.* Without thinking twice, Darlene dialed the number to see if anyone picks up. It rang for almost a full minute.

"Hello?" The woman sounded as if she ate cigarettes for dinner.

"Hi, Luke Craig there?"

"No. Sorry, wrong number."

The woman hung up right away before Darlene could apologize for bothering her. So the phone number was fake. What did Idris know that he wasn't telling her? At least she knew he was lying now.

As Darlene was leaving, she thought that maybe it wasn't any of her business. Maybe she should just forget about it all together. Locking the front door of the bookshop, she thought about calling Rebecca to see if they could meet up. It would make her happy, and Darlene could use some social interaction that wasn't about missing people.

As she walked around the side of the building to the parking lot, she stopped for a moment. Maybe she was being paranoid, but she swore that she saw something dart away from her car. The parking lot was tiny and dimly lit. It was behind the building that housed not only the bookstore but the other two shops next to where she worked — the coffee shop and massage parlor. The massage parlor was closed for the night but the coffee shop usually stayed open until 10:00 pm. It must have just been someone from there leaving.

Darlene began to walk again, clutching her keys in between her fingers. Why was she getting such a sense of dread? Was it stupid to keep going to her car? She had a mental image of those bad horror movies when the person decides to investigate the source of the noise instead of running away as quickly as possible. Darlene stopped and turned around. She would figure something else out... like call a taxi. As she walked away from her car, she heard a noise. She turned around and saw a blur coming straight toward her.

The force sent her flying. Darlene shut her eyes to brace for the impact but then she felt steely fingers wrapping around her waist and slamming her against the back of the bookshop, out of sight from the coffee store. Darlene was out of breath and opened her eyes.

The woman who stood over her was deathly pale and had blood-red eyes. Darlene felt terrified just looking at her. Was this the same person who had just tossed her as though she was a ragdoll? There was no way. The woman had dark red hair tied up in a tight bun and was wearing baggy clothing that Darlene couldn't make out. Darlene tried to wiggle away but the woman's grip was iron tight.

"Where is he?" the woman asked in a low voice.

"What?" Darlene squeaked. How could this woman be so strong?

"Idris. Don't play dumb with me." The woman moved her face closer to Darlene's.

Darlene felt as if ice had been doused over her. *Idris*. She supposed she had made her vow not to get involved in people's business a little too late. The woman continued to stare at her with empty, emotionless eyes.

"He's not with me," Darlene said through shuddering gasps, unsure of what the woman was looking for.

"Where was he last?"

Darlene was unsure how to respond. Fear flowed through her veins, as if her entire body had been drained of blood.

"Answer me!" the woman shouted. "Or I'll make you my meal right now."

Darlene was going to squeak a response when suddenly the woman tilted her head back and fangs popped out. She hissed at Darlene.

"Oh my god," Darlene mumbled. "Are you a vampire?"

This just seemed to piss the woman off. She picked Darlene up again and threw her back against the wall. Darlene hit the ground and grunted, tasting the blood that filled up in her mouth. This was crazy. She had to be dreaming, right? Or did this woman have fake teeth in her mouth, because vampires aren't real —

"Tell me or I will kill you right now." The woman crouched down next to Darlene.

Darlene looked up at her. "Idris said he was leaving town and had found the trail of his friend back home."

Darlene held her breath. She hoped the woman believed her lie. Could vampires sense when someone was lying? It was as if all the useless knowledge that Darlene read about vampires suddenly slid out of her brain and landed on the ground next to her. She had no idea if her lie even matched up with what was going on, but if she could get the woman to leave, then Darlene could tell Idris what was going on.

"Did he take the book with him?" the woman asked.

"Yes," Darlene lied. "He took some big book with him. I don't know what it was."

The woman pulled on Darlene's hair and yanked her gaze to meet hers. "If you're lying, I'm going to come back and drain you. Do you understand? The only reason I'm not going to kill you tonight is because I'm feeling fucking generous." When Darlene didn't reply, she yanked on her hair again. "Say thank you!"

"Thank you," Darlene mumbled, her face blushing with embarrassment.

The woman let go of her hair and stood back up, looking down at Darlene in disgust. Then she glanced around the parking lot and ran off so fast that she was just a dark blur against the backdrop of the few cars still around. The blur jumped high in the air and disappeared over the rooftops.

Darlene just sat there and managed to prop herself up against the back wall. Her mouth tasted of blood and her entire body ached from the physical trauma. She slid her cellphone out of the jeans of her pocket. The screen was cracked but she was able to get it to turn on. Darlene brought up her contacts and hit Idris' name.

***

The hotel where Idris was staying at must be the worst in town. He wasn't entirely convinced that this wasn't just a front for some prostitution ring, because the turnaround rate on his floor alone was ridiculous. Half the time, he couldn't sleep because the moaning was so loud and fake that he wished he could Change into a bear instead to hibernate. Idris turned up the volume on the tiny TV in his room but the picture was so fuzzy he could barely make out what it was. It reminded him of when he was a teenager and would watch the fuzzy channels to try to find a breast. He was thinking about going to bed when his phone went off.

He didn't realize it was his own phone at first. No one ever called him. *Darlene.* His heart jumped up and lodged in his throat. He was trying not to think about her all night. Idris knew that Darlene had given him her number because of the missing people they had been discussing and nothing more. But he still found his thoughts drifting to her too often. He told himself that she probably just butt dialed him as he answered.

"Hello?"

A long pause of silence, and then finally Darlene's labored breathing on the other line. "Idris." Her voice was rough. "Bookshop."

"What's wrong?" Idris asked, standing up.

Another long pause filled with her ragged breathing as Idris grabbed his car keys and opened the door to the hallway. "Woman. Vampire." Idris' blood ran cold. "Please."

The call ended. Idris was already taking off down the hallway toward his car. The moon was high in the air, spilling light over the parking lot as he slid into his old pickup truck. Female vampire. Idris didn't even need to ask Darlene to describe her to him. He knew who it was. Vivica. And if Vivica was coming after Darlene, then whatever was going on just got a lot more serious.

It took him fifteen minutes to get through town to the bookshop. Idris pulled into the parking lot and saw Darlene's purse, the contents strewn about. Her car was still there. The coffee shop looked mostly empty and only had two other cars down at the end. Idris got out of his truck and looked around. Then he saw Darlene. She was sitting up against the back door of the bookshop, her eyes closed. Idris ran over to her, crouching by her side.

"Darlene?" he asked, afraid that Vivica had done something horrible to her.

Darlene's eyes fluttered for a moment and then she looked at him. "Hey."

"Are you bit?" Idris asked, running his hands over her arms to check for any bite marks before tilting her head to each side to check her neck.

"No," Darlene mumbled. "She said that would be for next time."

"We have to get you home, okay? You can tell me what happened later."

Darlene tried shaking her head. "Can't move. My body is so sore."

"I'll get you to my truck."

"No. I'm too big."

Idris ignored her and picked her up in one swoop. Darlene made a soft noise of surprise but Idris was already walking to his truck. He couldn't explain that his werewolf strength rendered almost anything light as a feather. He managed to get her into the passenger seat. Idris started the truck up, and the engine purred to life.

"Where do you live?" he asked.

Darlene managed to mumble out her address before she fell asleep. Her breathing was soft and slow, but as far as Idris could tell she wasn't wounded. He was sure that Vivica tossed her around enough to give her bruises that would last for days. Darlene only lived about ten minutes from the shop in an apartment complex that seemed a little rundown. The gate was broken and allowed anyone through, and there was a huge party in one of the apartments near the back.

Darlene's apartment was in a secluded spot, which was good because it meant no one would notice a giant man taking her into her apartment. With her keys in hand, Idris picked her up again and unlocked the door. The apartment was small yet incredibly clean. There was a bookshelf in one corner next to a computer and a couch with lots of blankets on it. The kitchen was neat and orderly. Idris could see her bedroom behind the kitchen. He walked to it and placed her down on her bed.

Idris shut the blinds, just in case Vivica was still around. He looked around and saw a dresser with little trinkets, tiny figures of things from different TV shows and a lamp. He flicked the lamp on and dim light filled her bedroom. There was a painting above her bed of cats playing poker, which he thought was cute. The night table next to her bed had a framed photo. Idris picked up the photo. It was a couple years old, Idris thought, because Darlene looked a bit smaller and her hair was long, swept up in a bun. She wore a pale pink dress that shimmered in the photo. She was smiling in a way that Idris had never seen before. And she was holding hands with an extremely thin man with messy blonde hair. He was tanned and had bright white teeth. He was holding her hand loosely and had a T-shirt on with khaki shorts. And they were both wearing matching rings.

Darlene was fast asleep now, her chest rising slowly. There was no ring on her finger now. He looked back down at the photo. Darlene looked so happy, her eyes shining and bright. The man next to her looked a little less excited, his eyes not bright at all and his grip on Darlene not as tight. *They must have broken up, although her having his picture right here isn't a good sign.* Idris put the picture back down. He knew all about broken hearts and old loves. It seemed Darlene had one of her own.

***

Darlene was running. She kept trying to run faster toward the church. But the storm clouds were rolling in, covering the church with rain and wind. The wind stopped her from making it to the entrance. She had to get into that church. There was a clap of thunder and Darlene looked over her shoulders. The graveyard behind her was growing darker and skeletons were rising from the graves. Their mouths were open as if they were trying to speak, but she didn't want to hear them. Darlene turned back around and there was Austin on the church steps. The vampire had her arms wrapped around him, and she was biting into his neck, her red eyes flashing —

Darlene suddenly woke up and gasped for air. Sunlight spread in through the cracks in her blinds. She was in her room. Darlene tried to turn her head but her entire body ached and throbbed. Her mouth tasted faintly of blood. Her head pounded. She lay there, very still, trying to remember what happened. But the images seemed to twist with her nightmare, and she had a hard time remembering the truth.

"You're up."

Darlene painfully turned her head to the side and saw Idris in the doorway to her room. *Right* — she had managed to call him before the pain of being thrown around had become too much. He looked at her gently, his eyes soft in the morning light.

"Hey," she croaked.

Idris crouched next to the bed, uncapping a bottle of water. "I'm going to help you sit up for some water, okay?"

"Okay," Darlene croaked again, unable to find the energy to nod her head.

Idris managed to prop her up against the back of the bed but it was painful. Her entire body felt as if she had been hit by a car, especially in the front where Vivica had rammed into her. She thought of the stranger bearing down on her with those red eyes and it was as if she was taken back to that moment again. *Best not to think about it.* The water was cold and refreshing and before Darlene knew it she had drunk the entire bottle. Idris looked at her with concern in his eyes.

"How are you feeling?"

"Sore," Darlene replied. "All over. Thanks for getting me."

"Absolutely," Idris said. "As if I was going to ignore your phone call."

Silence filled the air and then Darlene cleared her throat. "I'll tell you what happened, but then I'd like to know exactly what is going on."

Idris nodded. Darlene wondered what he knew and if he was going to lie to her. He was clearly the reason that she was attacked. Darlene told her story, watching his face closely. He didn't seem puzzled by the description of the vampire who had attacked her, which made Darlene think he knew exactly who it was. He did seem surprised, however, when she mentioned that the creature had asked if he had taken the book with him when he left town. When Darlene finished, Idris was silent.

After a little bit, he finally spoke. "I need to look at the book, Darlene. *The Werewolf Code.* I need to know why Lucian sold it to you."

"The man who sold it to us is your missing friend?"

Idris nodded. "Whatever information he gave you..."

Darlene cut him off. "The phone number is fake. I already tried it. We can look up the address he gave though. And you can look at the book, but it has to be on the down low."

Idris held his head in his hands at this point and sighed. "I never meant for you to be dragged into this."

"Well, it's too late to freak out about that now," Darlene snapped, feeling irritated over the entire situation. "It's my fault, too. I shouldn't have looked into Brent. I should have just minded my own business. Now are you going to tell me what is going on or what?"

Idris looked up at her and chewed on his bottom lip, as if he was trying to think of what to tell her. Darlene suddenly felt afraid. This wasn't just going to be some run of the mill explanation. She still couldn't wrap her head around the fact that a *vampire* had attacked her.

"I'm not sure where to start," Idris finally said.

"Who attacked me?"

"Her name is Vivica. I've known her a long time."

"Is she really a vampire?"

There was a pause and then Idris replied, "Yes."

Darlene felt her head starting to throb again. "How can that be? How can she be a vampire? You're telling me they are real?"

"It's all real, Darlene. Vampires are real. Monsters you read about in legends are all real. They exist."

Darlene's vision went dim for a moment. This was way too much. She wanted to go back to bed. She pinched her skin on her arm and felt pain — no, she wasn't dreaming. She was awake for this insanity. The sad thing was she couldn't even tell Idris to stop being crazy. She had been attacked by Vivica herself.

"My friend Lucian has gone missing. And I'm trying to find him."

"Is Lucian a vampire, too?"

"No," Idris said. "He's a werewolf."

"A werewolf," Darlene repeated slowly.

Idris nodded. "He's a pack leader. I managed to trail him here. I was running cold until I heard you mention Brent. I thought the timing was funny, you know, about you mentioning someone killed by werewolves at the same time I was trying to find one."

"Brent was killed by werewolves? Was he one himself? He said online he was."

"No." Idris shook his head. "He wasn't. But I never saw that post you showed me of someone asking him to come back to Roman's Tavern." Darlene inferred from his tone that Roman's Tavern was a werewolf haunt after all. "Who lured him back to the club? Why was he killed? There are more questions than answers. And then you had a copy of *The Werewolf Code* that Lucian sold you — why did he sell you the book? Did he leave it there for me to find? Why did he run away?" Idris shrugged. "And now Vivica is involved, looking for me and the book. Vampires involved in werewolf affairs are never a good sign."

Darlene's breath came faster now as she looked Idris over. *Of course, he is so large and so warm and looks like he could tear someone in two if he felt like it. Idris is a werewolf, too.*

"I don't know what to do next. But if you're on Vivica's radar, that isn't a good sign. We have to get you out of town. Get you in a hideout somewhere... "

"Are you mental?" Darlene snapped. Idris looked at her in surprise. "If you think I'm skipping town and leave my entire life here to go hide out because of Vivica, you have gone mad. There is absolutely no way I'm leaving."

"Darlene, you don't understand. Vivica is going to come for you once she finds out that you lied to her. And now you know about werewolves and vampires. It's too risky. You have to get to a town with no packs or vampire nests."

"I'm not leaving." She crossed her arms, even though they ached and stared Idris down.

Idris stared back at her. "Why are you being so stubborn about this?"

"I'm sorry but you do not get to come into my life, rearrange it and mess it all up, tell me vampires and werewolves are real and then put me in...werewolf witness protection or whatever."

"What do you want to do then?"

"Let me help. I won't let you see the book unless I can help."

"And how are you going to help?" Idris shot back. "This is completely out of your element."

"Exactly. I'm your element of surprise."

Idris stood up. He was so mammoth that he seemed to take up her entire bedroom. He left the room. Darlene could hear him pacing in the living room, his big feet hitting the floor. She leaned back against the bed, closing her eyes. Her life might not be much but she wasn't going to run away. Darlene tried to imagine living in another town where no one knew her. No Maria, no bookshop, no Rebecca. Just…what? Her life almost how it was now minus the couple of things that kept her going. If Vivica wanted to take that away from her, then she'd go down with a fight.

***

Idris stared out the window of Darlene's room. The sun was high in the air. In the distance, children swam and jumped in the community pool, making a lot of splashes. Why was Darlene being so stubborn about this? Vivica could come back and kill her, but still she wanted to stay here and fight. Lucian had relocated others who stumbled across their secret. Idris never heard from them again and imagined they were living happy quiet lives. Not all the packs liked to do this. More than once, Roman had killed those who stumbled upon their secret or Changed them to get another member for the pack. Lucian never agreed on it. That was when the groups split off into two packs.

But Idris had never run into anyone who both didn't want to leave and didn't want to Change. Did Darlene just think she could live a normal life? No, because she said that she wanted to help him. What could a human do for him? Would she really not let him see *The Werewolf Code* unless he agreed?

Idris pulled away from the window and went back into Darlene's room. She had lay back down. Her skin was pale and bruises formed along her arms. She let out a grunt of pain when she turned to look at him.

"Here's the agreement. I don't want a human around me getting in the way," Idris said to Darlene. "But if you help me find anything useful in the book or some clue about Lucian, then we'll have an agreement. You can help me, and I won't try to get you to move away."

"Fine," Darlene agreed.

"No funny business, okay?"

"Fine." She shut her eyes before opening them again a moment later. "When do I have to worry about you changing into your werewolf form?"

Idris hadn't admitted to being a werewolf yet, but Darlene wasn't stupid enough not to pick up on it. "If I lose control of my emotion…or a full moon."

She nodded and before Idris could say anything else, she fell asleep.

Chapter Five

Maria grilled Darlene for a good twenty minutes about why she couldn't come in. By the time Darlene hung up her phone, she felt confident that Maria didn't believe one word out of her mouth. She debated texting Rebecca and saying hello, but she was unsure what to say. *Hey, Rebecca, got attacked by a vampire and now I'm trying to solve the case of the missing werewolf. Lunch next week?* In the end, she put her phone down and stared out the window of her bedroom for an hour, just thinking.

The thought of Vivica coming for her terrified her. But Darlene didn't want to run. She felt as if she had been doing a lot of that lately. She ran from Austin when she found out the truth. She ran from all her past friends and most of her family. And she ran from her life, becoming basically a shut-in who only went to work and spent the rest of her time online. It seemed silly to make a stand now, against a vampire who could kill her in one swipe, but it felt right to her.

Darlene was sick of thinking about Vivica. She had been trying to find something to give to Idris, some sort of clue that proved that she belonged on the case with him. The werewolf and the fat girl. *Don't. Don't start hating yourself right now.*

She stared at her laptop. Idris said he'd be back later to check up on her but didn't tell her where he was going. Darlene found herself wondering where to go first. She knew nothing about Lucian or *The Werewolf Code,* but she did know a little bit about Brent.

Darlene spent some time looking up things about him and tracking down his blog online where he talked about what it was like to be a werewolf. Idris confirmed he wasn't one and the blog made it clear he wasn't either. It was just entry after entry about struggling with being a werewolf that couldn't transform and how it was his "kin-type". Most of it went over her head. Brent struck her as a very sad guy who had just turned eighteen and seemed unsure of where to go in life.

She read post after post of Brent's struggles until she found the post that he made after he had gone to Roman's Tavern the first time.

Hi everybody. Going to Roman's Tavern was a bust. I heard it was a supernatural haunt in the area. I was excited about being accepted as a werewolf but it didn't go as planned at all. Some huge guy with bushy eyebrows jumped on me as soon as I told him I was a werewolf looking for a pack. He said I wasn't a werewolf and to stop trying to get attention. I was terrified because it looked like he was going to rip me apart. Some guy with glasses stopped him though, and I left soon after. The guy who saved me didn't give me either one of their names but thank the moon for him. I'm afraid he would have killed me on the spot!

Darlene jotted down some notes. *Guy with glasses — Lucian?* And was he stopping Idris from ripping this kid's throat out? She would have to ask him. Idris hadn't mentioned anything about being there the night that Brent showed up. She felt a cold sensation in her stomach — why didn't he tell her? The blog post didn't sound like Idris at all, but this was a long time ago. Who knew what happened to Idris since then?

Darlene went to Brent's final post of the blog. All it said was… *Wish me luck.* Darlene rubbed her eyes, tired. Where was the link? She had to be missing something. Who lured Brent back to Roman's Tavern? She searched for more, digging deeper until she found it — the name of Brent's mother.

It didn't take her long to find Brent's old address.

***

Idris felt as if a lot happened, but it led him nowhere. In fact, things just seemed to get worse now that he dragged Darlene into it. He couldn't believe how he just told her everything like that. If he ever found Lucian again, he would be in for a lecture from the ages. And since Darlene refused to leave and go into hiding, what would Lucian do?

Idris tried not to dwell on it. He took another sip of his coffee. He was at the coffee shop next door to the bookshop. Idris wanted to look at the book but knew that Darlene would have to be there to help look things up for him on the computer. His phone buzzed, and he looked down to see a text from Darlene: *I found Brent's address. Might be a lead. Also why didn't you tell me that you were there that night he first came to the Tavern?*

Idris sighed and pushed his phone away. The real reason was that he was embarrassed by his behavior that night. Lucian had stopped him from attacking Brent. And then when Roman accused Idris of being the one who murdered the kid months later, Idris had had enough. He wasn't sure what hurt more — that his pack leader thought he'd kill someone like that or that he was so close to actually killing Brent the first night he had come by. What if he had Changed and had no memory of killing Brent? But that wasn't right, because Lucian swore that they had been together that night. Idris remembered that too, but was terrified he was just making up memories that weren't real. Would Lucian try to protect him like that?

Idris could remember them drinking and watching a game at a bar nearby. Tensions had been high between him, Lucian and Roman. Lucian didn't like how Roman ruled the pack and was talking about leaving. But leaving a pack was a serious thing and Roman wouldn't take kindly to the threat of another pack close by. Lucian was second in command at this point and was trying to convince Idris to come with him.

Idris had been thinking about it, if only because his behavior had been getting so out of control he was concerned about his well-being. When he was around Roman's pack, he seemed to become even more worked up and would attack anyone who he thought had insulted him. Leaving the pack meant he could fully focus on gaining control of his werewolf side. Lucian was unlike any werewolf he had ever met before — calm, collected and kind. Under Lucian's pack rule, Idris might have a shot at redeeming himself.

But Idris hadn't decided to leave until Brent showed up dead and Roman had blamed him. Upset at being blamed for the death of a kid pretending to be a werewolf, Idris agreed to break from the pack with Lucian.

It didn't go well.

Idris shook his head, dispersing the memories from his mind. He looked back at his phone. Going to talk to Brent's mother would be the next best thing, at least until Darlene returned to work tomorrow and he could look through the book. He picked up his phone and texted, *Sounds good. I'll come over now. I'll explain about that night, too.*

He paid for his coffee and left.

***

An hour later, Darlene was wedged in Idris' ancient pickup truck, bouncing along toward the highway. Each bounce of the truck sent dull throbs of pain along her body. She had some pain reliever pills on her and took a couple more.

"This truck is terrible," Darlene mumbled.

Idris glanced over at her. "It's a classic."

"That's what people say when something is old and crappy," Darlene grumbled.

She didn't mean to sound so grumpy but the last thing she felt like doing was driving an hour to go see

Brent's mother. Darlene thought she'd have a day or two to figure out what they would say to her, but Idris wanted to leave right away. Darlene had agreed because she wanted to be there, too. Not that Idris was mean, but he was somewhat terrifying to look at if one didn't know he was a werewolf... which was something Darlene was still trying to wrap her head around. Werewolves, vampires...what else? Hopefully not zombies... she hated zombies.

Still, Idris is incredibly handsome and... she told herself to stop thinking because it was just going to lead her down a bad path.

"Why couldn't this wait?" Darlene asked.

"We only have two leads right now. Brent, which might not even be a lead, and whatever Lucian has in *The Werewolf Code*, which he shouldn't have gotten rid of anyway because only a true pack can have a copy. That means if anyone in my pack finds out Lucian got rid of the book or sees our copy is missing, we lose official pack status."

"Who revokes pack status?" Darlene asked. "Some werewolf council or something?"

"No. All the packs in the area vote in on major issues that affect all packs. That book lists absolutely everything you need to know about werewolves. It was originally started by the first pack and over the years other packs added to it until the version we have today. The only other pack in the area is Roman's, and he's out for blood from our pack."

"Why?"

She could see Idris hesitate, as if he wasn't sure what to say or where to start.

"You said you were there the night Brent first went to the bar," Darlene prompted.

Idris nodded stiffly and then began to talk. His voice was low and throaty as he told her how Brent arrived at the bar that night, claiming he was a werewolf. As he told her about wanting to start a fight with Brent, Darlene could see the torment in his eyes.

"I used to be like that," he said to her. "All the time. I wanted to fight everyone. The Change…it pissed me off. When I got bitten, I was furious. I wanted to take on the entire world and make them pay for turning me into a…monster. I was vicious for ten years. Vicious, Darlene. I did things that are so shameful that I will carry that burden until the day I die."

Darlene didn't know what to say. She couldn't relate on that vicious level. After she lost Austin, all she had left was her sadness. There wasn't any rage left inside her. Idris spoke about Lucian, how he wanted the pack to be kinder and not terrorize people so much.

"But Roman loved being the only pack in the area. Like I said earlier, if there was an issue that affected the area, all the packs would discuss it. Being the only pack in the area meant Roman was a king, of sorts. When Brent went missing and turned up dead by a werewolf, he blamed me… said I did it. But Lucian was there with me that night and he knew I hadn't. Roman tried to get the pack to go against me. That was when Lucian and I broke off to form our own pack."

"I'm sure that went well," Darlene said. "Seeing as Roman seems really levelheaded over things."

Idris cracked a smile, which made Darlene's heart flutter. "It didn't go well. The fighting was brutal. When it finally settled down, Roman and Lucian formed a truce. But the truce is barely holding together and now that Lucian is gone…" He trailed off, sighing.

Darlene looked out the window, seeing the trees whirl by as they kept driving. There was more to the story, Darlene could tell, but she didn't want to press it.

She knew how it felt to want to keep things to herself. Everything with Austin felt that way.

"So, you sort of explained werewolves to me," Darlene changed the subject. "How do vampires come into play? You seem to know Vivica?"

Idris sighed again and glanced at a car passing him. "Do you think anyone else on this highway is talking about this stuff or do they all get to play the license plate game?" He shook his head. "Werewolves and vampires are a terrible mix. They were around before us and see us as a hindrance to how they are supposed to live. Vampires are excellent at keeping themselves out of any sort of human affairs. And if they happen to be caught, they just turn whoever found them either into a vampire or kill them. No sweat off their backs...do vampires sweat?" Idris seemed to pause, as if this had never struck him before.

"Why do they think you're a hindrance?"

"Most packs don't want to kill a bunch of humans or want to control the human race, like vampires do. We just want to co-exist. But the vampires think humans are weak and would be better either dead or one of them. It creates friction. Werewolf packs try to stay away from vampires altogether."

"But you know Vivica," Darlene stated.

"Yes. Yes, I know Vivica. But after I first Changed, I searched for vampires. I found their nest. I was hoping to upset them so much they'd kill me. They didn't. I met Vivica instead, and we had a very unhealthy relationship for a few years."

"You tried to kill yourself?" Darlene asked, her eyes wide.

Idris shrugged. "Mind if we talk about something else the rest of the way?"

Darlene nodded, looking Idris over slowly. A werewolf who hated it and had tried to have a vampire kill him, tormented by Brent and now the possibility of Lucian being gone... She turned back to face straight ahead. Even though Idris had asked for a change of subject, they didn't speak the rest of the way.

Chapter Six

The house where Brent lived was quiet and at the end of the street. The paint on it was faded and there were three flower pots out front, all containing dead flowers. The roof was dirty, and the grass was brown in some spots. There was an old-looking Dodge Neon in the driveway with chipped silver paint. Idris could hear a dog barking but he wasn't sure if it was from a few houses over or this one.

He looked at Darlene out of the corner of his eye. He had shared too much with her, and it was his own fault. He was falling for her, as much as he wanted to trick himself into thinking he wasn't. The only other person who had known about Vivica and him was Lucian. Relationships between werewolves and vampires were strictly forbidden. They had a sick, twisted relationship. Idris was sure that Vivica would be back for Darlene out of pure spite and nothing to do with Lucian. How did she know about the book and Lucian anyway?

Darlene was already getting out of the car. The bruises on her skin had faded a little but she still looked rough for wear. Maybe Idris should have waited like Darlene had suggested. Perhaps it wasn't a good idea to show up to someone's home, a giant man like him and a woman with bruises all over. He was going to tell Darlene to stop but he was already getting to know certain movements she made — her walk told him she was on a mission.

Idris followed, admiring Darlene's behind before telling himself to stop being so distracted. She knocked on the door and they waited. Idris couldn't hear anything inside. Darlene waited another minute and then rang the doorbell. This time Idris could hear someone shuffling inside slowly toward the door. The door opened and Idris saw a tiny old woman, her hair going gray and her skin pale. She looked exhausted, as if she hadn't slept in years.

"Hello, my name is Darlene and this is my friend, Idris," Darlene said, extending her hand. "Are you Ms. Boots?"

The woman hesitated for a moment and then shook Darlene's hand, glancing mostly at Idris. "Yes. How can I help you?"

"I'm sorry to bother you," Darlene said, having clearly formed a plan that Idris hadn't bothered to come up with. "But we knew Brent online."

"Oh!" The woman's eyebrows shot up. "Please, please, come in."

Darlene glanced at Idris with a look that seemed to say *this is going better than I expected.* The two of them followed Ms. Boots into her house. It still looked as though Brent lived here. There were action figures on display on a table near the door and his shoes still by the front door. As Idris followed her to the living room, he saw a door down a hallway that had a werewolf poster on it. *Must be his room.* Idris wished he could go inside it.

Ms. Boots sat them down on a couch that smelled faintly of mothballs. An old cuckoo clock was ticking away in one corner. The TV looked old and the carpet faded. It was clear that they were tight on funds. A cat slept in one corner, purring softly. Idris felt depressed just being in the room. Darlene chatted about how adorable the house was, flattering Ms. Boots, who seemed to eat it up.

"It's so nice to meet Brent's friends. I was so concerned, you know. He spent so much time on his computer, and I never saw anyone he said he was talking to." Her hands began to flutter around her chest. "And then once he finished high school, he never left the house. He just loved his computer. You knew him a long time?"

Darlene nodded. "Yes. We both did. Brent said he had some things in his room for us, and we were going to meet up and trade them but then…so we decided to come up today to see if we could find them. If that's okay with you…?"

Ms. Boots nodded sadly, glancing again at Idris. "He…did he say anything about…leaving that night?"

It was directed to him, Idris realized. Maybe she thought since they were both guys he would have told him more. Idris shook his head. "No, ma'am."

"Brent was confused." She was speaking quickly now. "He thought he was a werewolf."

"Yes, he mentioned that," Idris said suddenly, deciding to go with whatever Ms. Boots said.

She nodded. "Okay, so you two know then. I think he latched onto that after his father passed away when he was twelve. Brent always kept to himself, you know? He liked to be alone a lot and once the Internet became popular…I should have watched him closer but

I don't know much about computers. He told me he found other people who were werewolves, too." Ms. Boots shook her head. "Some group they had."

Darlene glanced at Idris, as if to urge him on and Idris cleared his throat. "Did he say anything about going to that bar?"

Ms. Boots looked up, her gaze slowly becoming more focused, "No. The first night he went, he paid for a taxi with his own savings. We fought. I told him he was being ridiculous to go someplace that said it was a werewolf haunt or whatever. I told him he wasn't one, and he was going to get hurt. I had never seen him so angry when he stormed out and left. I stayed up all night. I tried telling the police this, you know, but they didn't think the werewolf thing was important. But I think it is."

"Why?" Idris pressed gently.

"Because the next time he left, the night he died, someone picked him up. I didn't see too much of him in the car but it was a beat-up looking thing. And he had shaggy hair and glasses."

Idris felt as if the walls suddenly caved in on him. Shaggy hair and glasses? There was no way...no way...they weren't at the bar that night. They were at

Lucian's place all night, watching TV and discussing Roman. How could Lucian pick Brent up?

Darlene, sensing Idris' sudden shock, took over. "Did you see anything else, Ms. Boots?"

She shook her head. "No, but I was screaming at him not to go. That I would…I would have to kick him out if he kept going to dangerous places like that. But Brent got in that car…" Ms. Boots went very still, as if she was fending off tears.

The room went silent. Darlene's big blue eyes darted between Idris and Ms. Boots but Idris wasn't sure that he could trust himself to say anything without grilling Ms. Boots with a million questions.

Darlene leaned forward and gently touched Ms. Boots' hand. "I'm sorry for your loss."

Ms. Boots looked up now at the two of them. "You two knew him. You knew he was a good kid, an honest kid who just seemed lost. I don't think something killed him in the woods. I think he was murdered. And I think that man had something to do with it. Please, believe me. The police thought I was crazy."

Darlene squeezed her hand. "I believe you."

Ms. Boots seemed to relax and nodded. "I haven't been in his room since the police came. I can't bring myself to...please, just take anything you need. Otherwise it will just sit there. Anything Brent wanted you to have or anything you want to remember him by."

Darlene stood up. "Thank you."

She walked by Idris and slipped her fingers through his, tugging him out of the room. The human contact made Idris' body feel hot all of a sudden. They walked down the hallway, past Ms. Boots' room, which looked as if she had moved into it. The sheets were thrown back in the bed and an old black and white TV was on by it, showing an old sitcom. Darlene looked down the hall and then at Idris.

"Was Lucian the one who picked him up?" she whispered.

Idris nodded, numbly, his fingers still wrapped around hers. "It sounds like it."

"What did you guys do that night?"

"We watched TV and drank. Talked about leaving the pack," Idris mumbled back. "I had so much to drink that night that I don't remember exact details, like what time he got there."

She chewed her bottom lip. "Let's look in his room."

Darlene turned to face Brent's door, her mind swirling. Had Lucian really picked Brent up on the night of his death? Was he the one who had told him to come to Roman's Tavern the night of the full moon? If Brent did everything by computer, like his mom claimed, then maybe they'd find a record of who contacted him off the site. The poster on the door was peeling off. If Ms. Boot's hadn't come in here in five years, then it truly would be untouched.

Darlene steeled herself, glancing back at Idris. She was aware of their hands touching. His body was hot to the touch, and his pupils were dilated. He looked extremely stressed out, as if it was all too much. She felt the same way, still trying to get used to werewolves and vampires and now this.

She opened the bedroom door slowly. It was pitch black in here. The blinds were tightly shut. Darlene flicked on the light switch. Dust swirled up into the air as the two of them stepped inside the room. The walls were plastered with posters of werewolves. A movie collection in one corner contained mostly supernatural films and old horror movies. There was a bed in one corner, still unmade, the covers thrown back as if Brent had gotten up in a hurry. A laptop was on a rundown-looking desk. Piles of clothes were on the floor and school books were strewn about the room. The air was musty and with each breath Darlene took, she could feel the dust fill her lungs.

Idris looked like a giant in a little boy's room. He looked around slowly. If they had expected something to jump out at them, then they were let down.

"You should look around his room. I'll check out his computer," Darlene said, going on a hunch that computers weren't exactly Idris' thing.

She could tell she was right by the relieved look on Idris' face as he nodded and turned to one corner of the room. Darlene slid onto the computer chair and booted up his laptop. It made a low noise, almost as if it was grinding awake. She imagined that it had been offline for five years, and she was thankful that it still booted up.

Brent hadn't password protected it, probably confident that his mom would have no idea what to do with a computer. The desktop showed a beach background and there were files over it. None of them caught her eye. She opened his web browser and went through his bookmarks. There was the forum he posted on as well as fan-fiction websites and a link to his blog.

She found a page to his email and clicked it. It was still logged in.

Darlene told herself that the cops had gone through all of this stuff already, and it was silly to think she could find something they hadn't. But the fact that Lucian had picked Brent up that night...

Darlene cast a quick glance over to Idris, who was lost in thought and holding a stuffed werewolf animal. It would have been a funny sight if Darlene didn't know the pain he was in.

She looked back at the email. Spam, spam and more spam was in the inbox. She quickly went through to five years ago, when Brent was using his account. Notifications on forum posts and his blog made up the chunk of the mail. Around the time he went missing, Darlene found an email from an address of 540w@springboard.com. She clicked it open and read the message.

Hi,

Glad to see you got my forum post. We met already, the night you came to Roman's Tavern. You should remember — we spoke briefly outside before you left. I have a proposition for you that will change your life. Can you come again on the night of the full moon?

Darlene frowned, lost in thought. Could this be from Lucian? She was going to ask Idris if he had seen Lucian talk to Brent outside the bar when he came over, holding a thin notebook.

"What?" Darlene asked.

"This book. Look." Idris opened it, and Darlene saw book pages rubbed onto the pages of the thin notebook. "This is from *The Book of the Ancients.*"

"What's that?"

Idris looked annoyed that he had to explain when he was clearly onto something, "Think of it as *The Werewolf Code,* only for vampires."

"Okay," Darlene replied slowly. "And Brent had these pages how?"

Idris shook his head. "I don't know. He got them from someone, maybe? I don't know how a regular kid would get this stuff."

"Look at this," Darlene said, and Idris leaned over her to read the email.

He smelled faintly of cologne and body-wash. Warmth radiated off of him, and Darlene had a mental image of curling up and resting against his chest before she shook her head to clear herself of the fantasy.

"Did Lucian talk to this kid then? Why would Lucian pick Brent up the night of his murder? How did Brent get paper drawings of *The Book of the Ancients* ? Did he answer this email?" His questions were rapid fire.

"Let me look," Darlene replied, clicking over to the *Sent* box and flicking through the emails there. "There it is," she said and pulled up Brent's reply.

Hey!

I'm super glad to hear from you. I did what you asked outside the bar the last time and managed to find a copy of that book you were asking about. I know you mentioned you couldn't show your face in that part of town. I broke in during the day when they were sleeping and managed to rub some pages on paper for you, but I couldn't steal the actual book. Way too heavy. Hope that is okay? So you're coming to get me on the full moon then? Glad it was you! When I got the message on the forum, I thought it was someone playing a trick on me. I know you said you'd contact me and not the other way around but I was starting to think you had forgotten about me. Glad to know that I'll see you soon!

Darlene started to feel in way over her head. Every time she thought she had a handle on things, slowly accepting the fact vampires and werewolves were a thing, something seemed to spring right up to send her back fifty feet. Idris clenched his jaw, staring at the computer screen.

"Do you know where the vampire book is located?" Darlene asked gently.

Idris shook his head. "No," he replied gruffly. "But apparently Lucian did."

Darlene pulled out a flash drive. "I'm going to back up what I can from his documents and save it on here."

"I'll bring this book," Idris said, shoving the thin notebook into his jacket pocket.

Darlene managed to back up everything Brent had in his documents and shut down the laptop. On the way out, they saw Ms. Boot snoring gently on the couch, her chest rising and falling slowly. Darlene felt a pang of pity for her. As they left, Darlene's phone rang. Idris shut the front door while Darlene took the call. It was Maria.

"Hey," Darlene answered. "Was I supposed to work today?"

"No," Maria said, but her voice sounded a bit funny. "I just heard that Jacob is missing."

"Jacob as in...the one we just fired from the shop?"

Maria heaved a sigh. "That's the one... went missing last night. I figured you should know. Cops came by asking questions so they might ask you some since he worked with us."

"Thanks for the heads up," Darlene said before saying good-bye and hanging up.

Idris stood in front of the truck, looking at her curiously. "What happened?"

Darlene shrugged. "Jacob, this guy who worked at the shop and we had to fire for being terrible, has gone missing. Maria gave me a heads up that the cops might come by."

"Missing?" Idris replied, his brow furrowing together.

Darlene walked over to the passenger side of the truck with a sinking feeling in her stomach. She couldn't shake the fact that Jacob suddenly going missing wasn't just a strange coincidence.

Chapter Seven

Darlene woke up as they pulled into her apartment complex. She had fallen asleep in the truck. The sun was already sinking below the horizon. She hated how quickly it got dark in the winter. She yawned and looked over at Idris, who seemed lost in thought.

"Let me walk you up," he said.

Darlene nodded, still rubbing the sleep from her eyes.

She was thinking about Jacob. He had gone missing last night after Vivica had attacked her. Her body was still sore, but she was feeling a bit better. Did Vivica find Jacob after she tormented Darlene? Darlene rubbed her head, feeling her headache coming back. She took a step forward and realized that Idris was still by the truck.

"What is it?" Darlene asked.

Idris just shook his head, and Darlene fell silent. Abruptly, Idris dashed out of the truck without saying a word. She looked around, a growing sense of dread in her stomach. Her apartment was out of the way from the main set of units, having been added on later. The parking lot was empty and an old playground nearby creaked from a small breeze. *Idris must be paranoid, he just isn't thinking clearly.*

Suddenly a dark shape burst out of the nearest tree. There was a flash of red hair and all Darlene could think was *Vivica!* She closed her eyes and braced for the impact of Vivica steamrolling into her.

But instead there was a roar and a gust of wind. Darlene heard thrashing noises and opened her eyes. Her mouth dropped open. Vivica was dodging out of the way of a wolf...no...Idris. He had Changed. Darlene's head felt dizzy. How could that be Idris? The beast in front of her was hulking in size, his fur bristling and standing up on his back. He snarled at Vivica and the teeth that were exposed could have easily torn Darlene in half. Vivica backed up, her fangs exposed, her red hair loose and flowing around her shoulders. Her eyes were bright red and angry.

Idris snarled and lunged off his hind legs. Vivica was fast but not fast enough. The two blurred together and rolled across the pavement. Darlene could only stand there, frozen by fear and knowing even if she wasn't, there wasn't anything she could possibly do to help. Idris was suddenly kicked back hard. He slid across the pavement and in a flash, Vivica was by Darlene's side. Her red eyes blazed. "You little bitch!"

Then she was taken down again. Darlene shifted to the left to get out of the way as Idris tackled Vivica to the ground, his snarls filling the air. Once again, everything became a blur. It made her head hurt. Darlene shut her eyes tightly, wishing it would all go away.

When she opened them, the mammoth creature that was Idris was still fighting Vivica. But Darlene saw something behind Vivica. She blinked and tried to look closer. Something transparent in the trees behind the apartment complex. Was that a… No. Darlene rubbed her eyes and when she looked again it was gone. No, she was simply going crazy.

Idris let out a snarl and suddenly his jaws clamped down on Vivica's wrist, yanking her down to the ground. She snarled back, yanking on her arm. There was no blood.

"Give us back the book!" Vivica cried. "Your friend said that you have it, Idris!"

"Oh no," Darlene breathed, realizing that she had thought Vivica had meant *The Werewolf Code*, not *The Book of the Ancients*. Shit.

Vivica heard Darlene, and her head snapped up. Idris saw that she was distracted, and he clamped down harder on her wrist and tugged her down to the ground, getting ready to rip her throat out. Darlene closed her eyes again, terrified. There was a grunt from Idris and then the wind whipped around her. Silence, except for Idris' labored breathing. Darlene didn't move.

Finally, someone spoke. "It's okay now."

Darlene's eyes fluttered open to see Idris standing in front of her. He tugged his jeans back on but was shirtless. He was cut like a rock, his muscles chiseled and his arms defined by pure muscle. She was going to open her mouth to speak but suddenly felt overwhelmed. The last thing she thought of was the glowing figure in the woods.

***

Idris watched Darlene sleep. Her chest rose and fell at a normal pace. He cursed himself. He had overwhelmed her. Given her too much to chew on and then Vivica turned up. She would have killed Darlene if he hadn't Changed. Seeing him in his altered form must have been too much for her. He rubbed his eyes. Everything that had happened was almost too much for him. He tried to backtrack.

From what Idris learned from Brent's computer, that night he had shown up at Roman's Tavern, he had a conversation with Lucian outside the bar. Idris tried to recall that night but he was a heavy drinker five years ago and his memory failed him. He could remember yelling at Brent, telling him to bugger off pretending he was a werewolf. Why did Brent even come up to them? Was it because of Lucian? He remembered wanting to fight Brent, but Lucian held him back and told Brent to leave. Lucian must have gone with Brent outside to talk to him. About what?

But Idris knew the answer to that… to steal *The Book of the Ancients.* But why did Lucian even need a copy of that book? The original was in some ruin somewhere, which meant that Brent found a copy of it among a vampire clan. He had broken in and transferred pages to the notebook. Idris pulled out the notebook and flipped through the pages. He couldn't read the language and didn't know what he was looking at. Frustrated, he let out a sigh and closed his eyes.

Vivica thought he had the book. Darlene must have lied and said Idris had it, meaning *The Werewolf Code,* but Vivica meant the vampire book. The whole thing made his head ache. He didn't understand any of it.

Darlene shifted and opened her eyes, mumbling his name. Idris went to her side, looking at her. Luckily, she remained untouched in the fight but must have passed out from shock. Idris helped her sit up and gave her water to sip. Darlene's big blue eyes looked at him, and Idris felt warm all over. What were these feelings that she brought up from inside of him? Lucian had been his mentor and it was as if everything he had known and loved about him crashed down around him and that made Idris want Darlene even more.

He did it without thinking. He leaned forward and kissed her. Darlene let out a soft gasp of surprise, but she kissed him back. A warmth that Idris had never felt before rolled through him. It wasn't the heat of being a werewolf. It was something more. Something deeper awakening inside of him. Idris backed away a little, tilting his face to look down at her. He wanted to make sure this was okay — that Darlene wanted this as much as he did. She nodded and that was all Idris needed.

His lips met hers again, and he kissed her. He wanted to kiss her hard and take her on the spot but he had to be gentle. He didn't want to hurt her because he knew she was still sore from Vivica throwing her around. He kissed along her neck and slid his hands down her sides. He liked the feel of her. She stiffened under his touch and not from the pain. *She's shy*. Was it because of her weight? How could he explain to her that the very thing she hated was the thing that made her so attractive to him?

"You're beautiful," he murmured gruffly into her ear.

"No," she breathed back, closing her eyes.

"Yes," he whispered, kissing down her neck.

"Guess this means I've earned the right to help you."

Idris smiled into her neck. "Guess so."

Idris wiggled his fingers up under her T-shirt, running his fingers along her belly. He loved how much of her there was. He felt himself harden in his jeans, almost painfully, as he ran his hands over her belly and down her sides, feeling her skin. His desire thrummed through him. Idris wanted her, all of her. Darlene looked up at him with those beautiful, big, blue eyes that were hazy with desire and he knew she wanted it as well.

Darlene felt her entire body quiver. She wasn't used to anyone looking at her the way Idris looked at her. She usually felt so shy over her size and how she looked, especially lying down, but Idris seemed only enflamed by desire when he slid her shirt over her head. He went slowly and tenderly, knowing her body was still sore. Her face was hot with embarrassment — what if he didn't like her without her clothes on?

But with her shirt off, seeing her in her bra, he let out a soft moan. Darlene watched as he tugged his own shirt off. Once again, she saw those clearly cut and well-defined muscles. She ran her hands over his abs, marveling at them. Idris was so fit and well built. His body was so warm, like touching a fire. Darlene remembered what she had read about werewolves — how they ran hotter than humans and always felt warmer to the touch. Darlene loved it.

Idris leaned down and kissed down her neck again, toward her bra. He let out soft moans as his hands would slide over her skin and squeezed it. *He likes it, he likes that I'm a big woman.* This time, she let out her own sigh of pleasure as he tugged down her bra, exposing her breasts to the cool air. Idris immediately rolled his tongue over her nipples before taking one in his mouth and sucking and then switching to the other one. Knowing that Idris liked her body this big, she felt more confident and ran her hands along his back, mumbling his name.

His warm hands teased her breasts, slowly kneading them with his fingers, while he sucked on her nipples. She could feel how hard he got, pressing against his jeans. Darlene wanted more. Her hands traveled to his jeans and gave a tug. Idris read the signal and leaned back as Darlene unzipped his jeans and tugged down his boxers. His stiff manhood throbbed, and Darlene took delight in the size of it. She had never been with anyone this large before.

Idris watched Darlene as she stared at him lustily. He loved how full her breasts were and how luscious and large her body was. He couldn't wait anymore. He gently nudged Darlene back to lying down as he slid her own jeans off, followed by her panties. The smell of her brought out the animal in him and drove him mad with lust.

"I need you right now," he groaned.

"Take me," she whispered back.

That was all Idris needed. He positioned himself accordingly and slid into her. Her warmth engulfed him. Idris let out a moan of pleasure, louder than any of his other ones. Darlene murmured something and arched her back. Her hair spilled out across the pillow, and her blue eyes appeared hazy and dark in the moonlight. She looked beautiful and tonight she was all his.

Idris grunted and slid in more. She was tight and seemed to send her own warmth through his body. Finally he was fully inside her. Idris leaned over her and began to thrust. He started off slow, making sure she was okay. Holding back was agonizing. She let out small whimpers of pleasure, whispering his name. Her hands pressed against his back.

"More," she mumbled.

He thrust deeper into her. Darlene threw her head back and let out a moan. He was so large that it felt like he was filling her up. Darlene pulled him closer to her. Idris' body gave off so much heat that beads of sweat formed on her brow. Their bodies slicked up and slid together as Idris pulled all the way out and then pushed all the way back in. She moaned for him to do it harder and faster. Idris obliged. Waves of pleasure raced through her entire being. Her eyes shut as she clung to him, forgetting everything else besides Idris deep inside her. They moved together like this, perfectly in sync, for quite some time until finally Darlene's hips bucked. She was going to come. Darlene mumbled Idris' name before taking all of him inside her again.

"Oh!" she gasped in surprise as her orgasm broke through.

Waves of pleasure rippled through her core. She matched his thrusts, moving against him as hard as she could. Her hair stuck to her face from their sweat as she rode her orgasm through.

As Darlene came down from her own beautiful orgasm, Idris began his. He yelled out her name and thrust inside her, grunting. He held down her hips and spilled his seed inside her, his eyes tightly shut. He shook against her. His entire body formed rivulets of sweat as he finished his orgasm. After he came down from it, Idris slid out of Darlene and lay down next to her.

They both fell asleep in moments.

***

The next morning, Darlene heard her alarm going off. She let out a groan. For the first time ever, she didn't feel like going to work. And why was it so hot in here? Darlene opened her eyes and for a second, the sight of Idris sleeping naked next to her didn't make any sense. And then it all came back. Last night. Their arms entwined. Idris kissing her. Having sex on her bed until late into the night. Darlene felt her face flush, and she closed her eyes. She was on the pill for birth control but she still couldn't believe she had slept with him. *Oh my god, what have I done?*

She hadn't been with anyone since Austin left her at the altar. The experience was so horrifying that Darlene had given up on life and was just going through the motions. To have the man she loved so deeply leave her — for a man, no less, not even another woman — had been enough to scar her till the end of her life.

Austin had been using her to cover up the fact that he couldn't be true to himself. He was gay and couldn't accept it. How many times had he thought to himself, *Darlene is fat and I'm doing her a favor?* She didn't know. After he left her at the altar, telling her that he was gay and couldn't go through with it, she had made sure never to reach out to talk to him again. She couldn't bear it.

On the other side of the bed, on the night table next to the sleeping Idris, was a framed photo of her and Austin. They had just gotten engaged when the photo was snapped. *Stupid, stupid, why am I thinking about this now?* She shouldn't be thinking of Austin anymore, but whenever she tried to throw the photo out, she couldn't bear it.

Darlene slid out of bed. Idris remained in a deep sleep, snoring loudly. She had to get to work. Idris didn't wake up during her morning routine of showering and changing. Before she left, Darlene hovered in the doorway of her room, watching Idris sleep. Should she wake him up? But Darlene didn't want to talk to him and have to discuss what they did last night. No. She shook her head and left her apartment, shutting the door softly behind her.

***

When Darlene parked her car at work, she saw that there was already a cop car in the parking lot. *Jacob.* In her lust for Idris, she had forgotten all about him suddenly vanishing. They must be here to question her. She took a deep breath and opened the door of the shop. Maria was chatting up the police officer, who was clutching a coffee from next door. He was laughing at whatever story Maria was telling.

As Darlene entered, Maria waved. "There you are. Officer Walsh stopped by to see you today… about Jacob."

Darlene walked over to him. He had a mustache that was too big for his face. His hair was slicked back and clearly dyed to hide the gray that was probably encroaching faster than he wanted. His eyes were wide and dark brown, and he gave Darlene a firm handshake. Cops always made Darlene nervous. Even when she did nothing wrong, she still felt nervous, as if they would arrest her on a whim.

"How can I help you, Mr. Walsh?" Darlene asked, hoping to sound like a proper adult.

"I'm sure you heard about Jacob Richardson. We're interviewing everyone who had contact with him recently, trying to gauge where he may have gone. I know he was recently let go from here."

Darlene nodded as Maria said, "Let me offer my office for you two to sit more comfortably."

Maria ushered them into her office and waved as she shut the door behind her, going back out front. Maria's office was decorated in all sorts of old Native American art she had collected from over the years. Officer Walsh sat on Maria's side, which Darlene found odd, almost as if she was interviewing for a job. She played with one of the blankets on the side of the chair she sat down on. Why didn't he just sit down on the couch next to her in the corner of the room? Could cops sit on couches with people? Why was she freaking out like this?

"This won't take long." He flipped open a tiny notebook. "Maria mentioned that with the schedules here, it didn't give you much of a chance to see Jacob."

"That's right," Darlene replied. "But I saw him more than our past employees. He wasn't...very good with people, I guess would be the best way to put it. He rubbed them the wrong way. I saw him a couple of times when Maria sent him home early, and I had to cover." She told herself to stop talking so much.

Officer Walsh wrote a couple of things down in the notebook, nodding. "Did you ever have a conversation with Jacob?"

Darlene tried to think. "Nothing important. Maybe just about the shop."

"Was he interested in the old books you sell here?"

"No. These are more for collectors and people interested in books that are in some strange subject areas."

He nodded. "Yes, I noticed you have a paranormal section. You must get some loonies interested in that area!" He laughed as if he told a funny joke.

Darlene bristled. She was one of the loonies he was making fun of. On top of that, he was wrong. At the very least, werewolves and vampires were real. She swallowed down any sarcastic remark she was going to make and forced a laugh.

"Yes," she replied. "What a lark." Darlene cringed to herself, thinking she sounded like she was eighty years old.

Officer Walsh didn't seem to notice that she was suddenly acting like an old lady and nodded in agreement with her. "Did Jacob ever mention leaving town or skipping out on anything?"

"No," Darlene replied, feeling useless with each question the cop asked.

"Did he have any debt that you were aware of?"

"No," she repeated, wondering why he was asking this when she had already made it clear that the two of them hadn't talked.

"Had he shown any interest in going into the bar down the street, Roman's Tavern?"

Darlene froze, taken aback for a moment. "Roman's Tavern?"

"Yeah, have you ever been there?" he responded. Darlene shook her head no, and Officer Walsh went on, "We have trouble there often. A lot of fighting and some pact there not to call the cops. Once in a while, some newbies will try to fit in there and are in over their heads. We spoke to someone who knew Jacob. Said he was thinking about going there."

Darlene shook her head, hoping she looked casual. "No. Sorry. No mention of Roman's Tavern. Not really my scene."

The cop nodded and stood up. "I think that'll be it."

Darlene stood up as well, and they walked out of Maria's office. Her mind was spinning. Why had Jacob been talking about going to Roman's Tavern? At first, Darlene thought that Jacob had merely run into Vivica somehow, and she had made a meal out of him. But now she was thinking that something far worse may have occurred. Officer Walsh said his good-byes. Darlene wanted him to leave so she could text Idris. She wasn't in a hurry to see him on account of how she felt since they had slept together last night. She pushed the memories out of her head. This was more important than that.

Finally after Officer Walsh left the bookshop, Maria returned to her office looking pained. Darlene managed to send a text off to Idris that said only one thing: *We need to go to Roman's Tavern.*

Chapter Eight

Idris stared at the ceiling of his hotel room, all the while thinking of Darlene when his phone buzzed. A new text message arrived. He didn't move to get it right away. He couldn't get the thought of Darlene and last night out of his mind. When Idris had woken up and found that she had left already to go to work without leaving a note or saying anything to him, he wondered if they had made a mistake.

Darlene was clearly still upset and hurt over her last relationship. What if she only slept with him as a rebound? Did he sleep with her out of his own desire or did he have feelings for her as well? Maybe he had simply been too ramped up from the Change and wanted some physical release. He closed his eyes tightly, second guessing everything.

Now wasn't the time to get wrapped up in some human woman, he lectured himself. Lucian had something to do with Brent. He told Brent to try to get *The Book of the Ancients*. Why would he need such a thing?

Then something else came to him. It struck Idris so quickly that he didn't know why he hadn't thought of it sooner. Darlene said that Lucian had told her that someone would come looking for *The Werewolf Code*. At the time, Idris thought the book was meant for him. What if it was for someone else? Whoever may have been working for Lucian was still going to come by for the book!

Idris sat up in bed and went to grab his phone. He had to text Darlene so she would know if anyone came by for that book to tell him right away. That was when he saw the text message from her. His heart thumped. He wasn't expecting any text from her. What was she going to say? Was she going to tell him they couldn't see each other anymore? Or that they made a mistake?

Idris opened the text message and read it.

We need to go to Roman's Tavern.

That was all it said. He was disappointed and relieved all at the same time. Darlene must have found something out, too. Idris stood up and grabbed his jacket. He headed out to the bookstore right away.

It took Idris only twenty minutes to make it to the shop. As he walked inside, he saw Darlene training the tiny old woman who had been recently hired. He felt his heart suddenly thump very hard in his chest. Idris tried to ignore it. Darlene looked up when he entered. She nodded at him before turning back to the woman… Mabel — that was the old woman's name. Idris wandered back to the supernatural section, looking for *The Werewolf Code.* He found it wedged between some book about ghosts and another about faeries.

Idris yanked it out and placed it on a table nearby. He didn't know what to look for, but there had to be a reason that Lucian would take the book from the pack and leave it here for someone to pick up. He idly flipped through the pages he knew so well. Glancing up, he made sure Mabel and Darlene were lost in conversation as he slid out Brent's notebook with the vampire paper scans in it. Why didn't Lucian have the notebook already? That must mean that he didn't kill Brent that night.

Idris glanced at what Brent had copied onto the thin pages. The language was old and hard for Idris to even understand. It looked like instructions on how to turn someone into a vampire. Why did Lucian need this? Why did he have Brent get these pages five years ago and then leave this book here now?

Idris stopped suddenly at a page in the book. It was near the start, explaining how to cause the Change in someone. In the corner were Lucian's initials. This page was meant for someone, too.

"What is he doing?"

Idris looked up to see Mabel looking at him. Her skin was withered and old. Her hair was a mess of gray tied up in a bun. Something about her unsettled him. It was the way she looked at him. Suddenly Idris wanted to get as far away from the old lady as possible. Had she always been this unsettling? He hadn't paid attention to her enough the first time Mabel showed up for her interview.

"He's just looking at a book," Darlene replied, her brow creasing in slight confusion over Mabel's sharp tone.

Mabel's cloudy eyes lingered on Idris with a clarity he didn't like. No, there was something off about her, he decided. He just didn't know what it was. Her gaze fell to *The Werewolf Code*. Idris turned his back to her so he could look at the pages better and block her stares.

Darlene started speaking again, telling Mabel about the computer system. Idris studied the pages that Lucian had marked off. Both of the books had creation pages marked. Why? He felt as if he was banging his head against a wall. A few minutes later, Darlene ushered him over.

"I don't like your new hire," Idris mumbled to her.

"You think she was acting funny too?" Darlene whispered back.

Idris gave a slight nod and then briefly explained the connection he found with the books. In turn, Darlene explained to him how Jacob had mentioned going to Roman's Tavern.

"We should go, but I don't like leaving the store unattended. Someone is going to show up for this book. We could lay a trap for them. But I don't want you going to Roman's Tavern alone," Idris whispered.

Darlene chewed her bottom lip in thought. "I might be able to get a friend who can stay here and text us if anyone shows up."

"Contact your friend. We'll go to Roman's Tavern tonight then."

Darlene opened her mouth to speak when her phone went off. Darlene pulled it out and looked at it. Her face visibly paled. Idris felt his stomach drop even though he didn't know what happened yet.

"What?" Idris asked, harsher than he had meant to.

"I…" She faltered and tried again. "I set up a search alert for anything to do with Brent."

"And?"

Darlene glanced up at him. "Brent's mother was killed."

***

Darlene had to wait until break rolled around for her to contact Rebecca about coming down to watch the shop after closing. She felt odd calling her, knowing Rebecca would want to know why Darlene was making such a strange request. She was trying to come up with the most believable story that she could muster. But Darlene still felt distracted.

The news of Brent's mother's death cast an even darker cloud over her mood. There weren't many details on how she was murdered, but police disclosed that it was a break-in gone wrong. Darlene didn't believe that for a moment. Someone murdered Ms. Boots after they talked to her. Guilt wracked her. It was her idea to speak to Ms. Boots about Brent and now she was dead. Darlene felt another headache coming on.

That, plus Idris' sudden strange feeling about Mabel added to the issues. She found it strange how Mabel focused on Idris when he looked at *The Werewolf Code*. She tried to remember what she knew about Mabel but found mostly hazy memories. Darlene had been too busy with other things to pay attention to some old lady who wanted to work at a book store. She remembered mostly that she came in with an umbrella. The rest of the time with her seemed like a blur. She would have to pay better attention from now on.

Trying to shove the rest of her concerns from her mind, including being so close to Idris earlier that she wanted to touch him again, Darlene pulled out her phone. She unlocked the screen and stared at the article about Ms. Boots that she left up. Darlene shook her head as if to clear her thoughts and called Rebecca.

It rang for a little bit until she answered. "Darlene?" Her tone sounded surprised.

"Hey, Rebecca," Darlene breathed. "How are you?"

"I'm fine," Rebecca said, sounding a bit cautious. "What's up?"

"I was wondering if you can do me an odd favor."

Darlene then launched into her story.

It was 9:30 at night when Darlene's friend, Rebecca, pulled up into the parking lot behind the bookshop. Idris had a bad feeling in his gut about the entire thing. Darlene said that Rebecca was up for anything and liked adventure. That was fine, but this wasn't an adventure. Idris wasn't sure who was going to turn up to claim the book. He couldn't get Mabel's eyes out of his head. *She's an old lady... there is no way she can do anything.* He watched Rebecca get out of the car. She had short hair and big glasses and looked as if she weighed ten pounds. She was wearing all black and looked like a walking stereotype of what an artist in France would look like.

She waved and walked over to them, her boots clacking on the pavement. Earlier, Idris asked Darlene what she told her friend. Darlene told Rebecca that someone was going to break into the bookshop but they couldn't let anyone know. She told Rebecca it was highly dangerous and to lay low and text if anyone broke in and to not engage with them. Rebecca would have to park across the street in the front where she can observe the shop from the safety of her car. Rebecca jumped at the chance without hesitation. Idris hated the plan. But he told himself there was no promise of anyone actually breaking in for the book tonight. The only reason it felt like it might end up being tonight was because of Mabel, Ms. Boots' death and Jacob's disappearance. Everything seemed to roll at a high speed toward something terrible.

"Hey!" Rebecca said, cheerfully, pulling Darlene in for a hug. "Takes forever to see you and once I do, it's for something weird like this." Her brown-eyed gaze settled on Idris, clearly amused. "You must be Darlene's…friend." The way she paused on the word made Idris feel like anything but.

He shook her hand. "Nice to meet you."

"Same. So, you guys just want me to sit and watch the shop till you get back?" This was directed at Darlene, who nodded.

"If anyone or anything goes through that door, text me, okay? Rebecca, I'm going to stress this again — whoever goes through that door is going to be highly dangerous. We can't go to the police. You have to make sure they don't see you." She was chewing on her bottom lip, and Idris knew Darlene felt incredibly nervous as well.

Rebecca nodded. "I get it. I'm just keeping watch from the car while you guys do whatever other mystery thing you're doing."

"You don't mind doing this?" Idris spoke up.

Rebecca looked at him. "No. I mean, I'm not dumb. I'm sure there is way more going on than whatever Darlene told me." In the darkness, Idris could see Darlene flush. "But whatever it is, she is including me. More than we've hung out together lately, anyway. Besides, I'm all for adventure."

Idris still felt uneasy. Adventure, sure. But throwing this girl possibly in the way of Vivica or someone else made him worried.

"Okay," Darlene said. "We're going to go then, okay? Be careful."

They hugged again, and Idris and Darlene headed over to his pickup truck. Rebecca headed over to her car to move it up across the street in front of the shop.

"This is a bad idea," Darlene mumbled, looking up at the moon.

Idris' looked up at it as well. "Why? The full moon isn't for another week." That reminded him that he would have to hide from Darlene — there was no stopping the Change on a full moon.

She shook her head. "No. About Rebecca. I feel guilty. And after Ms. Boots…" Darlene trailed off.

Idris paused and then rested his hand on hers. "You told her it was extremely dangerous. You made it as clear as you could without saying it had to do with the supernatural."

Darlene looked at him and then nodded. "Let's go to Roman's Tavern."

Now it was his turn to feel nervous.

***

It didn't take long at all to get there. Darlene scrunched up the edges of her skirt in her hands. She was wrinkling it but didn't care. Her brain felt as if someone had taken it, put it in a blender and then poured it into a cup. She worried about Rebecca. Darlene wished she had told her about the vampires and werewolves instead of just stressing how dangerous it was. She had known Rebecca for a while. She was a daredevil and loved doing crazy things and calling it art. Of course, as soon as Darlene tried to warn her how dangerous it was, Rebecca leapt at the chance. On top of that, the guilt over Ms. Boots seemed to be a living creature inside of her. Darlene felt as if she had killed her herself. And then on top of that was this knowing feeling about Mabel. Was Idris just being crazy about her? Darlene had to stop thinking about it.

They pulled up in front of Roman's Tavern. It was crowded, with motorcycles and old trucks parked out front. She suddenly felt even more nervous.

Idris said, "They won't like outsiders. You're with me, and that will help a bit, but no one will be friendly to you."

Darlene steeled herself and nodded, opening the truck door. It was chilly, too cold for a skirt, but she barely felt the cold due to her nerves. How had Ms. Boots died? Was it Vivica? Did Vivica kill Jacob too? Darlene found herself looking at the rooftops of the buildings, just in case she was lying in wait. But there was nothing that popped out at her.

"Ready?" Idris asked.

Darlene stepped up next to him, feeling anything but ready.

They walked up to the doors, and Idris pulled one of them open. They were large and wooden, splintered in spots. They stepped inside, and Darlene tried to take everything in at once. There was a rock band off to the right side, playing loud music with a lead singer that howled into the mic, the tendons in his neck tight from screaming out words Darlene couldn't understand. A group of people were dancing, for lack of a better word, in front of the band. It mostly looked like thrashing.

The entire place stunk of cigarettes and old booze. There was a bar that wrapped around the other side with tables that looked as if they would crack if anyone sat at them. Most people stood.

There was a second floor above them, which was too dark to see anything. People probably went up there to do drugs and make out. As Idris had warned her, people were glaring at her. She felt exposed. Were all these people werewolves? How large was Roman's pack? Did Lucian's pack come here, too? She couldn't ask Idris anything because the terrible music was so loud. How was she going to ask anyone if they had seen Jacob?

Darlene felt Idris' strong fingers slide through hers and a shot of warmth went through her. She closed her eyes briefly as Idris pulled her through the crowd toward the bar. Idris stopped suddenly, and Darlene walked into his back, letting out a grunt of surprise. She peered around him to see another man talking to Idris. The man had a missing eye and was gesturing at her. Idris yelled something back but it was hard to hear.

"…humans….mental?" the one-eyed man yelled, pointing to Darlene.

Idris shouted back, "Looking…missing boy!"

The man shook his head in disgust at Idris. Darlene could tell they had some sort of history together. *He must be part of Roman's pack.* Idris said they were part of Roman's pack up until Brent turned up dead.

"Roman!" the one-eyed werewolf yelled and pointed to one corner.

Idris said something back and then tugged on Darlene, leading her through the crowd. Everywhere she looked, people glared at her, mostly in disgust. She felt more aware of her size than ever. No one else was as large as her. She wanted to leave. Why did she ever want to go to this bar?

There was a rundown table in this corner. A man who looked like he had giants as parents sat there along with a trashy-looking woman with a shaved head that made her look sickly and a dress that probably cost twenty dollars around forty years ago. She glared at Darlene as well. Darlene averted her gaze. The man stood up and Darlene was struck by how large he was. He could probably kill anything that came toward him. *He must be the pack leader.*

"What are you doing, Idris?" the man grunted, getting very close to Idris. "Have you lost your mind?"

"I'm looking for the boy who just went missing, Roman."

"Not my concern if another human went missing. And who the hell is this?" Roman jutted his chin toward Darlene, who tried to look brave.

"Friend of the missing boy."

Roman sneered, "That all, Idris? She looks to be about the size you like."

Darlene felt her entire face flush red. *Asshole,* she thought, wanting to tell him off but not feeling like getting killed. The woman behind Roman let out a laugh. Idris growled and jerked forward, his face now inches from Roman. Darlene could only watch.

Roman was looking at Idris now. "You find your missing pack leader yet? You know, I've been hearing some funny things about your best friend lately. Heard he was fucking your old vamp girl. What was her name? Vivica?"

Darlene had never seen Idris so angry. She balked, wishing she could be anywhere else.

"Have you seen the boy?" Idris repeated.

Roman stared at him. "I didn't see him. You probably killed him though... just like you killed that kid five years ago."

That was enough for Idris to snap. Darlene thought it could have been the stress of everything that finally got to him. She wasn't sure. All she saw was Idris leap and knock Roman down to the ground. The two of them smashed against the table. Darlene jumped back and could only watch in horror as Idris slammed his fist directly into Roman's face. The woman at the table jumped and flew toward Idris. Idris shoved her away and two other people held the woman back.

Roman swung his fist toward Idris, connecting with his lower jaw. There was a disgusting noise. The music was still playing. Some people didn't even look over. This must be an every night thing. She wasn't sure what to do. How does one stop werewolves from killing each other? Idris picked Roman up by the collar of his shirt and slammed him against the wall before head butting him. Roman's nose began to bleed and Darlene felt pretty confident that it was broken. No one was going to break up the fight, she realized with a sinking feeling.

She turned around to see if anyone else was going to do anything about it, but no one moved. The group nearby watched as casually as if they were watching

TV. Darlene was just about to turn back around when she saw something that made her stop. Someone walked behind the bar... the curve of the neck and that shaggy hair. The person turned slightly to the left, and Darlene's heart thumped a bit harder.

Jacob.

Darlene snapped her head back to see Idris and Roman still fighting. Suddenly irritated at both Idris and the other pack leader, she stormed over to them. She yanked back on Idris' shirt. Normally that wouldn't have done anything, but he was taken aback and lost his footing, his knees hitting the ground. Roman was slumped against the wall, his face covered in blood and his breathing ragged.

"Can you get a grip? Both of you?" she snapped, louder than she had meant to because some people were looking at her curiously now.

Idris looked abashed. "Darlene..."

She yanked him up as he stumbled to his feet and hissed in his ear, "Jacob is here."

His eyes widened in surprise. Darlene looked at Roman one last time as the woman ran over and crouched next to him, glaring at Idris. Darlene turned around and made her way through the crowd.

"…Broke up the fight…"

"…Human getting involved…"

"Kinda cute for a big girl," said one guy as Darlene walked by.

Irritated, she flipped the man off as she picked up her pace, walking behind the bar. There were protests from the bartender but Idris said something that shut him up quickly. Darlene's heart thumped some more. Jacob was alive and here in this bar. Idris and Darlene burst through the back exit behind the bar, the music spilling out behind them. No one was there.

"I am sure he came this way," she said to Idris.

"You're positive it was him?" Idris said, trying to rub Roman's blood out of his shirt.

She nodded. "I swear it was him." She looked at Idris. "What was that about?"

"What?" Idris replied, clearly playing dumb. When Darlene didn't say anything back, Idris looked sheepish. "He pisses me off."

"Is that how werewolves settle disagreements?"

"Pretty much."

Darlene thought about making another quip when she saw a shadow move behind Idris. Without thinking, she took off toward it, pushing Idris out of the way. Idris chased after it as well. She could see the outline of Jacob's face in the darkness. He was against a brick wall that blocked the alleyway next to the bar. In the dim moonlight, Darlene made out the whites of his eyes.

And then suddenly, Jacob leapt up in the air and over the wall. It was graceful and fluid, like a bird. In a single motion, he was gone. Darlene stopped running and stared at the top of the wall. Her throat had gone dry. She knew that motion. Jacob was a vampire.

Just then her phone chirped in her purse. With a sinking feeling in her stomach, Darlene yanked it out. She got the text ten minutes ago but didn't hear it during the commotion in the bar. With shaking fingers Darlene opened up the text. It said one word.

Help.

Chapter Nine

They sped down the road toward the bookshop as quickly as they could. Luckily they weren't far and got there in a couple of minutes. Idris' heart was beating fast. He glanced over at Darlene, who looked as pale as a ghost. He cursed himself for wasting time fighting with Roman like that. Roman urged him to fight, made remarks to get under his skin, and Idris took the bait. He should have just walked away.

Instead he had quickly and easily fallen back into his old behavior. The same behavior he told himself and Lucian he would no longer do. He scowled at the thought of Lucian. So much for being on the straight and narrow, when Lucian was plotting and planning something for years behind his back.

And now Jacob was a vampire. Why did Vivica bother to turn that boy into one? And Roman…did he mean it when he said Lucian and Vivica had a thing going on?

"Stop!" Darlene cried.

Idris slammed on the breaks. He almost drove right by the bookstore, too involved with his own thoughts yet again. On the street, Rebecca's car sat where they last saw it parked but there was no Rebecca. The door to the bookshop was flung wide open, with light spilling out onto the sidewalk. Darlene flew out of the car. Idris cursed and took off after her, trying to stay by Darlene's side.

They ran into the bookshop. Books were strewn around the room, some with the covers torn off. The computer had been flung off the desk and was shattered. Some of the shelves were tipped over and the lights were flashing. Bulbs were popped, Idris realized as he tried to get used to the flickering lights. He ground his teeth, fighting off the urge to Change.

"Rebecca!" Darlene called. "Rebecca!"

"I took care of your friend," said a voice — one that Idris knew very well.

Vivica came around one of the bookshelves. Her red hair was loose and flowing over her shoulders. She wore all black. Her red eyes were dark and stormy. She would have been beautiful, if it hadn't been for the blood smeared around her mouth.

"No!" Darlene cried when she saw Vivica's mouth, lurching forward.

Idris pulled her back and behind him, putting himself between the two of them.

Vivica scowled. "Protecting her? Won't do you any good. Where is it?"

"Where is what, Vivica?" Idris replied, sounding like a tired father dealing with a spoiled kid.

Her eyes narrowed. "You had that girl protecting *The Werewolf Code*. I have that now. *The Book of the Ancients* — I need it. Where is it?"

"You're a vampire. You don't have a copy of it?"

"No," Vivica spat. "Our copy doesn't have what I need. And Lucian told me he'd have *The Werewolf Code* here plus *The Book of the Ancients*. So where is it?"

Darlene spoke up, "We never had that book."

Worry creased Vivica's face. "The pages then, the pages that stupid boy did five years ago. Give me those. I know you have them. I went to his mother's last night to find them. Lucian said Brent had them. And since I couldn't find our book, the copies he made would have to do."

"You killed Brent's mother?"

"I was hungry," Vivica replied coldly.

Idris tried to sort out what she said while stalling until he could figure out a way to take her down. "You're working with Lucian?"

Vivica began to pace the room now, her long legs making her look almost like a cat. "Lucian and I have been working together for years. You were just too stupid to see it, Idris. You believed anything I told you in our disgusting relationship." She shrugged. "But Lucian didn't want to do anything physical with me. Said it took things too far. So I had my fun... with you. Lucian had *The Werewolf Code*. But he needed *The Book of the Ancients* for his plan. Brent was the perfect patsy and so willing to get the pages."

"Why couldn't you get the pages?" Idris said as Darlene whimpered, still not seeing Rebecca. "It is your book, after all."

"Lucian didn't want our copy. Said it was missing too much. He knew of a copy that was directly from the original, from a rival clan. I couldn't go in and get it.

We got Brent to do it. Lucian told him he'd make him a werewolf if he did. Brent made copies of the pages we needed. All the information about turning, including the information that had been lost to the ages."

"That was five years ago," Idris countered, trying to cover Darlene as she moved closer to the ground, getting ready to crawl under an overturned table to get out of Vivica's line of vision. "Did you kill Brent and then decide against whatever ridiculous plan you had going?"

Vivica snorted, still pacing. "No. We didn't kill Brent. I don't know who did. That was when Roman told Lucian he had to go. Roman backed out of the plan then. Said the heat coming down on him was too heavy now that Brent showed up dead. He tried to pin it on you, but you didn't buy it. So Lucian split from the pack."

"Roman was in on the plan?" Idris repeated.

Vivica scowled. "That's right, pup. Lucian decided to lay low. Make Roman think he had given up on his plan. Buy Roman's trust with time."

Idris didn't know where Darlene was. He hoped she had somehow gotten around Vivica to Maria's office. Rebecca could be in there. Vivica was too involved in her own speech to notice Darlene had gone missing. She always did love to talk. Idris decided to keep her talking.

"So he stopped whatever he was doing for five years?"

"Yes. But he's been trying again. We need those pages though, from the book of our kind. You have to have them. I know you were snooping around for Lucian. I have that old human spy for me. Mabel. She's loyal to me. Thinks I'll make her a vampire before the cancer eats away at her. I won't. You know that. But she told me you were snooping around here for that book. I thought she meant the vampire one until tonight when she told me you were looking at *The Werewolf Code.*"

"Lucian said he left it here for someone."

"He left it here for me."

"Where is he?"

"He's in hiding. He wants me to get the vampire pages we need and *The Werewolf Code* and then he'll contact me and let me know where he is."

"Why is he in hiding?"

Vivica groaned. "You ask so many questions about things I can't tell you, Idris. The only reason I've told you this much already is because I thought you would want to know before I kill you right here, right now."

She bared her fangs and, in a flash, Vivica slammed into him. Idris went flying back, smashing against a bookshelf. He tried to clear the fog that settled around his head. Memories flashed by, now coupled with the truth. Lucian had used Brent to get the vampire pages. Someone had killed Brent. Roman knew Lucian's plan. Vivica had been with Lucian, who'd left *The Werewolf Code* for a vampire minion to pick up.

Whatever grand scheme Lucian had going, it wouldn't be enough to right the wrongs he had already created. Rage burned hot in Idris. Vivica stared at him, her pretty features twisted in a sneer.

"You going to Change on me, pup?"

Idris started to see red. *Yes, I am going to Change.*

But this time he welcomed it.

***

Darlene managed to crawl toward Maria's office without Vivica seeing her. She loved to talk. Darlene could tell by the tone of her voice that she relished every moment she crushed Idris over the memory of Lucian. As Darlene crawled behind the desk, she could see the door to Maria's office was nudged open a crack. Rebecca had to be in there. Darlene's heart pounded loudly in her ears. She was amazed no one else could hear it.

She crawled over to the door and slid it open painfully slowly. She hoped Vivica wouldn't notice. She needed Vivica not to notice so she could get inside.

From what Darlene could gather, Lucian was working with Vivica. Why did he leave the book here, of all places? Why couldn't he just meet up with Vivica and give her the book? Did he just want Mabel to steal the book and give it to Vivica? Darlene felt as if Vivica was being lied to in some regard about why Lucian left the werewolf book here, but she couldn't figure it out. Not now. Not when she slowly slid the door open and saw a pale hand jutting out from behind the couch.

Darlene crawled over as quickly as she could. The entire office was trashed. Maria's desk was cracked in two with papers all over the floor. The chair that Officer Walsh sat on only hours ago had been smashed against the wall. The couch was sitting on the floor, lop-sided. Darlene held her breath and looked behind it.

Rebecca was on her back. Her eyes were closed. Her skin was deathly pale. Her neck was covered in blood. Her glasses were smashed and lying by her side. Fear, cold and clammy, came alive in Darlene's stomach. She was going to throw up.

Outside the office, she heard a smash and then books falling. She closed her eyes briefly. Idris would have to handle Vivica. Rebecca was wounded because Darlene had thrown her into this mess. Darlene went over to her and felt for a pulse. She couldn't feel one, but she wasn't sure if that was because of her own fear clouding her brain. She fumbled for her phone to call an ambulance. Darlene tilted Rebecca's head to one side and her heart stopped.

Rebecca's neck had two little puncture marks.

***

"It's been a while since I've seen you Change, Idris. You know, since you were trying to be a good little dog."

Idris snarled at her. Vampires didn't have any scent. He wasn't sure what bookshelf she hid behind now. Every muscle in his body felt alive. With Idris in his werewolf form, the only thing he cared about was attacking and defending accordingly. Everything else faded. That was why he used to love the Change. He never had to think when he was in his werewolf form.

"I wonder if your new girlfriend found her friend yet. I was thinking about just killing her, you know? But I decided against it."

Idris growled, pacing the floor, trying to find her. There was a flash of red, and she appeared next to him. He pushed off the floor with his hind legs and smashed into her. The two of them went flying into a table, which smashed in half underneath them. Idris bit down on her shoulder and sunk his teeth in. It was like biting stone. Vampire skin was just layers of dead skin being held alive by some disgusting force. Vivica thrashed underneath him and kicked him in his stomach. Idris let out a whine and was suddenly thrust into the air before hitting the ground.

"I thought to myself, would Lucian kill her? No, he wouldn't. He needs loyal servants to come to him later, once he has figured it out completely."

Idris leapt to his feet again and ran forward, ready to clamp down on Vivica's face and destroy her. He was sick of hearing her speak. He bit down on her ankle and tugged. Surprised, she toppled to the ground. Idris raised his front paws and extended his claws, bringing them down on her back, hard.

Vivica let out a gasp. Idris wasn't sure how much pain he caused her. There were only a few ways to kill vampires and, sadly, clawing them in the back wasn't one of them. Idris didn't feel the usual satisfaction he got when he fought with someone, because he was fighting a vampire and no one actually alive.

Vivica rolled over and grabbed Idris' neck. She tossed him off, and he skidded across the floor. That was another thing he hated. Vampire strength made him feel like a rag doll being tossed around.

Vivica looked at him, her red eyes flashing with pleasure. "I turned her, Idris. I turned your new girlfriend's friend into one of us. And when Lucian figures out how to combine both vampire and werewolves into one species, she'll be the first in line for the fucking experiment."

***

Darlene spoke rapidly into her phone, "No, I need an ambulance here right away! There's been a break in, and my friend has been attacked!"

Rebecca still wasn't moving. Her chest had stopped slowly rising up and down. Fear clutched at Darlene. *No, no, this can't be happening. Not to Rebecca.* The operator said they were dispatching someone right away, and Darlene hung up.

"Rebecca," she whispered to her friend. "Please wake up."

She shouldn't have asked Rebecca for her help. Why in the world did she leave the safety of her car? What a mistake it was. Panic, rage and sadness boiled up inside of her. Tears sprang from the corners of her eyes. She killed her friend.

Rebecca's eyes suddenly opened. And they were red.

***

Idris threw himself at Vivica again, and they toppled into the wall. Vivica looked irritated, which was the best Idris could say he was doing. He hated to admit it, but he was outmatched. Vivica was an ancient vampire. On top of that, they had been together on and off for a long time and often would fight with one another. They knew each other's weaknesses.

Combining werewolves and vampires. What sort of fucked up idea was that? How could Lucian be plotting such a thing? He cast a glance over to Maria's office.

Darlene was in there. Was she safe if Rebecca truly turned?

Vivica loomed over him, ready to strike again. One of his paws bled from when she sank her fangs into him moments before. She tasted blood and wanted more. But suddenly a siren filled the air. Vivica's head snapped up, and she looked back at him.

"Your bitch must have called the cops," she hissed through her fangs. "Tell her I'll be back for my new baby."

And Vivica was gone, bursting through the nearest window into the night, scaling the walls of the coffee shop next door. The sirens grew louder. He needed to Change back and it had to be now. But it was hard to come down from the negative emotions he felt. He wouldn't be able to Change back in time.

***

Darlene let out a gasp of surprise and lurched backward. Rebecca sat up so quickly that it looked almost like a blur. Rebecca stared at her now, wide-eyed and panicked. She grabbed her neck, feeling it, making soft noises that Darlene couldn't make out. Rebecca suddenly let out a cry of sharp pain and looked down at her hand. She had accidently touched her cross necklace. Darlene could see the faint burn mark on her neckline as well as her hand.

Sirens. The ambulance was coming, but Darlene now regretted calling them. Rebecca heard them, too. With a scream, she wrapped her hand around the necklace and ripped it off of her neck, tossing it onto the floor.

"Rebecca," Darlene whispered.

Her eyes focused on Darlene for a moment. She looked terrifying, with her pale, dead-looking skin and blood smeared along her neck and T-shirt. And the bite marks. Those bite marks.

Rebecca let out another scream, and Darlene saw the fangs in her mouth. Then, in a flash, she ran past Darlene and burst out of the office. Darlene stumbled to her feet. She felt as if her head had been held underwater for too long. Her movements felt sluggish and slow compared to Rebecca's. She opened the door to Maria's office as the paramedics and cops burst in.

She was the only one left in the book store. Even Idris was gone.

Chapter Ten

Hazy. That was the only word Darlene could use to describe the next few hours. The police asked tons of questions that she stumbled through. She stammered out that her friend had gotten up and left. No, she didn't know where she had gone. No, she didn't know who had broken in or where they had gone. Yes, she was fine, she just had a headache.

It wasn't until Officer Walsh came into the room and gave her a cup of coffee that she became dimly aware of her surroundings. He sat across from her, and Darlene watched his mouth move but she didn't hear anything.

Rebecca. That was her only thought since she saw Rebecca's red eyes. Vivica turned her only friend into a vampire. And it was all her fault. She turned Rebecca herself by asking her to watch the shop... just like she had killed Ms. Boots.

"Miss Troop?" The sound of her last name jolted her back to the present day.

Darlene shook her head and tried to focus on Officer Walsh. "I'm sorry. What did you say?"

"I said that I had looked into your story a bit after your call came in. You were here at the station a few days ago, claiming you had information on Brent Boots."

That felt like a lifetime ago. Was it truly only a few days ago? In any case, she nodded.

"A neighbor of Ms. Boots said she saw someone fitting your description and another man visiting her the day of her murder."

Yes, it's my fault. All of it was my fault. If I had only minded my own business when Idris showed up. If I had only remained a hermit. None of this would have happened to anyone.

But instead she just nodded again.

"Miss Troop, I understand you're in shock from whatever happened at the book store. But I need to know why you saw Ms. Boots on the day of her murder."

Darlene opened her mouth to reply when suddenly the door to the room opened. Another officer peeked inside with a strained expression on his face.

"What?" barked Officer Walsh.

The man's eyes darted to Darlene. "There's a man here for Miss Troop. He won't leave. Demanded to see her now."

Idris. Darlene stood up quickly and, without saying anything else to Officer Walsh, pushed past the man at the door and walked down the hall quickly. Her heart thrummed with his name. She needed to see him. She needed to know that Idris, at the very least, was okay.

She burst through the door of the hallway and out into the main station floor. Her eyes scanned the area. Maria sat in one corner, talking to an officer with panic spread all across her face. Darlene half expected to see Vivica there, her hands held together by handcuffs, with her leg casually thrown over one side of a chair, staring at her. Then she saw him.

Idris stood in front of the main desk. His face looked drawn and his eyes tired, as if he hadn't slept in ages. His clothes were baggy, hanging off of him in odd angles, as if they weren't even his. Idris' eyes darted around, searching for Darlene. She moved forward now, toward the exhausted werewolf she suddenly wanted more than anything.

Idris finally saw Darlene. She moved toward him, as if she was a ghost. Her skin was deathly pale, almost as if she was a vampire herself. Her hair stuck up at odd angles, and her eyes had purple circles under them. Her clothes were wrinkled and her blue eyes seemed to have a funny look to them. His heart pounded as she walked over to him.

When Idris realized there was no way to Change back in time before the ambulance and police arrived, he fled. He hated himself every second he spent turning around and running out through the back door. He scrambled into the parking lot and jumped the brick wall, crashing into the bushes beyond. But even that wasn't good enough, because the police were soon checking the area, trying to find whoever Darlene had told them had broken into the store. Idris, still in his werewolf form, fled even farther away from Darlene. He ran into the woods to where Brent had been found murdered.

The emotions inside him were too strong to Change back. He never had this problem before. Normally, the rage in him would quell after a battle. The only time he couldn't Change back was during a full moon.

But now it was too much. There was no stopping the onslaught of feelings inside of him. *Combine both werewolves and vampires into one species.* The words kept repeating in his skull, bouncing around as if his brain had been turned into a dozen beach balls. How could Lucian be plotting such a reckless act? And why?

He reviewed everything Vivica said a million times over. Lucian got Brent involved to get the pages from the vampire book. He dropped the idea once Brent was discovered murdered by someone and didn't have the pages. He was trying the stupid idea all over again.

Something nagged at him though. Idris understood not having the vampire pages detailing the art of turning a victim. But Lucian *had* the book of the werewolves, explaining everything about how to turn someone into a werewolf. Why would he drop it off at the bookstore for someone to pick up, only to collect it for him again? It seemed redundant. Vivica claiming it had been for her and her spy, Mabel, seemed wrong. As if Vivica had been lied to.

Vivica killed Ms. Boots. But she didn't mention changing Jacob. Was there a link between Jacob working at the store and now being a vampire? Vivica rarely changed people into vampires. She hated taking care of the younglings. Idris knew she had changed

Darlene's friend out of spite and was going to leave her out to dry until she could experiment on her.

That meant there was a feral vampire out there somewhere.

It took Idris four hours to Change back. Once he did, he headed to the police station right away after Darlene didn't pick up her phone.

And now she was standing in front of him, her eyes no longer that bright blue he adored but a somber dark hue that showed nothing but pain. Idris let out a grunt and pulled her close to him, engulfing her in his arms, clutching her close. Her hands wrapped around his, and they stood there like that, in the midst of the police station and the buzz of activity, for quite some time.

***

By the time the police finally released Darlene, she felt exhausted and dirty. She craved a shower and sleep. Officer Walsh was furious that she left before her questioning was finished, but Idris had pulled himself up to full size and stared at him until he relented. But Darlene knew he'd be back with more questions. She had no problem explaining the things she had found about Brent online, but it was harder to come up with a convincing story about why she had gone to see Ms. Boots, who then wound up dead.

Darlene lied and said Rebecca came into town and wanted to pop in for a book before they met up. Then Darlene got the text, ran to the book store and found Rebecca wounded. She called 911 before the assailant attacked her, knocking her out. When Darlene came to, Rebecca was gone and the cops had just arrived.

Darlene knew that if the cops really started looking into the story, they would find pieces that didn't make any sense. Like the fact that Darlene had been at Roman's Tavern moments before when Idris had gotten into that fight. It wasn't as if they had lain low when they were there. Then Officer Walsh would come back with more questions that Darlene wasn't sure how to explain. He'd want to talk to Idris, too. Cops were going out to search for Rebecca.

Darlene didn't know much about young vampires. She barely knew anything about vampires in general, having not known they were real until recently. She found herself missing the days when she would read the supernatural books in the shop and knew it was all made up.

She thought back to the night in her apartment complex parking lot, when Vivica and Idris fought. The transparent shape in the woods nearby. The thought would come back to her once in a while, almost as if it was trying to tell her something.

"Darlene."

She shook her head and looked up to see they were at her apartment complex. She found herself gazing at the woods. But in the morning sunlight, there was nothing out of the ordinary to be seen.

"Let me walk you inside."

Darlene nodded and they got out of the truck. She suddenly wanted Idris. What did it say about her — about the fact that she wanted to sleep with him again just so she could stop thinking and feel as if someone truly cared about her? It probably said a lot, none of which actually interested her at the moment.

As she walked into her apartment and Idris stepped in behind her, Darlene turned around and kissed him. Idris let out a noise of surprise as she pushed herself against him, the door shutting behind him as she pulled at his clothes. Idris responded by kissing along her neck, mumbling her name. He smelled like the woods, Darlene noticed, as she tugged his shirt off. Her hands trailed over his muscles again, liking the feel of them under her fingers.

"You're so beautiful," Idris groaned in her ear as they toppled onto her couch.

This time their kisses were different. They were hard, fast and filled with a sense of growing dread, as if the entire world was going to change right before them and all they had was this moment. Darlene was Idris' rock, and he was hers. Gone were thoughts of the bookstore, Vivica's red eyes and Rebecca fleeing. Gone were images of Officer Walsh and Ms. Boots. All Darlene had was Idris undressing in front of her, enflaming her with desire.

She lay on the couch, looking up at him as he took off his clothes. Soon Idris only had his boxers on. Darlene saw his hard shaft straining against the fabric. She tugged them down and ran her tongue along his length. Idris shuddered as Darlene slowly, agonizingly, ran her tongue along him. Up and down, up and down. She looked up at him and when their gazes met, Idris let out a soft moan. Darlene liked being in control. She slid the head of his shaft into her mouth and sucked gently. Idris grunted in response as she then slid him out of her mouth again, teasing him.

"Darlene…" he groaned.

She liked how hard he was and how warm he was. He was even warmer than usual, if that was possible. Darlene took him back into her mouth, this time as far as she could take him. Idris moaned and arched his hips, forcing more of him in. Darlene let him fill up her mouth and throat, her eyes closing in delight. She loved how well he fit. Her underwear clung to her wetness as she worked him again. She moved her head up and down on him until Idris suddenly lurched away. She looked up at him in surprise.

"No more. Let me have you."

Darlene nodded and turned around on the couch, wanting him to take her from behind. Idris didn't even bother pulling down her underwear. He ripped them off of her. He pushed up her skirt and slid inside her. Darlene was so wet that she accepted him instantly. She moaned, the full length of him filling her up. Idris felt so amazing. He began to pump in her, hard and fast. She loved the feel of him. She loved that she could make him feel this good and how he wanted her this much.

Darlene moved against him, taking him all. His hands tangled up in her hair, and he pulled on it when he thrust into her. Darlene arched her back, her clothes stuck to her, throwing her head back, letting out a moan. Sucking him had made her so turned on that she was ready to come. Idris slammed into her, his breathing hard and heavy.

"Idris!"

Darlene shuddered, shutting her eyes tightly as her orgasm shook her. The pleasure vibrated through her body. At the same time, Idris yelled her name, louder than ever, loud enough that she was sure the neighbors could hear it. He slammed into her again, and she felt him coming, filling her up. This heightened her orgasm more. Darlene rocked her hips, milking him, moaning loudly, overcome by the pleasure of it all. Her mind was blank and empty. All she cared about was her orgasm.

Idris grunted too as he came, mumbling her name like a chant as he finished. Darlene slumped against the couch, panting for breath. He slid out of her and slumped to the floor, his chest heaving. Darlene rolled off the couch and moved toward him.

There, on the floor of her living room, the two of them fell asleep, entwined and naked.

Chapter Eleven

Idris knew this was a bad idea. But there was no way he wasn't going to see Roman that afternoon. If he ended up in another fight, then so be it.

He had woken up in Darlene's arms an hour ago. She was still sleeping soundly. Idris draped a blanket over her and left a note, explaining what he was going to do. He didn't like leaving her there. Was he falling for Darlene because she knew who he was and didn't leave him? Or was he falling for her because their situation made it almost impossible not to?

And what if he was falling for her because of only positive reasons — what about Darlene? She still had that framed photo of her ex on her night table. Was she ready for another relationship?

Instead of lying there next to her over-thinking it, he decided to leave and find Roman. He had to find out what he knew about Lucian and Vivica and their plan.

Idris pushed open the doors of the bar and was greeted with the same sights as the last time. This time Roman was talking to Mark in the center of the floor with Julie next to him. She saw him first and glared. She was there at the fight last night and would have probably torn Idris to shreds if Roman had allowed it.

"What the hell are you doing here?" Julie stormed over to him, her eyes already dilating, trying to fight off the Change.

Idris ignored her. "Roman, I need to speak to you."

Mark stepped in front of him. "He doesn't want to speak to you."

"What, Roman can't make his own decisions on who to speak to? He has to have his lackeys do all the talking?"

Idris knew that would be enough to irritate Roman, and he was right. Roman shoved Mark aside and walked over to him. His nose was bandaged up from where Idris broke it and one side of his face had swollen up. Idris won that fight. He had only a few bruises and nothing broken. Roman must be pissed.

Roman stood at his full height and looked down at Idris. "You come to play nice, pup?"

"We need to talk. Actually talk."

"I'm busy."

"With what?"

"Idris?"

Idris turned around to see who had called his name. On the second floor was a tall, lean Asian woman with her hair swept up in a messy bun. She was wearing jeans and an oversized T-shirt. Her eyes were wide. Idris hadn't seen her since her crying fit over Lucian. Liara — Lucian's'wife.

"Liara! What are you doing here?"

Liara walked down the steps. Her high heels made sharp noises against the stairs. She came over to him and hugged him. She always smelled like flowers.

"I haven't heard from you in a while. And nothing from Lucian either. Our pack is in trouble with both of you missing. And…" She hesitated, glancing over at Roman before lowering her voice. "Idris, our copy of *The Werewolf Code* is missing."

They both knew what that meant. Without their copy of the book, they were no longer a pack. Idris knew he would have to give Liara the book and discover who it was meant for later.

"Talk to me after this," Idris whispered before turning back to Roman. "Can we speak alone?"

Roman paused and then nodded. He brushed Julie off, who was telling him not to and walked up the stairs toward his office.

Idris turned and stopped in front of Liara. "The book is at a book store down the street. Leave, go right and keep walking. Get the book."

Liara seemed shaken but nodded as Idris walked by her. Whoever was meant to have the book would find out and be pissed off, but as long as Liara had it, they would still be a pack. If Liara claimed the book, she'd be pack leader next. It might be better for everyone if she was.

Idris stepped inside Roman's office again as he sat down at his desk.

"Listen, I don't want to talk to you. But it wouldn't do for us to fight again. Julie would just get on my ass. So whatever you want to say, just say it and leave." He leaned back, grabbing a cigarette out of his pocket.

Idris remained standing. "Five years ago, Lucian worked with Vivica to cross our blood line and create some disgusting hybrid. You knew about this."

Roman went still. Surprise flickered across his face before he managed to put a bored expression on. "Figured you knew."

"You knew I had no idea. Who killed Brent?"

There was a long pause now as Roman lit up the cigarette and watched the tip burn. Idris felt hot all over and itchy, wanting to lunge and beat the answers out of Roman. *Deep breathing, stay focused.*

"I did."

"Why?"

"I thought if Brent was killed, Lucian would give up his ridiculous plan. I knew he was using the boy to try to get pages from that damned vampire book. He needed information on both werewolf transformation and the full details of vampire transformations, which not all the copies have. I thought if I killed Brent, he'd lose his little helper and give up the plan."

"It didn't work, did you know that? Lucian is trying it again. Did you kill Lucian?"

"No. No, I didn't kill Lucian, although I wish I had. I don't know where he is. And I don't care. If he's dead, that means that ridiculous plan of his is dead, too."

"He's not dead. He's working with Vivica."

"That crazy bitch," Roman mumbled, taking a drag off his cigarette. "Listen, pup, I'll tell you the only thing I know about Lucian's disappearance. He told me he wanted the pack to reform. He didn't want to be pack leader anymore, and he didn't trust you to do it. He told me he was going to give me *The Werewolf Code.* Said he'd leave it in town and tell me where to pick it up. Never heard from him since, and now he's vanished. So you have your pack, but barely." He leaned forward, staring at Idris. "But once I find that book, your pack is under my control again, understand? And we can move on from this nightmare Lucian tried to bring to light."

Idris felt relief wash over him that he told Liara to get the book from Darlene's shop. And then that sick sense of betrayal washed over him yet again. Lucian giving the pack to Roman...had he really thought Idris couldn't handle the pack on his own? *Maybe I can't, but Liara can.*

"Roman, I don't like you. But you know that. You don't like me either. So listen to me when I tell you that

I don't think Lucian is dead. He's still working with Vivica. He sent her after me to try to get pages from the vampire book to learn more about the transformation. He may have promised you the pack, but he hasn't dropped his idea. He's just gone rogue."

"What do you want me to do? Not my concern."

"No, it is your fucking concern," Idris snapped, slamming his hands on Roman's desk. "You knew about this terrible idea and yet did nothing to stop it."

Roman growled, "I killed Brent! I tried to stop it. What the hell did you do, Idris? Fuck vampires and piss everyone off? You're still barely in control of yourself. Even now, what are you doing to stop it or are you fucking the bookstore girl, too?"

Rage filled Idris' veins as he tried to control his breathing before speaking again. "There's another thing to look out for. Vivica created a vampire and left her. The girl escaped. There's a feral vampire on the loose."

"Fantastic," Roman replied, his voice dry.

Idris stood back up, watching Roman smoke. "One more thing. Why was a vampire at your club last night?"

His gaze faltered for a moment. "What?"

"You heard me. You had a newborn vamp at your club last night. Darlene knows the kid. Around Brent's age. Why was he sneaking around here and not being attacked by your thug pack?"

"I don't know of any young vampire in my club." Roman spat on the floor and stood up, a growl coming from his throat. "I told you what I knew about Lucian. I told you I killed Brent. I told you I'm going to find out where Lucian put the book of our people and I'm going to dismantle your pack. I don't know shit about some kid vamp running around in my bar. But if I see him, I'll make sure I end him myself. Got it?"

Idris leaned close to him, inches from his face, close enough to smell the tobacco from Roman's breath. "If I find out you're lying to me about anything else, my next visit won't be so pretty." He took a step back. "You might want to put some ice on your nose."

Idris stormed out of the room, taking deep breaths, trying to control himself from Changing. As he turned the corner back out onto the second floor of the club, he ran into Julie. She thudded against him and bounced off before straightening up.

"Were you trying to eavesdrop on us?"

"No."

"You're lying."

Julie's small, thin frame was wrecked by hard drug usage over the years. Her eyes constantly looked on the verge of bugging out. Her tattoos were faded in spots and she was constantly dirty. She had missing teeth from poor dental care and constant fights with other females in the pack. Idris didn't know how she ever aligned herself with Roman but as far as he was concerned, they were a perfect match for each other.

But now as she stared at him, her usual hostility was gone. In its place was something weird — a look he had never seen before in her.

"What?" Idris snapped.

"That girlfriend of yours," Julie started, glancing over her shoulder. "You better be careful with her."

"Why?"

"She ain't like normal folk, Idris. I hope you weren't stupid enough to tell her what we is. Because it's going to come back on you, hard and fast. Especially if she ever realizes what she can do."

Idris' head thrummed with a dull pain, "What she can do? What are you talking about?"

"I warned you."

Julie slinked into the hallway and headed to Roman's office. Idris stood there for a moment, trying to make sense of what Julie had spouted before shaking his head and heading down the stairs.

***

Maria fiddled with the same book, opening and closing it, for over twenty minutes now, as she looked around the bookshop. Darlene never saw her so upset before. She cleaned up the store as Maria stood there, sending out wave after wave of confused, distracting energy. Darlene kept thinking about Rebecca — where was she right now? Then her mind would go to Jacob — who changed him and what was he doing? To Idris — should she keep sleeping with him? She liked him more than she wanted to admit, but was it only because of their circumstances? And now Maria was hovering, constantly looking at Darlene, clearly not believing her story at all.

Darlene was going to open her mouth and finally break the agonizing silence when the bell above the door rang out.

"We're closed," Maria said.

"Oh, I'm sorry…I was told to come here…"

Darlene turned around to see a tall, gorgeous Asian woman standing in the doorway. Her clothes were simple, but she radiated a sadness that almost knocked Darlene over.

"How can I help you?" she asked the woman.

"Idris sent me. He said you had a book here called *The Werewolf Code.*"

Darlene nodded and started to walk over to the woman when Maria grabbed her arm. "Darlene," she whispered. "When she leaves, I need you to tell me what is going on."

She nodded back, unsure of what to say. The woman kept glancing at Maria with confusion sweeping over her delicate features. Darlene introduced herself. The woman shook her hand.

"I'm Liara," she said to Darlene with her eyes still on Maria. "I'm a friend of Idris'. My husband left a book here for me."

Lucian's wife, Darlene realized with a jolt. She glanced behind her but Maria retreated into her office, the door locking firmly afterward. *Strange*, she thought, but relieved at the same time.

"Yes," she replied, turning back to Liara. "He did leave a book here."

Liara's eyes scanned across the bookstore now. "Oh my...what happened here?"

"We had a break-in last night. I'll try to find the book for you, okay? I'm sorry we're so disorganized."

"No, it's okay. I'm sorry to hear someone broke into your shop. That's horrible, truly."

Darlene looked around the shop in search of the oversized book. She knew Vivica left without it, but she wasn't sure where it ended up in the fight with Idris. She repeated her search in the supernatural section again, hoping it was still in the area.

"Did anyone get hurt?" Liara asked.

"My friend is missing."

"That's horrible!"

Darlene found the book wedged in between two similar sized books. She yanked it up from the floor and brought it over to Liara. Her face relaxed when she saw it.

Liara trailed her fingers over the cover and looked up at her. "My husband. Did he say anything when he gave it to you?"

"Just that someone would be coming by to pick it up."

Liara nodded, glancing around the bookstore again. "You, uh, know Idris well?"

"We're good friends," Darlene said, unsure of how to phrase it because she wasn't even sure where she stood with Idris.

"Well, I appreciate your help very much."

Liara nodded and glanced over at Maria's office again before leaving the shop, her high heels clicking loudly against the wood floor. The door closed behind her, and Darlene watched her go.

"Darlene?"

She turned around to see Maria peeking out from her office. "Yeah?"

"Can we talk?"

Darlene nodded and walked into the office.

***

Idris headed down the street to Darlene, tossing around what Julie said to him. It didn't make sense. Julie rarely made sense. She was turned into a werewolf at the age of ten by a rabid group of werewolves down south. They tortured her for days until finally turning her. The pack then abandoned her. Julie had to figure everything out about being a werewolf on her own. She met Roman when she turned nineteen. The two of them had been together on and off since then.

Julie was strong and had been through a lot. But she was prone to heavy bouts of substance abuse. Her mind wasn't all there, and she would spout a lot of crazy stuff. Idris had to stop thinking about it.

Down ahead on the sidewalk, he could see Liara. She clutched *The Werewolf Code* to her chest, taking long strides through the tourists crowding the sidewalk. She was focused with her mouth set in a determined line. When she saw him, she gave a small wave and walked over to him.

"Where are you heading?" she asked.

"The bookshop. Everything go okay?"

A strange look crossed her face. "Why didn't you tell me?"

"Tell you what?"

"An Exsul is working in the shop."

Idris' heart suddenly pounded. An Exsul…there was no way Darlene was a werewolf. He would have sensed it instantly. His throat felt dry.

"What? Darlene?"

"No, her boss. The older woman… Maria."

Idris shook his head. "Maria isn't an Exsul. No way. I would have picked up on that instantly. How could I miss a werewolf? On top of that, an Exsul?"

Exsuls were exiled werewolves. They had no pack and ran alone. There were various reasons one became an Exsul, and none of them were good. Idris would have sensed a werewolf as soon as he had entered that bookshop. Maria didn't give off any werewolf signals at all.

"She hides it with magic... but I know. She knew I could tell and hid in the office."

"Doesn't it mean that Maria knows I am a werewolf too?"

Silence hung between them, and Idris felt his heart beat faster.

"Roman said the book was for him," he told Liara. "That Lucian was going to give up the pack to him."

Liara's face paled. "What?"

"What if Lucian knew about Maria? What if he left it in her shop with another werewolf so it could be protected?"

"Idris, what aren't you telling me about my husband?"

"A lot." Idris walked away now, hurrying to the bookshop. "I'll have to explain later."

***

Darlene shut the door behind her and looked at Maria. She sat behind her desk with a tired expression. Her large glasses covered most of her face, and her white hair stuck up at funny angles. Her jewelry today was entirely lizard themed for some strange reason, and her shirt was a dark red that didn't match her yellow skirt. Darlene sat down across from her, wondering if she was going to get fired.

"Darlene," she said slowly. "I made a conscious effort to steer clear of inter-pack politics. When Lucian contacted me and told me about dropping off *The Werewolf Code* here until someone can come get it, I said fine. But I didn't want to know why he decided to relinquish the book and who would come to get it."

"Wait, what?"

"When Idris came by, I assumed he would get the book and leave. But I was wrong. He hung around and you began a relationship with him." Darlene began to speak, looking defensive. Maria held up a thin hand. "Don't. I've seen how you two look at each other. And now my shop is in ruins, and Lucian's wife came to collect the book. I should have put a stop to this earlier."

Darlene opened her mouth to speak again but her head was spinning. Nothing Maria said made sense. She was going to answer when the door to Maria's office burst open. Idris stood in the doorway. His eyes fell on Maria.

"Get away from her, Exsul," he growled at her.

"So Lucian's wife told you already?"

Darlene's gaze bounced between the two of them. "What is going on? What is an Exsul?"

"So what did you do to get banned from the packs, Maria? What did you do so badly that you were marked an Exsul? Let me see the tattoo… do you have the tattoo? Or are you using magic to block that as well so that no one else will know that you're an Exsul?"

Maria went stock still. Darlene looked at them both in confusion. *What is an Exsul? Does that mean Maria is…?*

"If you're an Exsul, why did you have *The Werewolf Code* here?" Idris continued. "Are you involved with what Lucian is planning?"

"Lucian was giving up the pack," Maria said stiffly. "He was going to become an Exsul as well. You know if you give up the book and dismantle the pack, the leader becomes an Exsul. He came to me, another Exsul, to keep it safe for whomever came to take it."

"Enough!" Darlene snapped and stood up, glaring at both of them. "Now both of you tell me what an Exsul is! I am not going to sit here and be left in the dark like this."

Idris crossed his arms and stared at Maria, who sighed. "Exsul is an exiled werewolf. We have no pack. We have no voice in pack affairs or anything affecting movements as a whole. We must be alone for the rest of our lives."

"You're a *werewolf*? Are you serious? This whole time?"

"Yes. I turned when I was fifteen. I became an Exsul ten years ago."

"Why?"

Maria shook her head. "I'm not talking about that. Not now. And especially not in front of *him*."

Idris grunted, "There isn't any good reason why a werewolf becomes an Exsul."

"My work is finished. Lucian's wife collected the book. My store is destroyed. There is nothing more I can give you or any of the other packs and nothing I care to give."

Darlene shook her head. She wasn't sure what to say. She wasn't even sure who to say it to. It was all too much. *Maria, her own boss, a werewolf? Was anyone around her normal? Was normal even a thing anymore?*

"You think you can just bow out now?" Idris said.

"I *am* bowing out now. I want nothing else to do with pack conflicts. I did what Lucian needed…"

They kept fighting. Their words swirled together and became one glob of noise that stuck to Darlene's ears. It seemed that everyone in her life was connected somehow to Lucian, and she didn't want to hear any more about it.

"That's it!" she yelled. "I don't want to hear from either one of you about this anymore."

She stormed out of the office, brushing against Idris who exclaimed, "Darlene?"

"No," she mumbled. "I shouldn't have gotten involved in this. What a nightmare this has become."

And she left the store behind, walking briskly to her car, hiding her torment. Darlene was grateful no one saw the tears falling down her face.

Chapter Twelve

Idris watched Darlene leave, a lump forming in his throat. He turned back to look at Maria, still sitting behind the desk, her expression unreadable.

"How come you didn't tell me you were one of us?"

"Why would I tell you? I would have to admit that I am an Exsul. It isn't as if you'd treat me with any respect because of it. Do the packs know that Darlene knows about them?"

He paused. "No."

"They'll be furious when they do, you know that, right? Especially because you didn't relocate or Change her. You'll be threatened with Exsul status by Lucian's wife."

"You're telling me things I already know."

Her eyes flashed. "You have Darlene wrapped up in things she shouldn't be wrapped up in. Now she knows about us and vampires and whatever else is going on."

"Did Lucian tell you why he was dismantling the pack?"

"No. He said he had something he wanted to try. Something that would make him an Exsul in the end."

"He wants to turn us into hybrids with vampires. Jacob, the worker you fired, who is missing — he's a vampire now. Do you know who changed him?"

Her face paled. "*Jacob?*"

"Darlene and I saw him at Roman's Tavern. Vivica, the vampire involved with Lucian, didn't admit to turning him. I know her, and she would have claimed it instantly. That means someone else did it."

Maria shook her head. "I don't know who turned that poor boy, but it's disgusting. The packs are disgusting and so are the vampires."

"Funny you should say that. Liara said you're using magic to block yourself from other werewolves. That's why I didn't notice you. So who is the witch that you convinced to help you?"

"None of your business." She stood up suddenly. "You need to leave. Leave Darlene alone if you know what's good for you. I'm an Exsul. Whatever happens with your pack doesn't interest me. But know this, Idris. If you don't figure out what you're doing, you'll be an Exsul yourself. You toed the line close for most of your life. Oh, don't look so surprised. I know about you. I know your anger and your rage at being a werewolf. I know how close you were to being tried for murdering that boy Brent. I wanted Darlene to find someone to make her happy after Austin cheated on her with a man, but not with you. Now get out."

Numbly, Idris turned around, thinking about what Maria said. He didn't know that Austin had left Darlene for another man. It explained why she was still hung up on him. Maybe he wasn't any better than Austin. Maybe Maria was right.

He stepped outside of the shop. The sun was setting, a brisk wind blew his way. Darlene's car was gone already. He shoved his hands in his pockets and stared out at the skyline. He wasn't sure what to do next. He had hit a dead end. Idris understood now what Lucian was trying to do — an idea that he believed in so much that he was willing to turn Exsul for it. Liara could lead the pack just fine. But could she survive what her husband was doing?

Rebecca was still out there, a feral vampire who had Vivica as her creator. Jacob was out there, too, turned by who knows. Lucian, plotting and planning with Vivica. Roman, who killed Brent without a second thought and would be extremely upset to know he had lost possible pack control already to Liara. And Julie's warning.

He had a bad feeling he couldn't shake.

***

Darlene drove around for a while, in an aimless way that she hadn't done in ages. She needed to figure out what to do next. She even considered packing up her things and moving away. She had enough in savings to get out of town and forget about all of this, like a bad dream. She was foolish to think she could help Idris. The whole situation was nothing but bad news, and it only got worse from here on out.

She ended up in her apartment parking lot. With a sigh, she got out of the car and walked toward her apartment. What she wanted was a long hot shower followed by maintaining a vegetative state on her couch, wrapped up in blankets and watching TV. She couldn't think of anything else that sounded as lovely as that did.

It all happened so fast.

Darlene heard a twig snap behind her. Turning around, all she saw was a blur and then her back was pressed against the side of the apartment building, away from the light. Her breath caught in surprise, and she could feel iron tighten around her wrists. With a gasp, Darlene realized she was staring directly at Jacob.

"Darlene," he mumbled.

"Jacob, what are you doing here?"

"I had to come get you. My Maker wants to meet you."

"Are you crazy? I'm not going with you."

Darlene tried to wiggle away and out of his grip, but it was as if she was chained to the wall. His strength was more than she could even understand. He seemed amused and watched her attempt to break free of his grip. He wore the same clothes as the night she saw him at Roman's Tavern.

"You don't have any choice."

Something hit her hard on the head and all Darlene saw was darkness.

***

Idris called Darlene twice but there was no answer. He told himself to stop calling her because it was clear she wanted to be left alone. But the nagging feeling in his stomach grew. He looked out the motel window, unsure of where to go next. Liara had texted him, demanding the full story of why the book had been with an Exsul. He knew he had to tell her the truth. Idris recalled how much she cried when she found out Lucian went missing. Now he would have to tell her that her husband was a madman, too. He cursed and threw on his jacket. He set out to head over to Darlene's place.

Idris swung open the door and found himself staring at Liara. Her hair was down and falling across her shoulders in a black sheet. She had an oversized jacket on that Idris recognized as Lucian's.

"You didn't answer my text," she said by way of greeting.

"I have to see Darlene."

"Fine, but I'm coming with you. And I want you to tell me what is going on. I'm…pack leader now." Her voice caught at the end, as if she didn't believe it.

Idris didn't feel like arguing, "Fine. Let's go."

***

Darlene drifted across the water. The sun beat down on her face. All around her was nothing but the ocean, quietly bobbing her along as she drifted. How did she get here? Her thoughts were slow and muddled, as if she was dreaming. Maybe she *was* dreaming. She couldn't remember the last thing she did.

Someone drifted by and called out to her. She turned her head to see a group of kids from grade school. Bullies. She was a pudgy kid, and they liked to make fun of her by pulling her pigtails and doing piggy noises. They floated by, calling out to her. Darlene ignored them.

There was someone else on the other side now. Austin. He was holding hands with his boyfriend. They were both in inner tubes, waving at her. Darlene felt rage engulf her. The rage was directed at Austin... at his lies... at the fact that he used her. But they paid no attention to her pain and then they were gone.

"I know what you are."

That deep voice, husky and dark, as if he was eating stones. Darlene looked above her and saw Idris, floating along his back as well.

"What I am?"

"You've always known, haven't you? From the books you've read. You just won't accept it."

"Accept what?"

"Your connection with things beyond this realm."

Darlene opened her mouth to reply but suddenly everything faded, and then there was only blackness around her.

Slowly, Darlene opened her eyes. The blackness crisscrossed with something. Trees, she realized. Stars dotted her vision, and she felt the dirt beneath her fingertips. She was outside.

"Oh good, you're awake." A soft, silky voice broke through the silence.

Darlene realized her head was tilted back against a tree trunk. She tried to move but her arms were tied around the trunk, her fingers brushing against the dirt. There was a man in front of her, walking slowly. His hair was messy, and his glasses glinted in the moonlight. She recognized him.

"Lucian."

"Nice to see you again."

Lucian walked over to her and crouched down. He was taller than she remembered. In the darkness, it was hard to make out his facial features. He walked with a gait that she didn't recognize from the store, as if he had been wounded. Fear gripped her as Darlene realized she was alone in the woods with him.

Lucian reached out and moved a strand of hair from her face, which made Darlene flinch. He laughed, a low laugh without any sort of humor in it.

"I thought I'd leave the book at your tiny shop for Roman and that would be that. I would do what I needed to do, be branded an Exsul if those narrow-minded fools decided upon it and have Roman take over the pack."

Darlene remained silent. She didn't want him to know his wife had come and gathered the book instead.

"But Idris was fast on my trail, trying to figure out where I had gone and why. By all accounts, nothing should have come out of his search for me." Lucian trailed his hand down to her wrist and squeezed just hard enough that tears sprung to Darlene's eyes. "But because of *you* and your interest in Brent, Idris never went away. And now you're here with me, and we're going to settle this tonight."

He stood up suddenly. Someone slunk out of the shadows. Jacob. He moved next to Lucian without a word and just smiled at Darlene.

"Prepare her. We've never tried this before and anything could happen."

Jacob's gaze flicked to Lucian briefly. "Master, you told me that I could be the one to drink the werewolf blood first."

Lucian waved his hand. "It will be so, but prepare her first. You're already a vampire. I'm sure you'll be able to successfully turn into a werewolf as well. We don't know what will happen with this one."

Panic surged through Darlene, and she struggled against the restraints as Jacob went over to her.

"Why are you doing this?" she finally gasped out through her fear.

"Because my Master knows the future. Vampires and werewolves as one creature. Imagine how we could rule the world. He's offering you an amazing chance, Darlene. You could become one of us. Rule with us."

"You're an idiot… the same idiot Maria had to fire. And he's an idiot, too, for this insane plan."

Lucian pushed Jacob out of the way with a low growl, crouching next to Darlene. Her palms felt sweaty, and her breathing was ragged as he stared her down.

"Did Idris explain what happens to people who find out about us? We either relocate them or we Change them."

"Idris said you always relocated them."

Lucian leaned in close and his breath moved against her ear. "I killed them." He backed his face away, staring at her again. "Idris didn't know. He didn't know a lot. He was too busy hating himself and everyone else for being a werewolf. I killed anyone who found out about us and told him we relocated them per the pack rules. Now I'm going to Change you. You're going to be our first human test subject to see if we can change you into the future." He stood up and looked down at Darlene in disgust. "Jacob. Prepare her."

***

As they pulled into the parking lot of Darlene's apartment complex, Liara dabbed at her eyes with a tissue from her purse.

"I don't understand any of this," she said. "How could Lucian want to give the pack to Roman? Become Exsul? Try this stupid hybrid thing out?"

Idris shook his head. "I don't know, Liara. His motivations don't make sense to me. It doesn't seem like the man we both knew."

She brushed the tears from her eyes. "Let's go find your friend."

Idris tapped his fingers along the steering wheel. "Did you…did you pick up on anything with Darlene? Something odd?" At Liara's questioning gaze, Idris spoke again, "Julie mentioned that she was different…"

Liara scoffed, "Julie's different."

She got out of the truck without another word. Idris followed. He saw Darlene's car in the spot ahead of them and walked over to it. Nothing appeared out of place. Was he being stupid? She was probably in her apartment, safe and sound. Liara walked along the

184

sidewalk, scanning the ground. Idris ran his fingers through his hair and was about to tell Liara that they should go back when she called him over.

He walked over to where she stood, against the side of the building, almost near the back, and she held something in her hand.

"What is it?"

Liara held out her hand. Darlene's cellphone. The screen was cracked down the center, the cracks branching out like spider webs along the glass screen.

Idris' heart lurched. "I'm going to follow the scent."

"You're going to Change *here*?"

"Something bad has happened. Are you going to come as well?"

"Alright, but I'm sending a text out for back up."

"To who, Liara? Roman's pack? We can't call our own. They're too far away and we can't trust Roman."

She paused for a moment and then shook her head. "Go. Change. Find her. I'll be right behind you."

Idris didn't wait another second. As he ran toward the forest behind Darlene's apartment building, he welcomed the Change. He felt his fingers elongate, the claws forming, his back hunching and legs shifting position. As he burst into the woods following Darlene's scent, he fought the urge to let out a howl to let whoever was with Darlene know that he was coming.

***

Jacob had Darlene lying on a slab of concrete with strange symbols gouged into it. There were shapes that depicted vampires and werewolves. Her arms were tied to a trunk above the slab but her feet were loose. She kicked and struggled but the ropes were too tight to break free. Behind her, Jacob and Lucian talked in low tones.

"The process is different for this one. She's entirely human. We don't even know if it will work," Lucian said.

"Let me drink your blood, Master. Let me see if I can complete the transition. This human will most likely die anyway, and we have nothing to fear. We're just going to see what goes wrong."

I have to get out of here. There has to be something I haven't thought of yet. Her eyes scanned the woods around her. Moonlight broke through the trees at some spots, shining down onto the ground. There was no way whatever they were planning would work on her. Jacob was right. She was going to die.

She heard a soft noise and slurping sounds as Jacob drank from Lucian. Lucian chanted something, some sort of spell, Darlene assumed. She controlled her breathing. They were distracted now and this was her only chance to escape. Darlene slowed down her breathing and closed her eyes. Her dream from before floated back to her. She was on the ocean... Idris telling her something was trying to break through to her — her connection with another realm — was it just dream gibberish? She recalled what she saw in the woods that one night, floating, ghost-like.

I've always known, she thought, sending her thoughts out around her. *Please, now I need you to help me.*

She opened her eyes. Behind her, Jacob made a strange choking noise but she couldn't see what was going on. In front of her, however, a shape formed out of a cloud of mist. Darlene focused on it to make it take shape, but mist was all she could bring to it. Her mind was exhausted even doing this little to the spirit in front of her.

I saw you, the night in the woods. My fear made you come into focus, didn't it? You're a ghost. I'm not powerful enough to hear what you're saying to me. But if you can hear me, please loosen my ties.

A shape ran past her — Jacob, toppling into the bushes, away from view. There was gurgling and terrible noises in the bushes as Jacob tried to Change into a hybrid. Darlene focused again on the spirit in front of her. Her head pounded as the mist wafted over her, dousing her in what felt like cold water.

Lucian slid into view. "I'm afraid Jacob is too ill to help us for this next part. It'll be just the two of us to witness your historic transformation."

Darlene sensed the ties around her wrists loosen from an unseen force. She barely paid any attention to Lucian as she kept her focus on the spirit. The ties fell gently to the ground, freeing her hands.

Thank you.

Darlene broke her focus on the spirit, and it faded away. Lucian came toward her, a knife raised, a crazed look over his face as Darlene slid her fingertips around a blade at the edge of the concrete slab. He raised the knife and at the same time Darlene lunged forward, slamming the blade into his chest.

Lucian let out a scream and stumbled back in surprise, his eyes wide. Darlene slid off the concrete slab as Lucian took another step back. She heard something crashing through the woods now, loud and vicious. Jacob had gone still in the bushes.

Then two werewolves burst through on the opposite side of the clearing.

***

Idris looked around the clearing, trying to understand what he was seeing. There was an altar with strange carvings. Lucian stood over it, clutching at his chest. Darlene stood nearby him, looking at Idris with wide-eyes. Liara let out a whimper and stepped toward Lucian. Idris nudged Liara back with his snout. She wasn't nearly as large as he was in werewolf form but she was faster. Liara dodged him before darting by Darlene's side and transforming back into human form quickly. Liara always had better control over her emotions than Idris.

Idris wanted to Change back but was momentarily stunned by what he saw. Lucian let out a gurgle and hit the ground on his knees. Blood bloomed out from around the blade that protruded from his chest. Idris felt time slow down.

"Oh my god," Darlene said. "He was going to — I just needed him to — I don't…" She looked stricken.

"Lucian!" Liara ran over and crouched in front of him, cupping his face in her hands. "I'm here now! It's okay. I'm here!"

"Liara…"

"It's okay. I found the book. I'm pack leader now. I won't make you Exsul. We can forget about all of this." She was crying now — Idris saw her shoulders shaking.

"You?" Lucian rasped. "No…no…Roman…"

"Lucian?"

There was another movement in the bushes and Darlene screamed a second too late. Something flew out of the bushes, faster than Idris had even seen before and slammed into him. He flew through the air and smashed against a tree, the wind knocked out of him. He let out a deep growl and leapt to his feet again, but could only stare at what was in front of him.

Jacob stood in front of him, but he wasn't a vampire any longer. His fangs were exposed, and his eyes turned a red color but his arms were disfigured, having the terrible claws of a werewolf. His feet were the same. Hair sprouted all over his body in random spots, at odds with his pale vampire skin.

A hybrid.

Jacob looked like a werewolf stuck in mid-Change. Idris pushed off with his hind legs, snarling and lunged at Jacob but he was gone in a flash. He reappeared behind Idris to sink his fangs into the werewolf's leg. Idris lost his footing and stumbled to the ground, kicking up dirt in an attempt to get Jacob off of him.

"No!" Darlene ran over toward them.

Idris howled at her, signaling for her to leave. Liara laid Lucian's body down, a pool of blood underneath him. Jacob spun and grabbed Darlene by the throat, lifting her up into the air.

"What did you do to him?" Jacob screamed in a distorted voice. "What powers do you have?"

"I don't—" Her breath cut off.

Idris took advantage of the distraction and ran into Jacob, slashing his claws and sinking his jaws into his side. Blood filled his mouth, and it tasted vile. Jacob dropped Darlene, who hit the ground with a thud. She rubbed her neck and gasped for air but was otherwise unharmed. Jacob spun and kicked Idris with his foot. His claws sliced into Idris, who let out a howl and fell back. He was Changing back — how could that be?

Jacob let out a low chuckle. "I have more powers than you will ever understand," he spat, glancing around the clearing. "I'm not done, do you understand?"

Idris felt his paws Changing back into human hands, his body slowly losing its fur and his snout morphing back into his proper face. Jacob ran past him and into the woods. Idris wanted to chase him, to get him back, but he could feel the wounds along his stomach oozing blood. Darlene appeared above him.

"He's gone." Her face was tear-stained. "Idris, hang in there! Idris!"

But darkness overtook him.

Chapter Thirteen

Darlene didn't like being with Roman's pack. They showed up right after Idris passed out. Liara had called them as back-up, but the danger, for the moment, had passed. Roman stumbled in on Liara crying over Lucian's dead body and Darlene tried to shake Idris awake. The pack had swooped in and taken everyone back to their pack headquarters, which was a warehouse just outside of town.

Now Darlene was lying in a makeshift hospital room, watching Idris sleep. She wanted him to go to the hospital, but Liara said that they always tended to their own. Someone had patched Idris up and now his chest was covered in heavy bandages. He was heavily medicated and sleeping soundly.

She felt dirty, gross and terrible. She kept staring at her hands, wracked with feelings of guilt from killing Lucian and relief that it wasn't her that was killed instead.

There was a spirit. She didn't make that up. Jacob had sensed something was off too. Darlene had seen a ghost in the woods the night Vivica and Idris fought. Her recent dreams hinted at it as well. She was always attracted to stories of ghosts and spirits, but she assumed that was her own creepy interests and nothing that indicated a power inside of her.

How could she have this power inside of her and know absolutely nothing about it? She chewed on her bottom lip, mulling it over. They were going to ask. They would ask how she freed herself. What would she say?

"Hey."

Darlene looked up at the whisper. Liara had pushed back the sheet that made up the door to Idris' recovery room. She had Lucian's blood on her clothes and her makeup was smudged from crying. Darlene wasn't sure if she was going to attack her for murdering her husband.

"Hi, Liara."

"Mind if I come in?"

"No, of course not."

Liara stepped inside and walked over to Idris' bedside, looking down at him. "The doctor said he'll be okay. Just needs to rest. I need to talk to you."

Darlene nodded and Liara came over to sit next to her on the couch they had put in the room.

"A lot is going on. Idris told me what he discovered. And that you know about us. And vampires. In a case like this where the pack leader is missing, Idris should have followed procedure. Relocation or Change. Nothing else. He's facing Exsul status because he failed to do either."

Darlene's heart skipped a beat. "What? No. Don't give him Exsul status. It's my fault. He didn't want to Change me, and I refused relocation. I wanted to help him. What was he supposed to do? The only other option would have been to kill me. Lucian didn't relocate anyone. He told me he killed them."

Liara shut her eyes briefly, and Darlene wondered if she had gone too far. "I am the pack leader now. I understand what my husband did and that he would become Exsul for it. But I need you to tell me what happened, and sparc nothing regarding my own feelings for my husband."

Darlene nodded and told her what happened with Lucian and Jacob.

***

Idris' eyes fluttered open. The first thing he felt was pain... all over. He grunted and clutched at his stomach, remembering what had happened. Jacob. The first werewolf-vampire hybrid. He had kicked Idris' ass and was now out there, somewhere, free.

And Lucian was dead.

"You up?"

Idris looked toward where the voice came from. Julie stood in front of a sheet. He realized with a start that he was at Roman's pack headquarters. Julie looked terrible, wearing clothes that were too big for her and dark circles around her eyes.

"Hear about your girlfriend?"

"Is she okay?"

"Oh, she's fine. But she's exactly what I told you... a ghost walker."

Idris' head ached. "Can you please get out?"

Julie sneered, "I done warned you, pup."

As Julie slid out of the room, Liara stepped in. Their eyes met briefly. "Hey, how are you feeling?"

"Been better. You going to tell me what's going on? Where's Darlene?"

"I sent Darlene home."

"You what? She's a target. By Vivica, Rebecca, Jacob, and who knows who else!"

"I sent Mark with her as a guard. She'll be okay. I just needed to talk to you."

Idris looked at her. "What? How bad is it?"

Liara paced the room, talking the entire time, explaining what had happened in the woods from her standpoint, as well as Darlene's. When she finished the debriefing, she stopped pacing and looked at Idris.

"You mean to tell me Darlene has some sort of…otherworldly power?"

"Yes, that's right. She didn't know about it until recently. I think communicating with our world has brought it out in her."

Idris sank back in the pillows. "Now what?"

"You're facing Exsul status, Idris. But with Darlene's powers, I can try to get the pack to side with you on it... that she is one of us... not a mere human. Therefore her knowledge of us will be tolerated. But, like you said, Roman is furious about the fact the book is in my hands and not his. He wants you to be Exsul. He's pushing for it. And you know all packs in the area weigh in on all decisions regarding Exsul status."

"Yes, I know." He closed his eyes.

"I'll do what I can. But we have bigger problems. Jacob is still alive. From what I can gather, Lucian turned him to a vampire. But how? And now we have a hybrid on our hands."

"We don't know if he can even live in that state. He could just die out there in the woods."

Liara nodded. "I sincerely hope so."

***

Darlene looked out the window of her apartment. The sun burned high in the sky but she still felt jumpy. Even with Mark posted outside her door, she felt nervous. Mark was still part of Roman's pack. She saw

Roman's face when he found out that Liara possessed the book and had taken over as pack leader instead of him. He was furious. Why would one of his own protect her?

Liara advised Darlene to lay low for a while because of her story and her direct involvement in killing Lucian. So it was back to being a hermit. Her phone was still out of commission but she didn't feel like repairing it right away. She wanted to sleep for a long time and hopefully wake up to find out this was all a bad dream.

Darlene heard low voices at the door, and her heart stopped for a moment. Then the apartment door opened and she saw Mark.

"Idris is here. I can get rid of him if you want. I would love to do it, personally."

"No, no, it's fine. Let him in."

"No fun," Mark said.

Idris moved past him, and the two glared at each other until Mark shut the door. *Like we have time for pissing contests.* Idris moved slowly, the pain written all over his face as he sat down on the couch across from

Darlene. She remained sitting in front of her computer. She could see the bandages under his shirt.

"How are you feeling?"

"Been better. You?"

"The same."

Silence filled the room until Idris cleared his throat. "I heard about…about the ghost thing."

"Everyone is expecting me to have all these answers, but I don't have any. I just knew there was a spirit there. In desperation, I called for it. It took no form at all. It was just mist. And now everyone thinks I can raise the dead or something and I just —"

"Hey, hey." Idris stood up and walked over to her side, wiping tears from her face. "It's okay. We'll figure it out together."

"You're facing Exsul status because of me, Idris. I should have listened to you and gone away somewhere. I'm so sorry."

Idris crouched in front of her, his eyes warm and kind. "Stop, Darlene. I told you, we'll figure it out together."

"But Jacob is still out there."

"The threat of the hybrid monsters or whatever Lucian called them has passed for now, okay? Jacob doesn't have his Maker anymore. It's a big blow. We have time to regroup before we have to worry about anything... plenty of time to figure out what is going on with you, okay?"

Darlene sniffled. "You mean it?"

"I mean it."

Idris tilted her face up to his, leaned down and kissed her. Her despair washed away. The warmth that Idris could always bring came over her, slowly and sweetly. Darlene felt her heart rate lower as he kissed her.

"I know we're both wounded," he whispered. "Literally and emotionally. But I want to be with you, Darlene... if you'll have me."

Darlene smiled back. "I'll have you."

It was silly, given all that happened so far, but for the first time in a long time, even though everything else was messy and crazy, she felt that her love life was back on track.

-To be continued in Book 2-

Book Two

Prologue

AT FIRST there was only the hunger. It pulsed through Rebecca, tricking her into thinking she was actually alive. But she knew better than that, didn't she? She spent most of the night staring into a mirror, seeing nothing in the reflection… as if she had been wiped from the pages of the history books completely.

They were looking for her. She saw posters plastered around town, asking for any information on where she had gone since the bookshop was ransacked. She kept her head low and chopped off most of her hair in exchange for the semblance of a normal hairstyle. She had gone back to try and find her friend, Darlene.

But the hunger clouded everything. It was too dangerous to talk to anyone. Then it became too dangerous to even stand near them. The smell of their skin, alive, with blood pumping just under the surface, was too much to bear. She had retreated into the woods.

Just as daylight approached, she stumbled across an empty cabin that overlooked the highway. Clawing at the floorboards, she managed to get herself into the ground before the sunlight could shine into the cabin.

Now it was the middle of the night and she was staring at the soulless mirror. She was almost glad she couldn't see herself. She didn't want to see herself. Because the mess behind her was already too gruesome. A hitchhiker had thought she could stay here the night as well...but she was fatally mistaken.

No, Rebecca didn't want to see herself in the mirror. She didn't need to, because she knew what the mirror would show. Her face, smeared red...her hands, coated in the hitchhiker's blood. Rebecca could just make out the girl's hand, sticking out from behind the makeshift bed, her fingers curled slightly, a slick pool of blood sliding out from underneath her body. It was her first feeding and she made a huge mess of it.

Rebecca closed her eyes and screamed.

Chapter One

"Am I under suspicion of anything?"

"No, ma'am."

"Truly? Because it honestly feels like you suspect me of something." Darlene crossed her arms and leaned back in the chair, staring down Officer Walsh. Normally, she had the utmost respect for police officers and knew Walsh was just doing his job. But she couldn't help but think of him as a pain in the ass.

"Listen, Miss Troop, I'm just trying to understand why you went to see Ms. Boots that night."

"And I told you a thousand times already. I tried to make you guys aware of the forum post by her son that I found. I was blown off here, so I went to his mother directly to tell her."

"I just don't understand why you're involved in an old case from someone who has no connection with you whatsoever."

"Why does it matter? I didn't murder her, and it feels like you're suggesting I did. Do I need to get a lawyer?"

Walsh paled. "No, there's no need for that, ma'am. They're just routine questions. What did Ms. Boots say when you went to her with your information?"

"She told me she had known already that he thought he was a werewolf. She told me that he fell in with the wrong crowd. She was very sad about it all. But she confirmed that someone picked Brent up that night. So my information was useless, like the cops said. Brent's mother already knew that someone came for him that night."

Darlene hoped her story sounded convincing. Most of the details were true. It was just the circumstances of the details that were fudged a little.

Walsh looked down at his notepad. "What about Roman's Tavern? Witnesses put you there last week. Your boyfriend got into a fight with Roman. No cops were called, and the two of you bailed afterward, from my understanding."

Darlene's heart thrummed. For a second, she wanted to shake Idris. Why in the world did he fight with Roman that night? Of course people would have seen them and word would have gotten back to the police. It was a vicious fight. She didn't know that Walsh had heard about the fight already though. Who blabbed?

"So?"

"So if Roman decides to press charges, your boyfriend will be in a lot of trouble."

"As far as I know, Roman didn't press charges. So what is the question?"

"Why were you at Roman's Tavern that night?"

"I can't go to a bar with my boyfriend?"

Walsh leaned forward. "I just find it strange that after I mentioned to you that Jacob was interested in going to Roman's Tavern that you ended there as well. And you seemed so interested in Brent Boot's death, that he had a connection to Roman's Tavern as well."

Darlene felt warm. She didn't like lying to the police. But it wasn't as if they would believe the truth anyway. *Well, the truth is, my boyfriend is a werewolf. His pack leader wanted to exile himself from the werewolves in order to craft a werewolf-vampire hybrid creature. No, don't worry – he's dead! Yeah, I killed him with the help of a spirit. Yes, I said spirit. Turns out, I have power over ghosts that no one understands, myself included. Jacob is a hybrid and is out there somewhere doing God only knows what. My best friend is a missing vampire, and her Maker is a crazy bitch. You are chasing leads that go nowhere because my insane social circle, including my werewolf Exsul boss, is on the case!*

Ugh. It sounded like a terrible anime.

"This is just a questioning, right?" When Walsh nodded, Darlene stood up. "Then I'm done for the day. I have to get to work. The bookstore re-opens tomorrow. Where are you on my missing friend, by the way... while you sit here and accuse me of murder?"

"No one is accusing you of anything, Miss Troop. We don't have any leads on your friend yet. Has she been in touch with you?"

"No," Darlene said, trying to keep the sadness out of her voice. "I'm leaving now."

Walsh shook his head as Darlene left the room. It felt as if every cell in her body was vibrating slightly, making her head hurt. She dreaded this police station now. Why did she ever try to tell them about Brent and his forum post? It just ended up biting her in the ass.

As she stepped out into the sunlight and slid a pair of sunglasses on, she thought of Rebecca. Still no sign of her. Darlene was hoping Rebecca would try to call her. She kept thinking back to Rebecca opening her eyes and bursting out of the room, into the night. Guilt immersed heavily in her heart. Idris warned her that newborn vampires were feral and dangerous. Usually their Makers remained nearby to help guide them through their ordeal. But Vivica had no interest in taking care of Rebecca.

Darlene got in her car, ignoring whispers from a couple of teenagers nearby. She knew they were talking about her negatively, making remarks on her weight. *I don't care. I'm above this shit.* If she repeated it enough times, maybe it would finally sink in.

She looked at her phone and saw a text from Idris. He asked how the meeting with Walsh went. Darlene paused, unsure of what to type. She was touched that he had texted her with everything else going on in his world. *My boyfriend.* The phrase seemed so foreign to her. How could Idris, such an imposing, strong and sexy werewolf, be dating her, of all people?

Darlene lectured herself again. She deserved this. She deserved to have a boyfriend who made her happy, was great in bed and clearly interested in her. She had to stop trying to ruin herself and not let herself be happy. It was easier said than done. With a sigh, she typed out a reply. *Okay, but he is asking questions about why we were at Roman's Tavern the night we saw Jacob. What about your end?*

She sent the text and pulled out of the parking lot, heading toward the bookshop. She had been putting in extra hours since the time Lucian had tried to kill her to turn her into a hybrid. Originally, Darlene was furious with Maria for keeping the fact she was a werewolf a secret – an Exsul on top of that – but she understood more now why Maria did it. Darlene learned as much as she could about Exsuls in case Idris received that as his sentence. Plus working at the bookshop kept her busy, which meant no time for thinking about how she had killed Lucian.

No, do not go down that road, not right now. Darlene turned down the main street. She was almost at the bookshop. She would be busy soon.

***

Idris read Darlene's text and sighed. He wasn't sure what to say. Should he tell her the truth – that Liara and Roman were meeting right now to discuss his possible Exsul status and if it could be dropped because Darlene had some sort of powers – or should he tell her everything was peachy? He knew if he mentioned the meeting she would be worried for him and want to see him. But frankly, he just wanted to be alone.

Idris was still trying to absorb everything from the last few weeks.

Liara had told him to leave town and go back to Hedge Hill. But leaving meant leaving Darlene. Yes, it was just thirty minutes away, but he didn't like leaving her exposed. Not with Vivica somewhere. And Rebecca. But if Liara ordered him to and he refused…you just don't refuse an order from the pack leader. Not even if you were second-in-command. Idris swallowed.

"Worried about your girlfriend?"

He looked up to see Julie. They were in Roman's Tavern and she had lit up a cigarette. She stunk of the warehouse where Roman's pack headquarters were. That place was filthy. He was surprised Liara had let him stay there for medical attention. His stomach and chest were still aching and raw, but at least they were healing. Usually werewolves heal at an accelerated rate, but whatever was in Jacob's talons made rapid healing impossible. The healing process seemed to be taking its sweet time.

Julie's fingers were tar stained from her constant smoking. Her shaved head had some stubble showing now. She was looking at him with a blank expression on her face.

Idris sighed. "What do you want?"

Julie shrugged. "If Liara asks you to leave town – I mean really asks you, from pack leader standpoint – are you going to say no?"

He hated how she always seemed to know what he was thinking. He didn't say anything.

She took a drag off her cigarette. "You know if you say no, pup, that means you're Exsul. You can't disobey a direct order from your pack leader. You might as well tell Liara now that you are going to say no. Saves Roman the trouble of fighting with her about your status."

"I can't be Exsul. Darlene can communicate with ghosts. She is one of our world."

Julie shrugged. "Doesn't matter to me, pup. But Roman will call bullshit on that. You know it, don't cha? You told her before anyone but me knew what she was." Her tone was full of pride, as if she won a prize.

Idris was saved from having to answer because just then Liara came into view on the floor above him. She was still speaking to Roman. Mark wasn't around. The one-eyed bastard was still guarding Darlene's apartment, which made Idris uncomfortable. Lucian was dead, but Jacob got away. Darlene had killed Lucian…

They were walking down the steps now toward Idris. Julie moved away from him swiftly, going up to Roman and wrapping her arms around him languidly. She licked his neck playfully, and Idris averted his gaze. *Gross.* Liara walked over to him. Her hair was up in a stiff bun, and her outfit was befitting a pack-leader meeting. She had a tailored dress shirt on as well as a pencil skirt, her high heels clattering loudly against the empty dance floor. Roman's idea of dressing up had been a button-up shirt with three missing buttons. He was already leaving to go back upstairs with Julie. Idris could tell by Liara's face that the news wasn't good.

"Roman won't accept Darlene's otherworld abilities as a reason not to sentence you to Exsul status. He says that you didn't know of her powers when you told her about our world. You didn't relocate her or Change her."

"But if I had done either, then it would have been a mistake, due to her powers."

Liara held up a thin hand – she was still wearing her wedding ring. "Idris, I know that. But Roman won't budge. He wants to take it to a region-wide pack vote."

Idris sighed and closed his eyes briefly. "Fuck."

"There's still hope, Idris." She patted his back gingerly.

Idris opened his eyes and looked at her. Circles under her eyes that hadn't been there when Lucian was alive now stood out against her skin. She looked tired.

"You should get some sleep," Idris said, standing up.

"You as well. You look wrecked. Go see Darlene. Let her know what's going on."

Idris nodded, a knot forming in his stomach. He slipped on his jacket and headed out of Roman's Tavern. The scent of Julie's cigarette clung to him. He suddenly craved a cigarette.

***

Maria handed Darlene a cup of coffee. A peace offering, Darlene realized, as she took it and thanked her. They fell back into the silence that had been filling the shop since Darlene had arrived. Maria turned back to the stack of books she was trying to reorganize. Darlene turned back to her own stack but glanced at Maria out of the corner of her eyes whenever she could.

Today, Maria was wearing yellow pants that looked like they were straight from the 70's. Her shirt was a button-up dress shirt with flared sleeves. Her white hair was still sticking up at all edges. Her jewelry was all the same shade of turquoise. Her face was drawn, and she looked tired.

"Have you heard from Mabel?" Darlene asked to break the silence.

"No. Not directly. Her home nurse called me yesterday and said that she had woken up with extreme memory loss. She was rambling about a vampire who was going to cure her cancer. They're moving her to a home."

Darlene shifted awkwardly, trying to hide her face from Maria's. She wasn't sure how in the loop Maria was with everything and didn't want to be the one to tell her anything she wasn't supposed to know. She'd leave that up to the pack leaders.

"Liara came to speak to me the other day."

This made Darlene look up in surprise. "Really?"

"She told me what was going on, even though I'm an Exsul."

"So you know Mabel was…"

"Under Vivica's control, yes. Basically Vivica's toy. Spying."

Darlene put a book away on one of the shelves and then turned to face Maria "Can I ask you then? What an Exsul is exactly? I mean, I know they are exiled from everyone. They don't have any sort of pack to go with or a voice in anything that affects werewolves in the region. But why? Lucian was going to become an Exsul for this terrible plan he had. I don't…" She ended with a shrug.

Maria's shoulders relaxed slightly, as if she was looking forward to talking about these things. "Packs have a lot of rules. All of them are listed in *The Werewolf Code.* If you do anything to endanger the pack, you can be penalized with Exsul status if either the pack leaders agree or they take it to the vote."

"What qualifies as endangering the pack?"

"You mean, did Idris truly endanger the pack by not relocating or Changing you?" When Darlene didn't answer, Maria sighed. "Relocation is tricky. Humans who know about them are relocated somewhere where no packs exist and hope for the best. You have to make sure they are in good mental health so there isn't any risk they would just blab about it later."

"Lucian told me he just killed them. Is that what you really mean by relocating?"

"No. Absolutely not. But I know Roman has done that on a few occasions. He claims it's safer than relocation, and he doesn't want to Change anyone."

"How can that be allowed?"

"The pack votes in agreement for it if Roman wanted to override relocation or Change. His pack is bloodthirsty. They don't think much of it."

"If…" Darlene chewed on her bottom lip. "If Idris is sentenced to Exsul status, what does that mean for him?"

A shadow crossed Maria's face. She turned slightly, tilting her head to look out the front window of the shop. "It's lonely. You will never again hunt with your pack or belong with people who are like you. Your people will ignore you. They will be cruel to you, out of fear for whatever you did that made you become an Exsul. They will believe you care more about yourself than the other werewolves. You suffer alone."

"Maria…"

She turned to face Darlene and held out her arm, turning it over to expose her wrist underneath a row of bracelets. There was a tiny tattoo there – a small moon with a line down the middle, jagged, like a crack.

"They see this tattoo, and they know who you are. Exsul. I lost everyone I hold dear because of what I did."

"Is there any way to get the status overturned? To become a regular pack member again?"

A tight smile grew on her face. "One. You have to save a pack from destruction."

Darlene frowned. "That doesn't happen often, does it?"

Maria locked eyes with Darlene. "It never happens." She looked down sadly. "I'm sorry, Darlene."

Chapter Two

Idris watched the evening news on TV in his motel room,. He had trouble paying attention. He kept thinking back to earlier in the day. There was absolutely no way he wasn't going to be handed Exsul status now. Roman's pack would all vote for it. Liara couldn't get her entire pack to vote in his favor. Quite a few people in his new pack didn't like him and would vote against him. He made a lot of enemies in his time before he finally decided to settle down.

There was a knock at the door. Idris slid out of bed and opened the door, wondering gloomily who it could be. To his surprise, Darlene's bright blue eyes stared up at him. Concern was written all over her face.

"I'm sorry to bother you. But you never texted me back. I was worried."

Idris moved aside to allow her to enter the room. "I'm sorry. I should have. I just…there's a lot going on."

Darlene looked around the room before turning to face him. "What happened today?"

Idris thought about lying, because he didn't want to make her worry, but found himself spilling the entire story about his possible Exsul status.

She sat down on the bed and sighed. "This is all my fault. I'm sorry. I should have just relocated."

Idris sat down next to her and put his hand on her knee. "It isn't your fault. And...there's no way I could have relocated you."

Darlene's eyes met his. "But now you're going to be an Exsul."
"We don't know that," Idris lied.

She looked so beautiful in the soft glow of the hotel lamp that Idris forgot about what a dump the room was, how Exsul status was hovering over his head and how if Liara ordered him to go back to Hedge Hills and leave Darlene, he could end up with Exsul status anyway. He leaned forward and kissed her hard, his fingers entwining in her hair.

"I missed you," she mumbled.

Idris grunted in response, pushing Darlene back on the bed, running his hands along her sides. His body felt as if every sense was on high alert. He had missed her, as much as the old part of him wanted to be alone. Would he risk Exsul status for this woman? He slid down to his knees off the bed, running his lips along her thighs. *Yes.* He moved her skirt up, running his fingers down her wetness, watching Darlene let out a small gasp of pleasure. *I would risk Exsul status for her.*

Idris pulled her underwear off and could feel how stiff he was in his jeans as he enjoyed the smell of her. He put his face in between her legs and began to lick, slowly, dragging it out, teasing her. Darlene whimpered, quietly begging for Idris to do more, touch her more, make her feel good and Idris broke, probing his tongue inside of her.

Darlene closed her eyes tightly as waves of pleasure moved slowly and leisurely through her body. She could feel Idris's tongue moving along her, gently brushing against her clit before moving down to her center. Her hands were tangled in his hair, and she glanced down. Seeing him in between her legs gave her a thrill that she had never felt before. Then his mouth softly wrapped around her clit, sucking on it just enough that her hips bucked and she could feel herself orgasm. Darlene came, mumbling Idris's name over and over, letting the pleasure overtake her. Her skin felt flushed and hot as Idris pulled away from her, standing up and taking off his pants and underwear.

He was stiff and hard, throbbing as he bent over her, sliding inside her in one swift thrust. Darlene arched her back and moaned.

"You like that?" he teased in her ear.

Darlene could only moan in response as Idris began to thrust inside her. He bit along her neck, gently, and sucked on her bottom lip, moving deeper and deeper inside her.

Idris grunted in her ear, "Tell me you like it."

"I love it," Darlene moaned in response as he slammed into her.

His breathing was hard and jagged now. Darlene knew he was going to finish. She lifted her hips to match his thrusts, urging him to finish. Idris thrust inside her, and Darlene orgasmed again. She clung to Idris as she came, moaning louder this time, knowing that someone could hear her but not caring. Idris was groaning as well, holding her hips as he came, moving slower and slower as they came together, clinging to each other.

Gingerly, he pulled out and collapsed in a heap next to her on the bed. Darlene felt unable to move, having come twice and both times so hard. Idris was panting, and he held her hand.

"I'm glad you came by," he whispered.

***

Idris watched Darlene dry her hair after the shower they had taken together. She looked gorgeous, but she thought she looked terrible. He could tell by the way she tried to hide behind things, like towels or doors, while she dressed. He wished he could find the words to tell her that he didn't care how large she was, he found her beautiful. He opened his mouth to speak when Darlene spoke first.

"Hey, look."

She pointed to the TV. A reporter stood by a cabin that had been marked off with tape.

"…no witnesses have come forward at this time. The identity of the victim has not been released. Once again, for those of you just tuning in, a brutal murder has been discovered just off Highway 44, where a Jane Doe has been discovered dead in this abandoned cabin.

What is unusual in this case is how the body has been drained almost completely of blood. We..."

"It's Vivica," Darlene said, moving closer to the TV. "It has to be, right? Draining the blood. There's probably bite marks. And it's so close to here."

Idris was already shaking his head, a cold feeling in his stomach. "No. It's Rebecca."

***

Darlene walked up to her apartment. Each step felt as if her legs were made of pure lead. Any pleasurable moments she'd had with Idris were seemingly erased when she saw that news report.

Of course it was Rebecca.

Like Idris said, Vivica would have never made such a messy kill. This spoke of desperation, of the need to feed, of a hunger that Darlene would never understand. It was all her fault.

"You're home late." Mark leaned against the wall, smoking a cigarette.

She had grown used to seeing him standing guard outside her apartment but felt bad about it. There was no risk of Lucian returning, and no one had seen Jacob since he ran off. As Roman's second-in-command, this must be terribly dull.

"Yeah," she mumbled. "I saw Idris."

Darlene slid her key in the lock, and Mark leaned over, sniffing her.

Darlene flinched. "What the hell are you doing?"

Mark grinned, although with his missing eye it made him look more scary than playful. "You smell like you've been fucked."

"Seriously? No wonder you've been banished to guard duty if that's how you fucking talk to people," she snapped.

Mark's eye widened in surprise. "Hey, girl, I just –"

"I'm not a *girl.* I'm a grown woman."

She opened the door and slammed it in Mark's face, locking it behind her. She could hear Mark grumbling on the other side of the door but didn't care. She threw down her things and plopped into bed, staring at the ceiling. Everything seemed to sink in on her at once. Killing Lucian, Brent's mother being killed, Rebecca a vampire and now murdering others...on top of her utterly useless ability to connect with spirits, which was seemingly dormant since that night she had used it to escape from Lucian.

Out of desperation, Darlene picked up her phone and brought up Rebecca's number. She composed a text and hit send before tossing her phone to the ground.

I'm so sorry.

***

When Darlene opened her eyes, she was in a field. Wedding bells rang at a church in the distance, but she knew they weren't hers. Someone moved behind her, and Darlene turned around. A woman stood there, but she had no face. Instead of feeling afraid, Darlene waved at her. The woman was dressed all in white and was incredibly skinny, so much so that Darlene felt concerned.

You're here.

"Yes," Darlene replied out loud. "I'm here. Where is *here*?"

The center of worlds. Where the planes connect. You are the only one who can walk between them.

"That's great. Seriously, awesome. But completely useless, at the moment. I have so many questions, and it isn't like I can just ask a doctor."

My sister.

A sudden gust of wind swept up, kicking sand up in Darlene's face, which made her close her eyes. She didn't realize there was sand around but she could suddenly smell the ocean breeze.

Ask Maria.

Darlene opened her eyes to answer but the woman was gone. She was on the shore of a beach. A giant wave came in, but it was pure red, as if blood was about to crash down on her. Darlene felt fear shoot through her and as she turned to run, she realized she was too late.

***

Darlene pulled into work the next day, groggy and bleary-eyed from a terrible night. She had foolishly hoped Rebecca would text her back, but of course there was nothing. Her dream had woken her up, drenched in sweat and afraid and she'd heard Mark talking to someone outside on his cellphone, even though the clock showed four in the morning. For some reason, knowing someone was outside brought her comfort, but it was still another two hours of lying there until she was able to drift off back to sleep.

But today was the shop's grand re-opening. Maria was taking it very seriously, and Darlene found that trying to remain upset at her for not sharing the fact she was an Exsul werewolf was proving to be too much effort with everything else going on. Her dream, or a visit from whatever ghost woman that had been, had told her to ask Maria about drifting between two plains. But how exactly does one bring that up in conversation? *Hey, Maria. So this ghost last night told me you might know something about the plane of the living and the plane of the dead? Also, do you know what a giant wave of blood means? Maybe my period is just around the corner?* It would be just her luck to get her period a week ahead of time.

To her surprise, the parking lot was crowded. The break-in and destruction at the shop had brought more media attention than anything else they had ever done in the past. Darlene got out of her car and headed toward the store. Her phone went off in her pocket. Officer Walsh. She sighed and hit the ignore button. She didn't feel like talking to him and was wondering if she could just ignore him completely. She didn't want to ignore a police officer, but he was asking questions that Darlene couldn't answer and kept returning to her as if she had something to do with the murder of Ms. Boots or something to do with Brent and Jacob.

To her surprise, Idris was waiting for her outside the shop. Darlene walked up to him, smiling. She could see girls checking him out and thought with a thrill that he was all hers.

"Didn't expect to see you here."

Idris shrugged. "My fault about the store, isn't it? I should show my support."

She lowered her voice. "I figured you wouldn't want to be here because of Maria…"

The last time that Idris and Maria had spoken, it had been a rather heated discussion about the fact that she had hid her Exsul status. Darlene was reminded suddenly of how Idris had demanded to know which witch had been helping Maria block her detection from other werewolves.

"I figured I can't avoid her forever. Especially since we might be in the same boat."

"You don't know that."

Idris looked away. "I didn't tell you last night, but Roman is pushing for Exsul status. It's being taken to a pack vote." He met her gaze. "It'll pass, Darlene."

Darlene felt her heart drop. "You don't know that –"

"I do. Now come on, let's go inside."

Idris turned away from her and went inside the store. Darlene watched him go, feeling clammy all over, before following him.

Idris was surprised by the public's sudden interest in the store, although he didn't know why. Anything out of the ordinary would drum up interest in a shop. A break-in resulting in a missing person's case seemed to be just the thing to bring customers in.

Rebecca. He tried not to think about her since the news report but failed. He knew that she had killed that Jane Doe. And how could she not? She had no one to teach her how to feed or how to control those urges. A feral vampire was an ugly thing and Vivica didn't care about the new baby she had created. She had been silent since the break-in, which did nothing to calm Idris's nerves.

Idris recalled his own Change and how the man who had bitten him, Atticus, had offered no help or suggestions either. *No, do not think of Atticus. Not here and not now.* Atticus only brought up bitter, angry memories. He didn't need any more of those now.

Darlene walked over to Maria, who seemed slightly overwhelmed by all the attention. They were short-staffed as well, seeing as Mabel was now in a home. Just another person Vivica had abandoned. Idris walked along the shop. Few changes had been made. The biggest change he noticed was the supernatural section was no longer in the back but had space in the front. He wondered if that was Darlene or Maria's doing. He found himself looking at the books. The first time he had seen Darlene, she was reading a book about ghosts.

"Hi." He turned to see a college-aged girl looking at him. "You here alone?"

"No. My girlfriend works here."

The girl glanced behind the counter and seemed confused. "The old lady?"

"No."

Her gaze fell on Darlene and back at him, seemingly confused at his interest in a big woman. He stared at her, willing her to say something to piss him off, but the girl merely smiled and turned back to the books, not wanting to pursue it. He was growing tired of everyone doubting his interest in Darlene, just because of her size. Idris stepped away from the supernatural books and headed over to the desk.

"Listen," Darlene was saying in a low tone. "If we can just talk…"

"Not here and not now, do you see how busy we are?" Maria said, brushing Darlene off and going over to the register to ring up a customer.

"Everything okay?" asked Idris.

Darlene's phone went off again. He saw her glance at it as Walsh's name popped up. She hit ignore.

"Should you be ignoring the cop's calls?"

Darlene shrugged. "He won't leave me alone. I think he thinks I did something wrong, Idris. And how can I refute that when I can't tell him anything that is actually going on?"

Annoyed, Darlene put her phone on the counter. A woman came up and asked about a book. Darlene nodded and walked off with the woman to show her. Idris suddenly felt useless. They were clearly busy, and there was nothing he could do here. Maria finished ringing up the customer and found herself alone with Idris. The tension between them made Idris avert his glance.

He finally cleared his throat. "I should probably head out…"

"What did you tell Darlene about witches?"

"What?" The question was so out of leftfield he could only blink. "Nothing."

"She came up to me just now wanting to know who put the magic on me so werewolves couldn't detect me." Her tone was low, and she was looking around through her thick-rimmed glasses to make sure no one was listening in.

"Well, Liara found you out, so obviously your witch isn't doing a great job."

Maria's lips tightened into a thin line. "From what I hear, you're going to be an Exsul as well, so you might want to stop being an ass."

He narrowed his eyes. "Who told you that?"

Maria turned away from him.

"Hey, who told you that?" he pressed.

At that moment, another customer came up to the register, and Idris stopped speaking. Maria began to ring the man's items up, and Idris saw Darlene across the shop, helping out another customer. He was about to go, feeling irritated over everything, when Darlene's phone went off. He swiped it up and answered it.

"What?" Idris barked.

"Who is this? I need to speak to Darlene Troops."

"It's Idris, Officer. She's at work."

"I need to speak to her right away. It's about Rebecca."

Idris's heart began to hammer. "Did you find her?"

"No. Please let Darlene know we need to speak with her at the station."

There was a click. Walsh had hung up. Idris stared at Darlene's phone, knowing that whatever it was wasn't going to be good.

Chapter Three

Idris held Darlene's hand as they waited for Officer Walsh. She looked pale, and her hand was clammy.

"Hey," Idris said. "It's going to be okay."

Darlene grunted in response, her gaze fixed on the door where Walsh would enter. They were back in the room Darlene had been put in for questioning last time. Idris accompanied her. Walsh would want to question her alone, but he wasn't going to allow it. He wanted to know what was going on with Rebecca as well.

Finally the door opened, and Walsh stepped inside. He seemed momentarily surprised at seeing Idris in there but sat across from them both.

"Normally, I wouldn't allow Idris to sit in on this," he began. "But this isn't any formal questioning so I'll allow it."

Idris was going to say something sarcastic, but Darlene gave his hand a squeeze.

"What's going on?" she asked, sounding worried. "You didn't find Rebecca. Did you find her body?"

"No. Listen, what I am about to tell you hasn't been released to the press, do you understand? It's confidential but your name has come up so…"

"Come up how?"

"Have you heard of the hitchhiker who was killed by the highway? In the old state police cabin?"

Both Darlene and Idris nodded. His heart was hammering. Did they suspect that Rebecca had done it?

"When we found the body, it was because we had gotten a tip from someone through our hotline. They said nothing except to check the cabin, so we did and found the body."

"But Rebecca doesn't hitchhike," Darlene said, sounding tired – Idris knew that keeping up the façade of being in the dark was taking its toll on her.

"Right. It wasn't Rebecca. It was a girl who had run away from home one state over. We don't know who called in. When we returned to the crime scene today, however, there was something new."

"New?" Idris replied, his throat growing dry.

Walsh put a slim brown packet in front of them. "I have to show you."

He slipped out a photograph from the packet and moved it in front of them. Idris tried to register just what exactly he was looking at. It looked like the wall of the cabin and splashed on it was one word: *Darlene.*

Darlene's breath caught as she read it.

"What is this?" Idris asked.

"This wasn't here the first night we discovered the body. It appeared only today. It's written in animal blood."

"This could be any Darlene," Idris said, trying to cover until Darlene managed to speak. "How do we know this is meant for her?"

"We lifted prints from the crime scene. They've turned up positive for Rebecca."

"Are you saying you think Rebecca murdered this girl? And left a message for Darlene? Doesn't that seem absurd to you?"

"I will admit it sounds far-fetched. But her prints are at the crime scene and on the wall where Darlene's name appeared. That's why we think it is meant for Miss Troops."

Darlene let out a strangled gasp for air. Idris turned to look at her in surprise. Her eyes were wide.

"I…I can't…I…" She looked at Idris pleadingly.

"She's going to have a fucking panic attack," Idris growled, standing up. "She needs some air."

Walsh looked alarmed. "Of course. I'm sorry, I –"

"Save it."

He took Darlene's hand and dragged her out of the room, through the station and outside. She had tears streaming down her face as they went to the side of the station. He grabbed her and hugged her tightly, stroking her hair as she cried. It was a keen wailing noise, which attracted stares that Idris fended off with his own glares.

Finally she moved away from him. "Sorry, I just…"

"Are you okay? Darlene, we knew…we knew that Rebecca did that…"

"I know." She hiccupped. "But I texted her last night."

"You *what*?"

"I texted her. Last night after I got home. That I was sorry. And that's how she answers me. A message slathered in blood on the walls."

Idris closed his eyes counted to ten to calm down. "Darlene, why did you text her? You realize if the cops find her phone and it works, we are fucked. She vanishes, kills someone and you text her that same night the body is found, with an apology?"

Her face had drained of color. "I hadn't…I hadn't thought of that."

He bit back the urge to say *clearly* and instead tried to focus on holding her. "We have to go back in that room now, okay? Are you okay to go back in?"

She wiped tears from her eyes and nodded, not saying another word. Idris took her hand, and they walked back inside the station. His blood was pumping quickly, and the stress was making him want to Change. He had to fend that urge off now. The last thing he needed was to turn into a werewolf in the police station.

Why had Darlene texted Rebecca? If they found her phone…

And if she had texted Rebecca with an apology and her reply was to write Darlene's name above a crime scene, what did that mean for them? Was Darlene at risk?

They stepped back inside the room.

Walsh stood up. "Are you okay, Miss Troops?"

"Yes. I'm sorry, it was just…a lot to suddenly take in. The break in, Rebecca vanishing, you telling me she murdered someone and now that message."

"I understand. I'm sorry it is so much. It's confusing for us as well."

They sat back down across from Officer Walsh, and Idris got the sinking feeling they were going to be there for a long time.

***

Idris's hunch proved to be correct. They spent two hours going over everything to do with Rebecca, why she would be suspected in a murder and why she would go and write Darlene's name in blood. By the time they left, it was almost dark. Darlene looked exhausted, and Idris felt as if he had been put through the wringer.

He was still frustrated with the fact that Darlene had texted Rebecca but he understood at the same time why she did. She felt as if Vivica turning Rebecca was all her fault and the idea that Rebecca had killed someone was just the terrible icing on top of the cake.

"Thanks for coming with me," Darlene said. "My car is still at the bookshop. Can you drop me off?"

"Do you want me to stay with you?"

"No, I'm okay, thanks."

Idris nodded, and they got into his truck. The ride was silent. Idris was still dwelling on Rebecca, as well as the Exsul status hanging over his head, and he was sure Darlene was thinking her own thoughts. He wanted to speak up – ask for them to share their troubles together – but when it came to relationships, he was out of his element.

He dropped Darlene off at the bookshop. She gave him a kiss but it seemed distant. He watched her get in her car and had the urge to call her back, but shoved it away. Idris drove off with a feeling that things were only going to get worse.

***

Darlene drove home in a daze. The entire day felt surreal. Every time she blinked, she saw Rebecca's message to her, written in blood. She kept hearing Idris in her head, asking why she had texted Rebecca and how it could lead back to her. But the guilt was eating away at her over Rebecca being a vampire. And now she had killed an innocent girl to feed.

She had wanted to talk to Idris more about how she was feeling but he had been acting off all day. She knew he was facing Exsul status because of her and was still grappling with the knowledge of what Lucian had been attempting to do and who he really was. How could Darlene have burdened him with her own problems when she was the reason for some of his biggest?

Darlene walked up to her apartment and saw Mark slouched against the wall, smoking a cigarette.

"When are you going home?" She hadn't meant for it to come off as rude as it did.

Mark looked at her with his one good eye, and Darlene wondered when he had lost it. "Roman says I can leave once we know you're not in danger."

"Well, that will never be." She went over to her door to unlock it.

"Hey, you okay?"

"Never better."

"Listen, I'm sorry for the joke I made last night. About what you smelled like. It was pretty crass of me."

Darlene paused and looked up at him. "Well. Yeah, it was. But thanks for apologizing."

"You're welcome."

Their eyes met, and Darlene shifted uncomfortably. "Listen, you should tell Roman to just let you go home. Guarding my apartment can't be interesting. And if I'm attacked somewhere else and you're here…" She frowned suddenly, and Mark stiffened. "If I'm attacked somewhere else, and you're guarding an empty apartment, what exactly are you good for?"

Mark didn't reply, taking a drag off his cigarette to delay. Darlene had a sinking feeling in her stomach and let out a groan of frustration.

"You're not even here to protect me, are you? Are you spying on this place for Roman? God, why am I so stupid?"

"You're not stupid. Hey, hey…" He grabbed her by the arm to stop her from going inside the apartment, "You're not stupid – this has nothing to do with you, okay?"

"You're guarding my home! I would say it does."

Mark let go of her. "We're just keeping track of Idris. With his vote coming up to Exsul status, we need whatever we can on him, okay?"

Darlene began to breathe harder and closed her eyes, counting to ten. "Get away from my door. Okay? I should have paid more attention to how stupid it was for you to be guarding an empty apartment. I don't want you here. Leave now or I'll call the cops."

Mark's eye widened, and then he looked abashed before shuffling off down toward the steps. Darlene slammed her apartment door behind her and shut her eyes tightly. How could she have been so stupid as to think Roman had sent someone to protect her and leave them stationed at her apartment? Of course they were going to spy on Idris. She thought about texting him and letting him know but decided against it.

She went to her room and lay down on the bed. She felt exhausted and was debating calling off work tomorrow. Was it so wrong that all she wanted to do was sleep for roughly a million years? Darlene turned her head to the side and saw her framed photo of Austin still by her bed. She pushed it off the night side table and heard it clatter to the floor. Then she turned on her side and fell asleep.

*****

Idris was halfway to his hotel room when he realized someone was following him. He pretended not to notice and that he had forgotten something in his truck. He turned around to walk back there, hoping to lure whoever it was away long enough to Change if he needed to. As Idris opened his truck door, he slowly scanned the area, trying to see who was following him. He heard the crack of a twig being stepped on behind him, and he whirled around.

"You're terrible at mimicking forgetting something."

Vivica. Idris cursed himself. He should have headed to the hotel room right away. Vivica would have had to be invited inside then, and Idris would have denied her that right and probably taunted her from inside his room just because he was in a bad mood.

Vivica's long red hair flowed over her shoulders. She was wearing all black, and her red eyes were dull. In the moonlight, Idris could see her nails had been sharpened and were painted black. He thought back to their toxic relationship – fighting, screaming and anger that always led to passionate, crazy sex. A couple of times, he let Vivica feed off of him willingly, although he would never admit something like that out loud. It'd brand him a freak to have a vampire do that to him.

Vivica said she and Lucian had never slept together. But what were they then? Did Lucian love her? Idris left out the part about Lucian being with Vivica when he told Liara the full story. He didn't think she could handle it.

"What do you want?" Idris mumbled.

"Just wanted to see how you're doing."

"I'm doing fine."

There was a blur, and Idris was pressed against the side of the truck. He could feel her pressed against him as she trailed her lips along his neck. Goose bumps popped up along his skin, and Vivica smiled.

"Oh, I just missed you. I know you're not doing well. I heard about your Exsul status."

"I'm not Exsul yet."

"Oh, but you will be." She tilted her face so that her eyes stared into his and pressed herself tighter against him. "I know you still feel our connection, Idris. Even though you're fucking that bookshop girl."

Idris tried to move away but Vivica's grip was like iron. "We have no connection, Vivica. Whatever we had was sick and disgusting. Whatever you had with Lucian was sick and disgusting. Why don't you get off of me and go find the vampire you made and forgot about? She's killing people now."

Vivica let go of Idris's waist and moved herself an inch away so that they weren't touching anymore. Idris was relieved. He didn't want to feel anything but negativity toward her, and the sensual way she had been pressing herself against him…

"Yes, I heard what that girl is doing." She shrugged. "Why should I care?"

"Because if the cops find her or anything about vampires is discovered because you let a feral vampire loose onto the town, your fellow vampire friends will stake you."

Idris saw a flicker of anger cross her features before her face collected itself into the neutral expression that he knew meant she was doubting herself. She crossed her arms.

Idris pressed his advantage. "You made her, Vivica. You turned Rebecca and you are her Maker. She's feral and bloodthirsty, and that hitch hiker won't be the last person she kills to feed. She may have killed someone else already."

Vivica sighed. "Fine. But I don't even know where she is."

***

Darlene heard something tapping… very gently but insistent enough that it woke her up. She faced the wall where her closet opened and couldn't see what was causing the noise. She hadn't been asleep very long, judging by the time on the clock. The tapping came again, and Darlene rolled over to look at the window in her bedroom.

She froze, and her eyes widened.

Rebecca was tapping on the window. Her hair was wild, and her glasses were gone. She was crouched like an animal, holding onto the side of the building, tapping on the glass. Her eyes were wide and tormented. Darlene got out of bed and padded over to the window, opening it up slowly.

"Darlene," Rebecca whispered, and her breath smelled like blood. "Did you get my message?"

"You mean the wall slathered in blood? Yeah, got that message. Haven't you heard of texting?"

Confusion crossed her face. "I thought I did...I...I don't know."

"Where have you been? We need to talk, Rebecca. You killed a hitchhiker."

"I know. You don't understand, Darlene. What the urge is like...how much I need to feed..."

"Why did you come here?"

"Will you invite me inside?"

"What?"

"Invite me in. I can't come in unless you invite me."

Darlene hesitated.

Rebecca saw the hesitation, and her eyes flashed. "You're not going to invite me? It's your fault I'm like this."

"I know! No, please, Rebecca, I invite you in."

She backed up as Rebecca slunk inside the apartment, looking around slowly. The way she carried herself was alien to Darlene. She looked like a shifty-eyed cat, about to steal from someone. Darlene felt uneasy.

Rebecca slowly walked around her bedroom. "Anyone else here?"

Darlene shook her head. "No."

Rebecca smiled, and her fangs were suddenly exposed. "Good."

***

Idris scoffed, "That's a load of bullshit, Viv. I know vampires have a connection to anyone they make. You knew when she killed that hitchhiker, didn't you? You could tell."

Vivica gave a low growl. "Why the fuck are you quizzing me? Why do you care? You never cared about anyone else I made before."

"Because you actually took care of the other ones you created, even if you did a half-assed job. This girl you changed out of spite. So 'fess up."

Vivica closed her eyes. Idris watched as she tried to feel her connection with Rebecca. He wondered if he could walk off, and she wouldn't notice but decided not to risk an attack from behind.

Finally she opened her eyes. "She's about to feed again."

"What? We have to stop her!"

"Stop her from doing what is her right?"

"She's going to kill again, Viv!"

"Then you better hurry. Because judging from the emotions she's feeling, I'll bet it's your girlfriend." Vivica sneered at him and then she was a blur, darting out among the trees near the hotel, leaving Idris alone.

Idris cursed and got into his truck, revving up the engine. He hoped he had enough time to get to Darlene's place before it was too late.

*****

Rebecca was a flash of dark colors, and Darlene landed against the bed. Rebecca was over her now, her fangs exposed and a glint in her eye that filled her with dread.

"Rebecca, stop!"

"I'm so hungry, Darlene. Do this for your friend, won't you?"

Darlene struggled, but it didn't matter. Rebecca's strength was ridiculous. Even Vivica or Jacob hadn't felt this strong. It was the power of a new vampire, someone who had just fed. It wasn't like Rebecca at all. Darlene let out a scream and then Rebecca clamped her hand over her mouth. She reared back her head, and Darlene saw the fangs in the moonlight before they pierced her skin.

Pain shot through her. Rebecca wasn't trying to be careful. This wasn't one of those loving bites you saw in sensual vampire movies that were basically softcore porn late at night. This was brutal and angry. She could hear the soft slurping noises that Rebecca was making. Her vision blurred, and she dully wondered if Rebecca was going to drain her dry like she had with that poor hitchhiker.

A growl filled the air, low and angry. Then Rebecca flew off of her, hitting the floor next to her bed. Darlene sat up, clutching her neck. A werewolf had Rebecca pinned down. *Idris,* Darlene thought, relieved. But the werewolf turned to one side, and she saw that it had a missing eye. It was Mark.

Rebecca sunk her teeth into Mark's front paw. He let out a howl and leapt back, knocking into Darlene's dresser. The room was too small for such a fight. Darlene tried to get up to help but the world spun in front of her. *I've lost too much blood.* Through her fog, she could see Mark knocking into Rebecca with his front paws and sinking a sharpened talon-like nail into her stomach.

A shape appeared just outside the open window. Something transparent, barely moving. A spirit. She wanted to try to connect with it, to get it to help Mark, but she was fading fast. Rebecca had taken more blood from her than she had originally thought.

Rebecca spun away from Mark, let out a hiss at him and leapt through the open window. She went through the spirit, which vanished at the same time. Mark growled, his front paw bleeding, and he turned to look at Darlene with his one good eye. Darlene's eyes fluttered, and she felt as if she was falling. She hit the bed and was swept up in darkness.

***

Idris parked his truck with a screech of the tires and got out of the truck, running up to Darlene's apartment. Her door was wide open. The tiny old lady who was her next door neighbor was coming out of her room.

"I'm going to call the police!" she said to him, and Idris disliked her more than ever in that moment. "Your girlfriend is ridiculous. I'm constantly hearing insanity coming from her apartment!"

"Yeah, yeah, I got it. Go to bed."

Idris walked into Darlene's apartment and slammed the door shut before the neighbor could complain again.

"Darlene?" he cried out.

"She's in here."

Frowning, Idris walked into her bedroom. He saw Darlene on her bed, asleep, with Mark sitting at the edge of the bed, wrapping up his arm. The room was trashed. Darlene's dresser was broken, and her bedroom side table was cracked in half.

"Rebecca?"

Mark nodded. "Bitch got in. Bit Darlene. She escaped. I don't know where she is."

Idris hoped Vivica was going after her. He went to Darlene's side and looked at her neck. Mark had bandaged it up already.

"Is she okay?"

"She blacked out. Lost a lot of blood. But I think she'll be okay. Rebecca was going to kill her though. That vampire is feral. Blood-thirsty. Crazy bitch."

Idris felt uncomfortable. He knew Mark had been stationed here to watch Darlene but wasn't sure how to say thank you for what he had done.

As if sensing what Idris was struggling with, Mark held up his good hand. "Don't. Don't thank me. Darlene had already figured it out. I was guarding the apartment on Roman's orders to spy on you. To make sure you get Exsul status. Darlene told me off earlier. I was coming here to apologize to her. She was pretty pissed off. That's when I saw Rebecca on the side of the apartment building, hanging out on the window."

Idris looked down at the sleeping Darlene. "You still saved her. I'll…yell at you another time."

Mark stood up. He wasn't as big as Roman but he still wasn't the type of guy anyone would want to mess around with. His missing eye made him scarier. Right now though, he looked exhausted. His pallor was sickly, and his hand was clearly still bleeding through the bandages.

"You got her now, right? I'm leaving."

Idris opened his mouth to say something but Mark stalked out of the room. The door slammed shut in the living room, and Darlene's eyes opened.

"What?" she mumbled.

"Hey. Hey, it's okay. I'm here."

Her hazy eyes focused on Idris, and one hand went to the bandages on her neck. "Rebecca…"

"She's gone. Darlene, listen to me, did you grant her permission to enter?"

"Yes."

"You need to revoke it. Okay? You need to revoke it right now. Say you revoke it."

Darlene managed to prop herself up now, looking at the window, which Idris got up and shut firmly. "I revoke Rebecca Gil's permission to enter my home." She looked around. "Was something supposed to happen?"

"No. But now she can't come back. How are you feeling?" He crossed over the destruction of her bedroom toward her, sitting down next to her, one hand on her thigh.

Darlene recounted what happened. After she finished, Idris kissed her cheek and checked her bandage. He pulled it off gently and saw two puncture marks.

"You should eat something. You lost a lot of blood." He got up to grab fresh bandages and cleaning supplies for the wound, as well as a cookie, juice and a banana to try to get something in her system.

Darlene ate quietly and winced a little as Idris cleaned out her wound. He thought of what Mark had said and decided not to bring it up now and stress Darlene out more.

"I'd like to sleep. Will you watch the apartment for me?"

Idris nodded.

Darlene looked at him sleepily, leaning back against the pillows. "How did you know that Rebecca was going to come here?"

Idris wanted to tell her he had seen Vivica, but when he remembered her pressed against him, he faltered. "I had a bad feeling."

Darlene nodded and drifted off to sleep. Idris tried to clean up her room as well as he could. He found the photo of Austin shoved off behind the broken night table, the glass cracked in half, shooting spider web like lines all over Darlene's face. *Good,* Idris thought as he cleaned up the glass.

After he was all done cleaning up, he got into bed next to Darlene and thought about what to do next. He needed Vivica to pull Rebecca in line. Otherwise, he was afraid he'd have to kill Rebecca himself.

Chapter Four

Darlene was running through a mist. She couldn't see anything in front or behind her. The mist created a low hum, which resonated throughout her body, making her skin aflame with heat. Darlene reached out, but her hand glided through empty space. Forever out of her grasp, the spirits remained around her, floating, silent, their secrets locked inside of them.

Her eyes opened suddenly. It was pitch black and for a second she could feel the smothering of Rebecca's hand on top of her mouth. She reached out wildly, as if to fend Rebecca off and hit something.

"Hey, hey, it's okay," Idris mumbled in the darkness, his hand grasping hers. "I'm here. Rebecca can't get in. You revoked guest rights, remember?"

Darlene relaxed and sat up. Her neck ached, but she felt a lot better. "What time is it?"

"Around three. Did you have a dream?"

"Yeah." But she didn't want to talk about it. "Will you kiss me?"

She could feel Idris's surprise, but all she wanted right now was someone to lean over and kiss her and make her fear go away. She didn't want to think about ghosts or vampires. She just wanted to feel Idris against her.

Idris leaned over and kissed her gently, as if making sure it was okay. Darlene kissed him back harder, letting him know that this was what she needed right now. He moved his hands to her sides and for once she didn't feel shy about her size. She let him run his fingers along her. His warmth was comforting, like laying outside at the beach on a perfect day.

He kissed her again and Darlene fumbled to take off his clothes. It was so dark she could barely see. Idris took the lead. He could see just fine in the dark due to his werewolf senses. She heard him undress and then he slowly took off her clothes, as if she was a prize he was unwrapping.

Darlene closed her eyes and let her other senses come alive as Idris kissed her and ran his lips along her skin. She could feel how hard he was against her leg as he moved along her body. Her skin felt as if it was being warmed by pure sunlight. Idris's stubble rasped her skin as he kissed along her breasts, holding them gently.

Then he moved and positioned himself to enter her. He went slowly, each inch going inside her at a steady rate, making Darlene sigh with pleasure. In the darkness, all she could feel was Idris and his warmth as he moved inside her. She wrapped her legs around his waist and pushed him in deeper. Idris slid one hand down and began to play with her clit as he moved inside her.

Pleasure shot through Darlene. She arched her back and bucked her hips as Idris fucked her and moved his fingers around skillfully. She began to moan as Idris moved expertly. She could feel her orgasm building up. Idris himself was beginning to shudder, his thrusts becoming harder and faster as he moaned her name.

Darlene began to come, bucking her hips and clinging to Idris as her orgasm ran through her. She shut her eyes tightly to the pleasure, digging her nails into Idris's back as he finished as well. He murmured her name as he slammed inside her, shuddering with the force of his orgasm. Both of them came together, entwined as the moonlight poured into the room.

Finally, Darlene came down from her orgasm and Idris rolled off of her, holding her hand tightly. All the bad thoughts were at bay. Darlene turned to the side and wrapped her arms around him, falling back asleep.

***

Idris awoke to his phone ringing. He opened his eyes and saw that it was morning. The sun shone over the destruction of Darlene's room. He was naked, and Darlene was sleeping quietly next to him. Her neck was still bandaged up, and her hair splashed over the pillow. She looked beautiful.

Idris saw it was Liara calling him, and he answered quietly, "Hello?"

"Hey. Are you busy? Mark told me about Darlene."

"Yeah. I'm still here. I was keeping watch. She revoked Rebecca's guest invitation though, so I'm hoping that'll be enough to keep her safe here. Have you heard from Vivica?"

"No. But she was never friendly with Lucian and me, like she was with you." Idris winced at her casual tone, wanting to tell her that Lucian was friendly with Vivica too, but Liara kept talking, "Listen, though, we think Rebecca…killed again."

Idris's heart lurched. "Who?"

"It's bad. It was a cop, Idris. If you and Vivica are still close, you need to tell her to get this in order before it gets even worse."

"Do you know who it was?"

"No, sorry. You'll have to look it up." She paused. "The real reason for my call is to let you know that the meeting for your Exsul debate has been announced. Two days from now, on Friday."

"So soon?"

"Roman is rushing it to a region-wide pack vote. I'm doing everything I can. But Roman has most of his pack convinced that since Darlene was told before her powers were exposed, it was a risk you shouldn't have taken. Plus...she hasn't exactly shown that ability since. They're doubting if it is even true... if she made it up."

"She didn't make it up," Idris hissed and found himself clenching the phone tightly.

"I know that, Idris. I can't make you leave town because I know you'll say no because of Darlene. I get it. I'm not going to give you a pack-leader order to go. But you need to be very careful, okay?"

"Thanks," Idris mumbled, knowing he should feel grateful Liara wasn't going to ask him to officially go back to the pack till the vote came in, but all he could feel was sick.

She hung up and with that sinking feeling in his stomach, Idris pulled up the news story of the cop who had been killed by Rebecca.

And even though he knew what he would find, seeing that it was Officer Walsh did his budding headache no favors.

***

Maria fussed over Darlene when she chose to come into work instead of calling in sick.

"How can I call in a sick day?" Darlene sighed. "We're short-staffed."

"I hired someone. I was desperate, so it's just some silly teenager, but that'll do until the interest in the book shop wears off." Maria pulled away from Darlene and looked at her critically. "I cannot believe your friend did this to you."

"She isn't my friend anymore. She's just…" Darlene shook her head, her brain muddled.

Maria lowered her voice. "I heard about Officer Walsh."

Darlene groaned. "God, I know. She did that, too. She's blood-thirsty and feral and insane, but she used to be my friend and this is all my fault. And now the cop looking into her own case is dead. How can things get worse? Oh, wait, Idris is facing Exsul status via pack vote on Friday." She looked up at Maria. "It isn't going to go well, is it? He's trying to downplay it, but Roman is telling people I faked my powers."

Darlene felt sick. She thought going into work was a good idea to keep her head straight but she felt anything but. Instead it felt as if a hatchet was being slowly driven into her skull. Rebecca almost killing her had been terrible. But now Officer Walsh was dead. Idris was going to become an Exsul and Roman's pack thought she had made up her powers.

Maria patted her shoulder gently, showing concern in her eyes through her thick glasses. "Have you seen anything since that night with Lucian?"

Darlene nodded. "I saw one last night when Rebecca attacked. But I had lost too much blood and passed out. I keep having dreams…of spirits…trying to talk to me. But they only show up in times of stress in the real world, apparently."

Maria got up suddenly and went over to an old wooden box she had on a cabinet. She opened it and leafed through it before walking back over, handing Darlene a thin, glossy card. Darlene took it and looked down at it. It had a name – Rosamund – and then a phone number underneath.

"What is this?" Darlene asked, looking back up at Maria.

"That is the card of the…witch…who has helped me for years to hide from werewolves. We didn't know a pack leader would ever come into the store, otherwise I would have paid her more to make the magic stronger so Liara couldn't have known it was me. But…" She shrugged. "Anyway, contact her. Your dreams said I could help you. I ignored you and refused you, but now I can't help but feel this is partly my fault. Reach out to Rosamund. Tell her I sent you."

Darlene's heart beat quickly as she looked at the card and then back up at Maria. "Thank you."

Maria smiled and left the office, shutting the door behind her. Darlene ran her fingers over the card with Rosamund's name on it. Her head pounded and her neck ached, but for the first time in a long time, she felt a sprig of hope.

On her break, Darlene dialed the number and listened to it ring for almost a full minute until a throaty voice answered, "Hello?"

"Hi, uh, this is Darlene Troops. I'm calling because Maria gave me your number."

There was a long pause, and Darlene checked to make sure the call hadn't dropped when the woman answered, "I'm Rosamund. Maria has mentioned you in the past. You work in her shop, don't you? But now you need my help."

"Yes. That's right."

"Tonight. I live in Hedge Hills. I'll give you my address." Darlene scribbled it down along with the time to meet. "Don't tell your werewolf boyfriend you're coming."

"How did you—"

But the call ended. Darlene stared at the phone before looking down at the address. Idris's pack lived in Hedge Hills. She felt uncomfortable lying to Idris, but there had to be a reason that Rosamund didn't want him to know. Darlene shoved the paper in her purse and walked outside to the store front. Maria was wrapping a book for a customer.

Darlene lowered her voice. "She told me not to tell Idris. How did she know about him? Why can't I tell him?"

Maria admired her work on the wrapping job before replying, "Werewolves don't like magic. She wouldn't want the pack to know she lives so close to them. Don't tell Idris, Darlene."

Darlene nodded and went out onto the floor to help the customers. She found herself glancing at the clock almost non-stop. She was anxious to see Rosamund tonight. Anything to focus on doing something rather than how wrong everything had become.

***

Idris parked his truck and looked out onto the graveyard. The sun was setting and the graveyard looked normal, devoid of anything sinister. There was a small group of people on one side, crowded around a grave, paying their respects. Other than that, it was empty. Idris turned off the truck and stepped outside. Everyone wore jackets so he slipped one on as well, just to make sure he didn't stand out.

He didn't know for sure if Vivica still lived in this graveyard. She liked to move around a lot. Vampires were solitary by nature and most attempts to form a community like the werewolf packs blew up in their faces. More than once, Idris stumbled upon Vivica staking a fellow vampire out of pure disgust over some small slight.

Normally, the last thing Idris would do was to seek Vivica out. But after finding out about Officer Walsh's murder last night, he needed to know if she was going to stop Rebecca or if he would have to do it himself. Idris walked through the graveyard toward the older section. It was run down and had a catacomb that was sealed off to the public that Vivica liked to hang out in.

As he approached it, Idris knew he was risking a brutal fight with her. Waking her up was a stupid idea, but he couldn't wait until later tonight. By the time the sun set, which Idris guessed was another hour or so, Rebecca would be awake and out around town, which was a risk he couldn't take. He needed to know if Vivica had some sort of game plan for taking her creation down.

The front doors of the catacomb had a *Keep Out* sign that Idris brushed aside. He pushed open the doors, which ground loudly across the tiles, sending up a flock of scared birds into the air. He used all his strength to press against the doors until they were wedged open enough so that he could get inside.

Idris tried to make out the catacombs in front of him but it was pitch black inside. The catacombs here used to be a tourist attraction until people started dying in them. It was actually vampires pegging off humans who were willingly touring their nests. Now Vivica claimed it as her own home for as long as Idris could remember. Once in a while, a group of teenagers would break in and go exploring. As much as Idris used to plead for Vivica not to, it usually resulted in the group's death. Vivica had lived a long time, almost two thousand years, and the only thing she never seemed to grow sick of was murder.

Idris pulled out his flashlight and illuminated the patch in front of him. Broken glass lay scattered along the stones, leading to a crude hallway that curved downward below ground level. Idris made his way to the hallway, ignoring the smell of death that permeated throughout the room.

"Vivica?" he called out, hoping he could wake her up this way.

There was no reply. Idris followed the curve of the hallway as it led to the main floor of the catacombs. He tried not to recall all the times he spent with Vivica in here. It made his skin crawl.

In the early years when Idris' anger and rage boiled inside him after he was Changed, his relationship with Vivica was right up his alley. She was sick and twisted and their rages fueling together offered up a relationship neither one of them could resist. They'd fight and scream at one another and then have mind-blowing sex. The fact that Idris had to keep it a secret from the pack had made it even more appealing for him. Vampire and werewolf relationships were frowned upon and would be cause for banishing a werewolf to Exsul status... so could trying to combine them into one hybrid monster.

Idris shook his head, not wanting to think about the fact that Jacob was still out there somewhere, doing God only knows what. Better to focus on the problem at hand. He called out for Vivica again as he stepped down into the main floor of the catacombs. The entire place had fallen into disrepair. Coffins were strewn open and bones littered the floor. Some were too fresh to be actually from the time period the catacombs were built and were only there thanks to Vivica.

There was a closed coffin in the middle of the floor. It was out of place due to the fact that it looked spotless. Vivica had never enjoyed a dirty coffin to sleep in – she was picky. Idris walked over to the coffin and began to yank it open. It glided open soundlessly and exposed Vivica.

She was fast asleep, deathly pale. Her makeup stood out against her skin. Red lips and black eyeliner. She must have gone out the night before. Her pallor told him that she hadn't fed last night. Her chest was still. Idris realized how vulnerable she was in this state. *I could stake her,* he thought with a jolt.

***

Darlene's car crested over the hill and she slowed down. Rosamund's house was somewhere along this street. She didn't want to miss it and then try to turn around. She was in an older section of town. The streets were narrow and almost all one-way, which was fun when Darlene got stuck behind an old man who looked to be roughly a thousand years old and could barely see over the wheel.

By the time she had managed to get out and away from the old guy, she was almost late. Darlene saw an old mailbox with the house numbers on it and realized she had made it. She turned sharply into the driveway and stared at the house, which was tiny and run down. A window was covered with a garbage bag and weeds grew all over the lawn. There was a broken *Welcome* sign hanging off the front door, which was clattering loudly in the small wind that had kicked up.

Darlene steeled herself and got out of the car. She walked up the pathway to the house and saw two cats hiding in shrubs, staring at her with big eyes. As Darlene walked up the patio steps, a smell of strong incense floated through the door. It made her eyes sting. The door was covered in citations from code enforcement over the state of the house and when she knocked on it, one of the papers fell off and landed in her hand.

The door opened with a lurch, and Darlene blinked. A young woman stared back at her. Her blonde hair was messy and long, flowing past her shoulders and down her back. Her clothes were too big and hung off of her at funny angles. Her eyes were wide and purple with a mouth that seemed a bit too large for her features. On the other hand, her nose was too small for her heart-shaped face. She looked as if someone had tried to draw a proper human being but didn't know how to draw facial features well.

"Darlene?" her voice was surprisingly throaty, and Darlene realized this was Rosamund.

"Hi. Uh, this was on your door and fell off." She handed her the citation notice from code enforcement.

Rosamund looked at it as if it were a bucket full of acid and knocked it out of Darlene's hand onto the patio. "Come in, come in."

Darlene followed her inside the house and worried about what she was getting herself into.

***

"Don't bother."

Idris leapt back. Vivica's eyes had opened and she sat up in her coffin, stretching out languidly, reminding him of a cat.

"Don't bother with what?"

"With thoughts of staking me. I heard you as soon as you came in. I just wanted you to think you actually had one up on me." She flicked her hair over her shoulder and smiled at him, her fangs exposed. "So what do I owe this honor?"

"I came to talk to you about Rebecca."

Vivica slinked out of the coffin and walked over to him. She pressed herself slightly against him and looked up at him with those blood-red eyes. "That's it?"

Idris pushed her back and shook his head. "Yes. That's all."

"How's your girlfriend?"

"Fine. Mark was there. He protected her until I got there."

"Are you okay with another man protecting your woman?" She moved so her breasts brushed against his chest, and Idris broke away from her, walking back to her coffin.

"Rebecca bit her."

"So what? Not my concern."

"And she killed a cop right after. You knew that, though, didn't you? You went out last night. Did you see her?"

Vivica sighed. "You're so bothersome. This is of no concern of yours."

"It is. The cop she killed was the one investigating her own disappearance. He had been asking Darlene about Rebecca. Things could lead back to her—"

Vivica hissed at him, "Are you here to make me give a damn about your girlfriend? Why do I care what happens to her?"

Idris growled, "I know you spoke to Rebecca. Tell me what happened, Viv."

At the sound of her old pet name, she softened a little and retracted her fangs. "I saw her last night. After she killed that cop. She was at some stupid night club. She was just dancing up on some guys. It was harmless."

"Did you talk to her?"

"No. Why would I talk to her?"

"You created her!" Idris growled. "This is as much your problem as much as anyone else's."

Vivica flashed over to him in a blur, pressing him against the back of the coffin, the weight of her body heavy on him. "She's my creation. I'll deal with her in my own way. I don't need you coming around talking about your stupid girlfriend."

"Are you jealous of her now?" Idris sneered, a low growl coming from his throat.

Vivica pressed her hand around his throat, gripping it. "It isn't my fault that you have bad taste, pup."

Idris breathed hard as Vivica squeezed his neck once before letting go. He shoved her off of him and then he was pushed back, landing on the floor of the catacomb, with Vivica straddling him. She leaned down to his neck, brushing her tongue along it which made him shiver.

"I know you still want me," she purred in his ear. "Why don't you just give in? That's why you wanted to see me, right? You want to fuck?"

Idris pushed her away, and Vivica rolled off of him. "Why do you have to be so crass about everything? It's gross." He stood up and looked down at her, sitting on the floor. "What club was she at?"

"*Seductions*. Let me come with you."

"No," Idris replied, turning to walk away. "Either you stake her or I'll do it myself."

Vivica laughed a low, throaty laugh that meant she saw right through him. Idris tried to ignore it as he walked out of the main chamber and back into the hallway. He didn't want to think about how much he had wanted her in that very moment she had pressed up against him. Old habits die hard. He didn't want to go back to that one.

***

Darlene looked around the house. Candles were lit all over the living room, and she could see two cats lying on the couch, fast asleep. The different scents of the candles blended together and made her eyes water. She tried to wipe them as Rosamund told her to follow her into a room off to the side. She followed her and stopped as she stepped into the room.

This room had a beaded doorway and voodoo dolls all along the walls. An oak table stood in the center with a crystal ball on top and two chairs, one at each end. Tarot cards were on the other side of the table. The rest of the walls had blankets on them. Candles were all along the floor.

"Is this your witchcraft room or something?"

"Most of it is for show. I run a fortune telling business on the side, and they come through the door back there." She pointed to the door behind the oak table. "They never see my real house. People coming to a fortune telling expect certain things. They have no interest in the realism of the practice. They want tarot cards and crystal balls."

"Do you tell them the truth?" Darlene asked as she shooed a cat off the chair and sat down across from Rosamund.

"Sometimes." She sat on the other side.

"Why only sometimes?"

"Some of them don't want the truth. I can tell by how they speak that they aren't interested in knowing their true future. So I tell them what they want to hear. It depends on the person."

"What about me? Can you do my future?"

"No." Rosamund turned to grab a box off the cabinet behind her.

"Why not?" Darlene pressed.

"You have too many spirits clinging to you."

Darlene felt a thrum of excitement. "So it's true, then. I can communicate with the other side?"

Rosamund nodded. "Yes, it's true. Dormant for so long though, which is curious. I can't see your future at all. Too many spirits are vying for your attention and yet you ignore them. Why is that?"

"I haven't been able to communicate with them. Only once. The second time I saw one there were…other things going on and I didn't get a chance."

"Maria said you run with the werewolves, yes?" She removed items out of the box now – they looked like different herbs.

"Yes. My boyfriend…but you knew about Idris."

"Yes. I hear rumors through the world. He is going to become an exile."

"That's not true," Darlene snapped. "You don't know that."

Rosamund's violet eyes flicked up to her. "I've been blocking Maria from other werewolves for ten years now. Yet she tells me one of the pack leaders saw through it. She asked why I didn't make it stronger. She thought she needed to pay me more. I told her the other day that it was because she wanted to be discovered."

"I don't follow."

Rosamund clicked her long nails together. They were painted purple, like her eyes. "Maria wanted another werewolf to see her. My magic cannot do all the work. Some work has to be done by the person themselves. Her will to be discovered led to the pack leader seeing her."

"And you're saying that Idris is the same with his Exsul status?"

"Yes, that's right. He may want it more than he even knows. Hold out your hand." Darlene did as instructed, and Rosamund put a small bag of different-colored herbs in her hand. "Eat these. One strand a night... fighting nothing that happens, do you understand?"

"This isn't like...weed, is it?"

"Don't be foolish," Rosamund said in a sharp tone. "This is going to open the restrictions you have placed on your mind. You need to be ready. Communicating with the spirit world is a lot of work. It isn't fun. But you need to stay positive, otherwise it won't work, like Maria and her magic."

Darlene nodded, looking at the bag. Some of the herbs were bright red and others a pale blue. She had never seen such a thing before.

"Another thing," Rosamund said. "Your friend. The vampire. She's only going to get worse. You need to end it or someone you love will be next on her hit list."

She stood up. Darlene followed her out of the room, her head spinning. "Anything else?"

"Your boyfriend. You still feel self-conscious because of your size. Do you know where he is tonight? No. You lied to him, and he lied to you."

"He lied to me, too? Where is he?"

"Clouded. Underground. Ex-girlfriend, maybe? Tangled memories."

Darlene's heart thrummed. Vivica. He had to be speaking to Vivica about Rebecca. That was fine, right? She told herself that he was trying to get answers and that made it okay. But she had a sinking feeling in her stomach.

"Thanks."

Darlene turned to leave when Rosamund cleared her throat. She paused and turned around to see her holding out her hand.

"Oh, right, sorry..." Darlene opened her wallet and looked for some money in there. "I didn't realize..."

"Witches have to pay the bills, too."

Darlene slapped a twenty-dollar bill down in her hand, which seemed to please her. She turned around and left, Rosamund shutting the front door behind her as Darlene shoved the bag full of different colored weeds in her purse. She had a headache from the different smells from the house, and her eyes were still watering.

As Darlene got into her car, she found herself looking up at the moon. There was something nagging at her brain. She pulled out her phone and brought up an app she had downloaded that showed the moon phases each night.

Tomorrow would be a full moon.

Chapter Five

"No, I can't come over, Darlene. You know that," Idris said into his phone, watching with dread as the sun set. "Full moon tonight. I have to get out of Dodge. Everything is...different on a full moon. Harder to control. You should stay inside the apartment, too. Rebecca can't get in there."

"Okay," Darlene agreed reluctantly. "But I'll be worried. What do you mean things are different on a full moon? How is it harder to control?"

"Most of the packs run in groups. They watch out for each other through the night and run in the woods. Lucian and I used to run together."

"Do you run with Liara now?"

Idris sighed and ran his fingers through his hair. "No. No, Liara asked...with the pack vote tomorrow, not to run with anyone tonight."

"You're going to be *alone*?"

"Yeah, but I'll be fine. I'm going as far into the woods as I can and will just stay there. Don't leave the house, okay?"

There was a pause, and Idris checked to see if the call had dropped.

"Idris," Darlene said suddenly. "Are you just going to the woods?"

"Yeah…where else would I go?" he replied, confused.

"Nowhere, I just…wasn't sure if you had an old friend you would go to or something."

"No. Just myself in the woods."

"Okay. Call me as soon as you're okay in the morning."

Idris promised he would and hung up, looking at his phone curiously. Something in Darlene's tone was off. He thought about what she had asked and frowned. Did she somehow know he had seen Vivica last night? No, that was ridiculous. And even if she did know, it had been for her benefit, to find out about Rebecca. There was nothing else going on besides that.

Idris sighed and made sure he had everything he needed. He had always hated the full moon. Running with Lucian made it a bit better but he hated how hard it was to stay in control. Yes, he was more powerful but he also felt more chaotic and angry at the world. He remembered his very first full moon, watching Atticus, his Maker, rip into a man who had accidently stumbled upon them, his sharp teeth biting into him…

Idris shook his head. Liara telling him he couldn't run with the pack had confirmed his worst fear – Liara knew he was being sentenced to Exsul status. Roman and Idris had never gotten along. Idris disagreed with the way Roman did pretty much everything as pack leader and in return, Roman hated how Idris couldn't accept what he was and get over it.

They were like oil and water. Idris never imagined that it would come back to bite him in the ass so badly.

For a second, he debated trying to find Maria. What did she do on full moons? But the thought of going to an Exsul and asking for advice seemed to only make it more real. He didn't want to call Darlene again to talk to her. She would only blame herself and say if she had relocated or allowed to be Changed then this wouldn't have happened. She was right, in that respect, but Idris knew that she had powers beyond anyone's understanding. Darlene belonged in their world, as much as Roman wanted to use that against him.

But Roman had a point, too. Idris didn't know about Darlene's powers when he told her about werewolves. He just felt a connection with her that he hadn't felt for another woman in a long time.

Thinking about the past didn't matter. Idris knew he needed to get ready to find a place to run in the woods and not hurt anyone. He'd think about everything else tomorrow.

***

Darlene screamed and covered her eyes. Nothing happened, of course, but seeing a spirit in her bathroom was jarring enough. She kept her eyes covered as she tried to regain her breathing.

She took her first herb last night and slept like crap. Nothing but nightmares and crazy dreams of spirits communicating with her – some were angry, complaining that they had been trying to get in touch with her for years, and others were upset because they were hoping she could somehow bring them back to life… thousands of spirits, all vying for her attention.

When Darlene woke up, she felt relieved… but not for long. After getting up and bumbling out to the kitchen to get a glass of water, a man in tattered clothes appeared in her kitchen. She shrieked in panic, prompting her annoying old lady neighbor next door to slam on the other side of the wall telling her to shut up. *I could have been in the process of getting killed,* Darlene thought ruefully as she stood in the opposite corner of the man.

"Sorry I scared you," the man admitted woefully. "I didn't think you'd actually see me today, of all days."

"How long have you been in my kitchen?"

The man turned to look at the clock and exposed a long gash along his neck, clearly life-threatening. "An hour. Sometimes I stand in your living room."

"What? How long have you – forget it! What do you want?"

"I'm just lonely."

Darlene let out a sigh of frustration. "Please…leave. I don't know the etiquette for this but you need to go, okay?"

The man shrugged. "Okay. Maybe tomorrow?" And he faded from her view.

Darlene realized now that she could see actual spirits, instead of just thin wispy clouds. Great, because it meant Rosamund's herbs actually worked. Bad, because it was a whole new realm of terrifying.

And now in her bathroom was someone who had clearly drowned. Seaweed wrapped around her neck and clung to her dripping wet body. Her water-logged clothes stuck to her in weird spots, and her eyes had gone milky white. Darlene tried to remember that she was in control and had asked for this, otherwise she feared something terrible would happen, like Rosamund had warned.

"Hey. Hey, hi...you..." Darlene said, finally lowering her hands to stare at the woman.

The woman sighed sadly. Darlene wondered if all the ghosts she saw were going to be this much of a bummer. The guy in the kitchen hadn't exactly been ready to party either.

Darlene's doorbell rang at that moment. She had gotten off the phone with Idris moments ago and knew it couldn't have been him. *Could ghosts ring doorbells?*

"Will you excuse me?" she said to the drowned woman and headed to the front door.

She looked through the peephole and to her amazement saw Mark. Darlene opened the door. Mark was dressed in loose clothes, clearly getting ready for the full moon.

"What are you doing here?"

"Nice to see you, too."

"Sorry," Darlene replied, abashed. "I just wasn't expecting it."

"Full moon tonight. Wanted to see if you needed anything before I head out to Roman's pack."

Darlene was taken aback. "No. I'm good."

"Idris here already then?"

"No, I didn't see him today."

"Oh. Shitty of him."

"No, it isn't," Darlene countered back, feeling defensive. "He has a lot going on right now. He has to spend the full moon alone."

"Liara banned him from the pack run?"

Darlene felt as if she was losing control of the conversation. "Don't tell Roman that, okay? Please. You know your pack leader is making sure Idris becomes an Exsul."

Mark crossed his arms. "You didn't know Idris before. When he was first Changed… he was an asshole."

"Well, he isn't anymore, okay?"

"Are you sure? Who is here and who isn't?"

Darlene felt her face flush. "What do you want, Mark?"

"You're all set for the night? You shouldn't leave the apartment, okay? Not with Rebecca still around."

"I know. The police station called me earlier for questioning. I haven't returned their call yet."

"Your friend got you in quite the pickle."

"I got her in one, too." Darlene found herself staring at his one bad eye, with the long slash over it, and wondered how he had gotten it. "Well, I'm fine. Thanks for checking up on me. You really don't have to do that. Roman released you from pretending to watch my apartment, didn't he?"

"I didn't come here because of Roman."

Darlene's heart skipped a beat and then she took a step back inside. "Thanks, Mark. Have a good full moon."

She shut the door and closed her eyes briefly. What the hell was that all about?

***

Darlene watched some terrible reality show later that night, with the moon high in the night sky and near freezing temperatures outside. She was wrapped up in tons of comfy blankets. It would have been perfect, except that drowned woman ghost stared at her from the bathroom all night.

Frustrated, Darlene turned to look at her head on. "Listen, are you just going to stay in the bathroom?"

The woman nodded mutely, and Darlene sighed. Just her luck. A creepy ghost was hanging out in her bathroom. She kind of missed the guy with the life-ending wound from this morning. She stood up and walked over to her window, looking out at the apartment complex. There were a few cars here and there but other than that, it was empty. The moon shone bright, illuminating the parking lot more than the lights did.

Darlene froze. Someone headed over to her building. She looked at him closer, pressing her nose against the window. He was gliding, not walking. A ghost. But this spirit gave her a bad feeling in her stomach. She opened the window and leaned out, trying to see it better.

That was when the ghost stopped and tilted his head up to look at her. Darlene's heart began to thud and her mouth went dry. *Lucian.* Lucian's ghost was out there, and it was coming to her apartment.

She slammed the window shut and looked around before heading over to the bathroom. The drowned woman stood in the corner, doing absolutely nothing.

"Hey, listen, I don't know much about ghosts yet. You have to help me." When the woman didn't answer, Darlene kept speaking. "This ghost is coming up here. I killed him." The woman's eyes widened at this but the fact they were milky white made it hard to read any expression. "How can I stop him from getting in here?"

"You cannot," the woman replied – her voice weak and raspy, like nails being dragged across gravel.

"You can speak! Okay, great, progress. What do you mean?"

"You say you killed him, did you not? He has the right. He has the spirit right to connect with his killer."

Darlene's heart felt as if it had been encased in ice. She cursed Rosamund and her stupid herbs and turned around to stare at the living room door.

***

Idris ran across a stream, getting his paws wet with mud and water as he chased after a rabbit. Boring and pointless, but better a rabbit than a human. The running felt good. It had been a long time, too long, since he had run such distance in werewolf form. He made sure not to run into Liara's pack and was now on the side of the mountain, sniffing the air. He could almost be at peace except...

There was a flash and then a shape landed in front of him. Idris bared his teeth and snarled but he knew with a thud of his heart who it was. Vivica looked down at him, dressed all in black again, almost perfectly blending into the darkness of the forest.

"Hey, pup. Heard through the supernatural grapevine you were spending the full moon alone. You won't let your girlfriend tag along? Afraid you'll eat her?"

Vivica was the last person he wanted to see. He was enjoying the solitude. He considered this night a dry run for what all the other full moons were going to be like – alone and away from his pack. Now Vivica was pacing in front of him. She clearly wanted him again. As soon as Idris showed any interest in moving on, she had to try to get him back.

Idris growled at her and took off, propelling himself forward with his hind legs, running past her. He lost the trail of the rabbit, but at this point he just wanted to get away from Vivica.

***

Darlene watched with horror as Lucian glided through the door. He looked exactly as he had looked the night he had tried to kill her. His chest still had the blade shoved in, and the blood had bloomed across his chest. Darlene's heart was beating quickly. She had no idea what ghosts could and could not do in the physical world, especially one who used to be a werewolf.

"Hello, Darlene." His voice sounded distant.

"Lucian," she breathed.

"Are you busy? I was wondering if we could talk."
He grinned, and Darlene suddenly wanted to get out of
there as soon as possible – but where?

"Talk? Really?" Darlene said as Lucian floated
over.

She shifted away from him, and they moved in a
slow circle until Darlene had the door leading outside
against her back. Lucian's eyes had a dull rage in them
as he floated in front of her.

"I was starting to think we would never be able to
talk. I just floated along. Checking up on everyone.
Idris. Jacob. Liara. Roman."

"You need to leave," Darlene said, hoping it
sounded menacing.

"No." Lucian grinned and wrapped his hands
around the blade stuck in his chest. "You should run,
girl."

All Darlene could taste in her mouth was fear. She
spun around and flew out the door, shutting it behind
her as if that would keep him inside. She had no idea
where she would go. The image of Lucian, pulling out

the same blade that had ended his life was too much for her. Ghost or not…she had to get away…anywhere…

Darlene barreled down the stairs, twisting around the corner to get to her car. Then she smashed into something hard, as if she hit a wall. She flew back and hit the ground with a thud, the breath knocked out of her.

But when she looked up, it wasn't Lucian above her. It was Rebecca. Darlene let out a gasp and tried to scramble backward but Rebecca's hand lashed out and grabbed her, holding her in an iron-tight grip.

Lucian appeared behind Darlene – she could feel him – and his mouth was near her ear.

"Foolish to listen to a ghost, girl. Especially one who can see who is waiting outside for her. Couldn't pass up the chance."

Darlene opened her mouth to scream but suddenly there was only blackness.

Chapter Six

Idris thought he was finally free of Vivica until she leapt down in front of him again, grinning. He growled a low throaty growl and was finally about to say forget it and attack her to blow off steam when Vivica paused. She tilted her head to one side, as if she heard something. That was when Idris heard it, too.

Roman's pack.

He cursed himself for foolishly trying to get away from Vivica. She had maneuvered him directly to where Roman's pack was running. They were coming over a hill now, howling together. Idris felt a stab of pain when he realized that he would never be running in a pack again. He turned to leave but it was too late. A chorus of howls went up to let Roman know he had been spotted.

Idris turned to glare at Vivica, to get her smug expression over with, but a funny look appeared on her face. She suddenly leapt up in the nearest tree. He watched her fly through them with ease and grace. Why did she suddenly leave? There was no way that meant anything good. Vivica would usually stay around to watch the chaos she orchestrated.

Roman's pack surrounded him now. He saw Mark off to one side, avoiding his gaze. Julie, a smaller werewolf with a missing ear, was next to Mark. There was a crack of twigs and then Roman broke through the crowd.

"Idris. Fancy meeting you here."

Werewolves don't speak out loud but through each other's minds. It sounded exactly like regular talking but always gave Idris a headache after. Roman's werewolf voice was booming and loud in his brain.

"I'm running alone tonight. Let me be."

"Yes, heard Liara booted you from the pack even before you were given Exsul status." Roman's sneer was heard through his voice as he took a step toward him. "But I would rather we settle things here. Tonight. Since you broke my nose last time, we should make sure we're even."

Idris tried to back up but the pack closed in around them, clearly gearing up for a fight. Roman was huge in werewolf form, even larger than Idris. He was a vicious fighter who never lost a fight. Idris knew Roman was out for blood.

"I'm not interested."

"You don't have a choice, Exsul. It's a challenge from a pack leader."

"But not *my* pack leader. Not my challenge to accept."

"Fine. Then everyone here will agree you attacked me first then, right?"

The pack howled in response. Idris's heart fell. There would be no way out of this then.

"Vivica," Idris said. "She set this up, didn't she?"

"That's right, pup. I talked to her the other day, mentioned how you broke my nose. Surprised she isn't here – she couldn't wait to see you die."

Rage filled Idris but he let it. He didn't try to control it. If this was what Roman wanted, then fine, this is what he would get. He'd kill him tonight and accept his Exsul status. He'd turn into exactly what they wanted him to turn into – a monster. An Exsul.

Idris let out a long howl.

***

Darlene's eyes fluttered open. Her eyes needed to get used to the darkness that was around her. She could see hints of the moon flitting in through cracks of boarded up windows. It smelled like blood in here, both old and new, and her back was pressed up against some uncomfortable wall.

It took some time, but her eyes finally adjusted. Things began to take shape – open coffins and bones on the floor. The musty smell of raw earth… she was in the catacombs, beneath the graveyard at the outskirts of town.

In the distance, she could hear two people fighting but couldn't make anything out. Darlene's feet were tied together but her hands were free.

"Do not." It was a raspy voice, soft and urgent.

Surprised, Darlene turned to one side to see the drowned woman from her apartment. For some reason, she felt relief at seeing someone she knew – drowned ghost or not.

"I untied your hands. But I do not have much power left." The woman looked around the catacombs. "This place is full of angry spirits. Can you see them?" When Darlene shook her head no, the woman nodded. "Your fear is blocking them. You might want to keep them blocked. They are not pretty."

Why are you helping me? Darlene thought this to the woman, not daring to speak out loud.

The drowned woman's gaze softened, her milky white eyes looking at Darlene. "I have watched you for a long time. You are the first person in a thousand years born with the sight to see us. I longed for another human to see me. To help my despair. I watched you for three years, waiting for the day you would see me and help me. But once you saw me, I realized that you have already helped me. Your presence has been soothing and comforting in a way I did not have during the first three hundred years I have been dead. You helped me. Now I will help you."

I don't know what to say. I didn't help you at all.

"You have. But I do not have much power left. It took almost all of it to follow you when the cursed one took you here and then to untie you. But I can try to do one last thing for you."

"What?"

"The cursed one and her Maker are talking in the other room. Your boyfriend, the werewolf, is going to be killed tonight by another. The Maker helped set it up. I can try to help stop it."

"Please!" Panic shot through Darlene at the idea of Idris dying.

"I will go. If you do not live through this, I will see you on the other side, Darlene Troops."

The drowned woman faded from Darlene's vision. Darlene's breath came hard and fast as she heard footsteps coming toward her. She made sure to pretend that her hands were still tied as Rebecca came into view.

"You're awake."

"Hey, Rebecca. Mind explaining to me what you're doing?" She hoped her tone sounded casual.

Rebecca walked forward and crouched in front of her. "I'm going to turn you, Darlene. You're going to be my best friend, and together we're going to kill and ravage and maim." She smiled sweetly, her fangs tucked safely in, making her look almost normal.

"Rebecca, this needs to stop." To Darlene's surprise, Vivica walked into the room, rage across her features. "You cannot turn anyone."

Rebecca's fangs popped out, and she turned around. "Yes, I can. Last night, you gave me the book with all the information about vampires—"

"Where is that, by the way? That shit was on loan, Rebecca. I don't have a copy anymore, and Idris refused to give me Brent's notes."

Rebecca went on as if she hadn't heard Vivica at all. "And I read that stupid book, and I realized that I want more. I don't want to do this alone. I want my best friend with me. It's because of her that I have this gift." She turned back to face Darlene and smiled at her. "That's why I killed Officer Walsh for you, Darlene. As a token of friendship."

"Rebecca, you have to stop this." Darlene's fingers wrapped around something behind her – a sharp piece of wood from amongst the debris scattered throughout the catacombs. "I'm sorry that I put you in danger. I'm sorry Vivica did this to you and is a terrible Maker, by the way."

"Hey!" Vivica scoffed. "You're in no position to be insulting me."

"Why? You're going to kill Idris, aren't you?"

Something shuttered across Vivica's eyes. "I'm not going to kill him. Roman is."

"Why?" Darlene demanded. "Why are you trying to kill Idris? What is Roman giving you for setting it up?"

Rebecca stood up to look back at Vivica. "You're going to kill my best friend's boyfriend?"

"I'm not getting anything from Roman. I'm getting Idris's death, which is all I want. Do you understand?" There was a blur of dark colors, and Vivica appeared next to Darlene, gripping her hair tightly. "Idris refuses to be with me again. It's because of you. He has to die, don't you see? He has to be with me or die."

Darlene shut her eyes briefly, hoping the drowned woman would get there in time to stop it. She couldn't imagine Idris, dead in the woods somewhere, waiting for the cops to discover him.

Rebecca spoke next, sounding irritated. "Enough of this already. I don't care about Idris. I'm turning Darlene now."

"If you think I'm letting you make this bitch one of us, you have another thing coming."

The two vampires stared at each other. Darlene's hand gripped the stake tightly. She was going to have to choose, she realized, between Vivica, a bitch in heels trying to kill her boyfriend, or Rebecca, a feral vampire who was going to change her into one of them if Darlene didn't do anything about it.

***

Idris bit down on the fur in front of him. His teeth sunk in, and Roman let out a loud howl, knocking Idris away with his front paws. His nails sunk into Idris and the pain blinded him for a moment. He writhed and managed to bring his hind legs up underneath Roman and kicked with all his might.

Roman went flying off of him and landed with a thump. Idris stood up on his legs but felt dizzy. His head felt cloudy, as if he was moving in slow motion. He had lost a lot of blood during the fight. *This is it, I'm going to die here.* He took a step forward, his front legs gave out and he went down. Roman bled heavily as well but was already getting back up onto his feet.

That was when Idris saw something slowly appearing behind Roman. No one else seemed to notice it, which made Idris know he was dying. Was this the white light everyone was always talking about?

The shape began to take form. Roman was on his feet now. It was a woman. She looked terrifying. There was sea weed hanging off of her, and her eyes were pure white. Her clothes were dripping wet, and she was slightly transparent. It was a ghost. Was she actually there? Had Darlene sent her?

Idris struggled to get back onto all four legs. His snout was covered in Roman's blood. The woman floated over to them now with one hand outstretched. Roman readied to leap toward him when suddenly the woman wrapped both her arms around Roman's neck and began to choke him.

Roman's eyes bulged in surprise as the woman held on. He began to thrash around, trying to breathe. Idris realized this was his chance. With a lurch forward, he extended his claws and jumped onto Roman, who was fading fast. The woman managed to hold onto his neck through all of it. Idris brought down his claws and clamped his mouth around Roman's throat. He was going to end this now.

***

"You can't just kill someone because they aren't into you, Vivica!" Darlene cried.

Rebecca pushed Vivica back. "I'm turning Darlene!"

"You're feral," Vivica sneered. "I'm going to kill you. It was a mistake to even turn you."

Darlene's hands dripped sweat as she gripped the stake. She was worried for Idris. What if the drowned woman didn't get there in time?

Rebecca pushed Vivica back again, but this time with much more force. She spun through the air and smashed against the wall, sliding down. Rebecca then turned on Darlene and ran toward her, her fangs extended and her eyes wild.

Darlene pulled the stake forward as Rebecca leaned over to bite her. She slammed it into her chest as hard as she could. Rebecca let out a gasp of surprise and looked down at the stake.

"You…"

"I'm sorry," Darlene said. "This is all my fault. I'm sorry."

Rebecca opened her mouth to reply but her body slowly turned to dust. Quickly and quietly, her body fell apart until she was only ash on the floor. Then there was nothing. Silence filled the catacombs.

Vivica spoke first, "You staked her."

"Only because she forced my hand. And I really do not want to spend forever with you. So are you going to kill me now, too?"

Vivica shook her head. "No. Rebecca needed to be put down. She was a liability."

She walked over to Darlene and cut off the ties around her feet, releasing her. At first Darlene didn't move, eying Vivica carefully.

"Go. Get out of here. Idris is probably dead by now."

Darlene wanted to stake Vivica, too. The vampire wanted Idris so much that she would kill him so no one else could have him. Darlene felt the rage fill her and she found herself slapping Vivica across the cheek as hard as she could. Vivica looked taken aback but Darlene ran off at full speed, to get to her car and get to Idris as quickly as she could.

Epilogue

Darlene paced the room in the warehouse. She was there for a full hour waiting to hear any news about Idris, her heart was pounding. She kept thinking about Rebecca breaking away into dust, and she choked back a sob. First Lucian and now Rebecca – when would she not have to get rid of people? She had turned her best friend into a vampire and then had to put her down herself.

And Vivica wanted Idris for herself and led him to his death because she couldn't have him. Behavior of a mad woman. Darlene sat down in a chair and shut her eyes painfully, trying to keep the tears from coming.

"Darlene."

She looked up to see Liara stepping into the room. She looked exhausted. The sun was finally up and everyone had Changed back into their human forms. Darlene waited at the warehouse until Roman's pack started to filter in. She saw Idris, tattered and bleeding, as well as Roman, looking deathly still as the pack brought them both in.

With everyone finally Changing back, she knew that she would get her answers.

"Idris," Darlene gasped. "How is he?"

"He's critically injured," Liara replied, stiffly. "We're...we're doing what we can. But Roman...Roman didn't make it. He's dead, Darlene."

"Vivica set it up. She wanted Idris to herself. But Idris wouldn't be with her. It isn't his fault. Roman wanted to –"

But Liara cut her off. "Darlene, stop. Please. Stop. A pack just lost its leader. It isn't something to be taken lightly. And Roman's pack is saying..."

"What? They're saying what?"

"They're saying that Idris started it. Called for the fight. And when Roman said no, he attacked anyway."

"They are lying!"

"Darlene, they passed an emergency vote."

Her heart swooped. "What does that mean?"

Liara looked painfully sad at that moment. Darlene's heart fluttered and she knew exactly what she was going to say before she said it.

"Idris was sentenced to Exsul status."

-To be continued in Book 3-

Book Three

Chapter One

IDRIS FLEXED his hand, wanting to rip off the bandage around his wrist. He knew what was under there and didn't care if it ever healed. But he was still too injured to do much of anything and ended up lying back down in bed. When Darlene finished work, she planned to come over to help take care of him. He found himself wanting to see her more than ever.

He had been foolish to even think about Vivica in a sexual manner again. He clearly took too long to give her the answer she had been looking for, because she made sure Roman got the fight that he wanted. She wanted Idris dead, all because he wouldn't go back into her twisted arms but chose Darlene instead.

Now Roman was dead. Idris was injured and still recovering. And he was an Exsul.

He stared at the bandage again. The tattoo was healing but it itched. Of all the pain and injustices he'd suffered recently, this was the worst.

Roman's pack lied and said Idris had started the fight even though Roman declined. The truth was that Vivica had led Idris right to the pack, and Roman had started the fight. Idris would have died if it hadn't been for the spirit that Darlene had sent to him, choking Roman and allowing him the upper hand.

He lived, but the packs voted to sentence him with Exsul status in an emergency meeting. As far as everyone knew and believed, Idris had killed Roman and defied pack law.

Now he was Exsul. Like Maria.

Like Attitcus, the man who had Changed him all those years ago.

For the first time in a long time, Idris felt lost. There was no pack, no rules to follow, just a lonely life ahead of him. He had Darlene, and he was happy he was with her, but he couldn't shake the fact that she wasn't a werewolf. At full moons, he'd have to run alone in the woods. He would have no voice in anything that determined the future of packs or laws. He would never read *The Werewolf Code* again.

Out of all the injuries on his body, the one that ached the most was the tattoo. It represented much more than an injury from Roman. It represented the loss of everything he knew and held dear.

***

Darlene checked over her shoulder before getting into her car. It had become a habit since taking Rosamund's herbs to help her connect with her spirit powers. She hadn't seen the ghost of Lucian since the night he lured her to Rebecca, but she still worried she'd see him again. She was also terrified that she would see Rebecca as well. How do you talk to the ghost of the vampire you had to stake? Especially when Darlene felt responsible for turning her into both.

Her phone blinked... a missed call from the police station. They had follow-up questions for her about Officer Walsh, but Darlene played dumb on every aspect. The new person in charge of the case, Detective Curry, seemed a lot lazier than Walsh. She was banking on that laziness and hoping he'd lose interest in questioning her after this. Rebecca had killed Walsh, in a misguided attempt to get the heat off of Darlene and show her how much she valued their friendship.

Darlene shook her head, trying to clear her mind of past ghosts. She had enough to deal with. Trying to figure out her own powers was a handful as it was. Rosamund's herbs had broken down whatever mental block she had, but sometimes fear clogged her from seeing everything. Sometimes her excitement meant she saw too many spirits at once. She had a follow-up appointment to see Rosamund tomorrow night but was secretly dreading it. Rosamund's house smelled weird, and she talked in strange riddles.

But Rosamund was the only one who knew about this sort of thing. And her herbs helped. Darlene just didn't know how to properly control it.

But tonight she had bigger things to focus on. She was going over to see Idris in his hotel room, which he had stayed in for over a month now. Darlene wasn't sure where he was going to go – now that he was Exsul. He had no pack to run with and nowhere to stay. Darlene had suggested he talk to Maria about it, but that only made him furious.

She knew that Vivica had a hand in setting up the confrontation between Roman and Idris, all because he wouldn't jump back to her. Vivica had the chance to kill her as well, but didn't. Darlene figured it was because she was so sure that Idris was dead, she didn't feel like killing her after Darlene had killed Rebecca.

Darlene knew nothing about Vivica other than that she was an ancient vampire with a deadly love for Idris.

Now Roman was dead, Mark was pack leader and Idris was Exsul. Not to mention hybrid Jacob was still out there somewhere. The whole thing made her head hurt.

Darlene drove out of the bookstore parking lot. Business had slowed a little since they reopened. Darlene was eager for it to go back to how it used to be – barely any customers and a big sale about once a month. That was what she preferred.

It didn't take long to make it to Idris's hotel room. The moon was high in the sky by the time she got there. She hated walking around at night, terrified that at any moment a vampire or something else would snatch her. Darlene had technically been kidnapped twice now and was completely over it.

She knocked on the hotel room door, and Idris called for her to come in. Darlene stepped inside. He was propped up in bed, watching the nightly news. He looked like shit, although she wasn't going to point it out.

"Hey. How are you feeling?"

"Great," he mumbled.

Once Exsul status was given and Idris's condition was stabilized, he had to leave pack headquarters. Darlene took care of him here the best that she could. He healed quickly because he was a werewolf and was almost fully recovered. She figured the reason that Idris dragged his heels about getting out of bed was because he was depressed.

"How was work?" he asked as she sat on the bed next to him.

She shrugged. "Same old. Nothing exciting."

Idris lapsed into silence. Darlene chewed on her bottom lip, unsure of what to say. Trying to get through to Idris was like trying to get a rock to talk. She wasn't even sure if he enjoyed her company. He refused to talk about his new status, although his hand kept tugging on the bandage around the tattoo that marked him as Exsul.

"Are you coming over tomorrow night?"

"I have to work till close," she lied.

Even though Idris had no pack now, Rosamund had strictly forbidden Darlene from telling him that Darlene was seeing her. She wasn't sure why, and Rosamund refused to tell. Maria didn't know either. She told Darlene that the only reason Rosamund would see her was because she was Exsul. Idris still had too many close ties to Liara's pack. Darlene didn't like lying about seeing a witch, but she didn't want to piss anyone off either.

Idris merely grunted in reply, not questioning anything. Darlene wasn't even sure if he was listening. She felt frustration build up inside her chest but told herself to stop. She couldn't imagine what he was going through – and she blamed herself for it.

She blamed herself for everything these days.

***

The hotel room was silent. Idris had his eyes closed and the TV muted. Colors danced against his eyelids. Darlene had left an hour ago, around ten. She usually stayed the night, but he knew why she lied and said she had to get home. He was terrible company and he knew it, especially tonight. He just didn't know how to change it. He didn't know how to ask for help either.

He didn't know anything anymore.

Liara's face swam into view when she delivered the news of his Exsul status.

"You know this is bullshit," Idris growled, barely awake in the hospital bed at pack headquarters.

"Roman is dead, Idris. The packs have voted. It is out of my hands."

In that moment, he hated her. It was irrational and stupid. She had done nothing wrong. As pack leader, she had followed the rules, even when he knew that her heart was still breaking over what Lucian had done. And he had made it even worse, in a fit of rage, when he told her that Lucian had been involved with Vivica.

"Why are you telling me this now?" she asked, staring down at him in the bed.

Because I'm furious, and I'm taking it out on you.

"Because you should know Lucian was cheating on you emotionally, at the very least," he said instead.

Liara left, and he knew he had made her cry. He was becoming someone he didn't even like.

There was a soft knock on the door, bringing Idris back to the present. He opened his eyes, frowning. If it was Vivica, he would stake her right now. He wouldn't even hesitate. His blood started to pump and he slid out of bed, looking for something to stake her with. The knocking came again, harder this time. He would just Change and lunge, he decided, as he slowly walked over to the door. He opened the door, ready to lash out at Vivica.

But he was stopped cold by the man in his doorway. Older, with crooked glasses and gray hair. Lines around his face and eyes. Slightly hunched over. Clothes too big for him.

"Idris," the man said, making Idris's blood run cold. "Heard you're one of us now."

The man pulled up his sleeve, exposing his Exsul tattoo. Idris's head began to pound, like an explosion going off in his brain.

This man had ruined his life and left him out to dry. "Atticus," Idris breathed.

Chapter Two

Darlene made her way up to her apartment. She saw someone in the hallway and steeled herself for whatever disaster waited for her just outside her home. *I need a new apartment.* She glumly made it up the steps.

To her surprise, it was Mark. He looked up when she got to the top of the stairs.

"Hey," he said.

"Hey, you lost or something?"

"No. Wanted to see you."

Darlene felt uneasy. She couldn't explain why Mark, who had been a glorified second-in-command when Roman was alive, was still hanging around, even though Roman had pulled him off of spy duty. But he still came around to check up on her. He had seen her before the full moon as well, making sure she was okay and to warn her not to leave the apartment. Now he was pack leader, and he was still here.

"Why? What's wrong now?" she asked.

"How is Idris doing?"

"You're kidding me, right? You came all this way to ask me that? How can you show your face after you lied with everyone else about what happened that night?"

Mark looked uncomfortable. "He was going to get Exsul status anyway."

"You don't know that. So what the hell do you want? Why do you want to see me?"

"I wanted to tell you that I'm pack leader now since Roman is gone. And if you need anything at all, you can just come to me, okay? The pack has your back."

"But not Idris's, right?"

"Idris never ran with us. He wasn't part of our pack."

"But you all lied about what happened. You knew that Vivica helped Roman set up the showdown. You just stood there as Idris was about to be killed."

Mark let out a huff of annoyance. "You don't understand shit about pack life."

"Maybe not," Darlene said, taking a step toward him, anger coursing through her. "But I know when I see a shitty person. Idris told me you lost your eye to Roman back when you were trying to become pack leader. You must have been so thrilled when it all worked out well for you. Roman ending up dead, and Idris an Exsul."

Mark moved quickly, and suddenly Darlene was pressed against the opposite wall in the hallway. He didn't hurt her, but he was close to her, his one good eye staring her down.

"What else did Idris tell you about that fight when I lost my eye? Did he tell you that he knew Roman was going to take out my eye beforehand? That he could have fucking warned me about it so I could have blocked the hit? No. He and his asshole friend Lucian knew that Roman was going to take out one of my eyes to win because Roman wouldn't have been able to beat me in a fair fight."

"I—"

"Save it. You defend a man you barely know. We all know he's been throwing himself nightly pity parties in his hotel room since he was sentenced with Exsul status. You ask how I could stand by and partake in that lie? How could he have stood by, knowing I was going to lose my eye to scum like Roman? Ask him that, Darlene, and you'll get your answer from me as well."

He pushed himself off the wall, looking at her. Darlene was breathing heavily. Mark spun on the heels of his feet and stalked off, leaving her alone. She shut her eyes and heard a door open.

"Of course it's *you* again." Darlene opened her eyes to see the old woman who lived next to her and sighed. "Making all this racket. I thought I heard a man's voice."

"You did. He just left."

The old woman scowled. "I thought it was maybe my boyfriend. I got a boyfriend now, you know."

Darlene walked over to the front door of her apartment. "That's great. Have a good night."

She shut the door behind her, hoping that she cut short whatever lecture her neighbor was going to impose on her.

"Bad day?"

The drowned woman floated out of the bathroom toward Darlene. Her appearance used to frighten Darlene – the wet clothes that stuck to her body, the seaweed around her small frame and her milky white eyes rotted from being underwater for so long – but since she helped save both Darlene and Idris's life, Darlene was feeling a lot more warmth for her.

"Hey. Just…people. It's complicated."

The drowned woman nodded. Darlene still didn't know her real name or anything about her life, including how she drowned. After she saved Idris, she was gone for a few days. When she finally appeared back in Darlene's bathroom, she said she had used up her energy for a while and it took some time to recuperate.

Darlene never thought she'd be grateful about coming home to a ghost. But that was the nature of her life now – utterly ridiculous.

***

"You need to leave," Idris said as he began to shut the door.

Atticus leaned forward and shoved his foot in between the door frame and the door, stopping him.

"Is that any way to greet your Maker?" Atticus asked, his breath smelling of whiskey.

Idris felt as if someone had dumped ice over his entire body. He hadn't seen Atticus in over ten years. He moved woodenly to the side, letting his Maker walk into the room.

"What a dump," Atticus said.

Idris didn't respond. He could only stare at Atticus in confused wonder. He had tried to block out any memories he had with Atticus. There were no good memories when it came to him. He had Changed Idris and led him astray, finally culminating in a disaster of a night that led him to be sentenced with Exsul status.

"What the hell do you want?" Idris asked, trying to sound menacing but failing.

"Heard through the grapevine you were given Exsul status. Like father, like son, huh?" He turned around and gave Idris a toothy grin that made him fight the urge to punch Atticus in the face.

"No. Because we're not related."

"Not like that, no. But I'm still your Maker. A father, in some respects."

"Nothing like a father," Idris snapped, the rage building inside of him. "Absolutely nothing like a father."

Atticus started going through his things. "This dump have a mini-bar?"

"You don't need anything else to drink."

"I haven't been drinking."

"Bullshit."

Idris stormed over to where Atticus was about to open the mini-bar, and yanked him back. Atticus's eyes flashed, and he backhanded Idris across the face. He saw stars for a moment and then the taste of blood filled his mouth.

"Know your place, kid."

Atticus opened up the mini-bar and grabbed a small bottle of vodka. Idris tried to quell the rage building inside of him. If he couldn't, he would go right back to where he had started all those years ago. He turned away from Atticus as the old man chugged the bottle of Gray Goose as if it were water.

"What the hell do you want, Atticus?"

"I have an idea that I want to run by you. I need a second-in-command and naturally, you are the first in line."

"Second-in-command to what? We're both Exsuls."

Atticus moved around to face Idris. The room was small even with just Idris and Darlene in it. Two werewolves standing in it made it seem crowded and stuffy. Idris suddenly wished Darlene was here. She'd be able to take control of the situation. Or maybe pull a ghost into the room to choke Atticus to death. Either or would suffice.

"Second-in-command for my pack."

"Are you insane? You can't have a pack, Atticus. You're Exsul."

"No, I can't have a pack of non-Exsuls."

The words hung in the air.

Idris narrowed his eyes at him. "What the hell does that mean?"

"Come on, boy, are you stupid? I'm forming my own pack. Of Exsuls, of course. They can ban us from the packs, but what if we have our own pack? Who can say anything then?"

Idris's head began to ache. Atticus always seemed to be able to bring about the worst headaches.

"You're drunk, Atticus."

"So?"

"So you need to leave. I don't need any more information about this stupid idea you have. Exsuls can't form packs."

"No, they can't belong to any true pack. Nothing says that we can't form our own."

Idris slowly guided Atticus to the door. He tried to do it in a way that he wouldn't notice he was being kicked out.

"Right, well, I'm pretty sure it says we can't form our own."

"No, it doesn't, boy."

Atticus was in the doorway now, slouching over. He never could seem to stand up straight, as if the weight of being such a total and complete asshole weighed heavily on him.

"What, you brushed up on *The Werewolf Code*?" Idris joked dryly, ready to shove him out.

"I sure did, boy. A few years ago. Right around the time that Brent kid was killed. Lucian made me a copy."

Idris froze, feeling as if he had been submerged in ice again. "He did what?"

"Lucian made me a copy. Heard he went off the deep end and is dead now but hey – he was never a good guy to begin with, was he, Idris?"

"Making copies of the book is forbidden. That includes giving one to an Exsul to start his own pack."

Atticus shrugged. "Doesn't matter, does it, boy? I have a copy. Means I can make an official pack."

Idris stared at him and then moved back slightly, letting Atticus back inside.

Chapter Three

Darlene finished putting a stack of new books away and walked over to Maria's office. Her boss was hunched over her computer with a look of pure focus on her face that let Darlene know she was trying to figure out Microsoft Excel again.

"Hey," Darlene said. "I'm all finished. Mind if I head out? I have to meet with Rosamund tonight."

Maria looked up. "Ah, sure thing. How are things going with...the whole spirit thing?"

"Better. At first, I saw ghosts literally everywhere. The stress of Idris being injured shot my focus to hell." She shivered, remembering how she saw ghosts everywhere, all shouting for her attention. "But I stuck with taking the herbs and now it's more manageable."

"That drowned woman still in your bathroom?"

"Sure is. No signs of leaving either. I'm pretty sure she considers us friends. She did save me and help Idris, so I can't be upset."

Maria laughed, her giant earrings of two cats hitting against her neck. "Worse friends to have, I suppose. Good luck tonight."

"Thanks. I'm hoping Rosamund can give me more tips on how to control it. I don't know who else to speak to about it."

"She is your best bet." Maria shifted in her seat. "How is Idris?"

Darlene frowned. "I haven't heard from him today, which is weird. To be honest, he's taking this Exsul thing really hard. I feel at a loss about what to do."

Maria sighed, looking down at her own Exsul tattoo. "It will be hard for a while. No pack. Being a lone wolf. It isn't easy. But we all have our crosses to bear. Idris will find a way. I did."

Darlene wanted to ask more questions and maybe for advice, but she was already running late to see Rosamund. She said good-night to Maria and headed to her car. The sun was setting. She chewed on her bottom lip, wondering what Idris was doing. She didn't want to go over to check up on him without contacting him first. Not for the first time, Darlene found herself wondering if she should try to talk to him. She didn't want to just bring up his behavior. She wanted to talk about their relationship.

Darlene wondered if she had jumped into things too fast with Idris. They had been so caught up in each other's worlds that falling into each other's arms felt natural. But the shiny veneer of their relationship was quickly fading.

She decided if she hadn't heard from him by the end of her visit with Rosamund, she would head there afterward. As Darlene drove past Roman's Tavern, she thought about Mark. She was still furious with what he had said last night but part of her couldn't help but feel that he had a point. But the way Mark kept checking up on her…

It was ridiculous to even entertain the idea that he was interested in her. Darlene still felt self-conscious over her weight. Austin had used her. Idris might like big girls but that must be a once in a lifetime thing, wasn't it? She refused to believe someone else could like her at the same time Idris did.

And what did that mean for her? How did she feel about Mark? One eye or not, he was still incredibly handsome in a rugged way. She knew that if she was thinking about him in that manner at all then she needed to talk to Idris.

The drive went smoothly and quickly. Before Darlene knew it, she was pulling up to Rosamund's house. To her surprise, the grass, which was usually growing like a forest, had been cut and there were no code violation papers on the front door. Two cats stood in the shrubs, hissing at her, but Darlene ignored them and rang the doorbell.

She heard the noise of something falling over inside and then the sound of a woman cursing before the door opened. The same sickly sweet smell of too many candles and incense floated over to Darlene, making her eyes instantly water.

"You're five minutes early," Rosamund said.

"Sorry, want me to wait outside?"

Rosamund was an odd character who Darlene still hadn't completely figured out. She tried asking Maria for more information about her, but even Maria didn't know too much. Darlene figured that Rosamund was around her age but just looked older due to her appearance. She had features too big for her heart-shaped face, which made her look innocent. Sometimes when Darlene popped by, Rosamund would be finishing up with a client – she was a fortuneteller in her spare time, but always seemed to try to liven her sessions up with her clients. Today, she wore giant glasses that made her eyes look like an anime character and an outfit that screamed psychic hotline.

"No, don't be ridiculous. Come in, but you have to sit. I just finished up with my last client of the day."

Darlene stepped inside the home and sat down on the couch, ignoring the cats that stared at her. Rosamund's living room was decorated like a grandmother's house from a horror movie. There were strange family photos everywhere and candles of different scents lit, which always left Darlene with a headache upon leaving. Her eyes watered from the lit incense in one corner, and she sagged into the couch when she sat down on it.

Rosamund went to the room that she used to meet with her clients. It was decorated like a tacky fake psychic. Darlene knew Rosamund made some fortunes up when she thought the person couldn't handle the truth. Darlene, not for the first time, wished she could ask her more about herself, but she knew Rosamund wouldn't answer any questions.

"Do you want some tea?"

"No, thank you."

Darlene learned the hard way that her tea wasn't the run of the mill sort of tea. She didn't need to repeat that lesson. Rosamund finally came out of the side room with her fake glasses and a layer of clothing removed, making her look a little normal, except for her blonde hair, which was sticking up all funny.

"So, tell me how things are going," she said to Darlene, petting a cat that had jumped up near her. "Your aura is a lot different."

"Good different or bad?"

Rosamund frowned. "It's a mixture. You have many spirits vying for your attention. How are you handling that?"

"Better," Darlene admitted. "Although if I'm feeling very stressed, it can be too much sometimes."

"The drowned woman – is she still in your bathroom?" Darlene had told Rosamund about her the last time she had seen her.

"Yeah. She seems fond of me since...since she helped me with Vivica and helped Idris with Roman."

"Ah, yes, your werewolf boyfriend. His energy is sticking to you." She waved her hands around, looking disgusted. "He is clinging to you in a negative way, do you know that?"

Darlene wanted to defend him, but she felt low when it came to Idris. She couldn't help but feel that he was pushing her away and wallowing in his misery. Darlene understood – she knew what it was like to lose something important. Austin betraying her and coming out as gay right before their wedding was a bad memory that would forever haunt her.

Rosamund kept talking, "Where is he today?"

"I haven't heard from him today," Darlene admitted, feeling stupid – what sort of girlfriend didn't know where her boyfriend was?

"I wonder if that is why your aura is tinged with darkness."

"Do you know if he is okay?" Darlene blurted out, absolutely hating to ask Rosamund to track down her boyfriend.

Rosamund stared at Darlene for a minute before closing her eyes, humming to herself. Darlene watched, unsure what Rosamund was going to tell her when her eyes fluttered open.

"Bad energy. Not like when he was seeing his ex-girlfriend. He's with someone. Male. Bad energy all around."

Darlene's heart gave a thump. Rosamund had once told her of Idris seeing his ex-girlfriend, Vivica. But it turned out that nothing had happened between them, which is why Vivica grew furious and helped plan the death match between Idris and Roman. This could be nothing, too. Idris could take care of himself.

Darlene told herself not to worry.

***

"Another round!" Atticus shouted at the bartender, and Idris cringed.

They were out at Waterfall Grove, near Hedge Hill, at some dive bar on the outskirts of town. Idris hadn't been in Hedge Hill since Lucian went missing and found himself comforted by the sights he had known so well – back when everything made sense.

Now everything was messy. He sat in a bar with Atticus, the man who had bitten him and Changed him, not only *not* punching him in the face but an Exsul like him. Had Idris become the man he had hated? He didn't know – that concern had faded somewhere around beer number five. Beer number seven had just been put in front of him.

Atticus had a copy of *The Werewolf Code*. He could form his own pack, and it would be a valid pack. Idris tried to think of where in the book it stated Exsuls couldn't form their own pack but failed to remember such a rule. The book had always stated they couldn't form a pack with other werewolves.

But a pack full of Exsuls…?

Atticus talked Idris's ear off all night. He revealed his great plans for the pack and how he wanted Idris to be second-in-command. Atticus said that the packs of regular werewolves were antiquated. Idris tried to brush aside what he said, but Atticus refused to leave.

And now they were at this bar, with Atticus still trying to convince him to join the pack. Why didn't he just leave? That was what Idris didn't understand about himself. He should have just grabbed his stuff and left. He didn't even text Darlene – he was too embarrassed about telling her what he was doing.

Idris needed to decide what he was going to do about them as well. If he was really going to do this and become part of Atticus's crazy Exsul pack idea, Idris knew that Darlene would speak out against it. He could almost hear her now, telling him what a terrible idea it was. That he should speak to Maria. That he should let it go.

But the more he stewed about his Exsul status, he knew that he couldn't just let it go and move on. There would be no quiet bookstore in his future. Idris's family had been a mess as a child. Atticus had been a terrible replacement father, but he was still that – a father.

Idris didn't think Darlene would understand that. And it wasn't even her fault that she couldn't. Pack life would be beyond her understanding. She lived without a pack, so she wouldn't be able to understand why Idris couldn't adjust to life without one. On top of that, a tiny, dark part of him blamed her for what happened. He knew it was wrong and he never said it out loud. But how could he have a relationship with a person he blamed like that?

Idris turned his attention back to the bar.

Atticus was thoroughly drunk again. Had he even sobered up? Probably not. He had dragged Idris to Hedge Hills to meet another Exsul, who was apparently gung-ho about the terrible idea of them forming their own pack. Idris had a sinking feeling that he would end up paying for their booze.

"Are you listening to me, son?"

Idris shifted in his seat, annoyed whenever Atticus made any reference to them being anything like a real family. "Yes."

"Listen, we do this together. You're my second-in-command. This will be our pack and we can make our own rules."

"I thought we had to follow the regulated rules in order for people to take us seriously. That's why you have a copy of *The Werewolf Code*."

A look of drunken confusion crossed Atticus's face before he nodded. "Right, right. I meant once we get everything organized. Once they take us seriously and realize our pack is valid. We're going to dismantle the way packs work. Create our own methods."

Idris merely nodded, taking a sip of his beer. He was buzzed, and everything appeared slow. Another guy walked up to Atticus. The two of them slapped each other on the back by way of greeting. This man was younger than Atticus, but still looked as though he

344

had been through some hard times. A long scar from a slash trailed along his cheek, and his hair was thinning.

"Idris, this is my main man, William."

William shook Idris's hand. "You can call me Bill."

Idris merely nodded. The alcohol made it hard to focus on anything. William pulled up a chair to their small table and lit up a cigarette. He was a burly, well-built man. Even if he didn't have the scar on his face, he looked as if he had been in a lot of fights back in the day.

"So, Atticus told me a lot about you."

"Has he?" Idris asked, saying it as a statement instead of a question.

William slid a cigarette over to Atticus, which Atticus promptly lit up. He offered one to Idris, who refused. He had quit smoking two years ago and knew if he tried it once he'd be back to chain smoking.

"Your old man here has some bold ideas," William said as he signaled for a beer. "Some brave shit."

Idris grunted, taking a swig of his own beer.

Atticus laughed. "Idris here is a bit hesitant about my plan."

"You have nothing to lose, right? We're all Exsul."

"Why are you Exsul?" Idris asked, feeling bold – it was considered in poor taste to ask why one was given Exsul status.

But William showed no sign of being offended when he replied, "I killed my pack leader in his sleep."

"Why?"

"He fucked my girl."

"So you took on Exsul status for her?"

"Yeah, that's right. She was furious. I killed her, too. She was with him."

Idris's head felt as if it was spinning. "Wait, you killed your pack leader and your girlfriend because they were sleeping together?"

"That's right, pup."

Idris bristled at the casual way William called him pup, but Atticus merely laughed. Idris decided he didn't like William.

"Anyway, heard Lucian's wife is in control of the pack in Hedge Hills. What a fuck-up of a pack that must be."

"Why?" Idris challenged.

"You can't have a woman run a pack. It just isn't right."

Idris felt irritated at the thought of this Exsul scum talking about Liara in that manner. "Don't talk about Liara that way."

Atticus laughed. "Are you serious, boy? Why do you have any loyalty to her? She didn't do anything to stop you from becoming Exsul, did she?"

He was right. Idris shut up, swigging from his beer as William went on with his ramble about females in charge of packs. William was wrong about females running packs. But it didn't surprise him that Atticus was working with some misogynistic asshole.

He ordered another beer.

****

Rosamund flipped through her tarot cards to organize them. Darlene chewed on her bottom lip.

"Any ideas then?" Darlene repeated.

She had asked Rosamund for tips on how to control the spirits when stressed. In reply, Rosamund sorted through her tarot cards. She now held up her hand to silence Darlene. Darlene chewed her lip again, thinking about what she said earlier about Idris. She checked her phone. Nothing. Where in the world could he be? Normally Darlene would say it was so unlike him to make her worry like this, but lately…

She watched Rosamund handle the cards and then something moved in the shadows behind her. Darlene jumped and startled a cat. A spirit walked through the room. It was an old woman with a bored expression on her face. She looked over at Darlene with mild to no interest before walking past her.

"Did you see someone?" Rosamund asked.

"Yes." Darlene watched the old lady glide through the wall out to Rosamund's kitchen. "She's leaving. I think."

"Interesting. You really do see them when you are stressed."

Darlene glared. "What am I, your science experiment?"

Rosamund shrugged. "I was curious to see what level of stress is needed to make one appear. Try to control your breathing."

Darlene grumbled but obeyed, focusing on breathing in and out. The old woman glided back into the room, but as she made her way over to Rosamund, she started to fade out of focus, like a bad television image. As much as Darlene didn't want to admit it, Rosamund was right. By simply controlling her breathing, the spirit faded away.

When Darlene finally nodded that the old woman was gone, Rosamund appeared thoughtful. "You came here for advice, didn't you? But I'm not sure what to tell you. There is no spell that I can cast that would help you block the ghosts, not without blocking your ability as well. Perhaps choose a less stressful life?"

"A less stressful life, seriously?" Darlene crossed her arms, and the old woman started to come back into focus – she promptly tried controlling her breathing again.

Rosamund stood up and left the room. Darlene trailed after her, almost tripping over one of the cats. She stopped when Rosamund peered at one of her bookshelves before pulling a book off the shelf. Darlene felt a trickle of excitement – was it going to be an ancient book about the spirit world?

She handed it to her, and Darlene looked down and frowned. "*How to Calm an Anxious Mind* – are you giving me a self-help book?"

"Yes, that's right. You wanted your powers of the other world to be awoken and now they are. But you can't have it all perfect, Darlene. You have to learn how to control it the best you can."

Darlene sighed, slipping the book into her purse. She felt annoyed but she wasn't sure if it was because Rosamund was right – she did need to control things better – or because her life was so messy.

Maybe she was just annoyed at herself.

***

Atticus pulled up into the gas station and barely braked in time to avoid hitting a cardboard cutout of some energy drink. Idris knew neither one of them should be driving. It was stupid and ridiculous and

350

liable to get themselves or someone else hurt. But he found talking to be extremely hard at that moment. He wasn't sure how much he drank. William had been kicked out of the bar when he started a fight with another patron. Idris wasn't sure where he had gone.

Atticus tried to get out of the car but his glasses had steamed up from his constant sweating. Disgusted, Idris got out of the car instead. He felt a vague sick feeling in his stomach, the signs of an upcoming throw-up fest. He was too drunk. Why did he get so stupidly drunk with those two assholes? He was one of them now, too, wasn't he?

Idris lurched over to the pump, staring at the keypad. How did this thing work again?

***

Darlene left Rosamund's house with a headache and the knowledge that she needed to control her breathing pretty much all the time to avoid the onslaught of ghosts. The book that was given to her was on her passenger front seat. She would read it, if only to tell Rosamund that it didn't work.

Darlene's gas light suddenly went on. With a sigh, she looked for the nearest gas station and pulled in. She slid out of her car. Two drunken idiots were at the pump next to her, talking loudly, slurring their words. The scent of alcohol almost knocked her over. The car had almost hit some cardboard cut-out. *They shouldn't even be driving.* Her hand hovered over the keypad. Should she call the cops? She decided to get the license plate number on the sly instead. She shifted and pretended to be looking at the store and peered around the pump.

And froze.

***

"Idris?"

Idris had tried swiping his debit card in the machine but it was like the machine didn't want his money. Was it free gas day or something? Maybe the attendant was offering to help…how come no one pumped your gas for you anymore? He turned around to tell the attendant off when Darlene came into focus. How drunk was he? Idris swore she had to work in the shop today.

But Darlene was moving toward him now, becoming clearer and clearer. Her face was twisted into a mixture of confusion and disgust. Idris tried to think about how bad he must look but wasn't sure what to say.

"What the hell is going on?" she demanded, in a tone that meant if he didn't pick his next sentence very carefully things were going to get ugly.

"I'm getting gas." *Nailed it.*

Darlene's face went from concern to anger. "I can clearly see you are attempting to get gas, Idris. The question is why? Why are you plastered? Why are you *driving*? Why are you ignoring my texts and not letting me know you are here?"

A lot of questions. Idris settled on the one he could easily answer.

"I'm not driving."

That was when Atticus leaned out the car window. "Hey, you're not driving! I'm driving!"

"Yeah, that's what I said," Idris snapped.

"Who the hell is this?" Atticus said, his eyes falling on Darlene.

"This is my girlfriend," he replied, unsure if he had mentioned her to Atticus or not.

Darlene's face showed that she didn't care.

Her head hurt. Darlene had been trying to stay in control this entire time but seeing Idris, drunk off his ass at a gas station, in a car with some other drunk moron who was *actually* driving, pissed her off. This whole time she had been worried about him, and he was getting *drunk*? Idris seemed to have no problem moving around now that he was out of bed. Anger filled her as he tried to explain who the man in the car was.

"Darlene, he's my...he's my Maker. He bit me."

Darlene understood what he was trying to say. The idiot in the car must be Atticus. He had mentioned him a few times to her and never in any sort of positive light. And the fact Idris was now standing in front of her, drunk and bumbling, did Atticus no favors for her either.

"Why are you with him?"

"I'm changing things up, woman." Atticus answered for Idris.

"Don't call me woman," she said to Atticus and then looked back at Idris. "You cannot be in a car with him. He's drunk off his ass and it isn't safe."

"I gotta get home," Idris slurred.

Darlene was about to tell them to get in her car – as much as she didn't want Atticus near her, but he was a danger to others driving. But then Atticus leered at her, and she knew what he was going to say next was just going to make things a lot worse.

"Idris, you didn't tell me your girlfriend was fat."

The rage that filled Darlene was so sudden that all control vanished. Suddenly the spirit world rocked into the physical world. She saw a beheaded ghost floating through a car nearby, holding his own head sadly. A little girl stood in the middle of the pathway to the store, singing a lullaby. Another woman in an old-fashioned dress looked as if she had stepped out of the 1800's.

More spirits kept appearing. Some noticed Darlene and vied for her attention, calling out to her for help, asking for the woman who could see them to please help ease their suffering on the mortal plane.

It was all too much.

***

Idris, oblivious to the color draining from Darlene's face, spun around to Atticus. "What did you just say?"

"Why you getting so mad?" Atticus slurred. "Just a question."

"This is my girlfriend! How dare you talk to her that way?"

"Why are you getting so mad?" he repeated. "You always liked bigger chicks. Except for...what was her name? The vamp? Now that was a woman! Unlike this one over here."

Darlene swayed on her feet before focusing on Idris. "Idris, I can take you home and you can forget about this guy."

Idris tore his glare away from Atticus to Darlene. "I don't want to."

"What? You want to stay here with this idiot?"

"Hey! You gonna let her talk about me that way?" Atticus yelled from the car.

He was right, Idris thought dizzily, taking a step toward Darlene. She couldn't tell him what to do. He was an adult and if he wanted to get drunk with his friend, then he had every right. The way Darlene looked at him felt chafing and restrictive.

"Neither of you can talk to each other like that," Idris declared, although judging by the look on Darlene's face, it had come out more slurred than he had intended.

"Idris, stop and just get in the car. This is ridiculous. He shouldn't be driving and you need to get home."

Idris looked at her. "No."

Darlene felt a surge of annoyance, which brought on more spirits. She shut her eyes tightly, counting to five. Why was Idris being such an absolute dick right now? She clenched her fists and then opened her eyes. "Idris, why are you being like this? Just get in the car."

But Idris's face twisted, as if something inside him snapped. "I don't want to get in the fucking car, Darlene. I want to stay here with Atticus. I'm sick of you telling me what to do."

Darlene's eyes widened. "Telling you what to do? You're kidding, right?" She felt as if she was sliding down a slippery slope, but between the spirits and Idris's behavior, she couldn't stop. "I haven't told you what to do once. While you've been sitting in bed, pretending you were too injured to move, and being grumpy and barely speaking to me, I never once told you to get your ass out of bed and do something about your situation!"

Idris moved over toward her, now clearly enraged. "Do something about my situation? The same situation that you put me in?"

Darlene was stunned into silence. The fact that Idris might have blamed her for his Exsul status had never occurred to her. But it clearly had occurred to him, lying there just the under the surface of his skin, ready to explode out of him.

"Do you mean that?" she finally asked, as a surge of spirits grew behind him, all with ghastly faces that made her skin crawl.

Idris, drunk as he was, realized what he said but just shrugged. "How could I not blame you? How can we even be dating?"

Another sucker punch to the gut. Darlene felt as if he had physically hit her. She tried to control her breathing but she failed. She shut her eyes again, wishing she could vanish. Was her relationship seriously crumbling in front of a gas station?

"Fine," she declared, opening her eyes. "Fine, why don't you just write this entire thing off?"

Atticus leaned out of his car, his eyes bloodshot. "Idris, you dumb idiot, get some gas in my car already!"

Idris stormed over to Atticus, wanting to punch him in the face. Why was he such a rude loudmouth? The rage that he tried so hard to subdue came back in full force. Idris's hands were clenched and he was shaking. People were looking at them, he realized. They must be making more noise than he thought. It wasn't as if it was impossible to tell how drunk they were either. He bet someone had probably called the cops on them.

Almost in reply, the police lights rounded a corner.

"Shit!" Atticus replied, trying to turn the car back on.

Idris knew Atticus would be busted for driving drunk. He wanted to stay and laugh at him. The urge to deck him in the face vanished once the cops arrived. Idris turned to Darlene. Her eyes were wide, and she looked on the verge of having a massive freak out. He regretted, dimly, in the back of his head, what he had said, even if it was the truth. He should have worded it differently or been kinder about it. Instead, she looked as if Idris had slapped her. Had he just broken up with her?

All of a sudden, Idris felt very sick. He leaned over and vomited. The taste of the caustic beer coming back up wasn't nearly as lovely as it had been going down.

***

Darlene tried to control her breathing as the police lights came into view. She was aware of Atticus insulting her and now Idris was puking. The ghosts were still crying out for her attention. She needed them to shut up. She took a deep breath, held it and focused on a point in the gas sign. She didn't look away from that sign. Slowly, the voices began to fall silent.

That was good enough for her. Darlene gave Idris a disgusted look and got into her car. She would hit another gas station – there was one down the street from this one. Darlene started her car as the cop car drove up to Atticus and Idris. A ghost leered at her through the passenger side of the car, trying to get her attention. His throat was slit, and the wound looked horrific. Darlene felt panicked enough for a moment to hear him call out to her.

She slammed on the gas and drove out of the gas station before Idris could even stop throwing up to see her leave. Tears burned at the side of her eyes. Everything that Idris said came back to her full force. Was it over for them then? Just like that, their relationship came to a head and turned to ash. How long had Idris been sitting on all of that? They were unhealthy for one another, but Darlene didn't want things to end this way. They both deserved better. Darlene knew she had to calm down.

At least until she got home.

Chapter Four

By the time Darlene got home, she wanted nothing more than to curl up in bed and sleep for the rest of her natural life. But Mark was waiting for her. She let out a groan of frustration. Her annoying old neighbor stuck her head out to see what the noise was all about. *Doesn't that woman have a life? Doesn't she have to sleep?* The woman narrowed her eyes at Mark and then shut the door.

"What? What could you possibly want today? I thought pack leaders were busy."

Mark didn't seem to be bothered by Darlene's bad mood. "I am. But Liara called me. Warned me Atticus was back. She got a call from Idris that he was in jail to sober up. You know anything about this?"

"Why does it even matter?" she said, opening her apartment door and letting Mark in after her.

"Because Atticus is bad news. If he's in town and you know why, it'd help me out a lot."

"He wasn't in your town though, was he? He would be Liara's issue."

"How do you know that?"

Damn it. She cursed herself for slipping up and basically saying she knew that Atticus was in Hedge Hills. And then Darlene wondered why she even cared about protecting a jerk like him.

"I saw him. Idris, too. At a gas station tonight in Hedge Hills."

If Mark was curious as to why she was in Hedge Hills, he didn't ask and instead said, "That isn't good. What happened?"

She gave a rundown of what occurred, not bothering to skim over Atticus making remarks about her appearance or Idris puking next to the gas pump. She even added details about their fight, shrugging at the end when Mark asked if they were officially broken up. She was angry and could feel it boiling under her skin. When she finished, Mark looked perplexed.

"None of that is good. Atticus is a slime ball. I get becoming Exsul isn't easy but falling back into line with him doesn't make sense. Idris wouldn't do that unless he lured him in with something."

"I have no idea what it could be. I don't even care."

Mark shuffled his feet in a manner that made him look like a school child. "Sorry all of that happened. I'd say don't let it bother you, but they are jerks so…"

"Well, if you wanted more information, I'm afraid I don't have it," Darlene said, trying to ignore the drowned woman peeking out of her bathroom.

"You okay?"

"No. I have a massive headache, and my boyfriend is a dick."

An awkward silence filled the room after her outburst. She hadn't meant to be so angry with Mark. He had been near her more than Idris had lately and that counted for something, even if he didn't think too fondly of Idris. Darlene wasn't thinking too fondly of Idris lately either.

She sighed, "I just don't know what to do. With Idris and me. I feel like we never even got a chance to be a proper couple, you know? We tried and life kept getting in the way."

That was putting it mildly. After Vivica trying to get him killed and Rebecca trying to kill Darlene, life kept spinning off the rails. Darlene wasn't sure if it would ever get back on the rails again. A ghost flickered into view, and she tried to control her breathing. She didn't want a repeat of the gas station incident, not while Mark was here.

Mark looked at her, concern crossing his face. Darlene found herself staring at him out of the corner of her eye, while she pretended to be putting her purse away on the kitchen counter. He was fit and burly, a little more rugged in a way that Idris lacked. His missing eye was scarred over. Darlene hadn't even gotten to ask Idris what happened that night.

"I'm probably not the best to be talking about Idris to."

"You dislike him that much?"

"I think he doesn't know how lucky he is to have a girlfriend like you."

The remark hung in the air, and Darlene found herself blushing, pretending to be looking for her cell phone in her purse. She had always suspected Mark of having feelings for her that were a bit stronger than just friends. He always seemed to show up when she needed protection, like when Rebecca had bitten her and he had saved her.

It was ridiculous to even be considering something like that, she lectured herself. Mark sensed the change in the air and moved back to the door.

"I should go. I just wanted to see if you knew anything."

"Did you really?" She blurted it out, unsure of where she was going with it.

Mark shifted again, this time facing her. "I wanted to see you."

Darlene felt her heart skip a beat as she looked at him. Had she wanted to see him as well? The thoughts in her head became messy and chaotic. Mark suddenly shrugged, as if answering a mental question, and took three steps over to her. He put his hands on the sides of her face, leaned down and kissed her.

Shock spiraled through Darlene. Without thinking, she kissed him back. His lips were dry and rough, and his hands felt calloused. She pressed herself against him, and Mark shrugged out of his jacket. It landed on the floor with a soft noise as he kissed her again. Unsure of what to do with her hands, she gingerly embraced his big burly shoulders. As they continued kissing, Darlene daringly fumbled with his shirt, trying to take it off. He moved her hands out of the way and took his own shirt off. Her chest rising and falling quickly, Darlene admired him. His muscles were well defined and the heat radiating off of him made her cheeks flush.

Mark pushed against her again, kissing her. Darlene took a step back and was pressed against the wall just outside her bedroom. She could feel his stiffness against her leg, and her stomach swooped. Her hands ran across his chest, pressing against his muscles. His body was rough. It was driving her into a frenzy.

Mark helped to pull off her own clothes now. When their bare flesh touched, Darlene gave a gasp of surprise. He was so hot, as if he had boiling water just underneath his skin. Their lips clashed together again, and they stumbled into her room, falling onto her bed as he tore her underwear off. She heard it rip, and Mark threw it onto the floor.

Then he opened her legs and slid down in between them. His tongue moved around swiftly, expertly. Darlene moaned and arched her hips from the sudden pleasure. His coarse hands ran over her thighs as he sucked on her clit. She couldn't stop moaning and threw back her head, wrapping her legs around Mark. She urged him to keep going, feeling almost possessed by desire.

At the last second before she came, Mark pulled away and entered her in one fluid motion. Darlene's eyes opened as he sunk into her. She moaned and he bit along her neck, small almost playful bites as she rocked against him. He slid one hand down and played with her as he moved into her slowly, almost painfully so.

"More, more," she begged, whimpering with desire.

"You want more?" Mark growled, his voice husky and rough.

"Please!"

"Moan for it."

She obeyed his command, moaning for him to fuck her properly. He grinned and then shifted so her legs were on his shoulders. He moved swiftly now. Mark pulled all the way out and then slammed back into her. The force of him was strong but Darlene reveled in it. Her skin was flushed and every sense was on high alert as he pulled all the way out, waited a second just to torture her and then thrust inside her. Darlene closed her eyes, clawing at his back, moaning so loudly that she was sure her old neighbor was going to complain. She kept clawing at him as he moved in her.

But even Mark couldn't tease her forever. His breathing became ragged, and his pumps became wild. He held her hips down, grinding himself deep inside her. He moved so quickly that Darlene could feel herself about to finish. The first wave of pleasure smacked into her body and she moaned, screaming as she threw back her head, clinging to him. As soon as she came down from the first orgasm, Mark wrapped his fingers in her hair and thrust again, this time connecting with her G-spot.

Another orgasm rocked Darlene. Her eyes fluttered, and she moaned loudly, chanting his name over and over as she came. Mark came along with her this time, holding her tightly against him as he finished. His chest heaved from the effort, and their bodies clung together from the sweat they had produced.

As they finally came down from their orgasms, Darlene lay next to him, exhausted. Her heart felt like it would explode. She couldn't remember the last time she'd had back-to-back orgasms like that before. Her thoughts felt muddled and hazy. Mark was trying to catch his breath as well.

Right before she fell asleep she thought, *what did I just do?*

Chapter Five

Idris wished he could paint all the windows on his truck black. His head wasn't just pounding… he was pretty sure it had cracked open and the contents had spilled out over the course of the night.

They had finally released Atticus and Idris this morning, after Liara came to get Idris. She refused to take Atticus anywhere, which was understandable because he was a slime ball. She didn't say anything to Idris the entire drive to the hotel and had dropped him off with an air of superiority that rubbed him the wrong way.

Idris spent the rest of the morning vomiting and popping headache pills as if they were candy. He tried to remember last night but most of it was blacked out. He vaguely remembered seeing Darlene in Hedge Hills, but that had to be wrong. Why would she have been there? If she had been, she would have taken him home. He debated texting her but wasn't sure what to say. What if she had been there?

The more Idris tried to recall the night before, the more his stomach churned. He had visions of yelling at her in the gas station, of telling her all the sick thoughts in his brain. He hoped he didn't really tell her that he blamed her for his Exsul status. But if he had...Idris wasn't even sure if Darlene and he were still together.

He spent the entire morning in bed in a confused state, watching TV and throwing up. He had gone through a gallon of water already but nothing helped his headache. That was when Atticus called. Idris must have stupidly given him his number last night. Atticus wanted to meet in a warehouse on the outskirts of town, opposite of where Roman's — or Mark's, Idris supposed now — pack met. He claimed he had something great to show Idris.

And now Idris was in his car, heading toward the warehouse, with a sinking feeling in his stomach. Meeting up with Atticus was stupid. Yet he still felt compelled to do it. When he got right down to it, the thought of having a pack again was all the motivation he needed. He wanted some sort of family and some sense of belonging. Even if that meant he had to be in a pack with Atticus and William...

The other part of him knew it was stupid on almost every level. But Idris couldn't help it. Every time he stared at the tattoo on his wrist, he felt so many negative emotions that he wished the earth would open up and swallow him whole.

He had on sunglasses but the sunlight still leaked through. His entire head was in so much pain that he could cry. Instead, Idris pulled up to the warehouse. Atticus and a few others were waiting outside. Atticus looked fine. Spending a night in jail, drunk as a skunk, seemed to roll right off his back... probably because he was an alcoholic.

Idris got out of the car and walked over to the group, wishing they'd go inside so he could get away from the light before he puked again.

Atticus gave a small wave. "You're here in the land of the living!"

"Barely."

"No matter, no mind."

Atticus turned and introduced Idris to the other Exsuls who would be in the so-called pack. Their faces and names all blended together. There were six men and one woman – who wasn't Maria. There was no way Maria would get herself wrapped up in this crap, and Idris knew it. For a second, he regretted being so terrible to her.

"Anyway, let's go inside. We got a lot to discuss. Bill is setting everything up."

Idris eyed the rest of the pack. They all looked rundown and out of luck. He assumed they had been given Exsul status a long time ago and this was mostly their last hurrah before they settled in to full-time alcoholism. When Idris looked at them, he saw his future and it terrified him.

Inside the warehouse, it stunk of mold and old diapers. Lit candles were scattered around the main room. William was there, setting up what Idris could only assume was the refreshment table and probably the only reason everyone else showed up – it was all booze. The sight of it turned his stomach, and he grabbed a bottle of water instead, not wanting to even be close enough to smell the stuff.

"Everyone, get settled," William said.

They all sat in a circle on chairs that creaked.

Atticus cleared his throat. "By now, we all know why we are here. We are going to be an official pack. You know that Exsuls can't join packs. But we can form our own. We have a copy of *The Werewolf Code*." Idris reminded himself to try to find out why Lucian had given a copy to Atticus. "Now all we need to do is set up the specifics. I will be pack leader. Idris here is second-in-command—"

"I challenge that."

Idris felt a flash of annoyance as William stood up. Two teeth were missing in the grin he shot Idris. He suddenly wanted to punch William in the mouth. Instead, he leaned back in his chair and looked at Atticus, waiting for him to shoot down the challenge. Only a pack leader could refuse a challenge for second-in-command.

But instead, Atticus smiled. "Ah, a new challenger approaches."

Anger swept over Idris, fast and furious. The grin on Atticus's face made it clear that he wasn't going to shoot down the challenge. He probably promised the second-in-command to both William and Idris. Idris knew the smart thing would be to agree to have William second-in-command. But he thought about how William had become Exsul. Letting a loser like that be second-in-command would only bring dishonor to a pack already filled with dishonor.

"I accept the challenge."

The small crowd mumbled to each other. Clearly they hadn't been expecting a fight at the meeting. Neither had Idris, but the rage coursing through his body demanded it.

This was exactly how you used to be like with Atticus, a small voice in his head told him, *and why you tried to break free. But look what good that ended up being for you,* the anger in him countered back, *you're Exsul now.*

"Okay, everyone settle down. You guys know the rules. First person too injured to fight or first person to give up loses. But…" His voice went up a little higher and the crowd shushed. "Seeing as we are dismantling the old rules, I'll throw in another one. The fight can be to the death."

The crowd of Exsuls roared with surprised excitement. William's eyes never left Idris. Idris opened his mouth to say something but then shut it. There was no point in speaking up against it. Clearly, some forethought had gone into this idiotic plan. He didn't know if the rule change came from Atticus or William, but he didn't care. If it came down to killing William, then fine, he would do it.

Atticus kept speaking, "Consider this proof of our new world, brothers and sister! This is how our pack will truly be among the new world. No more will we let the babies rule!"

The chairs were pulled back and the crowd made a circle around William and Idris. William ate up the attention, grinning and taking off his shirt.

"Great," Idris said dryly. "Are we undressing to the death?"

William scowled. Idris blocked out the rest of the noise behind him. He allowed his old self to take full charge of the situation. The voice in the back of his head that was trying to pull him back into reality faded.

Idris was ready.

***

A customer tapped Darlene on the shoulder, nearly causing her to jump out of her skin.

"Sorry! Sorry, I wasn't paying attention." She scrambled quickly, shoving the book she had in her hands back onto the shelf.

As the woman asked about a mainstream book there was no hope of them actually carrying, Darlene's mind drifted back to last night. What had she been doing?

How could she have slept with Mark? And yet the more she tried to tell herself it was wrong, the more she thought of how she hadn't heard from Idris yet. She felt irritated and hurt. And when she thought of her night with Mark…her heart skipped a beat.

She had woken up in the middle of the night from a bad dream involving a spirit who was trying to get her attention. Darlene had been slowly getting used to the bad dreams but this one involved the spirit of a child who looked to be no more than ten. He was saying a name over and over to her, but it was all foggy.

Mark was asleep. He hadn't stirred when she slid out of bed and went to get a glass of water. The drowned woman was gone. Darlene didn't bother to wonder where she had gone – she probably left when she saw how busy she was getting. Darlene rested her head against the cold fridge door for a minute. The clock said four in the morning.

First, she tried to make excuses. Idris had been a terrible boyfriend as of late, Exsul status or not. Maybe they had rushed into this relationship. Maybe the baggage between them was too much. Darlene didn't even feel as if they were even together anymore, not after last night. Idris made his feelings clear. He blamed her for his Exsul status and he wanted nothing to do with her. He stayed with Atticus and told her off. In the end, did it matter?

There was no way that she could keep seeing Idris, knowing she had slept with Mark. It made her feel too similar to Austin, who had cheated the entire time and didn't tell her until their wedding day. Idris would be furious over it, but better to tell him now than later… if he ever contacted her.

***

Idris stared directly at William, who had ripped off his shirt and was trying to work up the crowd in his favor, as if they had any factor in it. Although he supposed Atticus could change the rules whenever he wanted under the guise of his new pack law. Idris's blood was pumping hard. Ever since he fought with Roman and almost lost, he had been itching to prove his mettle to himself. If Darlene hadn't sent that spirit to him at the last second …

Darlene. He still hadn't contacted her.

With his distraction over Darlene, he didn't notice William coming over and throwing the first punch. Idris barely ducked and William's fist grazed the bottom of his jaw. He wanted to yell that Atticus hadn't even given the signal but there was no point – the fight had started.

William came after him again, but Idris moved swiftly out of the way. To his advantage, William was older, nearing fifty and too full of himself to realize when he was in over his head. As Idris turned, he delivered a kick straight into the back of his legs, sending him toppling to the floor.

William hit the ground but rolled over swiftly, growling. His hands twitched with the urge to Change. Idris backed up a little as William crouched and leapt off the ground with his feet, crashing into Idris. He managed to stay upright and delivered a punch to William's back.

But William had the advantage and delivered an upper cut into his stomach. Idris let out a cough and leaned over, the world spinning for a second as William spun and kicked him in the chest. The air squeezed out of his lungs in a rush, and Idris hit the ground, gasping. William came over and lifted his leg in the air to stomp on him with his boot. At the last second, Idris swung his fist. His hand had partially Changed and his long talons slashed at William's thigh.

In surprise, William lurched backward, his hands gripping his thigh as blood oozed out. *First blood.* Idris dizzily ignored the crowd behind him. William looked up at him, furious. His face was Changing now, his nose halfway into the snout of his werewolf form as he lunged toward Idris.

Idris felt his claws go down his back, reopening an old wound from Roman but he ignored the pain. He gritted his teeth and swung, his own Changed hand barely missing William's face. William was Changing rapidly now, out of control with his own emotions as he began to fully turn into his werewolf form. Idris knew he would have to Change to stay in the battle but he hadn't Changed since he was sentenced with Exsul status.

He found himself holding back.

***

Darlene knocked again but there was no reply. She looked back at Mark, who was leaning against the bannister, yawning. She felt an urge to snap at him but buried it.

"And you're sure Liara said he left jail this morning?"

"I'm sure, Darlene. But that's all I know. We don't keep tabs on the Exsuls."

"This isn't good. He's probably with Atticus."

"Not good. But not my problem. I came here to help you dump him."

She spun around and walked up to him. He wore a jacket and kept playing with a cigarette, clearly wanting to smoke it but not wanting to turn her off.

"Stop! Stop being crass about it, okay, Mark? This is important to me. Both of us fucked up last night, and we need to make it right. Idris was a dick and I wasn't exactly calm and collected with him either. I need to make our break-up official."

Mark shrugged. "Personally, I don't care for the guy."

Darlene crossed her arms and stared at him. There was something flickering behind him – a ghost, but she didn't want to see it and tried to keep her stress levels down.

Finally, Mark sighed and relented. "Fine, fine. What do you want me to do? I don't know where he is."

"We'll wait here for him then."

"Are you serious? Fine. But I'm having a cigarette."

Darlene sighed and leaned against the bannister next to him, staring at the wall, as if Idris would magically appear. Mark gave off a lot of body heat, so much that she felt as if she didn't need her own coat. She tried to not look at him out of the corner of her eye. It still felt odd to her that she had slept with him. Ghosts were flickering in and out of her vision. She closed her eyes.

***

William lunged again, and Idris barely dodged the attack. He could hear jeers coming from the crowd. He wiped the blood that dribbled into his eye and caught his breath. He needed to Change, but he was unable to. *What if I can't change anymore?* William leapt at him, teeth barred and growling. Idris spun on his heel and almost toppled into the crowd. Atticus stared right at him, anger across his face.

"What the hell are you doing, boy? Change! Or has your time being an Exsul made you this soft already?"

Atticus always knew how to piss him off. Idris turned around and felt the rage course through him as William snarled. He was an even uglier werewolf. Idris commanded himself to Change and slowly felt it. The process was a lot slower than normal and he had to fend

William off as he did so. But once it was completed, Idris could feel his feral instinct coming back to him.

The two werewolves circled around each other now. Both were bleeding and injured. William's eyes were wild with rage. Idris was feeling *déjà vu* being back in his werewolf form and fighting for his life.

Finally, William went after him. They toppled into each other and spun across the ground, all teeth and talons. Idris felt William bite his hind leg and he kicked wildly, knocking William back, slicing along his snout.

Idris wanted it to stop. He wanted William to agree that he had won but it was clear now that it wasn't going to happen. He was stupid enough to make this a battle to the death. Idris's only hope was that William would get too injured to move and this entire fight would end.

William shook Idris off and howled loudly. Idris's head pounded and his body ached. The cheers all blended together, and it felt as if his vision dimmed. For a split second, he longed for the times where he would go over to Lucian's and Liara's for dinner and watch TV. There weren't any of these fights and nothing he ever had to worry about. That was what he missed.

William attacked again, but it was sloppy. He was running out of energy. He limped on one paw and when he finally took another step forward, Idris used his remaining strength to knock William back down.

William didn't get up.

Atticus began to cheer, declaring Idris the victor and the new second-in-command. Idris slumped on the ground and closed his eyes. It didn't feel like a victory.

Chapter Six

Idris didn't return to the hotel. Darlene eventually gave up once the sun set. She was paranoid about running into Vivica, who had been lying suspiciously low since Rebecca's death. Mark drove her back to the book store, where she left her car.

Before Darlene got out of the car, Mark stopped her. His hands on her wrist made her think of last night and what they had done together. She flinched and pulled her hand away.

"Listen, Darlene, I know you're worried about Idris, but you should consider moving on."

"Why are you telling me this now?"

Different emotions crossed Mark's face before he suddenly decided on what he wanted to say. "Because I care about you."

Darlene opened the door of his car and left, shutting it swiftly behind her. She suddenly wished, wildly for a moment, that everyone would stop caring about her so much. She knew exactly what Mark was really saying to her. *Idris is in trouble, and you should expect the worst.*

As she walked up the steps to her apartment, her old woman neighbor came up the opposite staircase. Darlene shoved down a groan. The old woman saw her, and Darlene prepared for a lecture.

"Oh, it's you. Where is your boyfriend?"

Darlene passed by her – she smelled slightly like old cheese. "Down in the car."

She realized her error with a jolt that made her forget what she was doing for a second. She hadn't meant that Mark was her boyfriend…how could she have made such a slip of the tongue?

The old woman didn't notice and launched into her own story. "My *boyfriend,* you know, is coming over later. He is quite a young thing. Guess you won't be the only person making noise tonight!" she tittered and went back into her apartment, leaving Darlene in the hallway.

"What is wrong with my life?" she asked out loud, sighing.

"A lot, man."

Darlene glanced at the ghost who had appeared in the hallway – the man who had been in her kitchen a few weeks ago. She flipped him off before going into her apartment.

***

"Ow!" Idris exclaimed, shifting uncomfortably as one of the Exsuls finished stitching him up. "Were you made Exsul for your shitty medical skills?"

"Ass," the man mumbled, glaring at him.

Idris had open wounds all over. The man tending to him, Idris thought his name was Dave, tried to seal up his wounds to help him heal faster but instead caused Idris more pain than deemed necessary. Idris assumed that he probably wanted William in the second-in-command position. Idris didn't care either way. He was hung over and wounded all over.

William had left in a rage. Idris didn't care. He still thought William was a dick. However, nothing about their fight was enjoyable. There used to be a time when Idris loved fighting, loved the Change it caused and the rush of blood to the head.

This fight was ugly and dark. Exsuls watched. They fought over a position in a pack that was only going to cause them trouble. Idris suddenly wanted to see Darlene. Were they even still dating after he blew her off for over the past few days? His head gave a throb of sharp pain, and he wanted to go home.

Atticus came into the room. The warehouse had a small room in the back that they turned into a doctor's station, minus the actual doctor. He had a beer in his hand. The smell of it revolted Idris.

"Congrats, son. I knew you could do it."

"Why didn't you call off the challenge?"

Atticus looked at Dave. "Get out of here."

Dave looked surprised and shot Idris a glare, as if it was his fault that he was being booted out. Yet he took off anyway, shutting the door behind him.

Atticus moved toward Idris. "Why are you trying to undermine me in front of my pack?"

Idris groaned. "I wasn't trying to do that, Atticus. But it was a fight that didn't need to happen. And that stupid new rule about fighting to the death...you need new rules that make sense."

"Of course the fight needed to happen! The pack needs to know we are going to dismantle the old rules. They have to recognize our pack! We're meeting with Liara tomorrow."

Idris stared. "What?"

"You heard me. Tomorrow we're going to meet with her, explain our pack. She'll vouch for us. Then we just need Mark to agree, and we'll be a verified pack in this region."

Idris scoffed, "Liara isn't going to agree to verify our pack status."

Atticus's face twisted, and he lunged at Idris, his hand wrapping around his throat, growling, "Then why are you even here, Idris? You're my second-in-command, do you understand this? Lucian gave me the copy of *The Werewolf Code* when I first became Exsul. He said to me – he said *to me* – you take this book, Atticus. You are going to need it. When I heard he was killed, it all came to me. He wanted us to form a pack together, don't you get it?"

"What? He had you hold onto a copy of it for whenever he went through with his stupid plan?" Idris rasped through the hold on his neck.

"Lucian had vision." Atticus let go of Idris's neck. "His vision was too large, though. And I told him that when he came to me to ask about what it was like living with Exsul status."

"He came to *you*?"

Idris didn't know why he was so surprised. Everything he had known about Lucian was a lie. Lucian had told Idris repeatedly that Atticus was scum, an Exsul who had his status coming to him for the constant way he undermined the packs and caused trouble.

And now Atticus was telling him that Lucian had come to him for advice and given him a copy of *The Werewolf Code*. What pack had he stolen that from, Idris wondered.

"Yes, he came to me. He knew I would see things he couldn't think of. I told him – I told him it was hard but with his book, I had an idea for the future. Something we could all work together toward. Exsuls in their own pack. A breaking of the traditional rules."

"Let me guess – he was all for it."

Atticus took a swig of his beer. "Lucian had vision. I told you that. Just too much vision. But I wish he was here, I really do, because at least he had some vision – unlike you, Idris."

Atticus spat on the floor, as if Idris disagreeing with him was so disgusting that he couldn't even begin to fathom it. The thought of seeing Liara made Idris's stomach turn. Did it turn because he was afraid of her rejecting to verify their pack status or because of the shame in her eyes when she saw him with Atticus?

"I'm the closest thing you got to a father, kid," Atticus said. "And you keep letting me down."

Idris thought of his parents. His home life had been trash, which was how he had met Atticus. After he was Changed, he ran away from home. He didn't know what happened to his parents. As much as he hated Atticus, he was right. He was the only family he had.

"Fine. I'll be with you when you see Liara."

***

Idris couldn't work up the nerve to see Darlene until the next morning. He wanted to see her before the meeting with Liara. It was important to him to set the record straight with her. His hangover was gone but his body was wrecked. *I really need to stop fighting for a while.* He pulled up to her apartment.

Idris wasn't sure how furious Darlene was going to be with him. He felt confident now that he had seen her at the gas station, so he knew that she had seen him completely drunk and throwing up. His memory of the events of the night there were blurry, but he knew that he said some terrible things, practically breaking up with her. It didn't explain what Darlene was doing out of town, but it wasn't as if Idris had been in any condition to ask her.

Idris got out of the car and headed up to her apartment. He heard a door shutting and saw the old woman next to Darlene's apartment. He sighed. The woman only ever complained to him. Maybe this time, she'd just walk by him.

She didn't, of course. Idris could never remember her name. Maybe he never knew it. In any case, she stopped and looked at him.

"If it isn't the love birds," she said. "So noisy. Did you get those marks from your lovemaking last night? It was a lot quieter this time, at least. Did the other man join in?"

"Excuse me?"

"I said to Darlene when she got home last night the same thing – I have a boyfriend, too, so she won't be the only one making noise."

"Making noise?" Idris felt like he was in another conversation entirely.

The old woman winked. "The other night! I saw her with this one-eyed man. All that moaning after they went inside!"

She laughed and walked off toward the steps. Idris found himself staring at her door in confusion. Was this woman suggesting that Mark and Darlene had sex?

A sick feeling rolled across him that had nothing to do with his own injuries. The blood in his head began to pump, creating a headache so sudden that he wanted to scream. Darlene had slept with Mark. Mark had swooped in and slept with his girlfriend. Why, because he was Exsul?

He went up to Darlene's door and banged on it loudly. Blind rage filled him. He needed to get to the bottom of this.

***

Darlene woke up, groggy and confused. Someone was banging on her apartment door. For a minute, she thought police officers were knocking her door down to arrest her. After Rebecca killed Officer Walsh, she was concerned that they would come after her next. But whoever they put on the case was seemingly the laziest person alive. There hadn't been a peep from the police after an initial round of questioning over Officer Walsh's death. Rebecca said she had killed him to make Darlene's life easier – and Darlene knew she was a bad person for admitting to herself that it *had*.

But then someone yelled out her name and, with a start, she realized it was Idris. Darlene threw the covers off and ignored the drowned woman, who had returned last night without a word. She opened her front door and gasped.

Idris looked like a wreck. He was covered in bruises and his upper lip was cut open. He looked as if he had been in another fight, which wasn't what surprised Darlene. It was his eyes. They were big and wild, an anger inside of them that made her take a step back. In the surge of emotions she felt, she saw a flicker of a spirit behind her – Rebecca. The last thing she needed right now were spirits of people she knew coming to bother her.

"Are you fucking Mark?" he spat at her.

Darlene was stunned, wondering how in the world he had heard of that before she had gotten to tell him.

"Tell me!"

Darlene flinched and met his gaze. "I slept with Mark. I wanted to tell you the other night, but you never came back to the hotel."

"So I fall off the map for a few days and you fuck another man?"

He stepped inside her apartment. Rebecca floated into view behind him. Darlene wished she wasn't seeing her now, of all possible moments. The pain at seeing her friend was fresh and it felt as if a barely healed wound was being ripped open again.

"Idris, we need to talk, but I cannot talk to you like this."

Her tone was so measured that it only made things worse. He clenched his fists and let out a growl, knocking the lamp off her table, which shattered on the floor. Darlene tried to control her breathing, but Rebecca didn't move away. She moved next to Idris as if to say *give me the signal.*

"He voted to sentence me with Exsul status! How could you do this? How could you think this was okay?"

"Idris, you need to leave."

"Why, so you can fuck him again?" he sneered.

"You broke up with me. You blame me for your Exsul status. You can't crash in here and tell me how things are going to be!"

Idris was fuming. "You two deserve each other for what you did to me."

Darlene gave a small nod to Rebecca. Rebecca floated up in the air, her feet dangling underneath her, off the floor. Darlene could see the stake she had driven into Rebecca's chest from this angle. Idris was still yelling. Darlene wasn't innocent, but she didn't deserve to be talked to this way. Talking to Idris like this, in whatever weird head space he was in, was not going to do either one of them any favors.

Rebecca pulled back her hands and suddenly pushed Idris. Darlene didn't know if it was from her vampire strength or ghost strength, but Idris lost his footing and practically flew out the door. Rebecca then shut the door without touching it. Darlene heard it lock.

Idris began to yell through the door. "What the hell did you just do? Did you just use some spirit on me? This conversation is not over!"

"You owe me a lamp!" Darlene shouted in annoyance.

Rebecca stood by the door. She was fading. Darlene knew if spirits used too much power that they would fade from this plane and have to recharge. Rebecca used a lot by getting Idris out of the apartment, but she seemed to stay by the door in case Idris tried anything else.

But Darlene's quip about the lamp seemed to take the life out of Idris. She heard him leave. Rebecca waved at Darlene before slowly fading away. Darlene watched her go, her heart seemingly going with her. Too much had happened and all too quickly. Darlene ran over to her window and saw Idris getting into his truck, slamming the door shut and driving off wildly.

She wanted to tell him what was going on, but not like this. And why did he look like that? She knew that Atticus was no good, but there seemed to be more going on than Darlene could even imagine.

Darlene had the sudden urge to cry but she shoved it away. She was an adult and needed to act like one. Crying would do her no favors.

But she still felt like doing it anyway.

Chapter Seven

When Idris met up with Atticus at a bar in Hedge Hills, he was still fuming. He had the desire to punch someone in the face since he found out about Darlene and Mark. The only thing Idris could see was Mark putting his hands on Darlene and having his way with her.

And Darlene was so calm about it. She took his anger in stride and wouldn't even discuss it with him. She claimed she would speak to him when he calmed down, but Idris wasn't sure if he was ever going to calm down. He wanted to beat Mark to death.

Idris knew he had yelled at Darlene that night and told her off. Logically he knew they weren't even together anymore. But he ignored that voice and let himself be angry.

How could it be that the only person who hadn't lied to him was Atticus? Atticus had always acted the same, no matter what was going on. Yes, it was terrible and he sucked as a person, but what did it say about

Idris's life and the people he surrounded himself with if Atticus was the only one who was true?

He shook the thoughts from his brain. Idris didn't want to meet Liara at a bar, but Atticus would never pass up the chance to drink. No matter what, Idris felt that he knew Liara. He wasn't sure how it was going to go, but the nagging voice in his head said that she was going to stare at the two of them as if they were mental.

Idris walked into the bar and looked around. Atticus sat in a booth in the corner, drinking a beer. Idris walked over and ignored the pain in his body. He knew he looked like hell. He felt even worse. Atticus patted the seat next to him and Idris slid in.

"She'll be here soon," Atticus said by way of greeting. "Now, you let me do the talking. I got it all figured out."

Idris nodded. He thought about the night that Atticus had bitten him. They were drunk. Idris was young. Atticus told him there was a way Idris could be invincible, unstoppable. Idris was foolish enough to believe him.

His thoughts were interrupted by the appearance of Liara. She was dressed professionally, in a pants suit that meant she was offering this meeting the respect it didn't deserve. Atticus was dressed sloppily, and Idris looked like trash, too. Liara walked over to the table, her eyes wide with the surprise of seeing Idris there.

"Have a seat," Atticus said. "Want a beer?"

"I'll take a water, thank you."

Atticus frowned but ordered a water anyway. Idris ordered one as well, which only deepened the frown. Idris ignored it.

"How are you?" Idris asked.

Liara's eyes flicked away from Atticus to look at him. "Fine," she said stiffly.

Idris felt a twinge of annoyance coupled with disappointment. He foolishly hoped that Liara would look at him the same way that she did before... as friends. He remembered how he blurted out that Lucian was emotionally involved with Vivica. After that, he couldn't meet her eyes anymore.

"May I ask what this is about? Normally, I wouldn't agree to a meeting like this but because of our history…"

The waters were placed down in front of them and Idris took a big swig, wanting to blurt out everything. Instead, Atticus detailed his plan for his pack to be granted official pack status. The pack would consist of Exsuls only. They would make their own rules. Lucian had given him a copy of *The Werewolf Code*, which made Liara blanch. As he finished up his proposal, Idris could tell by the look on Liara's face that she was quelling her own outrage.

He didn't expect for her to turn it on him, however.

"Idris, you agree with this nonsense?"

Liara looked directly at him, her eyes ablaze with irritation and hurt. For some reason, the fact that she looked at him made him angry.

"What the hell does that mean?" he growled.

Liara's features showed surprise before she collected herself into a cool gaze that showed nothing. "It means that I can't offer you my support. The rules on packs and Exsuls are clear."

At this, Atticus launched into his evidence of how the text never stated that Exsuls cannot form packs.

Liara cut him off and held up her hand. "I'm not interested. Is this the only reason I was called out here?"

Idris felt the anger rolling off of Atticus. He tried to quell the conversation before it got out of hand. "Why won't you support us?"

Liara's eyes landed on him again, white hot fury crossing her face. "And you – after what this piece of shit did to you. You agree with this nonsense. You are all Exsuls for a reason. There is no pack status given to Exsuls."

"Your husband was going to become Exsul," Idris said before he could stop himself. "So you're in no position to treat us this way."

Liara's voice lowered. "If we weren't in public, I would scrape your eyes out myself, Idris. You two are pathetic. I'm done with this conversation. You do not have my support. You two deserve each other."

"Bitch," Atticus snarled.

Liara took her glass of water and threw it on him. The glass didn't explode but smacked him in the face, spilling water all over him. She was already out of the bar by the time Atticus collected himself. He started complaining loudly, wanting her to come back so they could fight.

Idris watched Liara depart and wondered who he had become.

***

Mark paced Darlene's living room, looking at her from time to time. She was surprised when he came by. She had texted him, explaining what had happened with Idris and he came right over. Originally, Darlene thought he was overreacting, but it seemed that he had his own story to tell her.

"Will you stop pacing? You're making me nervous. I've already had to deal with Idris and the ghost of my dead friend today. I don't need you freaking out on me either."

Mark stopped and promptly sat down. "Sorry."

"You want something to drink?"

Mark shook his head, and Darlene sat down next to him on the other side of the couch. The drowned woman peeked out of the bathroom. Darlene wondered where she was during Idris's outburst.

"Listen, I hadn't planned on dropping by, but I got a call from Liara."

Darlene listened as Mark told her what Liara had said about meeting up with Atticus and Idris. When he finished, she felt numb all over.

"He agreed with Atticus about this? He thinks Exsuls should have pack status?"

"I get that he's feeling lost. But Atticus is bad news. He was sentenced with Exsul status for non-stop violence against pack members. He's a loose cannon. He can't have his own pack. He's citing that our book doesn't state Exsuls can't form their own packs. Even if it is true, no one is going to verify them. Atticus brings out the worse in Idris."

"What are you going to do?"

"We can't do anything yet. But if they take things too far…"

Darlene felt a sickening feeling in her stomach. She could only picture the packs moving in on Idris and the others, ending the pack before it truly began.

"If he comes around," Mark said. "Try to talk some sense into him."

"I doubt he'll come around."

Mark sighed and stood up. "I should go. I just wanted to tell you this in person. If you feel like you're in any danger, call me. I'll come find you."

Everything had been so crazy since they slept together that Darlene didn't have any time to think about where they stood on things. Clearly, she and Idris had broken up. But did that mean that she and Mark are dating? Darlene wanted to bring it up but felt unsure of what to say. The worried look on Mark's face over the situation with Idris made her hesitate.

He walked over to her. "Liara's pack is keeping an eye on them. Just in case. If you want me to put protection here…"

"No." She shook her head. "I'm fine."

Mark paused and nodded. He leaned down and kissed her gently. His lips were rough, like before, and warm. Darlene responded to his kiss, kissing back softly at first and then harder.

Before it could go any further, Mark broke away and mumbled a good-bye, shutting the door behind him. Darlene watched him go.

"Hey," she said, turning around to the drowned woman. "Do you think you can do me a favor?"

The drowned woman floated out of the bathroom and nodded, her milky eyes staring at Darlene, questioning.

***

Idris stared at the hotel room ceiling. The television was playing some terrible daytime court show. After Liara left, Atticus was so worked up in a rage that he left as well.

"I'll come up with something," he said before departing.

Idris watched him go, feeling faintly sick. He came down from his anger. It seemed that he was always coming down from anger lately. He regretted the conversation with Liara, but was still irritated that she refused to support them. She was in no place to throw stones – not after what her husband had planned.

Idris found himself idly wondering about Jacob. The werewolf-vampire hybrid hadn't made a peep since the night Lucian was killed. He wondered if the Change had failed and Jacob had died somewhere in the woods. That would be for the best.

Of course, thinking about that night brought Darlene back into his mind. He hadn't heard from her since their fight this morning. Part of him wanted to find Vivica and sleep with her, but he couldn't even do that. She had led him to Roman and organized the fight that contributed to his Exsul status.

Idris ended up lying there instead. His emotions swirled around him, switching from anger and dislike to sadness and pain. A knock sounded from his door... did he just imagine it? But it came again, so Idris slid off the bed, his body protesting every moment, and opened the door.

Darlene stood in front of him. She looked pale and tired, as if she had been stressing out. Idris found himself looking at those beautiful blue eyes he was so charmed by and told himself to feel nothing for her. It wasn't easy.

"Why are you here?"

"I wanted to see if you were okay."

"With what? You cheating on me?"

"No. With whatever you are doing with Atticus."

Idris stiffened. "That's none of your business."

"I'm sorry I hurt you. But we had that fight and we pretty much broke up. I didn't mean to hurt you. But you hurt me as well. The timing for us being together…and our history…it just isn't right."

Idris didn't know what to say. Part of him wanted to shut the door in her face but something made him stop.

Darlene went on, "I'm not asking you to forgive me. But I am coming to you because I am concerned. I know you had a rough time with Atticus. I heard about you guys trying to form a pack."

"Who told you that? Mark?"

Darlene ignored his jibe. "I just don't want you to get in over your head, Idris. I know this Exsul status is hard –"

"No. No, you don't. You do not know how hard it is. And you know what makes it even worse? That I lost it *over you*."

"Idris, please—"

He slammed the door so hard the frame rattled. His breathing came hard and fast, and he found himself pacing his hotel room. Idris looked out the window to see Darlene walking away back to her car. He felt as if he had tunnel vision. He thought about her sleeping with Mark.

Idris knew he had been a bad boyfriend. He had been so roped up in his own problems that he never asked about Darlene and what was going on with her. He wallowed in his misery over the Exsul status and didn't bother talking to her about it.

But she had slept with Mark, of all people. He couldn't forgive her.

His cell phone rang. It was Atticus.

Chapter Eight

Darlene had been more upset by Idris's outburst than she had let on. Mark had given her his address, and thirty minutes later she pulled up to a duplex on the opposite side of town.

He let her in and she went willingly. In an effort to ease her mind, they slept together again. Darlene threw herself at him the moment she stepped inside, craving his touch and the rough comfort he brought to her. Idris's words faded as Mark entered her, mumbling dirty words in her ear, making her blush. He ravished her, telling her how much he wanted her from the moment he saw her.

Darlene knew he wanted her. With each thrust, Mark looked into her eyes as if she was the only woman in the world. It gave her sunshine in her dark moments. She knew they were doing their relationship backward – the more Darlene slept with Mark, the more she fell for him. But she didn't care.

She was on his lap, straddling him and rocking against him as he buried deep inside her, tugging on her hair. Mark moaned her name and expertly moved his fingers as she rocked against him, bringing Darlene to an earth-shattering climax that blocked everything else out.

Darlene's attraction to him was raw and animalistic. Their sex was unlike any she had had with a man before. It took her off the planet, to a world where the only thing she wanted or cared about were Mark's hands on her.

His face was buried in between her breasts as he came, grunting loudly, thrusting deeper in her as she rode off her own orgasm on his lap. They collapsed against each other in his bed, the afternoon sun slanting lazily into his bedroom. Their fingers entwined together as they collected their breaths.

In that moment, nothing else mattered.

***

The last thing in the world that Idris felt like doing was going out to the warehouse. But something in Atticus's voice gave him pause. As he pulled up to the front, the only other car there was Atticus's. A bad feeling settled in his gut.

Idris stepped into the warehouse. It was almost pitch black inside, with the afternoon sunlight peeking through sections of the broken windows up near the top. *If we ever were a real pack, I'd change us always having to meet in warehouses.*

"Atticus?"

There was no response. Idris walked past the table that served as the beer stand when he had the fight with William. Beer bottles were all over the place, some smashed against the floor. Broken glass cracked under his shoes. William was still recovering from his wounds, Idris recalled as he looked at where they had their fight. Idris hoped he didn't have to see him again for a long time.

"Atticus!"

This time Idris heard a muffled noise. Frowning, Idris headed toward where Dave had patched him up after the fight. He opened the door and stepped inside – and froze. It felt as if he had been hit with a mallet.

Liara was in the middle of the room, tied to a chair with tape over her mouth. Her eyes widened when she saw him, and she made muffled noises.

"What the fuck?" Idris exclaimed, walking over to her.

"Don't touch her, boy," a voice said lazily.

Idris spun around and saw Atticus sitting in the other corner. He looked slovenly and had two long scratches down the side of his face.

"What the hell is this?" Idris exclaimed.

"We're going to handle this. Together."

"Handle *what*?"

Liara made more noise now, muffled, trying to get Idris to look at her. He glanced down at her and saw panic in her eyes. She had a bruise forming on her forehead, as if she had been smacked there. The familiar feeling of rage filled him as he turned to stare down Atticus.

Atticus shrugged. "We're going to kill her."

***

Darlene almost drifted off to sleep when she lazily opened her eyes. The drowned woman was staring at her.

Darlene cursed and jumped up slightly in bed, clutching her chest. "You scared me!"

Mark looked over at her as if she was crazy. He opened his mouth to ask what was going on but then understood that Darlene was talking to a spirit.

"I am sorry. You told me to come get you if I found Idris doing anything bad."

Earlier on, she had asked the drowned woman to follow Idris and if anything happened to alert her right away. After Darlene's meeting with Idris at his hotel room, she was happy she had done so.

Now Darlene was nervous to ask what had brought the drowned woman back so soon. "What is it?"

"Liara is an Asian female, correct?" When Darlene nodded, she went on, "She is being held hostage at a warehouse with Atticus and Idris. Atticus plans on killing her."

"Oh my god." She started jostling Mark. "Mark, get up. Get up, we have to do something. Atticus is going to kill Liara."

That got Mark up almost instantly. He shot out of bed and grabbed his jeans, tugging them on.

Darlene turned back to the drowned woman. "Which warehouse? The city outskirts have so many." The recession had taken out a ton of businesses, leaving the warehouses like old fossils.

The drowned woman gave her an address. "Should I return to him?"

"Do you have enough power? Listen, do whatever you can until you know you're going to fade away and then come back to me before you do, okay?"

The drowned woman nodded and faded away. Darlene turned to Mark, who had a grim expression on his face.

"Let's go," he said.

***

"Are you crazy? We aren't going to kill Liara!" Idris shouted. "Why the hell would we do that?"

"Why wouldn't we do that, boy? You've been refusing to see the big picture this whole time! I should have made William my second-in-command. She'd be dead already."

Idris clenched his fists. "You're crazy."

"No, boy, you are. You think I was going to let this pack leader tell us *no*? Especially *her* – after everything Lucian has done? You think that would be acceptable to me? No."

"What the hell would killing her accomplish?" Idris snapped, moving himself in front of Liara to fend him off if needed.

"It sends a message, Idris. That we aren't going to take no for an answer. That Exsuls deserve their own pack. Isn't that what you wanted? You didn't want to roam alone. You couldn't handle it. You knew that about yourself. That's why you came to me, agreed with me, and became my second-in-command. You knew that about yourself."

Idris's heart pounded quickly. He hated that Atticus was right. He did want to belong. The thought of not belonging to a pack was almost the same as suicide. Being a werewolf was never easy, but the pack had centered him.

Or had Lucian been the one to center him?

Life with Atticus had only brought death, destruction and rage. It was a vicious cycle that Idris had settled into. One that he had managed to break free from with Lucian's help. And now he was right back where he had started. Finding out the truth about Lucian started a snowball effect and landed Idris right here – alone, with Atticus.

Idris unclenched his hands, breathing heavily through his nose, staring at Atticus. "You're right. I wanted a pack. Exsul status – it's not something I could ever do."

Idris thought of Maria, who hid herself from the other werewolves and opened up a bookstore. She had managed to find a life for herself away from pack life. It was quiet, but it was a life. He had been stupid not to listen to Darlene and go talk to Maria for advice. He had been stupid about Darlene in general. He liked her a lot, more than he liked anyone else, and he had pushed her away and wrapped himself up in a cocoon of pity and hate. No wonder she fled to Mark.

Atticus relaxed, thinking that Idris agreed with him. "I knew you'd see reason—"

"I do see reason. I've been an idiot. A fool for falling into your life of lies and stupid ideas. I don't care if I'm your second-in-command. I don't care if you have a copy of *The Werewolf Code* from Lucian. What happened to the pack he stole that book from, huh? What other lies did you and Lucian cook up together?"

Atticus narrowed his eyes. "Get out of my way, Idris. I will show you reason. We will dispatch of Liara together."

"No. I challenge you for control of your pack."

The words hung heavy in the air. Idris had never once actually fought Atticus. They had fought together loads of times, taking down idiots in petty fights and stupid bar bickers. Atticus was fierce and crazed. But Idris was not going to let him lay a finger on Liara.

Atticus stood up slowly, his hands twitching with the urge to Change already. "You sure about this, boy?"

"Yes. I'm dismantling the pack after you die. It's over, Atticus."

"We'll see about that," Atticus said and he lunged.

***

"You need to drive faster," Darlene complained to Mark as they rounded a corner.

"I really don't want the cops on my ass. Won't that slow us down?"

"Liara is going to be killed! If…if Idris goes through with this…he won't ever forgive himself, do you understand?"

"It won't matter, because if any harm comes to her, I'll kill him myself."

Darlene glared at him. "Enough. We have to save Liara and Idris."

Mark's fingers tightened around the wheel as he turned a corner so sharply that Darlene was forced against the window. "So it's true then. About the ghosts and you."

"You didn't think it was?"

"There were rumors…"

"You should have asked."

Something flickered across Mark's face – a memory. "When Idris fought Roman…suddenly, Roman stumbled. Like he was out of breath. It cost him the fight." His eyes darted to Darlene. "That was you, wasn't it? Through a ghost?"

Darlene nodded. "Yes. The same one is in the warehouse. If she sees a chance, she will do what she can to help. But her power is finite. We have to hurry."

"How'd you get a ghost on your side?"

"I just talked to her. Your packs might want to try that sometime instead of fighting all the time."

The warehouse was at the end of a dirt road. The sun was low on the horizon now and the air was chilly as the car pulled to a stop. Darlene flew out of the vehicle, not even checking to see if Mark was following as she ran up to the warehouse. She saw Idris's truck and felt relief at knowing he was still here. She hoped she wasn't too late.

Darlene opened the door to the warehouse and stepped into the main room. It was dark. She fumbled for a light switch and dim, flickering lights turned on. She barely had a moment to take in the smashed beer bottles and stench of pot and despair before a door in the back flew open and someone was being kicked across the floor.

"Idris!" she screamed.

Idris looked up from the floor, slightly curled up in a ball. His nose was bleeding, and his eyes were wild. He looked shocked when he saw her.

Then a werewolf came out of the back room. It was massive – Darlene had never seen one this large before, not even Roman. Blood covered his snout, and his red eyes fell on Darlene.

"Darlene, run!" Idris yelled.

Atticus ran on all fours toward her. Darlene froze. His teeth were long and jagged, his mouth opening to rip her face off. There was another flash, and Atticus was smashed to the floor. Mark, now in werewolf form, had taken Atticus to the ground. The two began to fight. Darlene tore her gaze away from the fight and looked at Idris.

"Change!" she shouted before heading to the back room.

She heard snarling and growling and yelps of pain but refused to look back. She shut the door behind her and turned around to see Liara tied to a chair. Liara's eyes widened with surprise at seeing her. Darlene ran over to her, checking her ties.

"Hey, we're going to get you out of here, okay?"

Liara mumbled something, and Darlene ripped the tape off her mouth. Liara gasped for air. "Idris!"

"He's fighting with Mark against Atticus. Liara, there isn't any time. Do you know of anything in this room that can get through this rope?"

Liara shook her head, her hair flying in front of her face for a moment. "No. I don't know. There are medical supplies in that drawer."

Darlene followed where Liara had pointed with her head. She heard a sickening snap outside and a howl that sounded too similar to Idris for her own liking. Darlene went over to the drawer, opening it and fumbling through it. She found a pair of medical scissors and a dirty knife – she didn't want to know from what.

Darlene rushed back over and got to work on setting Liara free.

***

Idris stepped forward. The world swung around him in varying colors. He was pretty sure his old wounds had reopened when he had Changed into his wolf form. He was losing blood. One of his back legs had been broken and every time he moved nothing but blinding, white hot pain shot through him.

Mark had Atticus clamped by his throat and was trying to grind his teeth through his neck. Atticus was snapping and howling. He was in no better condition than Idris but wouldn't stop. His rage fueled him. He wanted Idris dead.

Idris knew he had to finish it. He had to kill Atticus and be done with it. But his body couldn't operate correctly. Every time he tried to move, the ground moved from under him as if he was on a boat.

The back door opened, and Darlene and Liara spilled out of it. Darlene looked panicked. Liara looked angry. Idris knew what was coming next and tried to distract Atticus. He moved in front of Atticus and swiped with one of his paws. It was messy and barely connected – but it hid the fact Liara was Changing behind him.

***

Darlene watched Liara Change. She was fast, like lightning, as she leapt into the fray, jumping directly on top of Atticus. The male werewolves always seemed to be a little too slow for their own good. Liara was very fast. Mark released his grip on Atticus's neck as Liara sunk her sharp claws from her front paws into his back. Atticus howled.

The drowned woman appeared next to Darlene, looking at her curiously. "May I be of assistance?"

"What? Sure. Sure! Whatever you can do!"

The drowned woman nodded and vanished again. Atticus managed to get Liara off of him. The element of surprise was gone as he spun around. Darlene screamed. He was going to clamp down on Liara's neck and kill her. Idris lunged, clearly using the last of his remaining strength to strike.

The drowned woman appeared as Idris lunged. Idris landed on Atticus's back. There was a disgusting and horrifying noise of a spine snapping. At the same time, the drowned woman threw herself in front of Liara. It was as if Atticus had hit a wall. The drowned woman had made herself *corporeal*, Darlene realized with a shock. He connected with the ghost and went still.

Darlene held her breath but there was no more movement.

Atticus was dead.

Chapter Nine

Idris's vision became clear. He saw the hospital bed and the ceiling. The TV was playing bad daytime television. And then he saw Darlene. She stood up when she realized he was awake.

"Hey," she said softly.

Idris's entire body was numb with pain. It had been a day since the attack on Atticus. He had opted to go to the hospital. Mark was two rooms down. He was being released later on today, Idris had learned, but his own injuries weren't that simple. Broken ribs, broken nose, and broken leg – he was a mess.

He felt like a mess on the inside, too. He felt like an asshole.

"Hey."

"How are you feeling?"

"Terrible," Idris said.

"They're about to let Mark go. I just wanted to see you."

"Thanks. How is Liara?"

"She's okay. She was here earlier. She wanted to see you but you were out cold."

An awkward silence filled the air. Idris wanted to shift nervously but his body wouldn't allow it.

Instead he heaved a sigh. "I'm sorry, Darlene. I really messed everything up. I'm sorry."

"I know. You were lost. Are lost, still…maybe. I don't know." She looked exhausted. "But I know you're sorry. I am, too. For what I did and how I treated you."

"I didn't treat you so hot either."

She gave a sad smile. "Maybe so."

There was silence again. Idris wanted to say more – to try to explain himself and his behavior to Darlene. But now Atticus was gone. It didn't matter. He had lost himself to his Maker and had ended him. The only thing Idris could try to do now was redeem himself.

"Well, I should get going," Darlene said. "I'll talk to you later."

"Later. And hey – thanks. For everything. Saving Liara. Getting your ghost friend to help us out…again."

Darlene smiled a little and waved, leaving the room to go see Mark. Idris watched her go, feeling sadness mingled in with relief.

He had to focus on himself now. He had a lot of work to do.

-To be continued in Book 4-

Book Four

Chapter One

DARLENE DREAMT of immense power. She controlled any spirit that passed by her. They would bend to her will and do whatever she requested. The thrill of it made her feel more alive than she ever had before, even if she was in the world of the dead.

Then someone tugged on her skirt. Darlene looked down to see a young boy. She had seen him before, in a dream over a month ago, calling out to her. He looked normal enough, with blond hair cut close to his head and big blue eyes. He wore a torn, muddy soccer uniform.

"He's coming," the boy warned.

Darlene frowned and reached out for him, but he slid through her fingertips like water. He faded away, leaving her alone.

Darlene's eyes opened slowly. A loud noise could be heard from outside her apartment. She could hear people talking. Groggily, she looked over at her alarm clock, which showed it was a little past eight in the morning. She had hoped to get another couple hours of sleep in before the start of her shift at the bookshop.

She rubbed her eyes, thinking back to the dream she had. The dreams were growing more vivid lately. Darlene was starting to think they weren't even dreams but something more. Maybe she truly was in the other world while she slept. She decided she'd have to see Rosamund and ask if that was even possible.

Darlene sat up and was surprised to see the drowned woman peeking into her room. She only left the bathroom in times of emergency. Her milky white eyes made Darlene wish she could go back to bed.

Instead, she asked, "What is it?"

Darlene knew almost nothing about the drowned woman. She was hesitant to speak and was loyal to Darlene because she could see her and interact with her – apparently saving her from a terrible life of no one ever seeing her roaming spirit again. Her clothes were too ruined for Darlene to think of any time period that they could belong to. She had decided not to pry into the drowned woman's old life and merely accept the fact she had a roommate who lived in her bathroom.

"Your neighbor was killed," the drowned woman told her.

Darlene frowned. The apartment next to her on the right was empty, which meant… Her eyebrows shot up. The other apartment was home to the old lady who was constantly and consistently a pain in Darlene's ass. She would gripe about any and all noises Darlene made and threatened to call the police on a daily basis. However, lately, she had been bragging about having a boyfriend, which seemed to thrill her.

Darlene began to get out of bed. "Are you serious? Do you know anything else?"

"The body is unsightly."

Darlene didn't want to know what that meant. She put her hair up hastily and tugged a sweater on. It was winter now and even though the sun was out, it was sure to be chilly. Darlene opened the door to the hallway and found a swarm of police officers as well as paramedics.

One of the cops saw her and tried to block her from going into the old woman's apartment. "Ma'am, please step back inside your home."

"What happened?" Darlene asked, playing dumb as best as she could.

"Ma'am, please, go back inside."

Darlene tore her gaze away from the front of the old woman's apartment and looked at the young officer. "Is she okay?"

"Ma'am, an officer will be by to question you later. Please go back inside until this area is all clear."

The paramedics left the woman's apartment, carrying out the stretcher, which had a white sheet over it. Darlene's heart pounded. She was transfixed. The police officer was irritated, trying to get her back into her apartment. As Darlene took a step back, the old lady's hand slid out from under the sheet, and Darlene's breath caught in her throat. Along her wrist were bite marks – clearly a vampire's.

"Fine, I'm going," she snapped suddenly, stepping back into her apartment and shutting the door, catching her breath.

The drowned woman floated over to her, concern on her features. "Did you see the corpse?"

"I saw her wrist. Vampire bite marks. What did you see?"

The woman looked sad. "Wounds that matched those of one given by a werewolf."

Darlene felt as if her heart was going to pop.

***

"When I said get a normal job, I didn't mean here with me." Maria looked at Idris, her thick glasses making her eyes look like an insect's.

Idris shifted his weight uncomfortably. He hadn't thought this all the way through. That seemed to be his biggest problem regarding everything. His wrist began to itch, which it did whenever he was stressed and was being reminded of his own Exsul status. Maria never seemed to be bothered by her own Exsul tattoo, but she had been Exsul a lot longer.

That was the entire reason why Idris started visiting Maria. It had been two months since the debacle with Atticus, Liara and Darlene. In one fell swoop, he had blown up everything in his life.

His relationship with Darlene had crumbled and burned in front of his eyes, by his own hand. He had pushed her away and then lashed out in such a disgusting manner that she was now dating Mark, the leader of Roman's old pack.

Atticus, the man who had Changed him, a maggot on the planet, had somehow infested his way back into Idris's life. Idris had let him and the fault was with him. Atticus promised him a pack, which was the only thing Idris wanted back. Instead, he lost all sense of himself and who he was. He had ended Atticus's life, but at that point, the damage had been done.

Liara still treated him with respect, which Idris felt he didn't deserve. Yes, he had stopped Atticus from killing her, but he still had gotten upset when she refused to support their Exsul pack idea. As Idris recovered in the hospital, Liara had come to see him and said that she forgave him. She was forever a better person than he was. Before Liara left, she told Idris to forgive himself and work to be a better person.

Idris had taken her words seriously. The first thing he had done once he got out of the hospital was get out of that disgusting motel room he had been holed up in since Lucian went missing. He rented a small bachelor's pad on the opposite side of town, away from Darlene, in case he suddenly felt like seeing her. The next thing he did was take Darlene's advice and went to see Maria.

Maria had been an Exsul for a long time and used magic to hide herself from other werewolves, although it hadn't been strong enough for Liara. Idris had treated her like trash when he had found out about her Exsul status, something he had been too embarrassed to admit. But Maria was able to make a life for herself outside of the pack, now owning a book store that specialized in books no one wanted. If she could be content as an Exsul, why couldn't he?

"Speak up, boy." Maria crossed her arms – she was always tough on him, but in a motherly way that Idris never had as a kid.

"I don't have enough experience to get hired anywhere else," he mumbled, abashed.

"What did you do for work before this?"

Idris shrugged. "I fixed cars whenever I was able to find the work. Sometimes I protected people, like a body guard. Before all of this happened and I was second-in-command to Lucian, I helped him run his hardware store."

"So go work at a hardware store."

Idris cringed. "I…tried. The interview didn't go so well."

Understatement of the year. When the guy interviewing him role played as a difficult customer, Idris found himself irritated until he finally told the guy to Google what he wanted if he didn't want to listen to him.

Maria sighed, her bangles on her wrists clattering together. "Idris, you know why I don't want you working here."

He did. Darlene still worked here and having an ex-couple working together was something that made Maria nervous. It made Idris nervous, too, but there was no way anyone else would hire him with a blank resume where all his references were dead or paranormal.

"Can't I work in the back?"

"The back? You mean the closet where we put extra books?" Her face softened. "I'll ask around for you, okay?"

"Thanks, Maria."

"What are your plans for today?" It was the daily question she asked him, either by text or in person, to try to get Idris's head on straight.

"I planned on going to the library. Read there. Try to relax. I used to like to read. As a kid, I mean. Before everything happened."

Maria nodded in approval and opened her mouth to speak when the door to the bookshop opened. Idris turned around and saw Darlene fly in. Idris tried to control the way his heart beat quickly when he saw her. *You messed up and you don't deserve her.* He prepared himself for Darlene's glare when she saw him, but she barely glanced at him as she ran up to Maria.

"Jacob," she breathed. "He's back."

Maria stiffened. Idris's breath caught in his throat. Jacob – Lucian's vampire/werewolf hybrid who had escaped the night Lucian was killed. There had been no sign of him. Idris assumed Lucian's plan had failed and Jacob was dead somewhere. Darlene recounted the story quickly, ending with what her ghost had told her. Maria paced the floor.

Idris spoke first, although he loathed to do so. "Didn't she…" He realized he still didn't know her name.

"Gertrude, apparently," Darlene answered for him.

"Didn't Gertrude have a boyfriend recently?"

He hadn't wanted to bring that up, for the mere fact that Gertrude was the reason Idris had found out about Darlene running to Mark. But if that stirred up any memories for Darlene, it didn't show on her face.

"That's right. You don't think it could be Jacob, do you? I never saw him around but…Who else would be close enough to get to her?"

"Were there any clues in the apartment that could have been left for you?" Maria asked.

Darlene shrugged. "If so, there was nothing overt. Otherwise the cops would have been all over me again, like with Rebecca."

Idris chewed on his lip, thinking. "The only other person who was in on Lucian's plan was Vivica. And has anyone seen her lately?"

Darlene and Maria shook their heads. Idris hadn't seen her either, not since the night that Darlene had to stake Rebecca and Vivica had been so consumed with getting Idris back she had orchestrated his battle with Roman. There hadn't been any peep from her since. While that was a blessing, it was also worrisome. Vivica was not one to stay idle for long. Idris hadn't thought of her much since Atticus and the aftermath, but now that Jacob was back, a sick feeling formed in his stomach.

"I'm going to look for her in the catacombs," he said. "Maybe your ghost can help you get into Gertrude's apartment?"

Darlene nodded. "Good idea. I should wear gloves though, shouldn't I? I don't want anything of mine left at the crime scene."

Idris looked at Maria, who nodded gently at him to go and find Vivica. He zipped up his jacket, getting ready to go out in the cold. As he walked toward the door, Darlene called to him. He stopped.

"Be careful."

"You, too."

He headed out toward his truck.

Chapter Two

Darlene impatiently worked her shift, her mind wandering the entire time. The store enjoyed moderate success after Vivica destroyed it and they had reopened. That was three months ago now, and the store had mostly gone back to the way it was before the attack – quiet and empty. Darlene was next to the supernatural shelf, skimming a book about the supernatural world, searching for information on whether anyone could leave the physical world and go into the world of the dead while sleeping. She kept thinking back to the boy who had warned her that someone was coming. Maybe he had meant Jacob. He could have been a victim of Jacob's back when he first showed up in Darlene's dreams.

Darlene didn't want to run to Rosamund every time she had a question, and not just because her place gave her a headache. Her powers were growing stronger. Rebecca had helped her get rid of Idris when he found out about Mark and her, and the drowned woman was always by her side when she was home. Would it really be that much of a leap to be able to travel to the other side? Rosamund was correct in telling her that whenever she was stressed, she lost control of her powers, letting spirits communicate with her in an overwhelming fashion. Darlene had mostly gotten a handle on that, but they'd still badger her if she forgot to block them out.

The bell jingled, making Darlene turn around. There was Mark. He wore far less than anyone else would have outside in the cold weather but then, his body temperature was naturally warmer than everyone else's. Darlene still wasn't sure what she would label her relationship with Mark – they weren't exclusively together yet, even if it had been a couple of months. They weren't exactly seeing other people either. Darlene held back from committing to him, afraid she would run into it too quickly like she did with Idris. Mark sensed her hesitation and didn't bring up any conversation about their relationship yet.

"Hey," he said, walking over to her. "I wanted to meet you here instead of your apartment."

Darlene had asked Mark to come with her when they snooped around Gertrude's apartment. She wanted a lookout who wasn't a ghost in case anything went wrong. She closed her book and looked at him. "Why?"

Mark shrugged, avoiding her eyes. "Just in case Jacob was tailing you after dark."

He was concerned about her but didn't want to make a big deal out of it. Darlene tilted her face slightly away from him so he wouldn't see her smile and ran her fingers over the cover of the book.

"Sure, okay. Let me get my coat."

Darlene walked to Maria's office and stuck her head in. Maria was typing on her computer, her eyes focused. Darlene was glad that Idris had Maria helping him now. She knew Idris was a good guy, deep down underneath all his problems, and knew that being an Exsul was the reason he'd gone off the deep end with Atticus. They hadn't had a conversation more than a couple of times since Idris landed in the hospital. Anything Darlene knew, she had heard from Maria.

"I'm going to head out now, okay? Will you be alright?"

Maria snorted. "It would take more than a werewolf/vampire hybrid to take me down at this point. You be safe now, okay? Even if you have Mark with you." Maria didn't pry into Darlene's relationships with Idris or Mark, for which she was grateful.

Darlene slipped on her jacket and walked out with Mark. He followed her in his own car until they pulled up to her apartment. Darlene pulled her jacket tightly around herself. The wind had picked up and, with it, the first taste of what winter was truly going to hold. As they walked up the stairs, Darlene marveled at how silent it was compared to this morning. There was police tape across Gertrude's door but other than that, nothing gave any hint to the murder that had happened inside.

"You know, it's weird," Darlene said, facing the door. "She was always really annoying and I didn't know her name, but she still didn't deserve this. I never saw this boyfriend of hers either. I wonder if it was Jacob."

"Don't know. Either way, if it was him, he'd have wanted you to know it was, killing so close to where you live. Are you going to get your friend?"

Darlene nodded and went into her own apartment, approaching the drowned woman. She explained how she needed the door to Gertrude's place unlocked. The drowned woman nodded and slipped past Darlene. She always looked as if she was under water, with water dripping off of her, but never any puddles forming. Her milky white eyes used to scare Darlene but now she barely noticed them. The woman had helped her too many times to ever be a bother to her, even if she was always in Darlene's bathroom.

Mark and Darlene waited at the front door until they heard it click. Darlene learned enough about spirits at this point to know they could interact with the physical world for a limited amount of time. Once they hit their limit, they would fade back to the planes of the otherworld until they gathered their power again. The door slid open silently, and the drowned woman nodded at Darlene that she should come inside.

"What are we going to do about the tape?" Mark asked as he fumbled in his coat for gloves so that Darlene wouldn't leave any marks, and bags for her shoes for the same reason.

As if in response, the drowned woman pointed to the table near the main door. Darlene glanced over and saw a roll of crime scene tape thrown carelessly on it.

"That'll do it." She slipped on the gloves and bags for her feet.

She tore the tape down and stepped inside the apartment gingerly, waiting for alarms to go off. There was nothing. Darlene handed the crime scene tape to Mark, so that they wouldn't forget it, and he nodded, serving as lookout. The drowned woman stayed next to Darlene as she walked deeper into the apartment.

The first thing that struck her was the smell. It smelled like death, old death that had been sitting for too long. Darlene wondered when Gertrude passed away. She tried to recall when she had last seen the woman but couldn't remember. She had been so busy lately. Maybe if she had paid attention to the old woman...

No, it wouldn't do her any good to go down that road. Not right now. Darlene already blamed herself about Lucian and Rebecca. She steeled herself against the smell and walked into the living room.

***

Idris parked his truck just outside the cemetery. It was almost pitch black outside. The moon was covered by rapidly moving clouds. The wind would have chilled anyone else to the bone but Idris hardly noticed it as he made his way into the cemetery.

The thought of seeing Vivica filled him with dread. Besides their sordid history, she had still ultimately worked with Roman to make sure they battled. The rest of Roman's pack made it sound as if Idris had attacked first. The lie resulted in an early sentence of Exsul status.

Idris shook his head as he walked through the empty cemetery. Maria told him time and time again not to focus on the past and what happened to lead him to Exsul status. It would only drive him crazy. He reminded himself that the full moon was in another week. He spent the last two full moons holed up in a secluded area of the woods, as far away from life as he could get. It was lonely and depressing, but Idris avoided Mark's pack that way.

Idris made his way to the catacombs, looking behind him to make sure no one saw. He moved the wooden door aside and stepped inside. The stale air brought back memories of the last time he was here, when Vivica attempted to seduce him. Idris almost caved. If she had tried when Atticus was around, Idris was sure his resolve would have crumbled.

Idris wasn't even sure if Vivica would be *home*, for lack of a better word, right now. She could be out feasting. He smelled the air as he walked down the hallway that sloped downward into the ground and recoiled. The stench of something putrid caused Idris to gag. Preparing for the worst, Idris walked slower, until the hallway ended and it opened up into the main chamber.

Vivica's coffin stood in the middle, opened. Rebecca's ashes were still piled off to one side, from when Darlene staked her. There was no sign of what was causing the putrid smell.

Like a flash, Vivica appeared from one of the other rooms. She hissed at him but it seemed half-hearted. Her eyes flicked around the room wildly, as if checking for something. Her muscles were tense, but rigid, letting Idris know that Vivica wasn't actually going to attack him. Something was definitely wrong, and she was trying to hide it.

"What the hell are you doing here?" she sneered, showing him her fangs.

Idris pretended not to notice the smell or her odd stance and simply shrugged. "You've fallen off the radar. You told me that last time you fell off the radar, you and a fellow vampire massacred an Italian town back in 1730."

"Did I?" Vivica replied, trying to look innocent.

Idris crossed his arms.

Vivica retracted her fangs and straightened up. "So, you came here to catch up? I find that hard to believe, pup. What do you want? Heard through the grapevine that you and your girlfriend broke up."

"Don't even bother to try," Idris snapped. "Not interested. I figured you were up to something horrible and wanted to see if I should nip it in the bud."

A funny look crossed her face, so quickly that anyone else wouldn't have noticed it. But Idris did and he watched her closer.

"No. Nothing is going on. Sorry to disappoint. If you can leave now, that'd be perfect, otherwise I'll have to kill you."

Idris pretended he just noticed the smell, wrinkling his nose. "I can't say it smells like someone died in here, all things considering, but it does seriously stink in here."

Vivica's eyes darted around again. "I don't smell anything."

Idris nodded. "Might just be me then."

"You can go now, Idris," she hissed, and her fangs slid out. "Otherwise things are going to get ugly for you."

He held his hands up as a sign of innocence and began to back up. "Alright, V. You say you aren't doing anything then fine, I believe you."

Idris turned to leave. As he headed out of the catacombs, he knew that Vivica was hiding something – something big enough to make her look nervous. He couldn't recall the last time he had seen Vivica nervous.

It scared the hell out of him.

***

As Darlene walked into the middle of the living room, a strong, putrid smell churned her stomach. For a second, she worried she was going to throw up. Darlene closed her eyes and tried to control her breathing until the nausea passed. The living room was disorganized, with things thrown about everywhere. *Signs of a struggle*. Blood splattered on one wall that was covered with police tags. Nothing that proved their theory it was Jacob though.

Her phone vibrated in her pocket, and Darlene fumbled for it to see a text from Idris. *Vivica is hiding something – seemed nervous. Her catacomb stunk of something disgusting. Not sure what.*

She slid her phone away and thought about the message. This place also had a bad smell. Was it just a coincidence? Her heart picked up speed. What if the smell had something to do with Jacob being a hybrid? There had to be a reason the disgusting smell was in both places.

A quick walk around the rest of the apartment showed no signs from Jacob. It seemed silly that he would be so close to her for the past couple of months, finally kill Gertrude and leave no sign for her.

Then Darlene's heart skipped a beat. He had left a sign – but it would be something that *only* she could see. No one else could speak to Gertrude now...except for Darlene. Steeling herself against the smell, she moved out of Gertrude's bedroom and back to the living room. The drowned woman hovered nearby, staring at Darlene curiously as she shut her eyes. She had only practiced a little in calling spirits to her. Usually they just showed up. If she wasn't careful, Lucian was a happy regular in her torment, popping up whenever she lost control. The last thing Darlene wanted was him showing up.

Darlene called out to Gertrude. The otherworld opened up in front of her. For a second, she felt a sick sense of vertigo, as if she was spinning like a top down below. She focused her mind, moving through the spirits reaching out for her attention. Her ability to communicate with the world beyond was incredibly rare. Spirits had followed her since her birth, waiting for the day her powers would awaken. Now that they were here, they wanted nothing more than to get her to do their bidding. Darlene was terrified she'd lose her grip on the actual world and fall down into the other side, but she concentrated on the stench of the living room in an effort to keep her grounded.

She sensed someone or something approaching her. Darlene could feel it in her bones. Through the mist and the darkness, a figure took shape. Darlene called out again, and the mist finally took form. Gertrude appeared in front of her. It took all of her might not to recoil away from the sight of her mangled, terrifying looking body. Gertrude stared at Darlene with empty eyes.

"Do you have something to tell me?"

"He's coming," Gertrude whispered.

"Who, Jacob?" Gertrude nodded, prompting Darlene to go on, "Was he your boyfriend?"

Gertrude nodded again. "Yes."

"Did he say anything when he...when he did this to you?"

"He said for me to tell you that he is watching. He knows all about you. About your life and your abilities. He's been plotting and planning. You're next. Then all your friends. Then he's wiping out the packs. Be ready."

Darlene wanted to say more – at least wanted to apologize for getting the old woman wrapped up in this, but she was already fading away. She faded away and Darlene felt herself fall back to her physical presence in the living room, thick with the stench of death and Jacob.

***

On a whim, Idris didn't go back to the truck. Instead, he walked around to the side of the catacomb, moving as quietly as he could. Vivica's strange behavior made him think twice about just leaving. She was hiding something. Was she working with Jacob? She would be the only one left who would work with him. Lucian was gone, unable to help bring to fruition whatever grand plan he had worked up.

Idris found his way to the back of the catacombs, which was thick with bramble, making it hard to move stealthily. He gave up and looked over the top of the catacomb. It was a bit riskier but Idris took off his jacket and began to scale it. At last he saw Vivica. She wasn't alone. She was pacing, which was highly unusual for her, but someone else was near her. Idris tried to make out what Vivica was saying.

"…Idris here…knew something…"

The man replied, but his voice was so dry and raspy that Idris couldn't make out anything he said.

"But when?" Vivica asked, her voice raised. "You never should have brought Darlene into this. Leaving a message like that tips her off to our plan!"

Idris's heart beat faster. It had to be Jacob. There was no way it could be anyone else at this point.

The man growled and replied.

"Fine," Vivica snapped. "We'll stick with the plan, but you better hope you communicating with Darlene doesn't mean Mark raises his defenses. Now, get out of here. You seriously stink. It's putrid. What a horrific side effect. Bet Lucian didn't see that one coming."

Bingo. Idris slid off the catacomb roof, down into the bramble. He put on his jacket and made his way toward his truck. He had to warn Mark, even if it meant seeing Darlene and him together.

***

Darlene helped Mark tape back up the door. They shut it and the drowned woman locked it from the other side. It looked untouched, and Darlene hoped no one would pick up anything in the apartment. She had been incredibly careful not to touch anything and leave the bags over her shoes at all times. Mark and Darlene went back into her apartment as she explained what she had seen from Gertrude's ghost.

When she finished, Mark frowned. "So, he was spying on you then. He was dating Gertrude to keep tabs on you. Seems silly and a lot of work. Doesn't he have anything else to do?"

Darlene showed him Idris's text. "Seems to me that he isn't working alone. Vivica is helping him."

Her phone went off again at that moment and she read a new text from Idris. *I'm coming over! Don't let Mark leave! His pack is in danger! Be there soon.*

Mark read the text and started to pace the living room. Darlene wanted to pace the living room as well, but for a completely different reason. She hadn't had

Idris and Mark in the same room since they fought together against Atticus. Even if it was about Mark's pack, she was worried about the two of them being so close to each other. Idris hadn't mentioned their relationship since the hospital, but the last thing Darlene wanted was things getting awkward. It didn't seem to be on Mark's mind, however, as he waited for Idris to arrive.

When a knock sounded on the door, Darlene opened it to see Idris.

"May I come in?" he asked, so formally that Darlene almost felt bad.

She nodded and moved to let him walk inside.

Mark came over to him, asking about the pack.

"Vivica is working with Jacob, and he is mobilizing against your pack. They didn't know I was there. You can defend against them. They didn't say when. My guess is soon."

Mark nodded and got on his phone, calling up members of the pack. Darlene watched him in order to avoid Idris's gaze.

"Find anything on your end?"

She was relieved he hadn't mentioned anything uncomfortable. "Yes. That smell you mentioned. Must be Jacob, then. Gertrude's ghost relayed a message that he was coming for me, for all of us, and then to wipe out the packs."

Idris sighed. "I was really hoping he was dead."

"But what could he be using against the packs? You don't think he…he made more hybrids?" Darlene asked, the thought striking her for the first time and making her feel ill.

Mark got off the phone at that point and looked at Idris. "Can you come with us? Help protect the tavern?"

Darlene was shocked by Mark's request but not as much as Idris, whose eyebrows shot up so high they almost flew off of his face. "Are you serious?"

"Yes. You found the threat and we could use your help." He held up his hand. "I'll deal with any backlash from Liara's pack over having an Exsul help."

Idris nodded stiffly. "I would, but who is going to watch Darlene? She's clearly threatened."

Darlene crossed her arms. "I can protect myself."

"Your ghost power is great, don't get me wrong," Mark replied. "But you should have a werewolf here, too."

"Fine. I'll call Maria."

Mark snorted. "Maria? She's ancient by werewolf standards. Are we even sure she can still Change effectively?"

Darlene bristled. "I'm not letting anyone I don't know into my home. I know Maria. No, we haven't seen her Change, but it isn't as if you suddenly lose the ability to, once you're a werewolf, is it? You're implying that because she's old, she can't protect me. But I think she's the only other person who can, outside of you two."

Idris looked at his feet. Darlene swore she saw a smile showing through his calm expression – part of him was secretly enjoying hearing Mark get lectured. Mark shrugged and mumbled in agreement. She picked up her phone to make the call.

Chapter Three

"I'm sorry to bother you," Idris said into the phone. "But Mark asked me to call."

"*Mark*?"

Idris didn't blame Liara for the surprise in her voice. It was crazy to be calling her, to be warning her of Jacob and the threat against them. He knew that. Even standing in Roman's Tavern felt as if it belonged to another lifetime, an older version of him. Instead, he turned his back to the main floor, avoiding Julie's glare, which had been fixated on him since he walked in.

"Yeah, sorry. It's about Jacob. He's back. He's coming after Darlene. He left her a threat. He seems intent on going after her at the expense of turning a blind eye to other matters. But Vivica is working with him, too. They have an attack planned for Mark's pack but he wanted me to warn you as well."

There was long silence and then Liara said, "Okay. This is unexpected. Tell Mark thank you for the warning. And thank you for calling, Idris."

Idris mumbled goodbye and hung up, feeling uncomfortable at the soft nature of her voice. He told himself not to expect being constantly yelled at by her for what Atticus did, but he couldn't help it. He had still gotten upset with her. *No, stop. If Maria was here, she'd tell you to stop focusing on the past again.*

That wasn't easy. Roman's Tavern was filled with people from his past, all glaring at him. This was a pack that had lied about his fight with Roman so he would be sentenced with Exsul status quicker. He had killed their leader. No matter how much of a dick Roman was, he was still their leader. Julie, Roman's girlfriend, who had somehow known of Darlene's powers before anyone else had, had been staring him down since he came in.

Not for the first time, Idris wondered if Mark had some sort of malicious intent in asking him over here to help. The attack was going to happen soon and it was just a matter of when. But if it wasn't tonight, did Mark expect Idris to sit around here and hang out with everyone as if nothing happened? Idris walked into what used to be Roman's office, to see Mark behind the desk, putting down the phone.

"Liara has been warned."

"Great. I've been alerting anyone who isn't in the bar for a meeting."

"Is that wise?" Idris caught himself and shook his head quickly. "Sorry... sorry. Not my place to question you."

Mark looked at him with his one good eye. Idris flashed back to when he'd heard what Roman was going to do during the fight and his plans to take out Mark's eye. Idris did nothing to stop him. Atticus had told him to let Roman take Mark's eye because Roman was the leader they needed. Idris felt ashamed now, staring at Mark.

"What would you suggest?" Mark asked finally.

Idris cleared his throat. "If we're all in here, together, it could be easy pickings for whatever we're going up against. We know that Vivica is helping Jacob. You send in a small team to the catacombs. See if you can strike there directly while you hold down the fort here."

Mark gave a curt nod. "I'll give it some thought. In the meantime, why don't you wait down below? I'll let you know what we're doing shortly. Send Julie up, will you? She's second-in-command now."

Idris hid the surprise on his face as he nodded and left the office. Julie being second-in-command didn't exactly instill him with a ton of confidence. But it wasn't his place to say anything. Idris was trying to take that in stride – even as he walked around Mark's pack, he didn't truly belong.

***

Maria was a flustered, high-energy, multi-colored ball by the time she got over to Darlene's apartment. Her clothes were clashing, as usual, with her bangles and necklaces clattering around in a blur of color.

It had taken Darlene almost ten minutes to convince Maria to protect her.

"It's not that I don't care what happens to you, dear," Maria said. "You just have to understand that sort of thing is a long time behind me now."

In the end, in order to convince Maria to participate, it took an agreement for Rosamund, of all people, to come over later on and help protect the apartment as well. Darlene had nothing against Rosamund, except that she was odd and trying to get through to her could be frustrating. She also didn't understand why Rosamund would even agree to come over, seeing as she had always made it very clear that she tried to keep out of werewolf affairs.

But Maria was here now and Rosamund was on her way, so all Darlene could do was sit on the couch as Maria peeked around. In all the years that Darlene had worked at her shop, Maria had never been over.

"Not what I was expecting."

"How so?"

"I thought you'd have a cat, for one."

Darlene crossed her arms. "Why, you thought I'd be some sort of lonely spinster?"

Maria shrugged and peered out the window toward the parking lot, as if she was looking for something. She seemed nervous, and Darlene couldn't blame her. She never prodded about what exactly Maria had done to deserve Exsul status, because she knew it was a touchy subject, but she couldn't help but be curious. Some were given Exsul status due to murdering an important pack leader, like what Idris did, while others were given Exsul status for smaller acts that endangered the pack. In any case, Darlene was confident that this was the first time since Maria became an Exsul that she was asked to help out with anything pack related.

"Anyway, why is Rosamund coming? She's always been clear about avoiding anything to do with werewolf packs."

"We need her help. She downplays her abilities but she is actually quite powerful. She just gets roped up too much in her silly tarot card readings for foolish humans."

"I know so little about her," Darlene mused. "But she's never been one for open discussions. Perhaps it's just with me?"

"I wouldn't bother asking. I've tried for years but she seals up when it comes to anything about her past or werewolf packs. It took a lot of convincing to get her to agree to come here."

"You don't think she is a werewolf, do you? An Exsul?"

Maria shook her head. "No, I'd have known. She isn't. Maybe she has some bad blood with a pack that she wants to hide from. Who knows? In any case, with having her here, we make a good team."

Darlene looked out the window, waiting for Rosamund to appear, and sighed. "I just hope Mark and Idris are okay."

***

Idris drank a water by the bar, waiting for further instructions. He had his back to everyone, pretending he didn't sense the glares that were shot his way. He wished he was with Liara's pack. At least Liara wouldn't be glaring at him.

Someone slinked up behind the bar, grabbing a bottle of vodka off the shelf. It was Julie, looking as terrible as she usually did. If this had been a normal day, he would have asked how Julie had pegged Darlene's abilities before anyone else did. But that was before he had killed her boyfriend. He took a sip of his water instead, avoiding her gaze.

Julie poured a shot of vodka and downed it without a change of expression on her face. She appeared skinnier, if that was even possible, unhealthy. Was anyone looking after her now that Roman was gone? Julie had always been self-destructive, but her constant turmoil-filled relationship with Roman at least kept her grounded. Now she was likely alone. The thought racked Idris with guilt. *You were defending yourself. You would have been killed if you hadn't.*

Julie leaned over the bar to lock eyes with Idris. "How are you doing?"

"Uh. Fine. You?"

"Better," She paused, running her fingers along her shot glass. "You killed Roman."

Idris wished he could teleport himself away from this conversation. "Julie, listen—"

"I knew it was going to happen. I know everything that is going to happen before it does. You know that, don't you? I want to warn others of the dangers they face. But I never do. I can't play with fate."

Idris could only stare at her, unsure of what to say or what she was telling him.

Julie poured herself another shot. "Just remember that I know."

Julie took the shot and then walked off, leaving Idris at the bar. He let out a sigh of relief, happy he had avoided a freak-out moment from her. What was she saying? That she knew the future? Were there any normal beings left around him?

"Listen up." Mark's voice rang out and Idris shifted to look up at him, standing on the second floor. "Most of you are going to be staying here, holding down the fort. But I will be sending a team out to the catacombs. We know who is working with this Jacob kid. We know where she is. We can strike against them at the same time we defend our home base. But it's going to be dangerous. You might not come back. It's on a voluntary basis only."

Murmurs went up as members of the pack turned to look at each other and discuss if they would stay here with Mark or go to the catacombs. *He took my advice.* Before he could think twice, Idris stood up.

"I'd like to volunteer. If you'll have me."

Mark nodded at him. "You'll go. I'll hear no one speak against it."

The pack went silent, although Idris could feel glares sent his way. Julie stepped forward next and said she would go as well. *Great.* Three more people stepped forward. Two were men who were new to the pack, probably wanting to prove themselves. Dimitri and Peter. A woman volunteered, an older woman with gray hair named Amelia who Idris dimly remembered joining the pack a few years ago.

Mark nodded once the room fell silent. "Julie, get ready and head out. Idris knows where it is."

As he stared at the ragtag crew of people going to take down Vivica and Jacob, Idris wondered if he'd made a mistake.

Chapter Four

Naturally, the first thing that Rosamund did when she entered Darlene's apartment was to light a candle. The thing stunk of the woods, and not the enjoyable, pre-packaged scent of the woods Darlene could find in any candle store in the mall. It was the scent of the woods that had just been hit by a hurricane. She could almost smell the humidity and strange odor of stale leaves and something dead nearby.

"Great, smells lovely," Darlene mumbled, not bothering to hide the fact she thought it was a terrible candle.

Rosamund glared at her through her glasses. They made her look as if she was nearing eighty instead of just barely turned thirty.

"This cleans our auras, Darlene. It will help with improved focus and stronger minds."

Darlene looked around her apartment and wondered how her life had gotten so insane. The drowned woman hung out in her bathroom, a constant reminder of Darlene's power connected to the otherworld. Maria, her boss and an exiled werewolf, was standing guard by the window, watching intently. Rosamund, a witch, was pulling something else out of a giant bag she had brought with her. It was a far cry from her lonely nights after Austin left her alone at the altar. She couldn't remember the last time that she had hid on the couch, curled up in blankets, watching reality television.

Her phone went off and she saw a text from Mark. *My pack is holding the fort at Roman's Tavern. Idris and a small group are going to the catacombs to see if they can strike first.*

Concern filled Darlene. She didn't want Idris in over his head with going after Jacob and Vivica. They still didn't know what Jacob was capable of, besides the fact that he apparently stank. Vivica was an ancient vampire. Darlene had read that the older a vampire was, the stronger it became. Darlene had been thrown around enough by Vivica to know that she wasn't exactly weak.

Darlene told Rosamund and Maria what was happening.

Rosamund clicked her tongue against her front teeth. "Crazy, crazy, but I understand. Better not to sit idle."

Darlene used this as segue to what she wanted to ask. "Rosamund, what is up with you and werewolves? You didn't want any of them to know about you. You deal with Maria only because she is an Exsul. Why is that?"

"Darlene, I cannot discuss that right now. No, not with everything going on. Let's just say that werewolves and I – we have a history that goes way back and it is better left untouched."

Darlene wanted to say more but something about Rosamund's tone, casual yet with iron underneath, made her stop. She was feeling restless and didn't want to take it out on Rosamund.

"I hope they're okay," Maria said, changing the subject back to Idris and the group that was going after Vivica.

"Me, too," Darlene replied.

The only thing any of them could do was wait.

***

Idris took his truck and Dimitri took his car. Julie and Amelia rode with Idris in complete silence. Julie seemed lost in thought, and Amelia had a gloomy look on her face that clearly showed Idris she didn't think much of taking an Exsul along on the mission. Dimitri and Peter had made it clear that they didn't want to ride with him either. Idris tried not to let it upset him. He *was* an Exsul. He would have treated an Exsul the same way if the roles were reversed and he knew it.

As they pulled up to the cemetery, Amelia cleared her throat and leaned forward, holding a slim purse. "I brought these."

She opened up the bag and Idris saw five stakes inside.

Julie nodded in approval. "Everyone gets one," she said to Amelia and then narrowed her eyes. "*Everyone.*"

Amelia hesitated and then handed one to Idris, who held it firmly. It had been a long time since he held a stake. The last vampire he killed was over three years ago when he pushed him out into the sunlight, watching him turn to ash in front of his eyes. He had only ever staked one vampire but his technique was sloppy and it took three tries before getting the job done.

Holding the stake now made it clear that there was a distinct and real possibility that Idris was going to have to kill Vivica tonight. He knew he shouldn't even be concerned about it, but part of him felt odd even thinking about it. Vivica was still technically his ex-girlfriend, crazy or not, and their history made it complicated. They had always done terrible things to each other. But Idris couldn't forgive her for trying to kill him through Roman.

Would he be able to stake her tonight?

The group made their way into the cemetery, all holding their stakes.

Julie jutted her chin toward Idris. "You lead the way."

He nodded, feeling uneasy leading the pack toward the catacombs. He almost wished Mark had sent him alone, although that would have been madness. His tattoo itched on his wrist, and he fought the urge to scratch it. *It's all in your head.*

When the catacombs came into view, Idris realized something felt off. The air was heavy and the breeze had stopped. His heart picked up speed as he looked around the graveyard, searching for the source of his sudden disquiet. Julie moved behind him, as if she could sense it as well. Back in the old days, Idris would have made a joke – *thought you could predict the future* – but he didn't dare do that now.

It didn't matter. Before Idris could even say anything, something flew out of the shadows directly toward them. The smell was what hit him first. At the last second, Idris spun and pushed Julie out of the way. The creature ran into Idris. It felt as if a truck had hit him. He flew back, the darkened sky spinning in front of him before he hit the ground, narrowly avoiding a tombstone.

The creature loomed over him. In the darkness, it was hard to make out its features but he saw a flash of talons and a glint of fangs. A hybrid – and it wasn't Jacob. *He's made more,* Idris thought with despair as he scrambled to his feet. His stake had slipped out of his hands and was on the ground somewhere close to where he had fallen.

Dimitri ran forward, Changing as he ran, and lunged toward the hybrid. The hybrid spun around and knocked Dimitri back as if he were nothing more than a pillow. Idris pushed off with his heels and barreled into the hybrid, wrapping his arms around its neck. It struggled to get away from him but Idris held on. He held its neck firmly and with all his strength he turned his hands sharply.

There was a crack and the hybrid loosened, hitting the ground with a thud. Julie came over and staked the creature for good measure. They watched it turn to ash in silence before Julie looked up at Idris.

"You saved me."

"You'll probably have to return the favor."

***

Rosamund sniffed. "There has to be something else we can watch, right?"

"Nope," Darlene said, taking pleasure in making Rosamund watch reality television. "This is it."

Rosamund's varying expressions at watching bad TV was the only thing taking Darlene's mind off the fact that she hadn't heard from anyone in over an hour. *Maybe there isn't anything to report.* She couldn't shake the fact that there was, however. She had even secretly lowered her mental guard to watch the spirits passing through her apartment, terrified that at any moment, Mark or Idris would walk through. No one of interest came through though, leaving Darlene to wildly jump from scenario to scenario.

"Darlene."

Something in Maria's tone made Darlene stand up and walk over to the window. Maria had gone still. There was a dark shape lurching its way across the parking lot. Darlene strained to see what it was but couldn't make it out. Her stomach dropped at the sight anyway and she looked at Maria.

"I'm going out there," Maria said.

Darlene tugged on her arm. "No, you can't. You'll lead it straight to us."

"We don't even know what it is."

"Yes, we do," Rosamund said, her eyes closed. "It's a hybrid."

"And I'm guessing the rules about having to be invited in doesn't matter to a hybrid," Maria said.

Darlene looked around the room, as if some idea would come to her. "If we get separated, we have to meet up at Roman's Tavern, okay?"

"Fine," Maria said. "But I'm protecting you, as we agreed upon. So get ready."

Darlene looked out the window but the shape was gone. She regretted not going with Mark to Roman's

Tavern. Yes, they could be attacked there as well, but for some reason the greater numbers would have been more reassuring than her small apartment. The fear was making the spirits more vibrant, and Darlene shut her eyes when a particularly grisly one appeared.

A sudden bang against the front door made her almost jump up out of her skin. Maria moved in front of her and even Rosamund stood up, clutching a small vial in her hands. Darlene felt the fear run cold inside of her. The drowned woman glided over as well, finishing the pack around her. *Everyone standing by to protect me, and why am I more important than them?* She wasn't. Letting them take the full brunt of the attack from the hybrid seemed selfish.

"We have to get to my car," Darlene whispered as the door rattled again. "All of us. We're all going to Roman's Tavern."

Maria looked at Darlene. "I'm protecting you the entire way."

When the door rattled again, deep cracks formed in the wood. Darlene held her breath and let the spirits gather toward her. They seemed muted, eyes toward the door, as if they were waiting with baited breath to see what would show up.

I need your help, she called out to them. *I need you to help me stop this thing so my friends and I can get to safety.*

The next time there was a thump, the door exploded into the apartment. Darlene ducked as the wood flew over their heads. In the doorway was the hybrid. The stench that spewed off of it made her eyes water. It wasn't Jacob. Its body was contorted and changed into something that had both werewolf and vampire features. The cold hard pale skin of a vampire with patches of fur sticking out of it. Its feet were vampire but its hands were the claws of a werewolf with gleaming talons. It had fangs sticking out of its mouth, almost too big, as if they were created sloppily at the last minute. Ears pointed out of its head and its red eyes were staring straight at Darlene. It was hideous to look at it, and Darlene wished she could avoid it completely.

It let out a howl, a few pitches higher than a normal werewolf and lunged forward.

Now! The spirits in the apartment surged forward, slamming into the hybrid. The hybrid faltered, stunned by the impact of something it couldn't see. Rosamund threw a vial at it, which exploded against its face. A dark green cloud floated up around it, and it screamed, thrashing its claws around wildly. Darlene didn't know what the vial was or what it contained but the three of them moved past the hybrid, spilling out into the apartment hallway.

They took off running. The hybrid was out of the vial cloud and now running on all fours toward them. *We aren't even going to make it to the stairs.* Darlene was slower than the other two. As the stench of the hybrid settled down upon her, Maria suddenly stopped and moved toward Darlene. Darlene yelled at Maria to keep going but Maria leapt up into the air. She soared past Darlene and in one fluid motion, she Changed.

Maria threw herself toward the hybrid. Darlene had never seen her in werewolf form before. She was thin, but pure muscle. Female werewolves were naturally smaller than their male counterparts but faster, which was exactly what they needed against the hybrid. Maria sank her teeth into the hybrid's wrist, and Darlene felt someone else clamp her own. Rosamund's glasses had fallen off in the scuffle, making her look more approachable. Panic was written over her face.

"Darlene, we have to go *now*."

Rosamund tugged Darlene forward. She took one last glance at Maria fighting the hybrid before running down the stairs. They ran across the parking lot. The stress was making spirits flicker in and out beside her – tormented faces, peaceful faces, all sorts of spirits were looking at her. The drowned woman was behind her, following silently.

Darlene turned back to her as they made it to her car. "Can you help Maria? Please?"

The drowned woman nodded. "It will require such power that I will be unable to help you for a few hours. It will take me back to the otherworld."

"Please."

The drowned woman turned and floated back toward the fight. Rosamund and Darlene got in her car, starting the engine up and pulling out of the parking lot at high speed.

***

The entrance to the catacombs now had a sheet of metal shoved against it, over an inch thick and seemingly unmovable. The group tried to move it, but it didn't budge. Idris finally backed away from it, mulling over their options. He couldn't help but think that this was a way to guide them into the catacombs on Vivica's terms, which left Idris unsettled. They hadn't seen another hybrid since the one that had attacked them. There was no way that was the only one.

"There has to be a way we can go through here," Peter said, trying to move it on his own. He was brash and wanted to prove himself, which made him a liability.

"We won't be getting through there," Amelia snapped. "So stop trying."

Peter growled at her. Idris felt irritated but he remained silent. It wasn't his place to speak up. Luckily, he didn't have to. Julie stalked over to Peter and pulled him off the door, snarling at him. He quickly fell in line.

"I might know a way," Idris said.

Julie moved to go with him but Dimitri took a step forward, pulling Julie back. "We can't trust him. What if his way inside is a trap?"

Peter nodded as well and moved closer to Dimitri. "We should get rid of him, Julie. We can tell Mark it was an accident."

Idris felt a dull throb in his head. Were they serious? Here they were, moments from stepping inside death's house and these idiots were concerned about *him*. The group looked to Julie for the next word on what to do. Idris held his breath, not saying anything. He wasn't concerned about trying to get the others to side with him. They saw him as an Exsul and that was it. All he needed to do was get through to Julie.

Julie shrugged and looked at Dimitri. "We listen to Idris. Anyone touch him and they deal with me, understood?"

Dimitri's shoulders sagged. The rest of the group mumbled.

Julie walked over to Idris. "What do you suggest?"

Idris explained about climbing onto the top of the catacomb and going through the window. "It might make some noise but that is a risk we'd have to take."

"Fine, we'll do that." As she walked past him, she paused and lowered her voice. "Watch out for Dimitri."

Idris frowned, wondering if this was more of the psychic mumbo jumbo Julie claimed she could do.

Together, the group scaled the catacombs. Idris moved toward the skylight first, getting ready to smash it or find a way inside through it. As he got closer, however, he noticed that the skylight was already broken. His eyes widened, and he turned to tell everyone else to get ready when a hybrid crashed down onto the roof from a tree above.

The roof of the catacombs shook violently. It was old and unstable and couldn't handle the sudden pressure of the hybrid as well as the pack of werewolves. Amelia toppled off the roof as the hybrid swung one of its talons toward Idris. He moved back, barely getting away from it in time. Peter had Changed and lunged forward, barreling into the hybrid, who didn't budge an inch from the sudden weight tossed at it. It brought down its mouth toward Peter. This hybrid was slightly different from the other one. It was larger and its mouth had rows of fangs instead of just a normal set like regular vampires. Whatever Jacob had been doing in his spare time involved tinkering with the hybrid formula. Idris wasn't even convinced these things used to be human.

The mouth of fangs sunk into Peter's hind legs. Amelia jumped up in her werewolf form, sailing over the side of the catacombs and back onto the roof. The roof shuddered again, and Idris tipped forward dangerously. He grabbed onto Julie's wrist to keep her from toppling over. She seemed stunned by the hybrid, not moving, just staring at it. Amelia brought her front paws down onto the hybrid's back, her mouth clamping down on its neck. For the first time, the hybrid let out a noise – a low howl that sounded as if someone had taken the recording of a normal howl and put it down three pitches. Idris gripped his stake and ran forward at full speed, bringing it down toward its chest.

But the hybrid slammed Idris back with the side of one of its claws. He felt a dull pain shoot up his chest as he hit the roof. The hybrid shook violently, knocking Amelia back. Peter let go of it, falling at the hybrid's feet. It reached down toward Peter and before Idris could do anything, there was a crack and Peter's lifeless body was thrown off the roof down below.

Dimitri lunged forward, letting out a scream of rage over Peter's death. The hybrid was taken off guard, still in the motion of turning around after throwing Peter's body off the roof. Dimitri threw the stake, a careless gesture that normally would have brought on eye rolls from Idris's direction. But the stake sunk into the hybrid's chest and it crumbled into ash in front of them.

Dimitri looked back at Idris, disgust on his face, as if he personally blamed him for Peter's death. Then he hopped down into the skylight without waiting to discuss a plan with Julie. Amelia followed, having Changed back into her human form, not bothering to glance at Julie. Idris looked over at her, feeling the vague sense of control she'd had for a few moments now gone. She looked on vacantly, her eyes wide with horror.

"Julie," Idris said, shaking her gently. "We have to go. Inside. Come on."

He was unsure what it was that shocked her so. The hybrids were disgusting and strong, yes, but Julie had faced tons of attacks before. She and Roman had always fought together.

Idris let out a small sigh, realizing that Roman had always been there for anything stressful like this. Now he was gone, and Julie already had a frail mental grasp on everything as it were.

"Julie," he said firmly. "Are you coming into the catacombs? Your pack needs you."

Julie let out a shuddering breath and slowly her eyes refocused. She looked at Idris as if seeing him for the first time and nodded slightly.

Idris relaxed a little. "Your pack is down there. They don't like me here, Julie. Maybe I should stay."

"No." Her voice sounded like iron as she stood up. "I'm second-in-command. They will pay for their disobedience. Let's go."

Together they jumped down into the catacomb.

Chapter Five

Darlene and Rosamund pulled up in front of Roman's Tavern, almost crashing into a parked truck. Her head was aching, and the sky was growing darker with the threat of snow. Just perfect. She was amazed at the fact that they didn't run off the road. Her emotions were out of control, which meant spirits were looking at her non-stop while she tried to drive. None of them were Maria. She hoped that was a good sign.

Rosamund had gone pale and silent in the drive over to Roman's Tavern. "Looks like nothing has happened here yet," she said to Darlene.

Darlene nodded in reply and the two of them got out of the car, running over to the entrance of the bar as if they were being chased. The doors were locked and sealed and Darlene pounded on them.

"It's Darlene! We need to get inside!"

She had visions of the entire inside of Roman's Tavern being destroyed but fought them off. *I'd see their ghosts*. That wasn't exactly reassuring but calmed her down enough so that she hollered again to be let in.

The door finally opened a crack and someone peeked out.

"Let us in!" Darlene exclaimed.

The door shut, and she was about to freak out when it opened fully, letting Rosamund and Darlene inside. It shut after them and Darlene heard the locks fall into place. She looked around the bar and saw Mark rushing over. Relief filled her, and she threw herself into his arms. He hugged her tightly, his chin resting on the top of her head.

"You okay?"

In shuddering breaths, Darlene recounted the story. She kept her eyes shut, not wanting to see any spirits float near her as she recalled what had happened. She finished by saying they had left Maria behind.

"I don't know what happened to her," Darlene said, holding back tears. "Mark, if she...if something happened because of me..."

"I'm sure she's okay, Darlene. She's a strong woman... an Exsul who has made it on her own all this time. There is no way she was taken down by one of those things."

Darlene hoped he was right. She turned around to look at Rosamund, who had slunk back so far she was almost plastered against the wall. Darlene felt Mark stiffen next to her.

"Darlene," he whispered. "Why did you bring a witch into pack headquarters?"

"Well, I mentioned that someone was helping me figure out my whole spirit ability…"

"Right. I figured it was a spirit user or something else, not a *witch*."

"I didn't think it mattered," Darlene said, treading carefully, still not sure what the big deal was that a witch was here.

Mark looked down at her, his eyes wide. "No one told you?"

She shrugged. The pack was eyeing Rosamund now with extreme mistrust and even some loathing. Rosamund seemed to shrink into her overly baggy clothes. Mark stepped forward toward her and she flinched.

"A lot of the spaces here have been claimed but you can come to my office," Mark said. "Darlene, you too."

She nodded and Rosamund removed herself from against the wall, sliding toward Darlene and standing as close to her as possible. They trailed after Mark. Most of the pack barely glanced at Darlene. They were used to seeing her by now and knew of her powers. But the glares toward Rosamund were downright nasty. She tried to think back to what she knew about witches and werewolves. No new knowledge popped up in her head.

They followed Mark to the second floor, where Roman's office was behind what she supposed was the VIP lounge. The only time she had been here during business hours was when she and Idris were trying to find Jacob. Roman and Idris had gotten into a fist fight that had resulted in Roman's nose getting broken and his girlfriend staring Darlene down as if she were an alien.

They got to the back office area. Darlene had never been back here before and found herself looking around in interest. The desk was massive. A separate area had a cot. Darlene remembered Idris telling her that Roman and Julie used to fight all the time so Roman would sleep here. At the thought of Julie, she frowned.

"Where is Julie?"

"She's out with Idris and a few others at the catacombs."

Her heart dropped at the thought. "Have you heard anything?"

He shook his head and Darlene tried to control her breathing. Mark's eyes settled on Rosamund, who had taken a seat in the corner, looking uncomfortable.

"So, either of you going to explain to me what I am apparently missing?"

Mark spoke first, "Seriously can't believe you don't know, Darlene. Don't you read books all the time?" Darlene rolled her eyes and he went on, "Witches were the ones who created werewolves."

Darlene snorted. "What? Never read that before. Anywhere. Not even in bad werewolf-based fiction books."

"It's true," Rosamund replied. "Centuries ago. I mean so long ago that the fact we are still hated is ridiculous." Mark narrowed his eyes and Rosamund spoke a bit faster, "A witch created the first werewolf, yes. The curse was spread on throughout the generations and as you can see, runs rampant today with no intervention from my people."

"Your people started it."

"Someone I don't even know and will never know made the first werewolf. You guys hunt us down unfairly and go after us whenever you can."

Mark growled, "Your *people* erased the fact you created the curse from all lore. The only reason we still know is because of the original passage in *The Werewolf Code* that your people tried to erase."

Rosamund was wringing her hands now, her eyes darting around the room. "I, personally, have never done anything with your kind. I've even laid low. The only time I ever helped werewolves were Exsuls requesting my help to be hidden. Your pack doesn't need to chew me up or whatever they want to do."

"You have to protect her, Mark. She's been helping me with my abilities. I brought her here for safety, not so she could die here instead of at the hands of a hybrid."

Mark heaved a sigh and rubbed his face. "Fine, but the witch has to stay back here. She can lock the door and hunker down. I can't have her walking around the rest of the pack. With tensions running high already, I can't make any promises about her safety if she leaves the room."

Rosamund relaxed slightly. "Thank you."

"I wish you would have told me, Darlene."

"Hey, I had no idea about this blood feud. Why did the witch create the werewolf curse to begin with?" she asked Rosamund.

"Oh, nothing too special, I'm afraid. The usual. Man cheated on her, got married to another woman – not very interesting."

"Right, not very interesting. The entire story of how we all were created," Mark sneered, clearly irritated by Rosamund's flippant tone.

Darlene stood up. "Okay, enough of that. Rosamund, let's get settled, okay?"

She jumped up and scattered off to the other room where Roman kept his cot. Darlene looked back at Mark who just sighed again.

"Wish you would've told me."

***

Leaping down onto the main floor of the catacombs was akin to casually strolling into a pit of chaos. There were at least three hybrids down here, all startled by the fact they had been attacked. Dimitri and Amelia, who had Changed again, were battling the same hybrid, leaving the other two closing in on them. Idris looked around the room wildly. The coffin that Vivica usually slept in was overturned and empty. The room stunk so badly that his eyes began to water. There was no sign of Jacob or Vivica, which bothered him. Had they been alerted to their presence and left? The catacomb seemed to have an empty feeling that worried Idris.

One of the hybrids saw Julie and Idris. Julie began to Change in front of Idris, who did the same. As soon as he finished Changing, the hybrid was on top of them. It slashed at them and Julie leapt out of the way, going behind the creature to slash at it with her front claws. Idris jumped backward and then lunged, tackling the hybrid to the ground. His teeth sunk into its neck. It was as if he was biting into marble. The creature clearly had the skin of a vampire. The blood was old and tasted disgusting as it spilled into Idris's mouth. He remained clamped down on its neck until he broke through it, leaving the hybrid limp and on the ground, seemingly lifeless. Idris hoped that was enough to kill the monsters because Dimitri was the only one who hadn't Changed yet, and had a stake going.

The other hybrid ran over in a blur, so fast that Idris didn't have time to block the hit. He flew through the air, smashing against the wall and sliding down, landing awkwardly onto a coffin. Julie was fighting with the creature now. In the other corner, Amelia and Dimitri were trying to take down the other one. Amelia limped with one of her front paws and Dimitri tried to kick the hybrid to stake it, but missed.

Idris saw a flash of something near the main hallway – red. He let out a howl, letting Julie know he was going after Vivica. He leapt off with his back paws and barreled through the combat, hoping Julie could handle one of the hybrids by herself. He ran across the main room and up the hallway. Vivica was always faster than him. He hoped that she would get caught up with the metal door and have to slow down enough so he could tackle her.

As Idris made it through the hallway, Vivica ran up to the metal door. She stopped and began to lift it. It moved easily under her incredible strength – but she still had to stop running. Idris pushed off the ground and barreled forward, smashing into Vivica. She let go of the metal door and it slammed against the front entrance. She kicked Idris and sent him off of her and then held him tightly in her iron grip.

"Hey, pup, fancy meeting you here. Should have known even as an Exsul, you'd still be helping out those idiots."

Idris snarled and thrashed but her grip was tight. She squeezed his neck.

"I didn't want to do this. For real. I know you don't believe me because of the whole Roman situation but I just couldn't believe that you didn't want to be with me. I freaked out. I see that now. But it doesn't matter. I'm going to have to kill you now. Jacob is already making his way to the tavern to kill everyone there. He wants to wipe out as many werewolves as he can and change them to the smelly monsters he created. A new pack, Idris. No Exsuls. Just him and his second-in-command – me. Sorry I have to kill you and you won't see it."

Vivica tightened her grip, cutting off his air flow completely. If Idris didn't do something, she would strangle him right here and right now. He thrashed and felt himself lose control of his body, beginning to Change back into his human form. As his vision dimmed, his face morphed back into his human one, which gave him enough space in her grip to gasp for air.

Vivica seemed taken aback by his sudden noise, and Idris pressed his advantage. He shoved his hand back and struck her with his claws, which hadn't morphed back yet. Vivica gasped in surprise and let him go. Idris spun and kicked her directly in the chest, knocking her down. He yanked out his stake and moved toward her, ready to stake her.

He was thrown to the floor again. Vivica let out a cackle and she was a blur of red, chucking the metal door away from her and shooting out into the night. Idris felt blood rush out of his nose, and he dizzily wondered if he hadn't smelled a hybrid coming. He rolled over on his back and looked up to see Dimitri standing over him. Julie's warning floated back to him.

"Exsul scum!" Dimitri spat and raised a blade he must have kept on him.

Right before Dimitri was about to stab him, something grabbed him by the neck and dragged him down to the floor. Idris propped himself up, ready to fend off a hybrid, but it was Julie, still in her werewolf form. He watched as she took care of Dimitri and then looked up at Idris, her eyes trying to communicate with him. Since he wasn't in werewolf form anymore, he couldn't hear her but he knew what she was saying.

Now we're even.

***

Once Rosamund was settled, Darlene set off to walk around the bar and see what was in place to defend them from attack. Everyone had a job to do and they were doing it silently. There still no word from Julie or Idris. She paced the top floor, looking out onto the dance floor, wondering what could be going on. Mark was giving commands down below and she watched him, admiring him.

The more time Darlene spent around him, the more she found herself enjoying his company. He was comfortable in himself and was confident because of it. He was at ease being in charge of the pack. The rage that seemed to fuel Roman didn't exist in Mark. It was as if he was born for this role.

When he finished talking, he looked up to see Darlene and headed over to her. Her heart skipped a beat. He looked tired but his eye was fierce and awake, constantly checking to make sure that nothing was amiss. For the first time, Darlene felt a calm settle over her.

"How is it going?" she asked as he walked up to her.

Mark sighed. "We're as prepared as we're ever going to be but we're on edge as well. You guys were attacked but what do they have planned for us here? And I haven't heard from Julie."

Darlene was going to reply when Rosamund stuck her head out of the back office and waved at Mark. "I have a question."

"What?" he asked a bit roughly.

"If you clear it with everyone, I can put shields on the roof."

"You can *what*?"

Rosamund opened up her hand, which held three vials of different colors, "I can use these to help shield the bar. It won't be enough to keep the monsters out, but it will be highly effective. I won't do it without your approval. I'm sure one of your...pack members will think I'm trying to curse the place or something."

Mark paused, giving it some thought before he spoke. "Normally, I would say no. But since you've been helping Darlene, I know you're okay, witch or not. If you run into any problems, let me know. I have a guard up there on the roof. Let me know if you have any issue. Tell him...tell him pineapple."

"Pineapple," Rosamund repeated without inflection, almost afraid she would laugh.

Mark mumbled, "It's the code so they know the order is from a pack leader."

Rosamund rolled her eyes at Darlene and took off toward the roof. Darlene wiped the grin off her face as Mark turned around to face her.

"Come into my office. I'd like to spend time with you before the other shoe drops."

Darlene nodded, and Mark reached for her hand. She held his hand tightly, enjoying the warmth as they headed into his back room. They moved past Rosamund's things, to where Roman had his makeshift bedroom.

Mark looked down at her and smiled gently. "Things have changed a lot the last few months."

"They have. Seems crazy to think that a year ago we didn't even know each other," Darlene said, running her hands over a small dresser next to the cot.

"I just wanted…well, in case…You know…"

Darlene looked at Mark. She had never seen him at a loss for words before. She could feel herself blushing as he spoke to her.

"Don't," she said firmly. "We're all going to be fine. Whatever happens, we will take care of it together."

Mark nodded, although he still looked nervous. Darlene tilted her face to him and he kissed her. The kiss was gentle, unlike the rough kisses they would give to each other in heated moments of passion. This promised things to her that she had never considered with Mark before.

Darlene wrapped her arms around his waist and kissed him harder. They didn't know how much time they had left and both of them wanted to make the most of it. Mark ran his hands down the small of her back as they both moved toward the cot. It could fit two people, probably so Roman could make up with Julie here, Darlene thought as they laid down on it.

Mark undressed her now. His pace was quick but he wasn't rough. He treated her as if she was the only woman in the world at the moment and the only one who mattered to him. The bar was always a few degrees too cold for her own liking, probably because the werewolves' body temperature was naturally warmer. The cold air touched her skin, giving her goose bumps all over.

Mark undressed as well. Darlene watched him, marveling at his body. He had scars all over from years of fighting in the packs. He had a newer scar along his shoulder from his battle with Atticus. He unzipped his jeans and stood in front of her in his boxers. She blushed at the sight of him and pulled him close to her, kissing him again.

Mark ran his fingers along her bra, before unclasping it at the back. His hands traveled along her breasts before he moved down to kiss along them. Darlene let out a sigh, closing her eyes as she let the sensations of his tongue on her nipples overtake her. Mark pressed her down on the cot, kissing along her stomach and her breasts. She let out a shudder as he quietly removed her underwear and ran his fingers along her wetness.

Torturously slow, Mark slid one finger inside of her and moved it. Darlene let out a soft moan and arched her hips a little, wanting more. Mark obeyed, moving his finger a bit faster before lowering his mouth to her clit. Darlene bucked her hips in surprise and tried to keep her voice down. The last thing she wanted was someone coming in to make sure everything was okay.

Mark worked on her until she was on the brink of finishing. Right as the warmth built up in Darlene and she could feel herself about to finish, he moved away. Darlene let out a frustrated groan as Mark tugged off his own underwear and positioned himself above her.

She wasn't frustrated for long as Mark slid inside of her. He let out a small groan of pleasure as he moved all the way in. Darlene moaned and then bit her bottom lip to try to silence herself. She moved her hips against him, trying to take him in as deep as she could. Mark began to pump inside her, propping himself up as he looked into her eyes. Darlene wrapped her legs around his waist and moved in sync with him.

For those moments, there was nothing else they were thinking about but each other. Mark looked at her as if she was the most beautiful thing he had ever seen and in those moments, Darlene believed it. They moved together, breathing heavily in each other's ears as Mark thrust inside of her. Darlene could feel herself about to lose it and have her orgasm. He had gotten her so close before he had entered her and now was pumping inside of her faster and faster. He would pull all the way out and then thrust back in as deeply as he could, all while he looked deep into her eyes.

Darlene bucked her hips and sighed with pleasure, "Mark…I'm going to…"

Mark leaned down and kissed her hard, smothering her moans of pleasure as she came. Her orgasm was hard and intense, sweeping over her as she moved wildly against him. Her moans were muffled by his lips. The orgasm moved over her, spreading warmth throughout her body.

Mark thrust hard and then let out his own muffled grunt. He shuddered in her arms as he clung to her. Darlene wrapped herself around him, rocking her own orgasm to a finish as Mark let out small grunts in her ear. She turned his face so this time she could kiss him.

As they came down from their orgasms, Mark held Darlene tightly. The cold air was now a welcome sensation between her own warm body and Mark's body heat. She caught her breath and rolled over to hold Mark one last time before the battle began.

Chapter Six

As Idris ran through the graveyard, one look told him that Vivica was gone already. He missed his chance, all because Dimitri decided to kill him. He tried to quell the rage building inside of him. Now Vivica had slipped through his fingers, probably to wherever Jacob was, to mobilize against the pack. He let out a groan of frustration and heard someone approaching from behind. Idris spun around, but it was Julie and Amelia.

"Lost her," Idris said.

Julie's eyes narrowed, and she looked angry for a second. "All because of that idiot Dimitri. There isn't any point in sticking around here. We have to get back to the bar."

They returned to Idris's truck, leaving behind the other car because they didn't have the keys. As they drove back to the tavern, Idris tried to let what had just happened slide off of his back. But he couldn't help but be amazed by the fact that someone tried to kill him just because he was Exsul. He would have to be on his guard from now on, even without the threat posed by Jacob.

As they pulled up to the tavern, snow began to fall. The sky had been dull all day and now finally gave in, sending small white flakes down. Idris parked the truck and then held up his hand, squinting into the distance.

"What is that?" he hissed.

It wasn't a hybrid, but someone limping their way up to the front of the bar. Idris couldn't make out who it was but it was clearly injured. The figure turned its face slightly as it approached the door and Idris recognized the face. He opened the door of the truck, ignoring Julie's call to him and bolted over.

"Maria!" he exclaimed.

She turned to face him. Her glasses were gone and she had a long gash down the side of her face. Her clothes looked ruined and there was the scent of a hybrid on her, faint but still there. There were also strange black marks all over her clothing, as if a pen had exploded.

"Are you okay?" Idris asked.

Maria pitched forward precariously, and he caught her, helping her to steady herself.

She looked at him with tired eyes and nodded. "I might need a doctor."

Idris had a million questions to ask but her injury said it would have to wait. He scooped her up in his arms. By this time, Julie and Amelia had run over. Julie knocked on the door and shouted the word pineapple. The door opened without another second wasted. Idris wondered why the pack password was so weird.

There was a flurry of activity as soon as they burst into the main floor of the bar. Julie went over to Mark immediately to explain what had happened. Amelia ran off to find the pack doctor. Idris held Maria close and saw Darlene, safe but looking exhausted. She ran over at the sight of Maria and began to cry.

"Is she...? I thought she was..."

By this point, Maria had passed out but Idris nodded at her. "She's injured but should be okay as long as she sees the pack doctor. She was just outside, limping her way up here."

"Idris, she saved Rosamund and me. There was a hybrid and..."

The pack doctor ran up. He was an older man who must have been new to the pack because Idris didn't know him. They cleared a space for Maria on the bar. Usually, all wounded pack members would go to the warehouse at the edge of town but they were going to have to make due here.

"I'll take over from here," the pack doctor said.

Idris took that as his cue to back up. Amelia brought a sheet and draped it around the bar as a makeshift hospital curtain. Idris watched as she finished closing off the area and then suddenly felt exhausted.

Behind him, someone mumbled, "We listened to the Exsul and all we got for it are two dead pack members."

The insult rolled off his back and lay burrowed inside his chest, striking at his heart. They were right, weren't they? It was his plan to strike the graveyard and now Peter and Dimitri were dead.

Before Idris could think of anything else, Julie spoke up. "Dimitri was killed by me."

She addressed the pack now, speaking louder than usual. Idris turned around to see her up on the second floor, looking down at the pack.

"In the midst of battle, when Idris had the vampire who was working with Jacob within his grasp, Dimitri attacked him instead. He was going to kill him. His actions not only almost killed a werewolf but allowed Vivica to escape. We lost our chance."

There were grumbles but this time it was Mark who spoke.

"Anyone found to be treating our two Exsul guests as anything other than fellow werewolves will be answering to either Julie or myself. If you don't like it, you are free to leave."

Silence fell upon the pack. No one said anything, unsure of how to react. This was the first time that Idris could recall anyone spoke in favor of Exsuls. The moment was not lost on him. There was a woman standing next to Darlene now, eyes wide and shaking slightly. It took Idris a minute through the fog of being so stressed to realize what was so different about her. She was the witch, Rosamund, that Darlene had mentioned.

Normally the sight of a witch in a pack setting would have made Idris extremely angry. But seeing Rosamund, he felt nothing. He knew that witches were responsible for creating the first werewolves long ago but he didn't have the energy to blame her for that.

The pack dispersed now, and Darlene ran back over, asking questions about what had happened. Idris gave her a quick recap. He was about to ask about Rosamund and if she was the witch who had helped hide Maria from being detected as an Exsul when the power went off in the building.

Idris held his breath, waiting for it to come back, but there was nothing. He didn't know if it was because of the snow or if something was headed their way. Mark told everyone to calm down and then dropped another bomb on the pack.

"Rosamund has put shields up around the bar. As soon as a hybrid touches it, we'll be alerted and the shields will hold them off long enough for us to position ourselves for the attack."

The pack could have handled an Exsul or two but the mention of a witch using magic near them brought on a chorus of angry voices. Idris could barely make out anything in the darkness and moved back a few steps, away from the main hub of the yelling.

Julie spoke, her voice sounding irritated – the same voice she used when dealing with Roman. "Enough! I know how we all feel about witches! This was not something we chose to do lightly! But if you would rather have it so we didn't have any shields at all, then leave. No one is making you stay here! In the meantime, the shields are placed and are working so I don't want to hear anything else about it!"

The pack fell silent after Julie's outburst. The power suddenly came back on in the bar. Then Rosamund's eyes rolled up into the back of her head. People began to yelp, backing away from her as if she was on fire. Then she spoke.

"He's here."

***

Panic surged through the tavern at Rosamund's warning. Darlene looked over at Mark, who steeled himself for Jacob to appear. He went off toward the roof to get a better view.

Rosamund's eyes rolled back and she spoke again. "Vivica is with him. He has his hybrids as well. They are connected to him somehow."

Darlene followed Mark to the roof, with Julie and Idris trailing behind. She swallowed her fear in the attempt to remain calm. Spirits flickered in and out of her vision, like a bad TV connection. Before running up the stairs, she cast a glance down at Maria. Darlene couldn't see her because of the sheet but she hoped that she would be okay.

The group spilled out onto the rooftop. The snow fell down faster now with a wind that had kicked up, sending flurries up around Darlene's face. She looked down to see where Jacob was. The shield that Rosamund had put up was invisible but able to hold off the impending attack. At the center of the parking lot was a crowd of dark shapes. Darlene was able to make out a hint of red that must have been Vivica.

"Damn," Mark mumbled. "He really was out there creating more of them."

"Jacob didn't look like this the night Lucian turned him," Darlene recalled as the wind whipped through the group.

"Rosamund said they were connected – the hybrids and Jacob. If we kill Jacob, it might be enough to weaken the hybrids and take them down easily." It was Idris who spoke, much to Darlene's surprise. He had been silent since getting back to the bar.

"The shield won't keep them out for long," Mark added, pointing to a cluster of hybrids that were smashing against it. "We have to be ready for them when they break through."

Darlene took a shuddering breath. "Let me help."

Mark looked at her. "How?"

"I'll make a barrier."

"A barrier?" Idris repeated, as if Darlene spoke gibberish.

"Yes." She was talking quickly now. "A spirit barrier. Rosamund is here – she can help me. I can call spirits down and have a barrier in place. When the hybrids get to it, they'll be attacked by spirits. It'll give you guys an additional edge."

Both Mark and Idris shook their heads, but Julie look intrigued. "They wouldn't be expecting it."

"No way," Mark said. "You don't even know how it would go. If you could do it or not. You could get hurt."

"We could all get hurt. Are you really going to try to make me out as a princess in this battle or stand in my way? I'm doing it regardless," Darlene snapped.

Mark looked as if he wanted to fight with her more about it but thought better of it and turned back to look at the crowd. "Fine. I'll send Rosamund up."

As Idris and Julie headed back downstairs, Mark stopped in front of her and kissed her fiercely. "Be safe."

"You, too. After this, we'll take a vacation."

Mark smiled and then slipped off his jacket, sliding it onto Darlene instead. She pulled it closer to her, hoping to fend off the cold. Mark walked down the stairs, leaving Darlene alone. She looked out to where Jacob was and shivered. She knew she could do this – she knew she was strong enough to conjure the spirits necessary to block the bar. It would buy everyone time and maybe turn the tide in their favor. Every little bit will help.

The door to the roof opened, and Rosamund peered out. She wore Idris's jacket which hung loosely on her, making her look child-like.

"Did they tell you what I want to do?" Darlene called out to her over the wind.

Rosamund nodded and for the first time in a while, she smiled. "I'm ready."

***

Inside the bar, everyone was getting ready. Idris tried to stay calm but his nerves got the best of him. He found himself pacing in a corner, trying to focus on the task at hand. His thoughts kept drifting back to Darlene, up on the roof making a spirit barrier. It wasn't that he didn't have faith in her, he was just worried she would get hurt, or worse, while doing so.

But worrying about Darlene would undermine the entire effort everyone was about to undertake. If the shields fail, allowing Jacob's group access to the bar, there would be chaos. A few members of the pack volunteered to guard the main entrance. They were leaving now, some wielding weapons and some half Changed already. Idris watched them go, wondering if he should go with them.

"I want you to stay here," Mark said, to Idris's surprise. "Jacob knows of you through Lucian. Seeing you might be enough to throw him off balance in the attack."

Idris nodded, wondering how fighting in these close quarters would turn out.

"Another thing," Mark said. "If you see Vivica, will you be able to…?" He trailed off, the rest of his question hung in the air.

"Yes. I'll be able to."

Mark shifted uncomfortably. "I'm sorry about Dimitri."

"Not your fault."

The two of them stared at each other for a beat until Mark nodded. "Good luck."

Idris watched him go. The conversation wasn't much, but given their history, it was progress.

***

The snow picked up, making it harder to see as Darlene stood on the roof. Rosamund paced, mumbling to herself as she thought things through.

"The source of power is going to have to be you, Darlene. Essentially, what you are doing is using your body as a gate for the spirits to come through and form a barrier. You usually let the spirits do whatever they want as they communicate with you. You can't allow that to happen this time. You have to be in control."

Darlene nodded. "I understand."

"I can lend you my power so it doesn't drain from you all at once. But either way, you're going to be exhausted when this is done. Are you sure you're ready?"

"I'm ready."

Darlene did feel ready. All the practice and all the spirits she had seen – they all wanted the same thing, no matter what they cried out. They wanted to be useful again and to have a purpose besides just being a roving spirit. They would be able to help her today. She just had to stay in control.

Rosamund walked next to her and grabbed her hand. She felt better with her steady presence there. Rosamund knew a lot and her power would help Darlene. With that in mind, Darlene closed her eyes and tried to relax.

At first, nothing happened. The cold seeped into her bones the longer her eyes remained shut. Darlene fought down the panic that started to rise in her chest when she felt it. The world faded away. She didn't feel the cold anymore or even Rosamund holding her hand. Darlene opened her eyes.

She was back in the otherworld. Staring at her were the ghosts of her past – Lucian, Rebecca and Gertrude. All the people whose deaths she'd blamed herself for.

Darlene tried to be brave when she spoke. "Will you help me?"

Rebecca, who had never blamed Darlene for her being turned to a vampire, stepped forward first, nodding. Darlene's heart ached at the sight of her. Even when Rebecca wanted to turn her into a vampire, Darlene knew it was never from malice. It was due to a misguided friendship from her warped feral vampire mind.

Gertrude hesitated but stepped forward as well, grabbing Rebecca's hands. But Lucian's lips curled in disgust. Darlene hadn't planned on his help anyway. This was his idea that Jacob was trying to bring to fruition. He would love nothing more than to see Darlene die.

She ignored him. *He is beneath me.* To her surprise, Lucian began to fade away. He appeared surprised by this as well as he faded into nothing. Darlene felt a thrill go through her. *I hold the power here.* Rebecca nodded in agreement.

"You two are going to be the cornerstones of my barrier. I need others to help keep Jacob and Vivica out. We need to work together to bring them to me."

They both nodded, and Darlene started calling spirits forward. *Please, please, please,* Darlene repeated, hoping the barrier would keep building. She could see it, almost like a picture, of the bar with the snow kicking up, the darkness everywhere. There was something shimmering that she took to be the barrier.

It was growing, Darlene realized with a thrill. She just needed to make sure that she could keep it together.

Chapter Seven

Whatever Darlene was doing on the roof was causing the power to flicker on and off inside the tavern. The bar had suddenly gone ice cold. Idris wondered if it was because of the amount of spirits she was pulling into this world.

"Shield's down!" someone shouted from outside the bar, and someone else repeated it so everyone else could hear.

Idris's muscles tightened and before anyone could stop him, he left the bar, running out into the cold. His breath caught in his lungs as he saw the creatures moving toward the bar. The hybrids moved toward them, fast and in sync, as if they were being controlled. *Holding them off any longer is pointless.* Idris crouched down, ready to Change in case Darlene's barrier didn't hold. He wanted to get through the barrier.

As if sensing his thoughts, Julie suddenly appeared behind him. The air in front of them shimmered, which was the only indication that there was something there.

"The center barrier hasn't closed yet," Julie called out to him over the wind. "If we run now, we can get in before the barrier is sealed."

Idris knew that Darlene would kick him in the head if he went through with this. But it was the best way to save lives. The dark cloud of the hybrids moved swiftly. They would be against the barrier any minute now.

"I'm coming as well."

Maria's voice made Idris turn around. The doctor had stitched up the wound on the side of her face but she still looked like a train had hit her. How she was up and walking around was beyond him. He had to hand it to the old gal – she may have many years behind her but she was a fierce fighter. There was no time to tell her no. They had to run through the barrier *now*.

Another figure ran toward them, already Changed. The one eye let Idris know it was Mark. He wasn't going to stand by and let them cross the barrier without him. It was his pack, Idris thought, and he wasn't going to speak against him.

The four of them took off, each of them Changing as they ran. In front of Idris, the barrier shimmered with spirits he couldn't see. There wasn't much room left for them. For a split second, he worried that they weren't going to make it through. But he kicked off the ground and lunged, fully Changed. The four of them made it through the barrier as it shut behind them.

Ahead of them was a mass of hybrids. Behind them was a very pissed off Darlene.

***

Darlene guided spirits toward the barrier. The spirits linked together, holding hands and melding into one another to block out the hybrids. As she guided another woman spirit to the barrier, she felt a tremor that almost rocked her off her feet. Her connection with the real world shuddered for a moment and then she could hear Rosamund calling out to her.

"Darlene!" She sounded far away. "Mark, Idris, Julie and Marie went through the barrier!"

Darlene froze, shocked. She wanted to pull herself back into the actual world but the spirits had her rooted down in the otherworld, to serve as a connection for the barrier. She couldn't do anything to stop it. The barrier was almost sealed up by this point. Darlene could only watch in horror as the final grouping of spirits formed the rest of the barrier, effectively blocking the hybrids out. Her stomach plummeted as she thought of the group on the other side of the barrier.

Rosamund called to her but Darlene blocked her out. She knew what Mark and the others were trying to do. They were trying to end the battle before the barrier broke, saving everyone inside. If she let her emotions get the best of her, the barrier would be broken. As much as Darlene wanted to run after them, she knew that her spirit barrier played a pivotal role in the battle and she had to stay. She steeled herself and focused on the task at hand.

***

Running into the hybrids felt like running full on into a field of tanks. The creatures lashed out at the four of them. Idris ran past the putrid creatures as much as he could. He only had one goal… get to Jacob. He remembered Rosamund mentioning their connection. If Idris could get rid of Jacob, he was sure it would make the other hybrids easy to kill. Mark was next to him, running with him, looking for Jacob. Behind him, Julie was engaged in combat with one hybrid that had cornered her and Maria was offering coverage.

The stench of all the hybrids in close quarters was overwhelming. They were all horrifying to look at it, twisted and strange. Jacob had obviously been hard at work with Vivica to upgrade the monsters. One of them turned around and leapt at Idris. He maneuvered out of the way and spun around, sinking his teeth into its neck.

The creature flailed around and one of its talons connected with Idris's side. He let out a whine of pain and let go of his grip on the monster. Mark came from behind and lunged on top of it, tearing into it with pure fury.

Idris took this chance to run past the creature, his eyes scanning for Jacob. He couldn't see him in this mess but his eyes fell on a flash of red coming straight for him. *Vivica*, he thought as he moved quickly to the left. *Not fast enough.* Vivica grabbed one of his legs and tossed him into the air as if he were light as a pillow. Idris grunted as he smashed down onto the ground.

Vivica loomed over him. "I'm going to kill you now," she spat, fury over her usually cold features. "Don't think anyone will help you this time. Every human in this town is under our mind-control. They're sitting at home, staring vacantly at nothing. I'm going to kill you and then kill your ex-girlfriend."

Idris leapt back as she swiped at him. While they battled, he thought back to the years he had spent with Vivica. Their relationship had always been sick and twisted, something the old version of him had fed on. He should have known it would come to this… it was either him or her. In his wolf form, he couldn't stake her. He would have to go for decapitation at this point.

She slammed into him and he fell back. The hybrids gave them space, apparently sensing that Vivica wanted no interruptions. Idris snarled and tackled her down to the ground. She was always stronger than him. He wasn't going to be able to simply overpower her himself. Vivica flipped him over onto the ground and brought her fist down against his snout. She raised her hand again and a wolf came out from nowhere and smashed into her.

Vivica hit the ground, and Idris scampered to his feet. Maria, still in her werewolf form, had been the one to attack. She was limping and her wound had reopened, causing the side of her head to bleed darkly. She looked dead on her feet. Idris was amazed she hadn't Changed back into a human yet. Being wounded made the Change sometimes occur.

Vivica moved toward Maria. There was a flash of something silver and Vivica jammed something into Maria, who faltered and crumbled to the ground. With horror, Idris saw Vivica stab Maria with a long blade. On the ground, Maria Changed back into her human form. Rage swept through Idris, and he ran toward Vivica, taking advantage of her distraction.

With a howl, he was on top of her again, his jaws wrapped around her throat. He thrashed around, moving his teeth painfully through her marble skin. Vivica was stunned, struggling to get him off. Every negative emotion Idris had been feeling came out of him as he tried to bite through her neck. Vivica moved her arm back and punched him before swiping the knife toward him.

Idris jumped back, dodging the knife. They moved in a close circle. She had gashes along her neck, looking painful but already healing. Idris saw a movement behind her – *Maria.* She barely moved and each step she took left behind a bloody footprint. She wasn't going to make it, Idris realized. But she revealed something to him. A stake.

Idris made sure Vivica still had her eyes on him. She was so angry that she didn't notice Maria behind her. She crouched down, getting ready to leap toward Idris when the stake suddenly appeared through her chest. Vivica's mouth dropped open, and she looked down at her chest.

"Idris…" she breathed, looking back up at him, despair in her eyes.

Before she could utter another word, she began to turn to ash. Slowly at first, and then faster, her body turning to nothing, ashes being swept away with the snow. Maria fell down to her knees and smiled weakly at Idris, before collapsing. Idris ran over to her, nudging her with his snout but there was no movement.

He threw his head back and howled.

Chapter Eight

Darlene's grip on the barrier was slipping. Her strength drained quickly and she wasn't sure how much longer she could keep it. The real world was coming back into focus. Rosamund was weakened as well, holding onto Darlene's hand but on her knees next to her, sweat across her face. The snow fell heavily now and the wind was so strong that Darlene couldn't make out what was happening in the battle below. She heard one long howl that sounded so much like Idris she shuddered.

The entire barrier surged forward slightly before the spirits began to fade. Their strength also waned. They couldn't stay in the mortal plane anymore. Darlene fell to her knees, feeling the barrier fall apart. The dark shapes began to move toward the bar. Jacob was still alive – she just knew it.

Rosamund shuddered next to her. "Liara is coming."

Darlene turned to look at Rosamund, eyes wide. "What?"

***

Idris spotted Jacob. He wasn't nearly as morphed and tortured looking as the other hybrids. He still looked mostly the same as the first time Idris had seen him. Clearly, his experiments on advancing the hybrids weren't being done on him, at least physically. The barrier had crashed right after Maria passed away. Darlene must have run out of strength... or seen Maria's ghost.

Jacob moved at a rapid pace toward the bar. Idris got to his feet to go after him when Mark stopped next to him, in shock, facing the other way. Idris felt it before he saw them – werewolves. The snowfall was thick, making it hard to see. But as he turned around, one came out of the snow. Liara. She let out a howl and the rest of her pack followed after her.

"What are you doing here?" Mark exclaimed through their mind connection.

"You sent the warning but did you really think we would sit back and not help? I'm sorry we're late. What can we do to help?"

Mark glanced at Idris. *"Jacob is still alive and heading to the bar. Help us here on the ground."*

She nodded and howled again. This howl was loud and vibrated in the air as the packs ran toward the hybrids and Mark and Idris ran toward the bar.

***

Darlene felt relief that Liara's pack turned up. Better late than never. She wished she had been able to hold the barrier up a bit longer. Her head ached, white hot searing pain shooting through it. The spirit barrier had taken all her energy.

Of course that was the moment Jacob decided to appear in front of her.

He jumped up onto the roof as if it were nothing, looking at her with a grin on his face that seemed to mean he had been looking for her this entire time. Rosamund gasped when she saw him and gripped one of her vials. Darlene was too exhausted to be afraid. If he was going to kill her, she wanted Rosamund to get away to safety first.

Jacob began to walk over to them. As he got closer, Darlene could see the changes on his face. His skin was deathly pale, showing off all the veins underneath. His eyes had changed to look like a werewolf's at all times and his fingers were elongated, as if he was in mid-change. Up this close, she could see he no longer had just one pair of fangs, but his entire mouth was full of them.

"Just the woman I wanted to see."

Darlene didn't have the energy to muster up a witty insult. Instead, she probed for the one spirit she hadn't seen lately – the drowned woman. She felt for her out along the bar, using the last of her strength to summon her. *Please,* Darlene begged, *I know I ask so much of you, but I need you here.*

Jacob loomed over her and snapped her up by her neck as if she were a feather. Darlene gasped for air as his fingers closed around her throat.

"Your barrier was a cute idea but it didn't work. Even that other pack showing up means nothing. I'm going to kill you and turn all of you into my creatures."

Darlene gasped for air, her vision dimming. The drowned woman appeared behind Jacob suddenly but she was pale, barely holding onto this world. *She must have been part of the barrier.* Jacob gave another sick grin and dropped Darlene to the ground. She fell in a pile and looked up in horror as Jacob spun around and grabbed the drowned woman.

The woman gave a gasp of surprise, and he squeezed his hand around her chest. She vanished before she could help Darlene at all.

Jacob looked back at her. "I'm not falling for that again."

"Fine," Darlene gasped. "Fall for this."

The vial that Rosamund had slipped into her hands when Jacob had let her go was thrown into his face. Jacob screamed and clawed at his skin as it began to burn. Darlene realized it was holy water. Without thinking clearly, she lunged at Jacob, tackling him to the ground on the roof.

At the same time, Mark and Idris crashed onto the roof. Jacob was still being burned by the holy water. Rosamund rushed over and held out a stake to Darlene, who took it and looked at Jacob.

"If you visit me as a spirit," she threatened. "I will find a way to lock you into the pits of Hell."

She slammed the stake down into his chest. Jacob arched his back, trying to throw her off. He had extra protection there, she realized too late. He moved his arm to strike at her but Mark lunged forward, gripping his hand between his strong jaws. Darlene brought the stake down again.

Jacob tried again to attack her but Rosamund ran over and tossed another vial of holy water in his face. Jacob screeched, and Darlene managed to drive the stake in this time.

He crumbled to ash beneath her.

Idris Changed back swiftly into his human form, running to the side of the roof and pointing. Chaos reigned below. "The hybrids don't know what to do without him."

Darlene ran over as well and the group watched as the hybrids looked around, dumbly. The pack took advantage of this and began to wipe them out, one by one. In the swirling snow storm, the hybrids began to fall. All the energy sapped out of her and she crumbled to her knees, watching as the battle ended.

Epilogue

The sun was high in the sky and mostly covered by clouds. The snow that fell was light, an aftermath of the snow storm that had ripped through the town three days earlier. The graveyard was packed with mourners for Maria. It was her funeral, and Darlene's eyes were red from crying.

After Jacob's death and the wiping out of the hybrids, the town had gone back to normal. Idris told her that Vivica and Jacob had all the humans in town under mind-control. At first, she had found that hard to believe, but it ended up being true. No one in town could recall the attack on the bar. They all had fake memories implanted where the attack had been. It was impressive, if not terrifying, to see how strong Vivica and Jacob had become.

Maria's death hit Darlene hard. She had been crying on and off ever since she found out. Idris told her how Maria had killed Vivica and saved him from his own death. She had saved Darlene's life too, from the hybrid earlier on and by letting her work at her shop for all those years. The store remained closed until Darlene could figure out what to do with it.

That was another surprise from Maria's will, which was read out yesterday. She had drawn it up six months ago and had left Darlene the bookshop. Darlene found it strange how she now owned a bookshop. But it was a comfort that only Maria could have given her.

The funeral had just finished and people were beginning to leave when Mark and Liara stepped up to the podium. Darlene frowned. She didn't know Mark was going to speak at the last moment. It seemed odd but his face was collected, as if this was planned. Darlene's eyes fell on Idris, who was on the opposite side of where Maria was to be buried.

***

Idris hadn't noticed Mark and Liara up on the small platform that was set up at the last minute for the eulogies. He kept staring at the plot that now marked Maria's resting spot. His heart ached at the loss of a woman who had lived as an Exsul and had offered him comfort and support to get his life back on track. She died protecting him and the others. She had even left Darlene the bookshop.

"May we have your attention, please?" Mark asked.

Mark looked exhausted. There had been numerous funerals over the last three days from the pack losses. Next to him was Liara, who looked tired as well. Everyone fell silent.

"It isn't lost on any of us that Maria was an Exsul," Liara began. "She had been for a long time. She lived a quiet life but ultimately died protecting the packs. She gave her life for ours."

Mark took over at this point. "In light of that, we have determined that her actions taken to save a pack from danger falls in line with the requirements to lift Exsul status. So, officially as of today, posthumously, Maria is no longer an Exsul. As pack leader, I am exercising my right to allow her to be buried as an official member of the pack."

Stunned silence filled the crowd. Idris couldn't even speak. He had never actually heard of anyone getting their Exsul status removed. He assumed it had been a legend that was made up to give Exsuls hope. But people were already nodding in agreement with this and bowing their heads in respect to Maria.

Liara spoke up this time. "Idris, where are you?"

Idris took a step forward, feeling acutely aware of every eye now on him.

"Your help with the assault on the catacombs, as well as your help alongside our packs in combat and saving lives means we have also lifted your Exsul status. You are now officially a member of my pack."

Idris felt his vision blur for a moment and his mouth opened and closed, like a dying fish. *No way*, *this is a cruel joke.* But the crowd met this with approval as well and people came over to congratulate him. Idris couldn't believe it.

Liara came up to him, smiling gently. "Is that okay?"

"Of course!" he replied, almost shouting it as the news sunk in.

Idris had come home.

***

Darlene managed to get to Idris to congratulate him on his removal from Exsul status. The look on his face made it clear he thought he was dreaming.

"You deserve it," Darlene repeated as she hugged him.

"Thank you," Idris said, taking a deep breath to try to steady himself. "How are you holding up?"

"I'm okay," Darlene said. "I'm working on getting the shop ready to reopen next week. I suppose you'll be moving back to Liara's pack?"

Idris nodded. "It's for the best. I really want to throw myself back into it."

Darlene smiled and thought about the time they had spent together. Their relationship hadn't worked out and now Idris was leaving town. But Darlene felt at peace with what had happened. Idris had worked through his issues and come out on top. He would be happy being with Liara's pack again.

Mark walked up at this point to wish Idris good luck with Liara's pack. They shook hands, and Darlene marveled at the difference between the two of them. They got along now, as opposed to the years of pain now behind them.

Mark turned to Darlene and held her hand as Idris moved along to talk to more people.

"How are you holding up?"

"I'm okay. It's hard but…lifting Exsul status is truly an amazing act of compassion. Thank you for doing that for them."

Mark smiled. "I wish I could give you something in return for what you did with the barrier. And Rosamund too. Where did she go?"

Darlene sighed. "She left town right away. Said she had unfinished business to attend to, whatever that means."

Mark leaned down and kissed her gently. "I can't give you an award or anything but I want you to know I want to be with you for a very long time, Darlene, if you'll have me."

A sudden wind kicked up, but Darlene barely felt the cold. Instead, she realized for the first time in a long time that she didn't feel any spirits clawing for her attention. There was only silence…and peace. Happiness bubbled up inside her as she looked up at Mark. The thought of being with him for a long time made her heart swell.

She smiled. "I think that can be arranged."

Mark leaned down and kissed her. For once, everything in her life was perfectly in place.

-The End-

Get the latest update on new releases from the author at:

http://darladunbar.com/newsletter/

If you liked the stories, please take a moment to leave a review.

Here is a preview of **another story** you may enjoy:

Romeo Alpha: A BBW Paranormal Shifter Romance - Book 1

AMANDA WONDERED how the hell she had gotten so far away from home. When she walked, she usually didn't go past a couple of blocks, but she felt so different today. Something was pushing her further and in a different direction, and she wasn't sure what it was. But she didn't care at the moment, because she just wanted to walk.

Not thinking twice about where she was going, she let her gut instinct give her the direction she needed.

Her grandmother had always told her to go with her gut. She'd said human instinct was better than anything. "Intuition is a girl's best friend," she would say, and then they would both laugh. Talks she and her grandmother had always seemed to pop into her head at the strangest of times, like now.

Here she was, going for a walk, and wondering why she wanted to go in a different direction, and there was her grandmother's voice in her head, propelling her along. Amanda missed her grandmother more with every passing year.

Amanda paused and thought about her life thus far. She had just graduated from college and started working in the local animal hospital, but it wasn't quite like she had thought. She didn't see the care and passion she'd hoped to find in the industry. In the city, being a vet was all about how much money you could make, how many pets you could treat. And, at twenty-four, it was hard to be taken seriously.

Her two female roommates were nice, but they all just went their separate ways. They didn't eat ice cream and watch movies like on *Friends*. They didn't share secrets or even laugh or hang out. They really just slept in the same apartment, and they usually weren't even home at the same time. Except Amanda, that is.

Amanda was always at home, it seemed. She had nowhere else to go, really. The other two girls spent most nights out with their real friends or their boyfriends. Amanda lived a lonely life, but she was happy. At least, she was pretty sure she was happy. After all, she had an upstanding career, and she still had money left over from her savings.

Both her parents had been killed in a car accident years ago. Amanda had graduated from high school with no family there that day or on the day she graduated from college. It was what it was, though, and she knew that her parents watched her from Heaven.

The only positive thing was that her parents had been prepared and had made sure they left enough money and a big enough life insurance policy to help her out. They would be surprised but happy knowing how much that money had helped her in the years after their death. She was proud to say that she was able to live off of it through her college years. She'd never even had to get a job like most kids did. Amanda had been able to focus on her classes.

That freedom wasn't worth it, though. She would have worked three jobs at a time while going to school for one more day with her parents.

However, the account was finally starting to dry up, and she needed to think about what she would do. Sure, she had a new job that could pay her bills, but those loans were piling up with interest. Even a vet job only went so far.

Amanda sighed as she began the trek back toward the house.

Amanda liked her walks in the evening. It helped her to relax, enjoying the quiet time alone. And while Amanda wasn't overweight by any means, it helped slim her waistline, which showed those extra biscuits she liked every now and again.

She turned and began to make her way back to the townhouse she shared with her roommates, but stopped as she heard a noise

A rustling came from behind her, and she turned to see the bushes shaking. Looking over to the other side of the sidewalk, she saw those bushes shake as well. Not wanting to wait around to find out what was behind the leaves, she took off at a run. She swore she heard a growl come from behind her, but she didn't turn to see what was chasing her. That would only slow her down. As she reached the door to her home, she quickly turned the knob and went through headfirst. Shutting the door quickly, she looked out the window. She got a glimpse of a long black furry tail as something ran around to the side of her building.

"What in the world are you doing, Amanda?" Betsy stood there looking at her inquisitively.

"Something was chasing me."

"What?"

"I don't know what it was, but something big and furry was chasing me. I saw a long black tail just now when I walked into the house."

"You mean when you dove into the house?" Betsy's grin faded. "I'll call the game warden. If there is a big animal outside, then none of us need to go out there until they find it and get rid of it."

"Well, I don't want them to kill it."

"I know, silly, but if it's a wild animal, they can take it out to the National Forest and let it loose. The city is no place for a wild animal." Betsy turned and picked up the phone from the receiver.

Amanda stood in shocked silence as she listened to her roommate tell the person on the other end of the phone what had happened.

She knew from Betsy's tone that she and the person on the other end of the phone were questioning her sanity. They lived in a big city, and the closest thing they got to a wild animal was a stray cat or two. They didn't even get raccoons. If there was some huge animal like she thought, then it would make headline news.

Shaking her head in aggravation, Amanda turned toward her room. She suddenly felt silly and didn't want to have to explain what she saw to any more people.

"Amanda? Where are you going? They are on their way and might need to talk to you."

"Tell them it was a dog. Now that I'm thinking about it, it kind of looked like that couple that lives down the road's greyhound. Maybe he just got out."

"Are you sure, Amanda?" Betsy asked, turning and saying something into the phone.

Without saying another word, Amanda shut the door to her room tight and then quickly locked the door. She looked over her room and, seeing the window open and the curtains blowing in the breeze, she ran over to push the window pane down and lock it tight. As she stood there, she looked out into the woods that made up her backyard. There, in the distance, two yellow eyes stared back at her.

Suddenly, more eyes appeared, and it seemed the animals went on forever. She was amazed, since the woods behind her house were very dense and small. The dark night was lit with a full moon. A shiver raced through her as she stood there and stared into the first set of yellow eyes. She quickly shut the curtains and went to sit on her bed. She didn't think she would ever be able to fall asleep knowing what was out there. As she laid her head on the pillow, her mind wondered to large beasts with yellow eyes and sharp fangs. But she was soon fast asleep.

***

Amanda awoke with a yawn. It had been almost a month since the incident with what she now called a dog. She had agreed with Betsy that her mind had been playing tricks on her that night. There were often times when she was sure she felt eyes on her, and she would turn in one direction or another, looking. What she was seeking, she didn't know, but somewhere in the back of her mind, she just wanted to know if the eyes she had seen that night had been real or just part of her dreams that evening. She was still so uneasy about it that her walks seemed to get earlier and earlier each evening.

She was just about to walk out the door when her phone started ringing. She quickly grabbed it and pushed the button to answer it.

"Hello."

"Ms. Walker?"

"Yes?"

"Hello, Ms. Walker, my name is Ernest Montgomery. I am calling to tell you that your aunt has passed away."

"My aunt? But I don't have any family. You must have the wrong Ms. Walker."

"No, ma'am. Your father was Joshua Walker, correct? Mother Maureen Walker?"

"Yes."

"Then, I have the right Ms. Walker. It is your father's sister I am referring to. She unexpectedly passed away from a heart attack. I am very sorry for your loss."

"Oh, my gosh! I never knew I even had any family. I am very sad that I didn't get to meet her."

"Yes, ma'am. I'm sure. She was a nice woman. I have also called you to see if you can meet with me. I need to go over her will with you."

"Her will?"

"Yes, ma'am. Your aunt was a wealthy woman."

"Oh? Um, okay. When would you like to meet?"

"The sooner, the better."

"Okay. How about today?"

"That would be great. I am in Slatesville, in the valley. "

"Oh. Okay. That is just forty-five minutes from me. I can be there in a couple of hours."

"Sounds good, ma'am. I am at the *Montgomery Law Firm*. I am the only attorney in the town."

"Okay. Thank you, sir. I will see you soon."

"Yes, ma'am. I'll be waiting."

Amanda fell back on the couch, stunned, for what seemed like forever. Everything was pushed to the back of her mind as she thought about what she had just learned. She had a family. Well, she *did* have a family. Now her aunt was gone. Could there be others in her family who she knew nothing about? She didn't know, but she did know one thing. She wasn't going to find out sitting around here, twiddling her thumbs. She needed to get going fast.

Amanda headed for the kitchen. She wasn't surprised to see that no one was there. Of course her roommates weren't home. They were either in class or with their boyfriends.

Smiling, she made a cup of coffee and drank it slowly, thinking about what she might find out. Then, with a deep sigh, she made her way to her car. She looked at the small Honda with pride. It was a pile of junk to some, but it held a special place in her heart. She hadn't been able to get rid of her father's car. Instead, she had sold her own.

She looked down at the small picture he had taped to the dash near the speedometer. She was about six in the picture, and she had been holding her mom's cheeks in her hands as she kissed her.

She remembered the day like it was yesterday. They had just got to a cabin they vacationed in. She had enjoyed herself so much. The little cabin had one bedroom with a queen-sized bed where her parents slept and a set of bunk beds for her. They had stayed up late roasting marshmallows as her father told her scary stories about wolves and vampires. She had ended up in their bed, snuggled between the two of them. They had spent the next day hiking and walking trails and seeing tons of waterfalls and animals.

She had loved it and had never forgotten. It soon became a family tradition to go camping every year. After some of those trips, they didn't return home. Instead, they moved on to a different location. The constant moving had been hard on her as a kid, but she would have never told her parents that. She had felt like they were hiding something from her. Of course, she had been young back then and had blown it off as childhood curiosity. Now, with this new family member, she wasn't so sure.

Her parents had been very quiet people. They seemed cautious of everything going on around them and were even a little jumpy at times. Maybe there was more going on here than she thought. She needed to find out.

She wiped away a tear and go in the car. The car had a huge dent in one side and was almost fifteen years old, but it got her where she needed to go. She slid the car into drive and smiled to herself.

"Dad would be proud that his car was still running so good, wouldn't he, Trixy?" She and her father had named the car together.

Amanda turned onto the next road and made her way down the narrow two-lane road that led into the mountains. She had never been this way because her parents always went the long way around the mountains. They said they liked to take the scenic route.

She came to a small wooden sign that said *Slatesville—Welcome to your home away from home.* She smiled at the welcoming sign and kept on her way to the town. As she drove, she was amazed at how beautiful everything was. The low-hanging branches of the trees scraped the roof of the car every once in a while.

She was amazed at how many animals she saw. Deer acted as if they weren't afraid of her car. Raccoons were plentiful, and she jumped when a large black snake slithered across the road. There were people all around, and they watched her car curiously as she made her way down the street.

The town reminded her of a long lost western ghost town. It was a little spooky, and she caught herself checking the doors to make sure they were locked. The men nodded at her as she moved forward and many of the people smiled, although they held themselves back a little.

Amanda finally saw the sign that said *Montgomery Law Firm.* She pulled into one of the many vacant parking spots and slowly got out of the car. A handsome man leaned against the building she was about to enter. His brown eyes had flecks of yellow and orange in their deep depths. She smiled slightly, and the man just continued to stare as he looked her over slowly.

"Can I help you, ma'am?"

"I am just here to see Mr. Montgomery."

"Well, you're in the right place, Miss…?"

"Oh, Amanda. Amanda Walker. And you are?"

Something changed in his eyes as he smiled at her and made his way to her side. He held out his hand to her. "Name's Curtis Livingston."

"Oh. Do you live here?"

"Yes. I'm one of the controlling partners here in Slatesville. Well, I have to be going. It was good to meet you."

"You, too, Mr. Livingston."

"Please, call me Curt. Everyone does."

"Only if you call me Amanda."

"That's a deal, sweet lady." She flushed all over when he raised her hand to his lips and gently caressed her knuckles with a brief touch of his mouth. She felt the rise in temperature in her cheeks spread across her upper chest. She stood there and watched as he walked away from her down the street to slip inside a store. She felt foolish and realized that she had been staring. She shook her head, trying to think straight and clear the thoughts that were running through her mind.

Amanda was always aware that she wasn't the Barbie doll type of girl. Although she wasn't fat, she wasn't rail thin, which most men liked, either. Her waist and stomach didn't look like a washboard, although it didn't look like a bunch of bread dough either.

She instantly felt inadequate and quickly turned around to walk to the door of the attorney's office. Knocking, she was surprised when the door instantly opened. The man who opened the door wasn't what she expected. Mr. Montgomery was a short, pudgy man. He didn't wear a business suit, and he didn't seem stuffy at all. He was older and had a short goatee around his mouth. His hair was pulled back into a ponytail at the back of his neck, and he smiled when he saw her.

"You must be Amanda. You look just like your father, except for your eyes. You have your mother's eyes. Let's hope you didn't inherit your father's temper, though," he chuckled.

"You knew my father?"

"Oh, why yes, my dear. We grew up together, Josh and I. Have to say we got into a lot of trouble as kids, and your aunt Mabel was always there to wag her finger and tell on us. You see, there were the three of us; Joshua, Jeremiah, and I. We were called the three musketeers. Mabel wanted to be the fourth, but you know boys. We would never let her, so she always ran and told on us to get back at us for not including her; the little minx." He told the story fondly, and she instantly knew that this man held her family in the highest regard. She also knew he was her ticket to finding out the truth about her family.

"Do I have any more family that I don't know of?" She held her breath, as though she were a child again, asking if Santa Claus was real.

"I am sure you do, my dear. Unfortunately, your aunt was the last of your father's line. She couldn't have any children, and most of the family was killed in a fire in '90. I am sure there is still family on your mother's side, though. However, I must warn you that they are not the kind of people you want to know. Now, if you will come in, I will tell you about everything that now belongs to you."

"What?"

"Oh, my dear, you must know that your father's family had a legacy. You are the only Traverse left to take over the family business."

"What? I don't know what you're talking about."

"They never did tell you who you really are, did they? Oh, you poor child. I am afraid you are going to learn some things about yourself that are going to be hard for you. You must still be a virgin as well."

"I beg your pardon, sir, but I don't see how that's any of your damn business."

"No, my dear, I do not mean to be crude. I was just saying that you have never undergone the Change. It will happen, though. You recently turned twenty-four, and everything changes now."

"What change? What in the hell are you talking about?"

"They hid that from you, too? Oh my gosh. You don't know? Oh, Lord. Okay, first things first. You are now the owner of your family's estate."

"Family estate? So I have a house."

He smiled kindly at her. "Not just a house, my dear. It is what holds the legacy of your family name together. The estate has fifteen bedrooms with their own bathrooms and fireplaces, a kitchen, dining room, parlor, living area, office, library, Carolina room, staff quarters, wrap-around porch with two different sections screened in, pool, tennis courts and 300 acres. It was the pride and joy of your ancestor, Edgar. He was a distant grandfather of yours."

"Oh my gosh."

"Yes, ma'am. How about this? How about I get the keys and directions to the place? You go take a look at it, and then we can talk tomorrow about what you want to do. Stephan has been looking over things, and since your aunt's death, he has given everyone time off until you arrive and decide where to go from there."

Amanda wasn't sure she had the energy to deal with all of this tonight. "Unfortunately, it is very late. Is there somewhere that I can stay for a couple days and then I can go from there and take the day tomorrow to go look at the place?"

"That is perfect. Just give me a second, and I'll find a place for you to stay tonight."

Amanda sat quietly and listened to him talk on his phone. She didn't even hear his words as she thought of what she was going to do.

"I have gotten you a little cabin to rent down the road," he said, drawing her attention back to him. "It is in the woods a little but has electricity and such. On such short notice, I couldn't find anything else. It is only about ten minutes away. The key will be under the mat at the front door. Just go on in and make yourself at home."

"That is perfect. Thank you so much."

"You're welcome, my dear, and we will talk tomorrow. Say ten o'clock tomorrow morning? We will meet here and go to see the house together."

"Perfect. Thank you, Mr. Montgomery."

If you enjoyed this sample then look for **Romeo Alpha: A BBW Paranormal Shifter Romance - Book 1.**

Here is a preview of **another story** you may also enjoy:

The Awakening: The Daemon Paranormal Romance Chronicles, Book 1

THE LAST customer of the day was slowly leaving. Phoebe reached down to pet her dog, Ace, and moved to close up shop. Since graduating high school, she had worked in fairs across the country as a fortune teller, saving money. She did not know why, but when she touched somebody's hand, she could read their thoughts. Although she could not divine their future, she could make educated guesses that were enough to bring customers back. After saving enough money, she had finally opened up her own shop.

Removing the scarf from around her hair, Phoebe let her red curls cascade along her shoulders. Ace sniffed at some of his dog food while she reached over to grab her purse. Before she could close up, a knock at the door surprised her. In front of the door, she saw one of the most gorgeous men she had ever laid eyes on. Curious, she opened the door and let him in.

"Hello! How can I help you, Mr...?" She paused and waited for him to respond.

"My name is Apollo Mikos. Pleasure to meet you, Phoebe Williams." The blonde-haired man reached for her hand and shook it. Instantly, a vision arose before her eyes of Apollo and her rolling around in bed sheets.

Waves crashed outside the window—a storm was brewing. As the vision of Apollo entered her body forcefully, Phoebe pulled her hand back. The vision went away, but it left a slight blush on Phoebe's cheeks. Reading the minds of other people was occasionally embarrassing and often felt like a major invasion of privacy. Still, she found herself wishing that she could have held his hand a little longer to see where these thoughts took her.

Motioning toward the table and chairs reserved for clients, she asked if he wanted to sit down. Apollo just shook his head.

"I need your help with something, but not like that." He shrugged his shoulders. Tall and well-built, Apollo had blue eyes and chiseled features. He wore a dark black suit that made all of his muscles ripple beneath the fabric.

Confused, Phoebe looked over at him. "What do you mean?"

Sighing, Apollo looked into her eyes. "You will probably want to sit down for this." Still uncertain, Phoebe sat down and waited for him to speak again.

Gazing out the window, Apollo framed his thoughts. "I know your mother, Rhea. I also know what you really are and I need your help."

Phoebe was aghast. "What do you mean? I don't have a mother. I grew up in foster care after my mother left me there when I was two."

If you enjoyed this sample then look for **The Awakening: The Daemon Paranormal Romance Chronicles, Book 1.**

Here is a preview of **another story** you may also enjoy:

Devil's Advocate: A BBW MC New Adult Romance Series - Book 1 by Carla Coxwell

KRISTIE LOOKED at the sky as she pulled up in front of the casino. The air was chilly and the clouds were dark and threatening snow, which was the last thing Kristie felt like dealing with. She had been in her car for over ten hours, driving home from college for the holidays. Her back was sore and her legs needed to be stretched out. She wanted a hot bath in a Jacuzzi tub. She'd settle for a hot tub. But who was she kidding? There was no hot tub to be found at her parents' house and trying to have a hot bath without being interrupted was almost impossible.

Kristie had approached the holidays with an ever-growing sense of dread. It wasn't that she didn't want to see her mother, but every time she came home, it was like being suffocated. Her hometown had held more appeal for her when she was younger, back when her father was alive. Since he'd died and her mother had gotten remarried last year, Kristie had delayed going home at all. She had only met her step-father in passing and hadn't met his nephew, who he tried to raise on his own.

Kristie had saved up to stay at a hotel the entire break. It had made the most sense to her. It would cause the least amount of stress during her stay and give her space when she needed it. But when she had mentioned this to her mother, there was no way to mistake the sadness in her mother's voice for anything else. Knowing she was upsetting her mother by refusing to stay at home with her new family, Kristie had cancelled the reservation and agreed to stay at her mother's house instead.

She looked up at the casino where her mother had worked the last five years. Her mother worked in the back offices, far away from the lights from the slot machines and the sounds of people winning money. The casino was a little run down but brought in a steady stream of people who could afford the middle-level slots and risks it provided in a town that was mostly quiet.

The stale smell of cigarettes and alcohol hit Kristie in the face as she stepped inside. She looked around, seeing if anything had changed since the last time she had been here. Nothing jumped out of her. A few of the slots seemed to have been upgraded, but the carpet was still worn down and dirty and the place had an air of despair that made Kristie's skin crawl. She had never been to Las Vegas, but she imagined that the casinos there weren't as depressing.

Kristie made her way to the back and asked for her mother through the grate where an attendant was standing, looking at her cellphone. The woman went off to find her mother, and Kristie was soon ushered into the back offices. The casino décor quickly ended back here. Her mother's small office was near the back, shoved in a corner. The door was ajar, and Kristie peeked her head in.

Her mother was looking at the computer, squinting through her glasses to whatever was on the screen. When Kristie knocked on the door gently, her mother looked up and smiled. Kristie was startled to see she was going gray. The last time she had seen her mother, she had been a brunette. It was odd to see age creeping up on her. She came over to her and hugged her tightly.

"It's so nice to see you again."

"You, too, Mom."

Her mom urged her to sit down as she sat across from her at her desk. It made Kristie feel odd, as if she was interviewing to be her mother's daughter. Her mom didn't seem to notice, however, and smiled again. They made small talk for a while, mostly talking about Kristie's experiences at college. Kristie felt tired. She knew her mom meant well, but she really wanted to go home and nap. She was only here to get the address to her mom's new place.

"How are things with Lionel?" Kristie finally asked, feeling as if she didn't bring up her mom's new husband, she would never get out of the tiny office.

Her mom seemed to relax now that Kristie had brought him up, "He's great. Really, we're just wonderful. There are some issues, though..."

"Like what?"

"Well, it's actually one of the reasons that we wanted you to stay with us instead of a hotel. See, Lionel's nephew, Gray, is a bit of a handful. Lionel still feels responsible for him since he became his legal guardian when Gray was just a little boy."

Kristie wasn't following, "Okay..."

"He tends to run on the wrong side of the law, and we thought it'd be so great if you two could meet and maybe hang out."

The words hung in the air. Kristie felt a twinge of annoyance. She had thought her mother wanted her at the house because she had missed her, not because she wanted her to play nice with her new step-father's nephew. They weren't in grade school anymore. Trying to change someone set in their ways by sticking them with a goody-goody was a useless attempt.

Kristie took a deep breath and held it for a few seconds, letting the air out slowly. Her mother watched, a worried expression on her face.

"What do you want me to do with him?" Kristie finally asked.

Her mom, taking the fact that Kristie hadn't said no as a good sign, started to ramble. "Well, maybe just hang out with him. Show him what you do for fun. Maybe you two can go to the movies or something."

Kristie raised an eyebrow, "Go to the movies? What does this guy do for fun anyway that has you two so stressed out?"

Her mom avoided her stare and sighed, looking tired. "He runs with a bad crowd and doesn't like to listen. He's a good kid though. He's just lost."

"And you think I can fix him?"

"It wouldn't hurt to try, would it, Kristie? For me?"

Kristie sighed and nodded in agreement. How could she say no to her mother? She would always wish that her mother hadn't gotten remarried, but she didn't want her mom to be unhappy either. Her mom got up and walked over to her, hugging her tightly. Her mother's hugs had always reminded Kristie of being a little kid, outside playing till the sun set and running back inside for dinner. Back when her father was alive. Kristie shut her eyes tightly, willing the memories to leave her. She didn't want to think about her father right now.

Her mom finally pulled away and looked at her, smiling, "We'll have to really talk, you know, all about college and everything."

"Yeah, of course."

Her mom's eyes swept down her quickly, so fast that if Kristie wasn't used to it, she never would have picked up on it. She steeled herself.

"Maybe you and Gray can go to the gym. It'd get him out of the house and you could lose a few pounds at the same time," her mom said cheerfully.

Kristie mumbled in agreement and gave her mother one last hug before leaving the office. She should have known that there wasn't going to be any way in hell that her mother would have let an entire conversation go without making some sort of remark to her about her weight.

As she trudged through the casino, her mood lowered with every step. She regretted coming here for the holidays. Before her, they spread out in a bleak landscape. Dealing with her mother's 'helpful advice' in regards to her weight, and trying to show her loser relative by marriage around town. At the very least, she should have kept the hotel reservation.

Kristie dragged out the drive toward Lionel's house. Her mother had given her the address and it was close to the casino. A ten-minute drive didn't seem like enough time to prepare for whatever she was going to walk into. As she turned down the street where her mom's new house was, she found herself taking a deep breath. The first time, she just drove past the house. It was non-descript and had nothing of worth showing that made Kristie even notice it. Her mom had stopped gardening after her father died, and the front yard of this house was plain and dull.

Kristie pulled into the driveway. The garage door was open and a man was underneath a truck, working on it. She could only see his feet. Kristie got out of her car, grabbing her bags, and looked inside the garage. The man didn't look up when she shut the door of her car.

"Hello?" Kristie called out toward the man under the truck.

He didn't answer. Heavy metal was blasting out of a stereo nearby, but it was such an old stereo that the music sounded tinny. Kristie called out again, but the man still didn't answer. She knew that he heard her because he stopped working at one point and went still before resuming. She hoped this wasn't Lionel, because the guy was an asshole. *Probably his fantastic nephew.* Kristie trudged toward the front door, leaving the other guy behind. What a fantastic trip this was going to be.

If you enjoyed this sample then look for **Devil's Advocate: A BBW MC New Adult Romance Series - Book 1.**

Other Books by Darla Dunbar:

The Romeo Alpha BBW Paranormal Shifter Romance Series

The Daemon Paranormal Romance Chronicles

The Mind Talker Paranormal Romance Series

The Leather Satchel Paranormal Romance Series

About the Author - Darla Dunbar

Darla has been interested in paranormal romance since she was a teenager in high school. It was then that she discovered she could fulfill her fantasies through her writing.

Observing people and human behavior in the area of romance has always been one of her favorite pastimes. Combining that with an overactive imagination is a sure fire way of coming up with interesting themes.

19111084R00338

Printed in Great Britain
by Amazon